Madison's Mission

A Boldt Castle Story

By
Susan G Mathis

smWordWorks, llc
Fiction

MADISON'S MISSION by Susan G Mathis
Published by smWordWorks, llc

ISBN: 979-8-9876796-1-6
Copyright © 2025 by Susan G Mathis
Editor: Donna Schlachter

Available in print and e-book. For more information visit:
www.SusanGMathis.com/fiction

Visit her at www.SusanGMathis.com
sign up for her newsletter and please consider writing an Amazon review. Thanks!

PRAISE FOR MADISON'S MISSION

Susan G Mathis weaves danger, intrigue, love, loss, and faith restored amid class structure in her Gilded Age romance, *Madison's Mission*. Readers familiar with the beautiful Thousand Islands of will appreciate Mathis's historic detail and descriptions of Heart Island, its mysterious, unfinished Boldt Castle, and the natural beauty of the river and its islands.

—Cathy Gohlke, Christy Hall of Fame author
of *This Promised Land*

Your novel makes me want to pack my bags and head straight to the Thousand Islands! Thank you, Susan, for inviting readers on a journey to imagine what might have happened in Boldt Castle's earliest years, an enchanting monument to the Gilded Age. Susan captures its romantic, tragic history, and enduring charm.

—Melanie Dobson, award-winning author of
The Wings of Poppy Pendleton, another Thousand Islands story

If you love the Thousand Islands, this story will fill you with a longing to return soon! Madison's story is one of angst, heartbreak, and turmoil, but Mathis's satisfying conclusion rounds out the emotional upheaval to bring about the much-anticipated happy ending—but perhaps not the one you expect. As usual, an important life lesson is the central theme of this book, that being that nobody is ever truly alone who has God in their heart and love in their being.

—Donna Schlachter, historical romantic mystery author

If you enjoy a captivating story that whisks you away to the Gilded Age of The Thousand Islands, then read Susan G Mathis's latest release, *Madison's Mission*. Escape to a romantic setting, but be prepared for adversity, challenge, and even danger.
   —Davalynn Spencer, author of award-winning western romances

Once again Susan G Mathis has taken me into the Gilded Age on the Thousand Islands. This time there is a mystery to solve that sends Emmett and Madison on a journey of self-discovery and faith. I was whisked back in time to the Gilded Age on gorgeous Heart Island. Mathis never disappoints in capturing setting, dialogue, and culture of the time period she writes about, and she sprinkled just enough historical facts to keep me grounded in the setting.
   —Cindy Ervin Huff, Award-winning author

In her latest novel, *Madison's Mission*, Susan G Mathis takes us back to her beloved Thousand Islands at the end of the Gilded Age. The compelling tale is woven around Madison and Emmett who are attracted to each other but carry heavy burdens of loss, tragedy, and danger that threaten to keep them apart. As Mathis states so beautifully, "Their love was not born of ease but of perseverance, shaped by sorrow and refined by hope."
   —Janet Grunst, author of *A Heart Set Free*

Madison's Mission by Susan G. Mathis has wonderfully captured the essence of the Gilded Age. A must-read story filled with history, mystery, romance, and God's provision for His children.
   —Linda Shenton Matchett, best-selling author *Spies & Sweethearts*

DEDICATION

To my granddaughter, Madison, who inspired the wonderful character.

To my daughter, each of my four granddaughters, my son, and my son-in-law, who have always encouraged my writing. I am grateful for family.

To the Boldt Castle staff and volunteers who welcome hundreds of thousands of guests to the castle and island each summer. Every year, I am one of them.

To the Thousand Islands River Rats and especially to my faithful readers who love the river as much as I do. Thanks for your support in reading my stories, sharing them with others, and writing reviews on Amazon and Barnes & Nobles. You bless me.

ACKNOWLEDGMENTS

I hope you enjoy *Madison's Mission.* If you've read any of my other books, you know that I love introducing history to my readers through fictional stories. I hope this story sparks interest in our amazing past, especially the fascinating past of the marvelous Thousand Islands. Heart Island, Boldt Castle, and the Boldt family are real, and so are some of the amazing visitors to the castle, but please note that I took a bit of creative license in bringing this story to life, as some of the timing is a little different than recorded.

Thanks to you, my readers, for your faithful support and for staying connected. I love hearing from you. And a special thanks …

To Kathryn Gollinger, Boldt Castle Gift Shop Manager, who made sure the castle and island information was accurate. Thank you so much, Kathryn!

To Marianne McConeghy, who lives on Wellesley Island and made sure all the island information was accurate. Thank you so much, Marianne!

To Judy Keeler, my wonderful historical editor, who combs through my manuscripts for accuracy. Because of her, you can trust that my stories are historically correct.

To my fabulous Beta Team, Laurie, Barb, and Melinda who inspire me with your kindness, faithfulness, and wisdom. You are dear friends and a precious team.

To my amazing editor, Donna Schlachter, for being a great friend and for sharing your talents with me.

And to all my dear friends who have journeyed with me in my writing. Thanks for your emails, social media posts, and especially for your reviews. Most of all, thanks for your friendship.

And to God, from whom all good gifts come. Without You, there would never be a dream or the ability to fulfill that dream. Thank you!

Please stay in touch at susangmathis@gmail.com

PROLOGUE

The Thousand Islands, 1903

As the first rays of sunlight pierced the mist cloaking the magnificent Thousand Islands, George Boldt awoke to the symphony of nature—the gentle lapping of water against the shores, a chorus of songbirds, and the rustle of leaves stirred by a gentle breeze.

In all his fifty-two years, he'd never enjoyed such a tranquil summer retreat. These islands were his sanctuary. Here, dreams took shape amidst the rugged beauty of the St. Lawrence River, far from the hustle and bustle and heat of New York City, or Philadelphia, where he worked and lived. Here he could dream, think, plan.

George sighed as he donned his silk robe, leaving his precious Louise to sleep a little longer, and quietly moved out onto the balcony overlooking the river. This Wellesley House, perched on the edge of Wellesley Island, provided temporary respite until his latest and greatest endeavor—his magnificent Boldt Castle on Heart

Island—was finally done taking shape. This would be his crowning achievement.

His legacy of love.

His nose twitched with the slight scent of cow manure, but it meant the money kept on flowing. Wellesley House was all but surrounded by his massive Boldt Farms supplying fresh meat and produce for his luxurious hotels in New York City and Philadelphia. No…this cottage was but a temporary abode.

But soon Boldt Castle would be their summer home.

He shook his head, impatience and expectation mixing into a brew awakening his senses. Oh, how he loved every new project he put his hands to! As proprietor of New York's famed Waldorf Astoria, he possessed an unfettered imagination to innovate, improve, and impact his world. And he hoped what he accomplished transcended mere opulence now and into the future.

In the distance, he detected the sound of hammer blows across the water as the men commenced their workday at the castle. He honed his ears and eyes in the direction of the island.

A few years ago, he had dreamed of building a Rhineland castle as a Valentine's gift for his wife, Louise. He'd call it Boldt Castle—crafted from the very stones of the Thousand Islands, a monument to love, ambition, and the artistry of countless hands.

Now, over three hundred workers, from stonemasons to carpenters to craftsmen and artisans, toiled under the rising sun, pouring their own hearts into his monumental endeavor. He had ordered heart motifs be placed everywhere, in and around the rising castle and grounds, to signify his love. In the mantles and moldings. In the stained glass and furniture. In the fountains and gardens. Everything had to be perfect for his Louise.

Through every step of his career, she had been there for him. Through the ups and downs. By his side, encouraging, guiding, even offering her wisdom. And no matter what he created, Louise was his muse.

Boldt Castle, with its six stories and one hundred and twenty rooms, was to be more than merely a summer residence for her. For them. It was to be a testimony of his deep love and appreciation for his Louise, and--he admitted with a touch of chagrin—of his boundless aspirations.

Before long, it would be finished, complete with tunnels, a drawbridge, and intricately designed Italian gardens. A gazebo for her to sit and read in the fresh summer air. A dove cote, and, one day, a greenhouse. Maybe even a water fountain and pond.

His stone quarry on Oak Island provided all the material needed to finish the main building, and much was already completed. The Dove Cote and the peristyle archway, already complete, welcomed their guests to the island. The Power House, reminding him of his German homeland, and the architecturally unique Alster Tower, had also been completed. Louise loved the tower and affectionately dubbed it The Children's Playhouse, the one place on the island where they'd already enjoyed evenings of entertainment with family and friends.

George glanced back into the bedroom as Louise rolled over and moaned. His sweet, precious wife, her heart so weak—he shuddered to think, one day, he might have to survive this world without her.

No! Providence wouldn't let it happen. He needed her by his side. She was his partner, his inspiration, the strength of his life ever since they had wed. The mother of his two children.

He pondered his life journey while watching the sun peek over the St. Lawrence River and splash bright morning colors of pale blues and rosy pinks. Yes, his younger years had been interesting, and challenging, before he met her. And Providence, it seemed, had a hand in it all.

He'd grown up on a German island near a popular resort, so he'd cut his teeth on the hospitality industry from boyhood. At the tender age of thirteen, he'd emigrated from Prussia to the New World, alone, finding work in the hot city as a dishwasher. For years, he'd toiled in New York City hotel kitchens learning all he could, slowly gaining the reputation of being a talented, hard-working young man.

Then, at twenty-five, his break came when he rose to the position of managing cashier. An impressed guest offered him a job in the prestigious Philadelphia Club, and he grabbed at the opportunity.

And like the sun rising over the horizon and lighting the world, he met Louise, a fourteen-year-old spitfire and the boss's daughter. He'd fallen head over heels for her in an instant. His blood surged at the sweet memories.

That's when his life truly began.

A year later, even though he was ten years older, he married his darling Louise Kehrer, just fifteen. Yes, his rise from a poor kitchen worker to a hotelier was largely thanks to her father. And though his was also a tale of perseverance, Louise's steadfast support fueled his ascent. Together, they built a legacy to echo through time, their love story woven into the very fabric of their achievements.

"George? Are you there?" Louise's sleepy words wafted on the morning breeze. "George?"

After all these years, his name on her lips still thrilled him. He turned to face her. "Yes, my darling. Sleep a little longer. I'm right here, watching the sunrise."

"All right. Just for a few more minutes."

When her words faded to silence, he grinned.

How he loved his Louise!

Together they'd built the famed Bellview and Stratford hotels in Philadelphia, and Louise added innovatively feminine touches like fresh flowers and room service—until then, unknown in the hotel world. Such a wise woman!

As he built his hotel empire with his wife's support, love, and womanly wisdom, they focused on catering to the ultra-rich, including the Asters and Vanderbilts, charging the highest prices but offering unique and desirable amenities and drawing a loyal clientele.

Then, in 1893, William Waldorf Aster asked him to be the proprietor of the Waldorf Hotel in New York City—for a million-dollar salary a year! He smiled at the memory. What a day that was!

His wealth now secure, he came up with a brilliant plan. He leased the Astoria Hotel next to the Waldorf property and cleverly merged the two into the world-renowned Waldorf-Astoria Hotel.

George chuckled. "Well done, old chap! Well done."

"Did you say something, dear?" Louise mumbled from her bed. "Are you talking to the smartest man in the world?"

"No, my love. I'm just talking to myself."

He waited for her lilting laugh at their inside joke, but silence ensued.

Good. He didn't want to wake her, so he returned to his memories, clicking his tongue at the brilliance of foreclosing on Nikola Tesla's Wardenclyffe Tower, a wireless transmission station. A little out of his hotelier expertise, but an interesting endeavor.

And, thank the good Lord, all the while, Louise had faithfully journeyed with him. His years of effort and hard work, his fame—and his wealth—were secure. He and his precious wife were millionaires who wanted for nothing—and he'd give her the world if he could. His two children, George Jr. and Louise Clover, too. They would never be in want the way he had.

George lifted his head to the heavens, and with a grateful smile, offered a prayer of thanks to the One who'd mercifully led him thus far. Thank God. They'd never suffer as George had as a child.

Still, he never forgot his humble beginnings. The memories made him grateful for even the smallest blessing. So long as he drew breath, he helped others and passed on the blessing whenever possible. Though well-known for being a strict but caring employer, his staff both respected and revered him—and Louise, too. He encouraged his staff to rise in the ranks like he had, and many of his employees spent their entire lives faithfully working for him, knowing he'd treat them fairly.

A soft knock tugged him from his thoughts, so he quietly moved to the door and opened it, placing a finger to his lips. "Shhh. She's still sleeping. I'll leave you to it, miss."

Louise's lady's maid curtsied, and he left to dress for the day. Miss Madison Murray. How had she become such a treasured part of his wife's life?

In this world of grandeur, the young Irish immigrant had stepped into the opulent halls of their residence when his wife's previous lady's maid, Madison's Aunt May, suddenly died. But before that sad day, the maid had recommended Madison so highly that his sweet Louise hired her with nothing but a short personal interview. She hadn't even conferred with the housekeeper.

Yet, Madison had proven to be not simply another maid. Her nurturing spirit and compassionate ability to sense the needs of those around her soon endeared her to Louise. And, he had to admit, to himself. Since his wife was often confined to her room because of her fragile heart condition, Louise found comfort in Madison's presence—and he did, too.

Over the ten years that Madison had cared for his Louise, the relationship between the two women had blossomed into something deeper than employer and servant—it became one of trust and companionship. Louise saw in Madison a reflection of her own youth, a gentle spirit reminding her of the dreams she once held dear—and his dear wife told him so more than once.

Yet, he still wondered about the girl his darling Louise called Madison—not Murray like most wealthy women would. Beneath the surface, he suspected, Madison harbored a yearning for more— a whisper of hope that danced just beyond reach—and a sadness, too, that clung to her like a shroud.

George shrugged as he sauntered into his dressing room to prepare for the day. What was it about this young woman that so intrigued Louise—and himself? As with everything in his life, only time would tell.

CHAPTER 1

May 1903

Heart Island

Thousand Islands, NY

Madison Murray stood at the Alster Tower window overlooking the St. Lawrence River. The budding leaves of spring cast a soft, green haze across Heart Island. Her entire being ached from the beauty before her, mingled with a feeling she could not shake—a mixture of gratefulness and unworthiness.

She had poured all her strength into serving Mrs. Boldt, not only as a maid but as a companion, especially in these last difficult months. Yet, her own heart carried scars, hidden beneath the veneer of her duties.

She whispered a prayer, "Lord, grant me the strength to keep my past buried and to serve faithfully."

Madison tiptoed around the Alster Tower Venetian Room, preparing her mistress to rest but ready to be at her side when needed.

She helped Mrs. Boldt recline on the velvet fainting couch and covered her with an elaborate, soft quilt. "May I get you a glass of water or a bite to eat, missus?"

Mrs. Boldt sank into the pillow and closed her eyes. "Thank you. No. I need to rest awhile."

Madison curtsied, though her missus wouldn't see her sign of respect. She owed her that, and so much more. After all, her work as Mrs. Boldt's lady's maid had come as a lifeline, a chance to escape the shadows of grief and start anew, though the melancholy of it still lingered. Determined to honor her aunt's memory by serving the missus with unwavering loyalty, she had stepped into the role with both hope and trepidation.

A decade of care created a deep bond of love and loyalty between her and Mrs. Boldt, who felt more like family than anyone. Having lost everything, Madison had made it her mission to care for and protect the fragile woman who had shown her such abundant kindness.

She adjusted Mrs. Boldt's pale green skirts, pleased the missus had chosen the more matriarchal—and more comfortable— bell shaped full skirt and blouse. Though only forty-one, as her health diminished, the missus had refused to succumb to the fashionable Gibson Girl s-silhouette and the very uncomfortable corset it required, mainly so she could breathe more easily. And on days like today, her mistress refused a corset altogether, desiring to dress simply and comfortably.

Madison held back a grin as she slipped off Mrs. Boldt's shoes. Simple was a matter of opinion, for most of the missus's blouses had more than a dozen buttons and hooks in the back requiring help to dress. She didn't mind. She'd help her with anything, anytime.

Once the missus settled, Madison moved to a nearby chair and sat. She glanced around the beautifully ornate room reminiscent of the Italian city of Venice, her missus had told her when they first came to the island. For now, Alister Tower was the only structure they used on Heart Island, and these days, Mrs. Boldt often rested in the first-floor Venetian room rather than climb the steep steps to the opulent bedroom above.

Constructed from red sandstone, the Children's Playhouse, as Mrs. Boldt sometimes called it, resembled a German tower Kaiser Wilhelm had built. For the past three summers, the Boldts had hosted a plethora of events here, first opening the tower with a banker's association banquet and continuing with dinners, music performances, and the like. Here Mr. and Mrs. Boldt, their young adult son, George Junior, and their beautiful daughter, Louise Clover—along with many a guest—enjoyed the two-lane bowling alley, billiard room, and library while they waited for the castle to be completed.

Mrs. Boldt groaned and opened her eyes. "No need for you to watch an old woman sleep, dear. Take a walk and be back in an hour, please."

Madison hurried to her side and tucked the blanket around the fragile woman. "Are you sure you don't want me to stay, missus?"

Her mistress, whose weary eyes held a flicker of warmth, smiled. "I'm sure."

Madison fiddled again with the quilt, ensuring her lady was comfortable before bobbing a curtsy and quietly stepping out of Alster Tower into the spring sunshine.

Madison hesitated under the heavy stone entrance, concern etching deeper into her soul. She trembled at the harsh inevitability of what lay ahead, and her heart clenched.

From the moment Mrs. Boldt awoke in the morning, the woman's strength waned more each day, little by little, as if she had a leak that couldn't be plugged. The missus' once vibrant countenance no longer held the vivacity it had. Instead, her pale, drawn features replaced the life once so freely exuding from her, even though her mistress was but eleven years older than herself.

Yet Mrs. Boldt maintained her amiable attitude, a smile gracing her face. Even in her frequent moments of pain, an abundant kindness governed her actions. Just last month, Madison dropped the missus's expensive powder and spilled it all over the new Persian rug, but the missus forgave her amiably. Indeed, Mrs. Boldt was always charitable, treating Madison as a valued family member, and sometimes as an invaluable confidant.

Madison's eyes misted. She loved her mistress.

As a ship passed by Heart Island, Madison let out a quivering sigh. What would happen if? No! Nothing could happen to the missus. Surely the doctors could help her.

The Boldts were wonderful employers, and she never wanted her employ to end. Ever.

Madison had often viewed the couple's interaction as she hovered nearby, ready to meet the missus's every need, while Mrs. Boldt and her husband lovingly bantered, discussing their plans for the hotels they developed. The couple dreamed, planned, and worked together beautifully. She'd never seen two people so utterly connected, and she marveled at their intimate alliance.

She scowled. Her parents certainly were neither connected nor a team.

Now, in sweet and intimate partnership, the Boldts envisioned the grand castle as it rose stone by stone. The workers had already completed several outbuildings—the magnificent archway and most of the peristyle led visitors into the sheltered harbor. A stone dove cote, or the hennery as Mrs. Boldt called it, awaited a plethora of birds both for eating and admiring. The extravagant Powerhouse, with its three-sided clock tower, already chimed on the hour, every hour, and brought power to the island. Although still in the planning stages, the Italian Garden awaited a fountain centerpiece and the commissioned marble statues all the way from Italy.

She chuckled at the knowledge she so often heard, but held close. Information only she and Mr. Boldt's butler kept as secrets of their post. They didn't even discuss what they heard with each other, pretending not to be privy to the intimate plans Mr. and Mrs. Boldt shared. Like good servants should.

As Mrs. Boldt had grown weaker, Mr. Boldt's devotion to her grew stronger. Madison admired how deeply he cherished his wife, respecting her more openly, honestly, and adoringly than anyone she had ever seen—man or woman. More than a mother with her newborn babe. More than a bride on her wedding day.

"Blasted heart troubles!"

Madison swallowed the lump in her throat. The woman, who, by her very nature, had a heart bigger than the Heart Island her husband had designed for her, now struggled to keep it beating. Why would God allow such an infirmity to happen to such a fine woman?

She turned from the river and gazed at the magnificent Boldt Castle rising from the rocky island. The couple's monument to their love and partnership.

Madison took a deep breath of the crisp May air laden with the scent of early blooms and the faint tang of the river. She meandered toward the castle, her steps echoing in the momentary quiet of the island.

The warning signs had been there for months now—Mrs. Boldt's declining health, the hushed conversations among the staff, and the increasingly worried demeanor of her husband. As Mrs. Boldt's lady's maid, she was privy to the inner workings of the family's challenges. But what would her future be if she wasn't serving her mistress?

As she strolled along the gravel path winding through soon-to-be Italian gardens, her sense of foreboding hung heavy in the air. Did Heart Island hold its breath in anticipation of what was to come?

Lost in her thoughts, Madison rounded a bend, almost colliding with a man coming from the opposite direction. He was tall and lean, with a rugged handsomeness catching her off guard. His eyes, a striking shade of gray, held a mixture of concern and curiosity as they met hers.

"Forgive me, miss." He tipped his cap before removing it, revealing brown hair swept back from his forehead, his voice low and velvety. "I didn't mean to startle you."

She gathered herself quickly, smoothing down her apron with nervous fingers. "No harm done, sir. I should have been more attentive."

He smiled faintly, a gesture softening the intensity of his gaze, his sun-kissed hair blowing in the breeze. "Aye, are you one of Mrs. Boldt's attendants?"

"I am. Her maid."

Madison was unaccustomed to conversing with strangers, especially not handsome ones who appeared out of nowhere.

"I've heard she hasn't been well. I've been prayin' for better days ahead. How might she be farin' today?"

She hesitated, weighing her words carefully. "Thank you, sir. She has good days and not-so-good days. Today...she's resting."

His expression darkened a shade or two. What emotions lay beneath his polite façade? "Aye, I see. Please convey my best wishes to her. I'm Emmett O'Connor, by the way."

"Madison Murray." She bobbed a curtsy and gifted him with a tentative smile. "It's nice to meet you, sir."

The man inclined his head. "Likewise, Miss Murray. If you don't mind me askin', how are you findin' it here on Heart Island?"

She paused, unsure of how much to disclose to this stranger. Yet, something in his demeanor put her at ease. "Mrs. Boldt is pleased to see the progress on the island. I've been her maid for ten years now, and she has been part of the planning all along. She's a fine woman, and she has been good to me."

Mr. O'Connor nodded, a wink accompanying a slight smile. "Aye, I've met her a time or two. She has a generous heart. It's good you've found favor with her."

She stole glances at the man, curiosity tugging at her. "And what about you, Mr. O'Connor? Are you also in the Boldts' employ?"

He chuckled, the warm sound echoing through the quiet surroundings. "I oversee the castle's construction. I'm the construction engineer."

"Really?" Madison blinked, sucking in a breath. "It is quite a daunting feat, I'm sure, sir."

He nodded proudly. "Aye, but Mr. Boldt spares no expense in creatin' his vision of a fairytale castle for his beloved wife."

He waved a hand for her to proceed, so they walked together up the winding path, the castle looming larger with each step. When they reached a place where scaffolding hugged the castle walls, workers bustled about with tools and materials.

Madison gazed up in awe at the intricate stonework and towering spires. "It's...breathtaking."

He smiled, his deep gray eyes alight with passion. More than a head taller than she and clean shaven, he looked more the part of a wealthy businessman than a construction worker. But a deep scar over his left eye likely betrayed his demanding work.

"Thank you. It's a crackin' fine labor of love, really. Each stone is placed with care, every detail crafted to perfection. Is this the first time you've seen it up close?"

Madison nodded, pressing her lips together so she wouldn't gawk. They wandered through the construction site as Mr. O'Connor returned his hat to his head and explained the challenges and triumphs of building such a structure on an island. She listened attentively, drawn in by his enthusiasm and the fascinating world he described. She pushed aside the worries which plagued her earlier. Instead, she immersed herself in the tale of stone and dreams he painted with his words, as though she were a character in his personal fairy tale.

As they circled back toward the main path, he glanced at her, his features softening with a hint of concern. "Forgive me if I've jabbered on too much about work. I get carried away when I talk about the castle."

Madison shook her head, a smile tugging at her lips. "No, not at all. It's refreshing to hear someone speak with such passion. Thank you for sharing with me, Mr. O'Connor."

His smile widened, genuine warmth spreading across his handsome face. "Please, call me Emmett. And the pleasure was mine, lass."

They stood for a moment, a comfortable silence settling between them. Madison glanced toward the castle, its turrets reaching toward the sky, and then back at Emmett. Amidst the construction and the quiet beauty of Heart Island, a strange and unexpected connection to this man whose dedication shaped the very stones around her caught her by surprise.

Emmett tipped his cap and nodded, tossing her a playful wink. "Nice to meet you, Madison. I best be gettin' back to work. Can't be shirkin' my duties. Have yourself a fine day."

He strolled down the path, leaving her to ponder the encounter as she resumed her walk. There was something intriguing about Emmett—a sincerity in his dedication to building the castle, perhaps, or in the shared sense of unease about Mrs. Boldt's condition.

As she neared the end of her walk, she glanced back at the castle. Its elegant facade stood in stark contrast to the menacing malady accosting the precious Boldt matriarch. She couldn't shake the feeling the days ahead would hold challenges far greater than any she had yet faced before.

Yet, perhaps there might be unforeseen surprises as well.

~ ~ ~

Emmett sat at his castle construction desk, a stack of castle blueprints spread out before him. He and the masonry foreman had set up shop in what would become the staff dining room. While currently a bare-bones room, one day would be embellished with finery fit for an upper-class family rather than staff. That was the way the Boldts did things.

His fingers traced the intricate lines of the castle's latest designs, but his mind wandered back to the brief yet memorable encounter earlier.

Across from him, his colleague, Garrison, perched on the edge of a chair, his curiosity evident in the Cheshire-cat grin on his whiskery face. As the masonry foreman, Garrison and he worked closely together, though the man had only joined the team a month prior.

Finally, his friend could restrain himself no longer. "So, tell me about this young woman you met. What's she like?"

Emmett leaned back, a smile tugging at his lips as he recalled the pleasant meeting. "Madison is Mrs. Boldt's maid, though she strikes me as much more than a domestic servant."

Garrison raised an eyebrow. "Oh? How so?"

Emmett's thoughts muddled, as if he were piecing together an intricate puzzle. "Her eyes are the color of the river on a stormy day—dark blue with a depth hintin' at countless untold stories. Blathers. It's hard to look away from them."

He sounded like a lovesick schoolboy, even to his own ears, but he didn't care.

"Interesting," Garrison murmured, his lips pinched together as if holding back a guffaw. "What else?"

"She has this hair—burgundy fadin' to a soft, mellow brown. It catches the light in the most peculiar way, almost as if it's made of autumn leaves."

Garrison chuckled. "Poetic, Irish baird. Tell me more."

"She's got a splatter of freckles and this tiny turned-up nose makin' her look like a pixie. It's charmin', really. She's petite, barely five feet tall, but there's a strikin' strength about her. She moves with a kind of quiet determination. Aye, and she's obviously Irish, like me, though I couldn't tell from which county she hails. Not Cork, for a certainty."

Garrison's eyes danced with amusement. "You assessed all this on your first encounter? Quite the Sherlock Holmes, old chap. What did you talk about?"

"It was quite enlightenin', actually," Emmett said, a hint of admiration in his voice. "She's inquisitive and sweet, with a gentle nature. I found myself openin' up to her more than I intended."

Garrison's eyes widened as he leaned in. "Did she say anything about the Boldts?"

Emmett nodded. "Aye, she admires and respects them greatly, I'll give you that. When we talked about the castle, she listened with genuine interest, and her curiosity about the construction was refreshin'. It was as though she saw not just the stone and the mortar, but the dreams and ingenuity creatin' somethin' so grand."

Garrison grinned. "You've clearly been taken by her, old chap."

Emmett shrugged, a tentative smile rising, despite giving his friend more fodder with which to tease him. "It's not just her beauty and her countenance. It's her spirit, really. There's a quiet strength to her, a rare blend of kindness and resolve. I think there's more to her than meets the eye."

Garrison studied Emmett's expression, his chuckle giving away his amusement. "Well, she's made quite an impression on you. I bet my eye teeth you've made quite an impression on her as well. Sounds like a story worth unfolding."

Emmett chuckled softly. "Perhaps. For now, though, I'm just lookin' forward to seein' that this castle gets built. Let's get on with it, shall we?"

And they did. After discussing the next steps on the exterior edifice, Emmett led Garrison to the scaffolding on the south side of the castle. "I'm not too sure this crew has what it takes."

Garrison nodded. "I agree. Several of the men are rather shoddy with their building standards, and I've had to correct them twice for overlooking safety measures. They may be building just the scaffolding, but they could endanger our men if they aren't careful. We have to monitor them. On one, in particular."

Emmett huffed. The *one* was the second assistant of this season, and it wasn't even June. "I will. Count on it."

Because he surely couldn't depend on the *one*.

CHAPTER 2

Madison sat beside Hazel on the Wellesley House verandah, the soft breeze of the Thousand Islands rustling the tiny new leaves around them. The moment's stillness contrasted sharply with the churn of emotions inside her. She glanced at the footbridge connecting the tiny Tennis Island, a favorite spot of hers to ponder the day, before turning her attention back at Hazel.

She'd often observed her dearest friend and colleague, the head housekeeper, Hazel Preston, with a mix of admiration and a hint of apprehension. Preston, as everyone called her, carried herself with an air of authority that demanded respect. When in private, the two women used their given names—Hazel and Madison—and for that she was grateful.

As the head housekeeper of the Boldt family—wherever they resided—Hazel's wisdom and authority held Madison—and the entire household—steadfast. The woman's graying brown hair swept up with the grace of a swan's wings, an image making her both dignified and a tad whimsical. Her tiny, starched bonnet, seeming almost too delicate to restrain the authority she wielded, added a surprising height to her otherwise diminutive frame.

Abundantly plump, her expressive, thick eyebrows conveyed a silent strength and intelligence, often saying more than any words might. With the raise of a brow, she could bring a servant to tears or appear to read her mind. Other times, she filled a much-needed matronly role.

Adopting that trademark expression, Hazel peered at Madison and, in her usual calm tone, shared thoughts on life and work. "I've spent my whole life in service and never regretted a day of it. There's a deep peace in knowing you're fulfilling God's will while helping others."

Madison nodded and took a sip of her water, her gaze fixed on the sparkling river in the distance. She struggled to fully absorb Hazel's words, fear gnawing at her mind. "But Hazel… what happens if you lose the one person who's everything to you? Again and again? I love Mrs. Boldt. The whole family."

Hazel turned, her gaze soft but knowing. "Losing those we love is part of life, dear." The gentle tone conveyed much experience on the topic. "But God never leaves us, even when we feel alone. I know it's hard, Madison, especially with all you've been through. But He will carry you through whatever comes next."

Yes, Hazel was present when her Aunt Mary died and left her alone. Hazel saw. She knew.

The ache from her past rose in her chest once again. "I can't help but think about Mrs. Boldt. She's all I have. If anything happens to her…" Her voice trailed off as the depth of her fear pressed down on her chest. "What will I do?"

Hazel's hand settled on hers, warm and comforting. "I understand. I know you love her, and she loves you in return."

Madison shrugged, a storm of doubts still swirling in her heart. Hazel's words were meant to comfort her, but her fear of losing the last person who had given her a sense of belonging engulfed her. Instead, she remained silent, allowing the quiet to settle between them as she gathered the strength to face the uncertainty of the days ahead.

"You'd better prepare the missus for her trip to the castle. They're leaving in a quarter hour, and Mr. Boldt insists she accompany him to see the castle's progress. I'm coming, too, as they want to enjoy an El fresco luncheon at the island gazebo. Settle your heart and tend her well."

Madison stood and curtsied. "I will, ma'am. Thank you for your kind words."

Before long, Madison settled Mrs. Boldt onto the *Kestrel,* the Boldt's steamer. Then she took a seat in the rear next to Hazel, the sun shining warmly on her face.

As the Heart Island dock drew closer, the castle standing tall in the distance drew Madison's gaze. Its imposing silhouette always proved both awe-inspiring and intimidating. Yet that familiar sense of unease bubbled up inside her.

Hazel sat beside her, talking animatedly about the weather, but Madison barely heard her. Her thoughts focused on the future, on what might happen if Mrs. Boldt's health continued to deteriorate. She couldn't shake the feeling that the life she treasured here could slip away at any moment.

Mrs. Boldt coughed weakly, and Mr. Boldt wrapped his arm lovingly around her. At the moment, the missus didn't need Madison.

"Do you think Mrs. Boldt will be all right?" Madison whispered, struggling to mask the fear in her voice. "No platitudes, please."

Hazel glanced at the missus. "Honestly, I don't know. But I do know God has a way of caring for those He loves, and you must trust Providence."

"What if..." Madison began, her voice barely audible over the launch's motor and the breeze from offshore. "What happens then? I mean, what place will I have in this house, in this world, without her?"

Hazel gave Mrs. Boldt and Madison, a curious glance and lowered her voice. "If He takes Mrs. Boldt, He'll provide for you. You must trust Him." Hazel patted Madison's hand again, her touch warm but firm. "You have a servant's heart and a giving spirit. These traits will never go unnoticed. You've earned your place here, and you're stronger than you think. Stop fretting."

Madison wanted to believe it, but the doubt lingered. She couldn't help but wonder if, in the end, she was nothing more than a servant to them.

As the boat pulled near to the dock, her thoughts turned murkier. The Boldts, with their grand estates and world of luxury, would never *really* need someone like her—especially if Mrs. Boldt was no longer there. She loved being a part of their family, if only as a servant.

When the steamer stopped with a soft jolt, Madison's gaze flickered toward the shore, her heart racing as they disembarked. Mr. Boldt took charge of his wife while she followed a few paces behind. The burden of her thoughts only grew heavier as she stepped onto the dock.

"Welcome. I'm Garrison and will take you to the castle." The man stood by the water's edge, tall and broad-shouldered, with dark eyes piercing straight through her. He flashed a grin, and her cheeks burned.

Goodness. Had he noticed her looking his way?

After a few words with Mr. and Mrs. Boldt, the couple took the lead to the castle. Madison and Garrison followed, while Hazel headed to the gazebo with the boatman carrying the luncheon supplies.

Garrison leaned close and grinned. "So, you're the one Emmett's been talking about. He'll meet us in the Great Hall and will be happy to see you. He's been pining for you for days."

Madison blinked, taken aback by the sudden attention. "I…" she stammered, unsure of how to respond to such a personal comment. Emmett, talking about her? Pining? Finally remembering her manners, she curtsied. "Pleased to meet you."

Garrison's smile deepened, as if he found her reaction amusing. "It's good to finally meet you."

Madison's entire face burned at the comment as a second man slithered up beside Garrison. He was leaner, with sharp features and a cold, calculating air about him. He barely acknowledged Madison. "I'm Bruce Clawson, the assistant foreman." His eyes scanned her with a discomforting intensity. "More than an assistant, really."

A shiver ran down her spine, but she forced a smile, hoping she could mask the unease his presence caused her. "Good day."

Bruce gave a stiff nod but offered no further pleasantries. His haughty demeanor left a lingering distaste in her mouth. One she couldn't ignore.

Garrison, on the other hand, seemed amiable, his smile still lingering as he turned to lead them into the castle. "Come on then, let's join them. The castle's a beautiful place—although I'm sure you've seen enough of it already."

Madison nodded, her thoughts scattered in a world of *what ifs*. And as they walked toward the castle, she wondered just where she truly fit into this grand, complicated world.

~ ~ ~

Emmett ran a calloused hand over the granite stone in front of him. The cool smoothness beneath his fingers reminded him of a chilled melon fresh from the field. Every stone they laid was a step toward a building far greater than any of them could imagine.

It had taken six years to get to this point—years of hard work, sacrifice, and a relentless belief in Mr. Boldt's vision. "Ah, Boldt Castle will be a triumph like no other." He smiled as he waited for the Boldts and, he hoped, Mrs. Boldt's maid.

For Emmett, work was worship, his devotion woven into the fabric of the structure. This castle was more than a building—it was a monument to what could be achieved with creativity and determination thanks to Mr. Boldt's vision—and his team's hard work. Each strike of the hammer was like a prayer, an offering of an accomplishment bigger than himself.

But the satisfaction he took in the process was often challenged by those who didn't see the work the same way.

As the group arrived, he hurried to greet them, his boots echoing off the stone floor of Boldt Castle's wide verandah. "Welcome Mr. and Mrs. Boldt."

He glanced at Madison and gave her a quick nod. Her gaze dropped. And was that—he smiled—yes. A blush creeping up her neck. Ah, the innocence of the lass.

The Boldts entered the castle, and Mr. Boldt's eyes shone with a mixture of pride and curiosity. This castle was his masterpiece. And a little bit Emmett's, too.

He waved a hand toward the towering stone archways. "Aye, this here's the grand entrance hall." There was beauty in the angle the light hit the stone, the way the massive staircase rose high above them. "The lads are doing a fine job with the stonework. Took a few tries, but it's all comin' together step by step."

Workers scurried around the site, moving with purpose. Some waved at Mr. and Mrs. Boldt as they passed, some bowed, others gave a quick nod.

But they also acknowledged him, and their respect brightened his day. So did the hum of activity, the steady rhythm of hammers and chisels. It wasn't just that the men honored him. They trusted him, too. He'd earned their esteem, and it was good.

Mr. Boldt's eyes flickered over the space, nodding. "Impressive, Emmett. How long do you estimate before this is fully finished?"

"Ah, with the pace we're keepin', I'd say we'll have much of the first floor done by the end of the season." He adjusted his stance. "After this, we'll focus on the finer details about the place. It'll be a crackin' beauty, mark my words."

"Then, I approve." Mr. Boldt nodded. "Very good. Continue on then."

"And this," Emmett continued, leading the small group further into the hall, "the grand staircase is takin' shape well. As you planned, it rises from the center, leadin' to the upper floors. It'll make quite the statement when your guests arrive, I reckon."

Mrs. Boldt, walking beside Madison, leaned in slightly, whispering loud enough for him to hear. "He's quite proud of his work, isn't he?"

Madison nodded, casting him a soft smile. "As he should be, I expect."

Emmett's face flamed at the compliments.

Mrs. Boldt turned to him, a gentle grin warming her words. "You're enjoying the work you're doing here, aren't you?"

"Aye, I am, Mrs. Boldt." He bowed a tad, his voice softening for a moment. "This place…it means more than simply stone and timber to me. I've seen it take shape, stone by stone, and it's been a long road. But we've come so far…" He gestured expansively, sweeping his arm to take in the room, "and we're almost there."

Mr. Boldt joined his wife. "You've been overseeing this project from the start, Emmett. You must know every inch of this place by now."

He flashed a grin, his pride swelling. "Aye, sir, I've been privileged to see every stone laid, every beam placed. I've overseen it from the cornerstone and would be mighty proud to see it to the finish. There's not an inch of this place I don't know."

Mr. Boldt smiled. "Thank you for your faithful, hard work. I'd like to see the library now, please."

"Aye. This way."

He led them to the almost completed library, the respect in Mr. Boldt's words touching him deeply. It was a small thrill, but one he'd earned. He stood an inch or so taller knowing how the Boldts appreciated what he did. And the fair lass, Madison, seemed to appreciate his work, too, for her smile widened and her cobalt eyes sparkled.

He joined Garrison, where his colleague was adding the last touches to an elaborately carved American chestnut mantelpiece. A grin played at the corner of his friend's mouth, and he shot a knowing glance at Madison.

Thankfully, Garrison greeted the Boldts rather than mention the fair lass. "Mrs. Boldt, if you please, notice the faces of a boy and girl on either side of the fireplace and a haggard woman here." He pointed to a figure with a witch-like nose. "Remind you of Hansel and Gretel? Your husband suggested it. A nod to his German heritage, I s'pose."

The missus's eyes twinkled. "Thank you! Won't our grandchildren be delighted, husband? And the leaded-glass door frames and built-in bookcases are lovely, too."

"Nothing but the best for my queen." Mr. Boldt chuckled. "I hope one day we'll have a boatload of grandchildren, but we must be patient. Neither George Junior nor our darling Clover are yet betrothed. Shall we catch a breath of fresh air on the verandah, darling?"

Mrs. Boldt nodded, and without another word, the couple stepped onto the adjoining porch. Madison stood at the threshold, ready to attend to her mistress's needs.

Emmett's heart warmed. What a blessing this faithful maid must be!

As the couple returned to the room, the Boldts took in the space with an appreciation for it, and although polite, their interaction seemed almost intimate. Their dream was coming to life.

Garrison returned to his work polishing the wood. Madison turned her eyes away as if to give the couple privacy. He suspected she felt the same as he. The Boldts had a way of enfolding each other into an invisible embrace that could make you blush.

When the Boldts, Madison, and he left the library and returned to the Great Hall, his assistant foreman, Bruce, stood off to the side, clipboard in hand, a faint scowl marring his face. The man was a surly sort, always focused on his minimal authority to enforce strict discipline.

Bruce glanced at the Boldts and gave the nearby worker a little shove. "Step up your pace, you lazy toad."

The worker cowered at his rough treatment but hammered harder.

Emmett muttered under his breath, more to himself than anyone else. "Respect is earned, Bruce." There was more to leadership than simply being a cruel taskmaster.

"Pardon?" Madison asked, stepping up next to him. "Did you say something?"

"Ah, nothin', miss."

He cleared his throat and waited for the group to inspect the Great Hall one more time. Their smiles and whispers revealed they were pleased.

He glanced over his shoulder, catching the faint sound of Bruce's voice, low and grumbling behind him. The words were too distant for him to make out clearly, but he could guess well enough. Bruce had been muttering about *the overly ambitious foreman* for days now. It was always the same with him—never a kind word, never an ounce of respect for anyone else's way of doing things.

Not even for him as his superior.

Emmett's jaw tightened. He didn't let it show, of course. He was the foreman here, and if there was one thing he'd learned— a leader needn't waste time on petty complaints. He had a job to do, and he wouldn't let anyone, especially Bruce, distract him from his mission.

Squaring his shoulders, Emmett set his focus back on the task at hand. "Shall we continue?"

Mrs. Boldt sighed, reminding him of a wilted daisy. The poor woman was exhausted. She shook her head, addressing her husband. "Another time, dear?"

"Of course, darling." Turning to Emmett, Mr. Boldt snapped a nod. "Thanks for your good work. Carry on."

"It's an honor to serve, sir." He bent low this time, showing his employer honor he was due.

Madison smiled and mouthed *Goodbye*, before following the couple out of the vestibule and onto the verandah.

They were gone, but the murmurs behind him grew louder.

Bruce again. "Too much enthusiasm, the Irish Mick. You can't build a castle on prayer. Such a fool!"

Emmett's fists clenched, but he didn't turn around. He wasn't about to let Bruce get under his skin. Instead, he prayed quietly, his voice barely more than a whisper. "Lord, give me patience and the strength to hold strong and steady."

He wasn't perfect. He knew it. Sometimes his temper flared, when his pride got the better of him. But this castle was worth it. It was more than just stones and mortar. It was a dream in the making, and he wouldn't let anyone stand in the way.

Trouble was, the company had hired Bruce with lofty accolades and kinship, too, so he was obligated to work with the man and hope he'd eventually become part of the team.

Fortunately, the workers who looked to Emmett for guidance had already made up their minds about him. They respected *him*. Not Bruce. They trusted *him*. Not the foreman. They saw the work *he*—not the assistant—put in, the care he gave to every detail.

They understood one thing—when Emmett O'Connor said something would be done, it would be done right.

And this meant more to him than any grumbling from Bruce or anyone else. Still, the man remained a thorn in his side, a constant source of dissension and discord. What to do?

He wiped the sweat from his hands, took a deep breath, and surveyed the Great Hall once more. The steel framework that would one day hold an extravagant stained-glass dome was taking shape, and soon enough, the Italian Carrara marble staircase and floors would be installed. He could already envision it in his mind—the finished product, elegantly grand, a monument to what they had all worked toward.

His eyes narrowed slightly as he spotted Bruce glaring at him from the shadows. The assistant foreman was no doubt waiting for an opportunity to undermine his authority. Again. Bruce yearned for a position of power, but he would never truly understand. Or attain it. Some men led with fear, but Emmett believed in earning loyalty, not demanding it.

It wasn't about power—it was about respect.

Taking one last look at the grand hall, he stood tall, shaking off the tension in his shoulders. He had a job to do, and as long as he had the strength to see it through, he would.

Nobody—especially not Bruce—would stop him.

CHAPTER 3

Madison stood near the lilac bushes beside the Wellesley House, their vibrant purple blooms a stark contrast to the worries weighing on her mind. She inhaled deeply, letting the delicate fragrance wrap around her like a comforting blanket. The great outdoors was one of the few places where a sense of calm, away from the anxiety that so often gnawed at her as she cared for her ailing mistress, brought her peace.

This flower garden was her sanctuary. The worries plaguing her during the rest of the day vanished here, in the presence of God's creation. But even more, she wanted to gather a bouquet to surprise her missus when she awakened. Mrs. Boldt loved lilacs, but she rarely ventured to the garden beside the house these days.

Her thoughts drifted to yesterday's castle visit. What had Garrison meant by saying Emmett pined for her? She shook her head slightly, rolling her eyes at the very idea. Pined? It made little sense.

Yes, the castle foreman was kind, polite, and willing to lend a hand. He had a way about him, making people feel at ease. But pining? Ridiculous. And what did this Garrison know of him, anyway?

She snipped a fully bloomed clipping just the right length for the missus's Italian crystal vase. Mrs. Boldt would love them. As she cut another, her thoughts wandered to the Boldts.

They had been so proud of Emmett's work, and rightfully so. She had witnessed the admiration in their eyes as they spoke of his contributions to the castle's construction. He wasn't simply a worker. He was the heart of their project. The soul of Mr. Boldt's declaration of love for his wife. The workers, too, honored him. They addressed him with reverence, a man who obviously knew his craft and commanded respect without demanding it.

But then there was that foreman. Bruce Clawson. She shuddered at the thought of the man. She'd heard rumors about him, and none were good. He had an unruly air about him—slick, harsh-talking, and far too arrogant. His presence made her skin crawl. And the way he looked at her when he thought no one was watching…she shivered at the recollection.

A sudden rustle in the leaves brought her back to the present. Emmett? She hadn't heard him approach until he stood right next to her. His presence startled her, and her hand fumbled with the basket she was holding.

"Blathers! Forgive me, Miss Madison." His accent wrapped around her name like a song. A flutter danced in her chest at the sound of it. "I surely didn't mean to scare you."

"It's...it's all right." She steadied her breathing. "It's good to see you, sir." She smiled, though her heart raced. "I was quite taken by the wonderful work you do. Mr. and Mrs. Boldt spoke of nothing else the rest of the day and again this morning at breakfast."

Madison glanced at the lilac bushes, brushing a stray flower petal from her dress. Her eyes fell back to his steady gaze. She reached down to pluck a weed from the garden, anything to keep her hands busy. She wanted to appear unaffected, but her mind was far from calm. "How did you come to work for them?"

Emmett leaned against the side of the house, the edges of his shirt sleeves rolled up to reveal muscular forearms from years of hard work. His posture was relaxed, but there was a spark of pride in his eyes.

He paused for a moment before replying. "Aye, I work for the Hewitt firm—G. W. & W. D. Hewitt, the architectural firm out o' Philadelphia. They specialize in designin' churches, hotels, and large residences. When they were hired for this project, they chose me to manage the construction."

She listened intently, fascinated. "What does your role entail?"

He smiled, glancing up at the clouds drifting by. "I handle the day-to-day operations. Correspondence with the firm, managin' the construction team, overseein' deadlines, and makin' sure everyone stays safe on site. I work with the other managers to keep things runnin' smooth—keepin' the work within budget and on schedule. Meetin'—or exceedin'—the quality standards the Hewitts expect. It's a challenge, but I enjoy it. Aye, I do."

He paused, his eyes glinting with enthusiasm. "I spend a fair bit o' time with the blueprints too, and I enjoy every page. Those plans are intricate—every detail counts, ya see. The Boldts have created an incredible masterpiece, they have, and I enjoy the challenge o' bringin' it to life."

She listened with rapt attention as he spoke. The way he carried himself, so professional and yet so approachable, made him intriguing. And his enthusiasm for his work was much like hers. Emmett clearly had a passion for the intricacies of construction, for the blueprints, and for the challenge of bringing grand designs to life.

As they spoke, she realized how comfortable she felt in his presence. His steady voice calmed her, and she finally felt a connection with someone new, not from her past. His company conjured feeling she wasn't sure about.

She smiled softly, tucking a stray strand of hair behind her ear. "It must be a lot of responsibility."

"Aye, lass, it is. But I don't mind." He gave her a wink and a wide grin. "It's so fulfillin' to see a project come together. When I step back, and I see the work done well…there's satisfaction in it. From what I've seen, you, too, have a similar dedication to your own work."

She nodded, her heart fluttering unexpectedly. She had always admired faithful service, but seeing someone who truly loved their job—someone who thrived in it like she did—was refreshing. Most of her colleagues did what they were told, but lacked the enjoyment of it. She related to his devotion, and it captivated her in ways both exciting and confusing.

She needed to move the conversation to safer soil.

Madison hesitated for a moment before asking, her voice soft, hoping she didn't come across as nosy. Or forward. "Where do you stay when you're not working on the castle?"

Emmett shifted for a moment, his eyes flicking away from hers, as if the question had caught him off guard. For a split second, she saw something in his gaze—something deep or painful—but it was gone before she could fully grasp it.

"In the Yacht House on Fern Island." His words were slow and deliberate. "A small room. It's quite enough."

Madison furrowed her brow, sensing there was more to it. "Did you grow up here, or are you from Pennsylvania where your employers reside? Do you have family nearby?"

His jaw tightened, and his posture stiffened. "I *had* family." Bitterness crept into his voice. His tone darkened, and the shift in the atmosphere chilled her. The temperature dropped with the tension between them. "It's painful to talk about 'em."

The words hit her harder than she expected. She hadn't meant to bring up troublesome memories, but his demeanor shifted, as though he was closing off from her.

"I'm sorry." She regretted the question because it caused him pain. "I didn't mean to upset you."

He ran a hand along his jawline, his eyes briefly meeting hers before turning away. "Aye, lass, it's not your fault." His voice was so low, she wanted to lean in closer to catch every word. But she hesitated. "I just...I don't like to talk about it."

She'd crossed a line.

Madison nodded and looked down at the ground, her heart heavy with unspoken words. She had meant to ask a simple, safe question, but instead she'd erected a wall between them that hadn't been there before.

For a long moment, neither spoke. Emmett seemed lost in his own thoughts, and an uncomfortable silence stretched between them, a gulf of grief and loss hanging over his words too great to bridge in a single conversation.

When he finally spoke again, his voice was softer, though still distant. "I…I lost everyone when I was nineteen—parents, siblings. A fire. I wasn't...I wasn't there to save them."

The words were only a whisper, barely audible, but Madison detected agony. She reached out, wanting to offer comfort, but hesitated, unsure if he would welcome it.

His eyes flicked to hers once more, this time with a hint of apology. "I don't often talk about it, my lovely lass. It's just better that way. Please don't share this with anyone. It's a private matter."

Deep hurt narrowed his eyes, a pain he carried like an invisible load. The air between them had shifted completely.

She wasn't sure what to say now, so she nodded, knowing some wounds were too deep to heal with a single conversation. "Of course, sir."

She turned to the bushes and snipped three more clippings, slipping them into her basket. "But now, I better get back to the missus. She may wake at any moment. I hope you have a good day. And again, I'm sorry I asked so many questions."

"Aye, my lovely lass. It's all right. Good day to you."

But was it all right? His eyes said otherwise.

~ ~ ~

Emmett's chest tightened as he walked away from Madison, his boots crunching softly on the gravel path. His pulse quickened, and his mind raced, the words he'd spoken echoing in his ears.

A fire? I wasn't there to save them? He kicked at a solitary pebble on the pathway, sending it skittering into the underbrush. If only he could do the same with his words. "I'm such a dunderhead."

His heart sank as he replayed the moment in his head. He never, ever spoke of his past. He had sworn to himself no one would ever know the truth. The truth of his failure.

But Madison had a way of drawing it out of him, as if she reached into his chest and pulled out what he was hiding, no matter how tightly he kept it locked away. His breath came in shallow bursts as he fought to steady himself. He didn't want her to see this side of him—the broken man he'd become. The one who couldn't save his own family.

But now she knew.

No one had ever known. Not Garrison. Not the Hewitts, nor the workers, nor the few friends he'd made along the way. He'd kept this part of himself buried, locked up, never to be shared. His heart had turned cold with guilt, so cold he allowed no one close enough to chip away at it. Not even for a moment.

Yet with Madison, that wall had crumbled in an instant.

Why had he told her?

He shook his head, furious with himself. She didn't deserve to carry the burden of his past. And yet, there was something about her. The way she looked at him with those gentle eyes. The way she listened as if she actually cared.

Nobody had ever cared like that. She made him vulnerable in a way he couldn't understand, a feeling he resented. He slowed his pace as he reached the edge of the property, his fingers curling into fists.

She hadn't meant harm, of course. She'd only asked a simple question, and she didn't deserve such a heavy answer. But now the wound was open, the scar raw, and he felt it—the sting of guilt, the gravity of the lives he hadn't been able to save.

He whispered into the wind. "You should've been there, Emmett. You should've been the one to protect them. God! Why didn't you save 'em?"

The thoughts spiraled through his mind, consuming him once again. He'd been so focused on the future, on the task at hand, on burying his heartache in his work. He had forgotten how quickly his pain could return, how easily it could awaken.

And now, in an instant, Madison had slipped past his defenses. She'd never understand. And if she did, she'd never forgive him.

He still saw her face, the way her eyes softened, how her lips parted as if she wanted to offer words of comfort, but she hadn't.

She didn't need to. It was the way she'd simply accepted his silence, the way she hadn't pressed him for more. She had understood, even without him explaining further.

But that didn't make it any easier.

He headed across the tiny footbridge to the Fern Island Yacht House, his mind a whirlwind of conflicting thoughts. His instincts told him to pull away, to put up the walls again, to shut her out as he had with everyone else.

But his heart—his heart told him differently. Madison's presence was the first breath of fresh air after years of suffocating. She made him feel...seen.

And it terrified him.

He stopped walking and scratched his chin, his teeth clenching with resolve. No more. This ends now. He couldn't let her in.

He couldn't afford to let anyone in.

Emmett took a deep breath, the heaviness of his decision pressing down on him like the granite cornerstone of the Boldt castle. It would be better this way—better if she didn't know him, didn't know his history, didn't see him for what he truly was—a man who had failed those he loved most.

He returned to the Yacht House, grabbed a skiff, and headed for the castle, his face set. He needed to get to work. He needed to forget.

But Madison's face lingered in his thoughts, the way she had looked at him, the way she had listened so carefully. And for the briefest moment, he wondered if there was a chance—just a slip of an opportunity—that he might let her see more.

But no. He quickly squashed the thought, the burden of his vow heavier than ever.

No one would ever know the truth. Not even her.

When he entered the castle, he silently joined Garrett already at his desk, preparing for the day. The man was not merely a fellow worker on the castle project. He was someone Emmett turned to when the weight of his world was too heavy.

Garrison was the sort of man who could laugh at anything, and yet there was a sharpness in his eyes making him easy to confide in—though he wasn't sure how much he wanted to share about this.

Garrison looked up from his desk, his brow furrowing as he took in Emmett's somber expression. "Good morning, chap. Something on your mind?"

He hesitated, then slipped into the chair across from him. He scratched his chin, his thoughts tangled in knots. "I feel like...like I've lost control. I never even meant to let it in."

"Let what in? Or should I say who?" Garrison leaned back in his chair, taking a swig of water before setting the glass down. "Go on, then. Tell me what's weighing on you."

Emmett sighed, his shoulders heavy with emotions he needed to control. "It's Madison. She has this way about her...I can't explain it, but it's like she sees through me. Not the facade, not the 'engineer' or the worker—just...me." He paused, his throat tightening. "And it scares me."

His friend raised an eyebrow, the usual cheeky grin fading into a more serious expression. "She broke through? You've always been one to keep your distance."

"Aye. I know." He clenched his fists, and the burn of frustration rose in his chest. "I don't know what it is about her. When she looks at me, it's like she sees through the walls I've built. Like she knows the parts of me I've long buried. And it's too much. I didn't want any of this. I didn't want to care."

Garrison studied him quietly. "I see. But you're human. You can't keep shutting down your heart forever."

He shook his head sharply, embarrassment bubbling over. "Nae. I've got no business lettin' her in, Garrison. My past...what's behind me...it's not somethin' I can share. It's not somethin' I can burden her—or anyone—with."

The room was silent for a long moment. Then, Garrison responded with a gentleness he had never expected. "The past cannot be outrun forever, my friend. It'll follow you, whether or not you like it. But it doesn't mean it has to define your future. And it doesn't mean others will see you as the broken man you think yourself to be. If she's pulling at your heart, maybe it's because she sees more than your scars."

Emmett rubbed his temples, his mind spinning. "I don't know how to trust her. Or anybody else. I only know I can't trust myself." He stood abruptly, pacing back and forth across the small room. "The guilt, the shame—it's eatin' me alive. I can't let her see me like this, Garrison. I can't let her know the real me."

Garrison's gaze softened as he stood, moving over to stand beside him. "I understand. I do. Guilt will eat you up if you let it. But don't let it destroy the special friendship knocking at your door. She's not the one who caused your pain, but she might just be the one to help you heal."

He stared at Garrison for a long time, unsure how to respond. Deep down, part of him knew his friend was right. He'd always kept people at arm's length—put his work first, buried the pain. But now, with Madison, the walls felt weaker, the distance between them smaller.

"I don't know what to do with this." The folly of the decision pressed on his chest. "But I think I want to."

Garrison clapped him on the shoulder. "You don't have to figure it all out now. Just...be honest with yourself. Whatever happens, it'll be better than keeping it locked away."

He nodded, but the doubt still lingered, gnawing at him. Could he really open up to her? He didn't know the answer, but one thing was certain—he was standing at a crossroads.

And he had to choose which path to take.

Just then, Bruce rounded the corner, his smirk and narrowed eyes making him appear even more of a scoundrel than usual. "What ain't you being honest about, O'Connor?"

Bruce? How much had he heard?

CHAPTER 4

In the following days, Madison looked forward to her brief encounters with Emmett—conversations and tiny moments where they laughed together, shared a quiet word, or simply enjoyed each other's company in the warm sun. She never realized how much she could enjoy time with a man, or how easily he would put her at ease. And day after day, she looked for him, seeking his smile, his laughter.

Yet, an invisible wall separated them. Why?

Her heart clenched at the sad truth. Perhaps he'd realized that friends were all they could ever be. For she, a simple maid, was far below the station of an important engineer.

So be it. Better to have a friend than no one.

As she headed into the castle, workers bustled around like bees in a hive. The pounding of hammering. Swishing of sawing. Metallic clanking of chisels on stone. Grunts of men heaving heavy stones. How he kept it all in motion was anyone's guess.

For weeks now, his crew had been working on the Reception Room, and he'd invited her to see it. When she stepped into the room, she gasped. It was already a most beautiful room, one to welcome visitors to the castle, where a butler would serve refreshments while guests waited for the Boldts to greet them.

Plaster molding, embellished with mythological sphinx and other strange creatures, caught her attention. How interesting the Boldts were! Even after ten years, they surprised her with their creativity.

Disrupting her reverie, a commotion came from the room to her right. The Billiard Room. She peeked around the corner, and a shiver ran down her spine.

Emmett mirrored Bruce's aggressive stance, his face red and eyes narrowed. His voice rose as he addressed the rogue. "Your threats and innuendos have no place here. And you'll not do shoddy work nor risk anyone's life with your foolishness." His Irish brogue thickened in his anger, his surge of righteous indignation evident. "Do ya understand?"

Instead of answering, Bruce walked away with a sneer. Madison shrank back, still able to view the spectacle of an underling's disrespect for authority and position.

Emmett shook a finger. "I'll not let this place be desecrated, even by the likes of you."

Madison stepped back another step, her breath catching in her throat as she processed what she had observed. Emmett, the man whose laughter warmed her heart, angered in the face of Bruce's disrespect. Bruce, the sniveling toad was, she suspected, a strange and dangerous fellow.

She shuddered. Maybe Bruce was more than strange. Perhaps he was dangerous.

Yet, even in an altercation, Emmett's passion for his work, for the integrity of the castle, shone through every word he spoke. She shook off a pang of fear for him.

She pressed herself deeper into the shadows as her friend ran a hand through his dark, unruly hair. The frustration etched on his face made her chest ache. This anger was a side of him she hadn't seen before. He carried the honor of his work like a badge, refusing to let anyone tarnish it.

Her fingers trembled as they rested on the cool stone wall. She should leave—she didn't belong here—but something held her back. Perhaps it was the way his shoulders slumped, as if the argument had drained him. Or perhaps it was the way her heart tugged her closer, against all reason.

Before she could decide, his voice startled her. "Who's there?"

She froze, scolding herself for not slipping away when she had the chance. There was no avoiding it now. She stepped forward, her face flushing as she met his gaze.

"It's me, Emmett. I didn't mean to…" She faltered, her words stumbling over themselves. "I came to see your work in the Reception Room. I just happened to…overhear."

His eyes softened, the harsh lines of his expression easing into a gentle smile. "Ah, Madison." He rubbed the back of his neck sheepishly. "Didn't mean for you to see this. Not my finest moment, I'll admit."

She shook her head quickly, her curls bouncing against her ears. "No, you—you were right to stand up to him. Bruce…he seems…" She trailed off, unsure if she should say what was truly on her mind. "Unreasonable."

"A bully." He finished for her, his voice tinged with disdain. "Aye, he's that and much more. I won't let him compromise the safety of the men or the beauty of this place. The Boldts deserve better than shoddy work, and so do the lads puttin' in the hours."

Madison nodded, admiration flowing through her. "I've met no one who cares so much about his work."

"'cept you, I 'spect, lass." He chuckled, a low, rich sound, making her cheeks heat again. "It's not just work for me. Someday, this place will stand as a monument to dreams—to what can be built with faith, sweat, and vision."

His words stirred something deep within her, a yearning she hadn't realized she carried. To be part of something bigger, something meaningful. But she quickly pushed the thought away.

She was a maid and nothing more. Never would be.

"Still," he continued, his voice dropping a notch in volume. "I hate for you to have seen me in such a state. A bit of a temper on me, I'm afraid."

"I didn't see a temper." Madison surprised herself with her boldness. "I saw a man who stood for what's right."

For a moment, they simply faced each other, silence hanging between them. His gaze searched hers, as if deciphering a puzzle he couldn't quite solve. Madison shifted under his scrutiny, her hands twisting the fabric of her apron nervously.

Finally, he broke the silence, his brogue curling around the words like a warm embrace. "You've a kind heart and keen mind, Madison."

Her lips parted, but no words came. What could she say? That she felt the same way about him? That his kindness, his passion, had touched her life more than anything she had ever known?

Before she mustered a response, approaching footsteps echoed off the walls, shattering the moment.

Emmett straightened, his expression slipping back into professionalism. "Best we not linger here." His tone was brisk, but not unkind. "Bruce's surliness may not be spent just yet, and I don't want you endangered. May I show you the Reception Room?"

She nodded. Danger? Was Bruce more than creepy? Was he a villain?

She shook off the thought and followed him to the center of the Reception Room. "Oh, Emmett, you've outdone yourself. This room is magnificent! The craftsmanship, the refined elegance and classic details…it's simply breathtaking. Like so many of the Boldts' creations. Its soft cream tones, ornate plasterwork, and intricate ceiling details immediately draw the eye upward."

He chuckled. "You have a way with words, lass. Aye, the oval medallion ceilin', surrounded by delicate floral and scroll motifs, reflects the craftsmanship of the Boldts' vision. And the walls, framed with decorative plaster reliefs, add texture and depth. These elements give the room a formal and harmonious feel, don't you think?"

Madison nodded. "I do. And these large windows let in the lovely river light, highlighting your craftmanship and creating a sense of openness. I envision the draperies will be rich and tailored, with swags and tassels to complement the overall decor."

He swept his hand wide. "Aye, and this fireplace and its marble mantel serves as a crackin' fine focal point. The missus has ordered a large mirror to reflect the light and visually enlarge the room. Still, this room is only as grand as the dreams and talents shapin' it. So, it's not truly finished, is it? Not until Mrs. Boldt breathes life into it with her own special touch."

Madison's fingers brushed against the polished wood paneling, enjoying the banter. "And she will. I can imagine this paneling, so rich and warm, framed with paintings of the river and the islands. Perhaps a grand portrait over there reflecting the Boldt family's legacy."

He smiled. "Aye, a fine idea. And what would they have for furnishin's? Velvet settees, I'm guessin', to match the elegance o' the room?"

She nodded. "Perhaps deep jewel tones. Emerald green or ruby red, with golden trim. Regal, but inviting. And over by the windows, a pair of armchairs, so guests can admire the view of the river while they sit and talk."

"You've got a grand imagination, Madison."

She giggled at the compliment. "And perhaps flowers to soften the room. And rich Persian rugs. Deep reds and golds, tying everything together. They'll make the room feel grounded, even with all its splendor."

His smile softened, a touch of tenderness in his eyes. "And see how the polished wood floorin' has a subtle geometric inlay, adding an additional layer of detail and craftsmanship? It's grand, but it's the womanly touches that'll make it truly elegant."

She glanced out the window, remembering her duties. "I'd love to stay, but I must get back to the missus. Thank you for showing me this."

"The pleasure was all mine, lass. And Madison, may your heart be light and happy, may your smile be big and wide, and may your pockets always have a coin or two inside. It's an Irish proverb I wish to give you."

"Thank you."

Madison curtsied, her heart warmed as she turned to leave. This was the real Emmett. Not the angry one. As she walked away, she caught one last glimpse of him standing in the elegant room he was so proud of. The man who unknowingly was capturing her heart.

In an instant, she realized just how dangerous her feelings had become.

~ ~ ~

Emmett returned to his desk with a light step, despite the earlier confrontation with Bruce. Madison's presence lingered in his thoughts. She had made all the difference in his day. As usual.

He glanced out the small window near his desk, sunlight streaming in and catching dust motes in the air. The rhythmic sounds of construction echoed through the building, a reminder of the work they were here to accomplish.

Garrison looked up from his plans. His eyebrows arched in curiosity. "Did you show her? Did she like it?"

He dropped into his chair, the wooden frame creaking slightly, and he leaned back with a sheepish grin. "Aye, I showed her. Might've waxed too lyrical about all the architectural details, mind you, but she liked the room just the same."

His heart quickened as he recalled Madison's face, her eyes lighting up at the sight of the carefully designed space. "She had the most wonderful ideas for how to embellish it. Furnishings, paintings, drapes. The lass would add a fine womanly touch to anything she put her hand to, I reckon."

Garrison chuckled, setting his pencil down. "I'm sure she didn't mind you gabbing her ear off."

Warmth crept up his neck. "Maybe, but you know how I am—I could talk the ear off a donkey, especially when I get flustered. And she has a way of gettin' me all in a tangle."

Garrison nodded with a knowing smile. "Seems she does, old chap. But you've got the gift, Emmett. How many times did you kiss the Blarney Stone before you emigrated, anyway? I hear it'll set you to gab."

He laughed, the sound rolling out rich and full. "Ah, away with you! I don't need the Blarney Stone. I came by it honest, from my dear mum."

Their laughter mingled with the lively chatter of the workers in the adjoining room. The camaraderie among the crew was palpable, their voices rising and falling like the tide. It was a comforting backdrop to the day's work, reminding him he was part of a larger team working toward a shared vision.

Here, amid blueprints, timber, and the scent of sawdust, Emmett was in his element. The workers respected him, not just for his skill, but for his leadership. They followed him willingly, their trust in him evident in the quality of their work.

All except…

His smile faded as a shadow passed over his thoughts. He let out a heavy sigh and rested his forearms on the desk. "I had a row with Bruce this mornin' and Madison overheard. I can't keep dancin' around the man's vitriol or his incompetence. I fear he may gather a rabble around him."

Garrison's expression sobered. "I agree, but since the Hewitt brothers hired him directly, you're kind of caught in a pickle, aren't you?"

"Aye." He ran a hand through his hair. Time for a visit to the barber. Maybe next week. "Bruce's arrogance and stubbornness are a detriment to this project. He's already alienatin' the men, and if he keeps it up, it could endanger the work. I don't want to escalate things, but if he forces my hand…"

Garrison leaned forward. "You'll have to handle him without letting it fester. If he undermines you, the crew will notice, and that's what will breed resentment." He gave him a half-smile. "But you've got Madison in your corner now, eh? She may give you the wisdom to handle this with grace. Besides me, as your esteemed counsellor, of course."

Emmett smiled at the thought of her. "Aye. She's got a way of seein' straight to the heart of things."

"And maybe she can soften Bruce up while she's at it," Garrison teased with a wink. "Lord knows you've already got your hands full, keeping the rest of us in line."

They shared another laugh, but the underlying tension lingered. Garrison leaned back in his chair. "You'll figure it out, Emmett. You always do. And remember, not every fight's worth picking. But if it comes to it, you've got the lads on your side. They trust you. That counts for a lot."

He nodded, though his jaw tightened. "Aye, but I don't want to divide the men. Unity keeps this entire project movin'. If Bruce stirs the pot any more than he already has…"

Garrison clicked his tongue. "Just tread carefully. A wrong step with Bruce, and the Hewitt brothers might start asking questions neither of us wants to answer. He has their ears."

He sighed, drumming his fingers on the edge of the desk. He hated the precarious line he had to walk. On one hand, Bruce's attitude and incompetence were festering problems. On the other, alerting the Hewitt brothers would feel like admitting failure in managing the team. And where would this leave him? A weak leader, perhaps even dispensable. The thought twisted like a knife in his gut.

He couldn't let that happen.

Before Garrison could say anything more, a loud crash came from the adjoining room, followed by a chorus of shouts. Both men shot to their feet.

"What now?"

Emmett hurried toward the sound, his brows knitting together. He entered the room to find a stack of timber scattered across the floor, several pieces cracked and splintered. A handful of workers gathered around the scene, their expressions a mixture of annoyance and concern.

At the center of it all stood Bruce, his arms crossed and his face set in a scowl.

"Blathers! What in the name of heaven happened here?"

Emmett's tone came out sharp but steady as he surveyed the mess.

Bruce turned, his face flushing. "It's not my fault!" He jerked a thumb toward one of the younger workers. "Jimmy there wasn't watching where he was going and knocked the lot over. I told him to secure the pile, but you know how these greenies are."

Jimmy, barely out of his teens, blinked with wide, anxious eyes. He pointed to the far side of the room. "That's not true, sir. I was over there. I wasn't even near the timber!"

The other workers murmured their agreement, so his gaze shifted back to Bruce, who was now glaring at the group as though daring them to contradict him further.

Emmett inhaled deeply, fighting the urge to lash out. He willed his tone to be even but laced with authority. "Bruce, you were the one responsible for organizin' this load, weren't ye?"

Bruce's jaw tightened. "I might've been, but I gave clear instructions to—"

"That's enough!" Emmett held up a hand. His brogue thickened as his frustration bubbled just under the surface. "I'm not interested in your excuses. For now, I want this cleaned up, and the damaged timber assessed. We can't afford delays, d'you hear?"

The workers nodded and got to work, though a few cast wary glances at Bruce. Emmett turned on his heel, the tension in his shoulders aching.

By the time he reached his chair, he dropped into it with a weary sigh. "That man's goin' to be the death of me." He rubbed his temples. "I swear, if I didn't have Irish patience in me, I'd have him out the door already."

Garrison leaned against the desk, his arms crossed. "So, what's the plan? You can't keep sweeping this under the rug. He's a liability, and the lads know it. Sooner or later, the Hewitt brothers will too."

"I know, but if I go to them now, it'll look like I can't manage my own team. What kind of leader does it make me? Weak, that's what."

Garrison shook his head. "One who's tryin' to save the project before Bruce tears it apart."

Emmett leaned back, staring at the ceiling as if it might offer divine insight. "If I act too harshly, I risk alienatin' the lads or drawin' unwanted attention from the Hewitt brothers. But if I keep lettin' Bruce run unchecked, the lot of us might pay the price."

Garrison gave him a steady look. "You've got to do what's right for the crew, Emmett. They trust you to lead. If Bruce starts undermining their trust, it's all over."

Emmett clenched his fists, frustration and determination burning in his chest. "I'll talk to Bruce myself. One more chance. If he doesn't shape up, I'll deal with him—quietly. No need to bring the Hewitts into this unless I've got no other choice."

Garrison raised an eyebrow but didn't argue. "Be careful, Emmett. Bruce is a snake. Push him too hard, and he might bite back."

He nodded grimly. "Aye, he's a cladhaire all right, and I can't let him poison this crew. One way or another, this ends before it gets out of hand."

Garrison smiled. "Cladhaire? And that's Irish for?"

"A villain, a rogue, a skilamalink."

His friend guffawed. "I think cladhaire describes Bruce best. He's all those and more."

He clapped Garrison on the shoulder. "I think that be his name."

As the workers continued cleaning up the mess, the reality of his decision settled over him. There was no easy way out of this, but one thing was certain—he couldn't afford to falter now.

His leadership—and the project's future—depended on it.

CHAPTER 5

Madison's breath hitched as she bolted upright in her bed, her body drenched in cold sweat. The nightmare had returned, as vivid and haunting as ever, yet different. She closed her eyes, willing the images to fade, but they refused, playing out again in excruciating detail.

She was back in Ireland, just seven years old. The air hung heavy with the scent of damp earth and smoke. Shadows danced ominously across the walls of their small cottage, cast by the flickering firelight. Her father and brother sat at the wooden table, their faces lit with a warmth she hadn't seen in years.

A rare moment of peace in those turbulent times. Father wasn't intoxicated, for once. Mother was off helping a neighbor birth a baby.

Then came the knock—sharp and insistent. Her father stood, his broad shoulders tensing as he exchanged a wary glance with her brother. Her heart raced in the dream, just as it had on that dreadful night. The door creaked open, and there stood Bruce, his face a mask of cold cruelty.

Bruce?

The confrontation escalated quickly. Father owed him gambling debts. Accusations were hurled. Voices raised. And then, the flash of steel.

She screamed as her father lunged to protect her brother, but Bruce was faster. The knife glinted in the firelight as it plunged into her father's chest. Her big brother's cry of anguish echoed in the room as he charged at Bruce, only to meet the same fate.

Her legs felt like lead as she struggled to move, to scream, to intervene Instead, she froze, powerless to stop the horror unfolding before her eyes. Blood pooled on the wooden floor, its metallic scent mingling with the smoke. Bruce turned to her, his eyes dark and menacing, and for a moment, she thought he would come for her too.

But then the scene shifted, as it always did in her nightmares. She, left alone in the silent cottage, the bodies of her father and brother lifeless on the ground. The fire sputtered, casting long, ghostly shadows that mocked her grief.

Bruce? He wasn't the murderer. Mr. McTavish was.

Her hands trembled as she clutched the quilt closer. The dream was always the same, except for Bruce, but the pain returned every time. She pressed her palms to her eyes, holding back the tears. It was more than a memory—it was a reminder of all she had lost.

Yet, Bruce reminded her of McTavish in more ways than one.

She picked up her Bible from the bedside table. "Lord, give me strength to face this onslaught. To overcome this memory. Help me find peace." Flipping to the Psalms, her eyes landed on familiar words. "Yea, though I walk through the valley of the shadow of death, I will fear no evil: for Thou art with me; Thy rod and Thy staff they comfort me."

But she did fear. She hadn't found comfort. Ever.

By morning, the storm within had passed, but her frazzled nerves felt as though they had battled it all night. She dressed, smoothed her apron, and made her way to Mrs. Boldt's quarters, carrying a tray from the kitchen laden with tea and a slice of toast. When she entered, the sight before her made her stop short.

Her mistress sat propped up in bed, her face pale and drawn. The swelling in her legs and ankles had worsened, and her breathing came in shallow, labored puffs. Still, she managed a small smile as she entered.

"Ah, my dear." Mrs. Boldt's voice was weak but warm. "You look as though you haven't slept a wink. The storm must've kept you awake."

Madison set the tray down and perched on the edge of the bed, taking Mrs. Boldt's frail hand in her own. "It wasn't just the storm," she admitted. "I couldn't stop thinking about you. You're not well, and it frightens me."

The missus chuckled softly, though it twisted into a cough. "Oh, my dear girl, I've lived a long and blessed life. I hate that I'll be leaving one day, but only in the good Lord's time."

Tears prick her eyes. "Please don't say that, Mrs. Boldt. I couldn't bear to lose you, too. You've been like a mother to me since I came here."

Mrs. Boldt's expression softened. "And you've been like a daughter to me. I know it's an unusual relationship between maid and mistress, but I believe Providence brought you into my life. Which is why I must tell you…I've been praying for you—praying you find the strength to carry on, even when it feels impossible. The Lord never abandons His children, you know, even when the road is dark."

Madison wiped at a tear slipping down her cheek. "I know it in my head, but in my heart…it's hard to feel Him sometimes. Especially at night, when the silence is so loud, and I feel so alone."

Mrs. Boldt squeezed her hand. "You are never alone, my dear. Even when you can't feel Him, He's there, holding you. And you must remember, you have people who care for you, too. You've brought light into this house, Madison. Your kindness, your service—they're a gift."

Her emotions threatened to overwhelm her. "You've given me so much, Mrs. Boldt. I just wish I could do more for you."

"You do more than you realize," Mrs. Boldt said with a gentle smile. "But if you want to do something for me, promise me this—when the time comes, don't let grief steal your joy. Live fully, love deeply, and trust that God has a plan for you."

She nodded, though her heart was heavy. "I'll try. I promise I'll try."

The older woman leaned back against her pillows, her eyes closing as exhaustion overtook her. "It's all I ask, my dear. Now, let's not waste the morning with tears. Pour me a cup of tea and tell me what you were reading last night."

Madison reached for the tea, her hands steadier now. "Psalm 23," she said softly. "It says that even in the darkest valley, we're not alone."

"Ah, a good choice, and heed it well." Mrs. Boldt murmured, her voice barely a whisper. "Say, would you mind, dear, to fetch me a bouquet of those lilacs? They brighten up this room so and leave such a nice fragrance."

"Of course, ma'am." Madison nodded quickly and bobbed a small curtsy out of habit, the hem of her apron fluttering as she turned. Her shoes tapped lightly across the polished floor as she made her way to the garden beyond the veranda beside the house.

The missus's lilacs stood tall, draped liberally over their branches, dancing in the breeze, the scent intoxicating. Madison reached for a bunch, careful not to snap the stems too harshly. As she worked, the sound of footsteps crunching on gravel pulled her from her thoughts. Could Emmett be paying her a visit? It would be a treat.

"Well, well. Here I thought the lilacs were the loveliest thing in the garden, but I appear to be mistaken."

Madison froze, her fingers tightening on the blooms. She turned slowly. Bruce leaned against the white trellis. His hat was pushed back, exposing the smirk permanently fixed on his face.

"Good morning, sir."

Madison dipped her head but didn't lower her gaze. A dull unease settled in her chest.

Bruce strode closer, his boots dragging through the loose earth. "I'm surprised Emmett lets you wander off on your own. Or is it that he doesn't mind what you do?" His tone dripped with false concern, but his eyes flickered cruelty. "Some beau he is."

Madison's cheeks flushed. "I don't know what you mean, sir."

"Oh, I think you do." Bruce's grin widening. "The Irish lad's got trouble written all over him, you know. The Boldts may keep him on, but they're fools for it. I'm kin to the architects. Your

Emmett's a scrapper—a man who doesn't settle down for anyone. He's not worth your time. He'll only break your heart."

The words hit like stones, but Madison stood firm, heat rising beneath her collar. "Emmett's worth ten of anyone who talks like you."

She cringed at her thoughtless reply. She should have considered her words before speaking them.

Bruce's face darkened, though the smirk lingered. "Ah, so you're defending him. Careful, girl. A pretty face like yours will be wasted on the wrong sort."

"I'm not wasting anything."

Her hands shook as she clutched the lilacs. The blooms delicate blooms released a cloud of perfume, reminding her to treat them gently lest she bruise them.

Bruce stepped forward, forcing her to take a step back. "It's a shame, Madison. I could show you a better way. I…I am better."

She turned sharply, still gripping the flowers against her chest. "Good day to you, sir."

His low chuckle followed her as she hurried toward the house, her skirts swishing furiously. *Someone better*. His words rang like an ugly echo, taunting her all the way back to Mrs. Boldt's bedchambers.

But was Emmett really a scrapper? Only time would tell.

Emmett walked along the shore of the St. Lawrence River beside Madison, his hands tucked into his pockets. The fading sunlight painted the sky in brilliant strokes of orange and pink. The rays reflected on the Heart Island Powerhouse as they sauntered toward it. She clasped arms around herself, more from the unknown than the cool evening breeze, he guessed.

"What's botherin' you, lass?" He hoped his Irish lilt added softness to his insistence. "Tell me, now."

She hesitated, glancing at the rippling river. "It's Mrs. Boldt. She's so frail, though she still insisted on entertaining company tonight. It's too much for her. Even Mr. Boldt says so. Each day, she seems weaker. I don't know how much longer…"

Her voice broke, and she bit her lip, stifling tears.

He stopped and faced her, his tone gentle but earnest. "Ah, Madison, you're carryin' the weight o' the world on those wee shoulders, aren't you? It's not right for someone so tender to be burdened like this."

She shook her head. "She's been like a mother to me. I'd do anything for her, but watching her slip away—it feels like I'm losing part of myself all over again." She looked up at him, her eyes searching his. "Do you ever feel like life keeps taking from you, and you have nothing left to give?"

His jaw tightened, and he looked down at the ground for a moment, seeking an answer. "Aye, I have, lass. More times than I'd care to admit. But you've more strength than you know."

She offered him a small, weary smile before her gaze drifted to his face. "I've wanted to ask you a question for weeks." Reaching up, she brushed a stray curl from his forehead. "Might I ask, please, where you got this scar?"

He froze for a second, his hand instinctively reaching up to touch the jagged mark over his left eye. The scar, a pale line etched into his tanned skin, had been with him for years.

The ugly gash, a reminder of the risks he'd taken in his line of work, spoke volumes more than any words ever could. He dropped his hand and let out a slow breath.

The memory replayed in his mind.

The year had been long and difficult, filled with storms, setbacks, and the constant pressure to complete the Boldt Castle Powerhouse on schedule. As the leader of the construction crew, he worked alongside his men, not just because of his impressive physique or his years of experience, but because of his resolute dedication to the task at hand. Through rain and wind, he never asked the crew to do anything he wouldn't do. It was the way he had been raised—hard work was a virtue and sacrifice for the greater good was a given.

The accident happened one afternoon, when the winds were especially fierce. A section of bridgework collapsed, the wood splintering and crashing down. Closest to the falling debris, in a split second, he'd thrown himself into harm's way to protect one of his men. He hadn't thought twice before running into the chaos, using his body to shield a younger worker caught beneath the timber.

The impact had been swift, the edge of a broken beam slicing across his face. Blood poured from the gash over his eye, but he barely flinched. His men rushed to help him, but he refused to be carried off, insisting the other injured man be seen to first. Only after the crew was assured of the young man's safety did he allow himself to be patched up.

He never spoke of it again. Until now.

He shrugged, waving off her concern. "A workplace accident when we were buildin' the Powerhouse. I wasn't quick enough to duck."

Madison gasped softly. "How awful! I'm sorry, but I'm glad you're all right."

He pressed his lips together, though a dark shadow passed through in his gray eyes. "Aye, but it taught me an excellent lesson. I've gotta protect my men, no matter what."

Her fingers lingered for a moment near his temple before she let her hand drop. "I'm sorry you went through that. But the scar doesn't define you, Emmett. If anything, it makes you look more distinguished."

He smiled faintly as he permitted a flicker of warmth to break through his guarded emotions. And with her few words, the scar had become a badge of honor. "Ah, you've a gift for seein' the good in folks, don't you, lass? Even when they can't see it in themselves."

They stood in silence for a moment, the river lapping softly on the shore. Finally, he spoke again. "Mrs. Boldt's lucky to have you, Madison. And if there's anythin' I can do to help, you need only say the word."

Madison's smile softened at his words. "Thank you, Emmett. Just having a friend here—it helps more than you know."

He gestured toward the Powerhouse, its elaborate design silhouetted against the shimmering St. Lawrence River. "Have you ever been inside, lass?" His words came out in a rush, betraying his excitement. "I can give ya a proper tour."

She tilted her head, studying the towering structure connected to Heart Island by its elegant arched stone bridge. "I've only admired the outside, so I'd like to. But…is it safe? It looks rather—"

He chuckled, a deep, warm sound matching his thoughts of her. "Aye, lass, it's sturdy as the day it was built. And don't you worry—I'll keep you safe, here, there, or anywhere."

Her cheeks flushed at his words, but she nodded and followed him as he led her across the bridge. The wind carried the faint scent of the river as their steps echoed against the stone.

Together, they crossed the stone bridge, the river breeze rustling his hair and almost sending his cap into the river. When they reached the heavy oak door, he pushed it open with a firm hand, revealing the powerhouse's inner workings.

Inside, the air smelled of coal and oil. The high-ceilinged room was dim, illuminated by the glow of the electric lamps. The hum of machinery echoed faintly, and the massive generators stood like iron giants in the center of the room.

He motioned to one of the steam generators. "This is what keeps the island alive. She's a beauty, isn't she? Runs the lights and pumps water to the castle and to Alster Tower. Without her, the place would be dark as a tomb."

Madison stepped closer, her hand resting lightly on the iron surface. "It's remarkable." She leaned forward, looking all the way to the floor below. "To think all of this was built for one man's dream. George Boldt truly spared no creativity or expense."

"Boldt's a man who knows what he wants." He leaned against a nearby railing. "And he's got Fred Shutieb, the chief electrician, runnin' the entire operation. Coal's brought in by barge through the door over there by the waterway. It's no small feat, keepin' it all in fine workin' order."

Madison turned toward the open doorway he pointed to, through which the river sparkled in the fading light. "It's extraordinary. I never really thought about how the water and electricity make their way to the castle or to Alster Tower. And the chimes going off just now—they're lovely. I hear them every half hour. They remind me of home."

"Ah, the clock and chimes tower?" He clicked this tongue. "You've a good ear, lass. Those silver chimes came all the way from England, ya know. Westminster style, they are. I've been told you can hear 'em clear across the river, four miles away."

She smiled, a wistful look in her eyes. "We had bells in my village back in Ireland. I heard them ringing every Sunday morning, even from my room."

His expression softened. "You miss it, don't you? Ireland."

Madison nodded, her voice quiet. "Yes. But being here, seeing this…it makes me feel like I'm part of a grand plan. Like I belong."

"You do belong, lass." He tilted his head, his gentle gray eyes locking with hers. "You've a kind heart, Madison. You bring somethin' special to this place. To the Boldts."

Her cheeks flushed, and she glanced away, smoothing the fabric of her dress. "Thank you, Emmett. This means a great deal."

"Come on, then." He broke the tender moment with a grin and a clap of his hands. "There's more to see. If you're not too weary, I'll show you where the coal's kept."

She chuckled, following him. "You're quite the guide. Perhaps Mr. Boldt should add 'tourmaster' to your duties."

"Ah, if it means spendin' time with you, lass, I'll take the title gladly."

He teased, his laughter echoing warmly through the powerhouse. But if offered the opportunity, he'd grab hold of it with both hands and never let go.

As they left the main room, the steady hum of the machinery blended with the sound of the chimes ringing faintly. He smiled, a sense of wonder and peace settling over him. For the first time since arriving at Heart Island, he felt grounded—to the place, its history, and to the lovely lass walking beside him.

CHAPTER 6

Madison sat by the Wellesley House windows in the missus's boudoir. Early evening rays streamed through the thick panes and spilled onto the floral-patterned carpet. Outside, the pretty little bridge, the tiny stream, and the glistening waters of the St. Lawrence River stretched far and wide. An ironic scene of serene beauty, sharply contrasting with the pang of loneliness within her chest.

She held the delicate stack of letters in her lap—Louise Clover and George Jr.'s handwriting looping gracefully across the fine stationery. She unfolded the first letter to read aloud, its words painted with vibrant imagery of a bustling New York City.

Dearest Mother,

The season is in full swing here in New York, and Clover and I are quite swept up in the social whirl. There are balls every week—grand affairs filled with music, color, and laughter. The Astors held a particularly splendid evening last Saturday, where every fine lady wore a gown glimmering like starlight.

We met so many new faces at the Vanderbilt reception—everyone is abuzz with talk of the summer season ahead. And, dearest Mother, Clover assures me we shall come to you this summer, as we always do. She says there is no place in the world that soothes her soul like the Thousand Islands, and I quite agree.

We do miss you terribly and long to see you again. Until then, we send you all our love and pray this letter finds you in good health and good spirits. Know you are always in our hearts, even if we are far away.

Yours with much affection, George Jr.

A small sigh escaped Mrs. Boldt's lips as she turned her gaze out toward the river, her expression tender and distant. Another few ounces of life leaked out of her.

Madison glanced at her mistress, whose thin lips curled into a wistful smile. "It sounds like they are well, ma'am," she offered gently.

Mrs. Boldt nodded faintly but said nothing. So, Madison carefully folded the letter and picked up Clover's, a dainty envelope smelling faintly of lavender. She continued reading.

Dearest Mama,

Oh, how I miss the smell of lilacs in the gardens and the sound of the river at dawn. New York is lively, yes, but it cannot compare to the peace and joy of our summers with you. We have danced and dined and smiled until our feet, our stomachs, and our faces ache, yet every grand hall feels empty without you nearby.

Do take care of yourself, Mama. Promise me you will rest and walk in the gardens when the weather allows. George and I cannot bear the thought of you being unwell. We will come as soon as we can, bringing laughter and company to you once again.

With all my love, Clover.

Madison lowered the letter and looked up once more, her heart aching at the subtle loneliness in the missus's eyes—a loneliness mirroring her own. She understood what it meant to miss family, to long for voices that only now reached through ink and paper.

"They love you dearly, Mrs. Boldt. I hear it in every word." Madison folded the missives and handed them to the woman. "They are so devoted to you. And now you have something to look forward to. Imagine, summer with your children."

Mrs. Boldt nodded, her voice soft but clear. "They always loved the summers here…the sunshine, the laughter…" Her gaze shifted to Madison, observing her with quiet intensity. "It's a gift, isn't it? To hold family close, even in a letter."

"Yes, it is." Madison nodded, thinking of her own family now gone—her parents, her brother, her aunt—and wondering if heaven carried letters as tender as these. "A dear gift."

The missus motioned toward her vanity, her fingers tapping gently on the polished wood of her armchair. "Fetch me the brooch I wore last evening, please. I want to tell you a story about it."

She stepped into the adjoining bedroom, her gaze skimming the scattered trinkets—delicate brushes, a crystal perfume bottle, and an assortment of gleaming pins. Her brows knit together as she searched, lifting a silk handkerchief to peek beneath it. "It isn't here, ma'am."

Mrs. Boldt's brow furrowed, and a faint crease lined her otherwise smooth face. "Goodness! I must've left it in Alster Tower last night."

Her voice dropped, the words laced with both concern and a hint of urgency. "Please go and fetch it, Madison. It's a family heirloom, you see, passed down for generations. I couldn't bear the thought of it…wandering off."

She hesitated. The way Mrs. Boldt said spoke prickled at her nerves. "Of course, ma'am." She glanced at her employer's troubled expression. "Don't worry. I'll find it."

The older woman leaned back in her chair, the candlelight catching on her earrings as they swayed. "Be quick about it, dear.

The tower can be shadowy at this hour, and I'd rather you weren't lingering."

Madison gasped for a breath as she turned toward the door. Alster Tower always seemed too quiet at night, its hallways shrouded in shadows and whispering of scary stories. Clutching her shawl tightly, she stepped into the dim corridor, her footsteps echoing faintly behind her.

She hurried toward the Yacht House and stood on the edge of the dock, her shawl pulled tightly around her shoulders to brace against the brisk breeze, where she waited for a skiff. Her eyes drifted toward the Yacht House, where two figures caught her attention.

Thomas Roberts, the boatman with a mop of unruly hair and big brown eyes, stepped shakily away from Bruce. The boatman's pale face and stiff gait made Madison frown.

When the boatman reached her, he gave her a weary glance as he prepared the boat. He didn't even ask where she was going.

Goodness, he must be exhausted.

"Mrs. Boldt sent me to fetch something in Alster Tower." Madison explained. "Are you…all right?"

Thomas jumped slightly at the sound of her voice, turning to her with wide, wary eyes. He hesitated, his gaze darting briefly toward Bruce, who stood by the Yacht-House door with his broad shoulders and dark glare. He worked up a casual grin, though it faltered.

Madison tried to mirror his expression, but Bruce's villainous stare traced a cold chill up her spine.

He shook his head. "It's nothing, Miss Madison. Just…a conversation."

Madison narrowed her eyes, unconvinced. "If anyone's bothering you, tell someone. You don't have to keep it to yourself."

He glanced nervously over his shoulder. Bruce remained, arms crossed, his presence looming in the distance like a storm cloud.

A chill coiled deeper into her spine. There was danger in the air. Bruce's glare conveyed enough menace to send a warning.

When they set sail and were far from Bruce, Madison leaned toward Thomas. "What's going on? You can tell me."

He groaned, his voice barely above a whisper. "He warned me to keep my mouth shut…about him."

Madison frowned, her protective instincts flaring like a fire. "About what? Has he hurt someone? Or done something?"

He shook his head quickly. "The way Bruce talks, the way he looks at people…like he's always planning... I just…I can't say more."

Madison's expression softened, but the tension in her chest only deepened. "If there's mischief going on, someone should get to the bottom of it."

For now, though, she was here to fetch Mrs. Boldt's brooch, but this would not be the end of the matter. The truth needed to be uncovered, and Madison had to find it—no matter what danger lay ahead.

When the boat bumped against the dock, Madison jolted from her thoughts. The sky had darkened, and clouds rolled overhead as though the heavens themselves sensed secrets lying in wait. She climbed onto the dock, the boatman following hesitantly, and together they made their way toward Alster Tower.

The imposing structure, its stone walls weathered but sturdy, rose like a sentinel against the gray sky. The door loomed at its base, the heavy iron handle cool beneath Madison's touch.

She pushed it open, the hinges groaning like an old man waking from a long sleep. Inside, the air was cool, still, and carrying the faint scent of damp stone. The evening shadows filtered through narrow windows, casting thin, golden bars across the floor, but the shadows seemed thicker here—alive and shifting.

Madison moved forward, each step echoing faintly. "The brooch must be here somewhere," she murmured, more to herself than to Thomas. She hurried to the Venetian Room and her eyes scanned the room—the grand chamber where Mrs. Boldt frequented. In the far corner, atop an old sideboard, an object glimmered faintly.

"There."

She stepped toward it. The brooch was even lovelier than she'd remembered, an intricate piece of filigree holding a deep sapphire at its center. Mrs. Boldt would be pleased.

As Madison reached for the brooch, an icy prickle skittered down her neck. She froze. The sensation was unmistakable— someone was watching.

Slowly, she turned, scanning the room. The tower was still, save for the faint flutter of a curtain in a distant window. Thomas stood near the door, his face pale, his eyes darting nervously. Was it just her imagination?

His voice broke the silence. "Madison?"

She forced a small, reassuring smile as she slid the brooch into her pocket. "It's all right. Let's go."

But her steps quickened as they crossed the chamber and slipped back outside, the heavy door thudding shut behind them. The shadows grew thicker now, the wind sharper against her skin.

As they made their way back to the boat, she couldn't shake the feeling that unseen eyes followed her every move.

Watching.

Waiting.

~ ~ ~

The next morning, Emmett loitered near the Wellesley House, lingering as if he had a vital task to attend to. But really, he hoped to see Madison before heading to Heart Island. He did this more and more lately, especially after nights spent dreaming about her—her laughter, her eyes, the way she walked with quiet determination.

What had gotten into him? He felt like a lovesick schoolboy. Well, maybe he was.

He chuckled. "Ah, pull yourself together, lad. She's just a friend."

He shook his head as he stooped to inspect the cellar door. The handle was loose. It would take only a few minutes and a screwdriver to fix it. Another item for his mental list of chores. A practical excuse, though he knew full well why he was really there.

The house sat in the quiet of the early morning, just barely past seven. The sun was already warm, promising a fair day ahead, but the river wouldn't really come alive for another hour. He was about to stand when the sound of a window opening made him freeze.

"Good morning, Emmett. What are you doing?"

The words sent a thrill through him, but he pretended not to notice. Madison peeked out, her dark hair loose over her shoulders and her face. Lovely, though tired, and bathed in the golden morning light.

His heart gave a foolish lurch. "Morning, Madison." He gave her a half-smile, doing his best to sound casual. "Couldn't sleep, so I thought I'd check to see if the house needs any repairs."

"Repairs? At this hour?" She shook her head but release a faint smile of her own. "Wait there. I'll be down in a moment."

As she disappeared from view, he straightened and wiped his hands on his trousers, quieting the sudden burst of energy in his chest. A wry grin tugged at his lips. He felt ridiculous, standing there like an awkward lad, excited to see her as though they hadn't just spoken yesterday.

Aye, lad, you're hopeless.

Still, the spark in his chest when she finally emerged on the veranda hitched in his throat. Her pale complexion and dark circles under her eyes made him frown. She looked like she hadn't slept a wink, yet she was radiant all the same. The loose braid in her hair had already come undone, strands escaping to frame her face in the soft morning light.

"Lord, have mercy. You look like you haven't slept a wink. What's troublin' you, m' lady fair?" He kept his voice gentle, and his brogue softened the words further. He tilted his head, studying her. "Not more nightmares?"

She sighed, hugging her arms close to herself as the morning breeze stirred around them. "It's nothing, really."

"It's not nothin,' I'm sure." He stepped closer. The rise in the tone of his voice spoke volumes of his concern for her. "I can tell somethin's weighin' on you. I know you too well by now to believe otherwise."

Her lips twitched into a faint smile, though her exhaustion was plain. "Do you, now?"

He grinned, leaning back slightly. "Aye, I'd say so. You've got the same look I've seen on others who've spent the night wrestlin' with worries they can't shake."

Madison hesitated, her gaze dropping briefly before she met his eyes again. Perhaps his steady presence—his openness—would chip away at her hesitation.

"It's Bruce." Her voice, low but clear, conveyed the urgency of her worry. "And Thomas."

His lightheartedness faded, replaced by a serious edge. "Go on."

Madison looked over her shoulder toward the door before taking a step closer, lowering her voice to a whisper. "I'm worried about Bruce…he doesn't sit well with me. He threatened Thomas yesterday, and at Alster Tower last night…" She trailed off, shaking her head. "I can't explain it. It felt like someone was watching me."

His brow furrowed. "Bruce?"

Madison took a deep breath and shrugged before revealing everything—Bruce's threats, Thomas's fear, and the unsettling feeling someone watched her at Alster Tower. His mood darkened as she spoke, his easy charm replaced by a hard knot of resolve.

"And you're sure Thomas's not imaginin' things?"

She shook her head. "No. Bruce is dangerous. I feel it."

He was quiet for a moment, his jaw tight. Then he gave a curt nod. "You were right to tell me. We'll not leave this alone."

"Emmett…" She hesitated, her voice low. "Be careful."

His jaw tightened more, his worry deepening as he listened. "And you've been carryin' this by yourself all night?"

She shrugged again, though the worry in her eyes betrayed her. "What could I do? Thomas's terrified. And—" She stopped herself, shaking her head. "It doesn't matter."

"It does matter, Madison," he said firmly. "If Bruce's up to no good, I'll not stand by and let him cause harm. Leave the matter to me."

For a long moment, they stood there, the morning breeze carrying the scent of blossoming roses and river water. She met his gaze, concern passing between them—a quiet understanding, perhaps, or an unacknowledged trust growing stronger with each passing day.

"Thank you, Emmett." Her features softened, and for the first time that morning, her smile reached her eyes. "You've helped more than you know."

"Anytime." He willed the warm tone back into his words. "Now, go on back inside and tend to the missus. I'll fix this cellar door before I head off."

"Emmett—"

He waved a hand, flashing her a teasing smile. "Can't have loose handles about, now, can we? You'll owe me a cup of tea for my troubles."

Madison laughed softly, shaking her head as she turned to go. "Fine. But don't dawdle—you've a boat to catch."

He reached out and briefly touched her arm, soft and warm. "Don't you worry, my lamb. Garrison and I will take care of this."

She grinned then retreated inside, her steps lighter than before. When she was gone, he turned back to the cellar door, rolled up his sleeves, and pondered the cellar door handle. But his thoughts lingered on Madison—on her courage, her concerns, and the way she trusted him.

He knew now what had gotten into him.

And for once, he didn't mind it one bit.

When he got to his office in Boldt Castle, Garrison was already hard at work. "A bit tardy, my friend."

By now, he had worked himself into a frenzy. "We've got to talk about Bruce. Now."

"Okay," Garrison rubbed his hands together as if to start a fire, then leaned his forearms on his desk. "What's this about?"

Emmett crossed his arms, glancing around to ensure no one was listening. "I believe Thomas has been threatened. Madison says Bruce has a dark way about him, and she's worried."

Garrison raised an eyebrow. "Bruce. He's always been a wily one. Now, he's dangerous? Can't say I'm surprised."

Emmett nodded, his mood grim. "Bruce is more than a thorn in our side, Garrison. He's a cladhaire. I'll not have Madison—or anyone else—caught in his snare."

Garrison's grin returned, this time more teasing. "Ah, so it's Madison you're worried about, is it?"

He shot him a look. "Don't start."

"Oh, I will." Garrison pushed away from the door, grinning slyly. "You've got that puppy-love look about you, Emmett. Like a man ready to fall headlong into trouble for a lass who's well short of his social standing."

"Garrison—" he warned.

"Oh, don't deny it." Garrison folded his arms. "She's clever and bold, and you—well, you've always had a soft spot for the brave ones."

He sighed and rubbed the back of his neck, stifling the faint smile tugging at his lips. "She deserves better than to get mixed up in this mess."

"And maybe," Garrison said lightly, "she deserves someone brave enough to stand beside her."

He shot him a wry look. "You're insufferable."

Garrison laughed. "Aye, but I'm right. Come now—let's deal with Bruce first. Then we'll see if you've got the courage to chase after the lass."

He shook his head, but couldn't quite suppress a smile. As they returned to work, his mind lingered on Madison—on her strength and stubborn resolve, on the way her worry had softened when she looked at him. Garrison's words echoed in his ears.

Maybe she deserves someone brave enough to stand beside her.

And he realized that he'd face any danger—Bruce or otherwise—if it meant keeping Madison safe.

CHAPTER 7

Madison barely slept that night, though her room was dark and quiet. Her mind had been a tempest of unanswered questions and foreboding thoughts. The air itself seemed thick with secrets, pressing down on her as though warning her to tread carefully.

So, with the first light of dawn breaking onto the river, she grabbed her shawl and hurried out of the Wellesley House. She'd heard it was Bruce's day off, so she wouldn't waste the opportunity to find answers while he was gone. The missus wouldn't be awake for hours, giving her a perfect window to investigate without interruption.

As the Yacht House came into view, two boatmen already busied themselves for the day ahead. The river shimmered in the morning sun, deceptively calm compared to the storm brewing in her heart. As she approached, she willed a smile to express calm, hiding the unease churning inside her.

"Morning, gentlemen. I was wondering if I might ask you a few questions. About Thomas…and Bruce."

The two men froze, their casual banter fading into a tense silence. They exchanged wary glances.

Finally, the older of the two—a man with skin like weathered leather and hands that bore decades of hard work—cleared his throat and stepped forward. "Thomas's a good man," his voice gruff but kind. "Hard worker. Always on time and polite."

Madison nodded, folding her hands in front of her. "And Bruce? He visits here often, doesn't he?"

The man hesitated, his gaze flicking toward the trees lining the shore as though Bruce might step out from behind one at any moment. When he spoke again, his voice was lower, tinged with caution. He nodded.

"Best avoid him, miss. There've been whispers of dark things. He lives nearby, but I reckon he's not the man he pretends to be. Some say he's been mixed up in…business that doesn't belong here. But nobody wants to cross him, and he has familial favor with the Hewitts. Some sort of kin, I'm told."

Her frown deepened, suspicions growing with every word. "What sort of business?"

The man shook his head sharply, his jaw tightening. "Best not ask too many questions, miss. Bruce doesn't take kindly to folk meddling in his affairs. You'd do well to keep your head down."

"I appreciate your concern." Madison measured her tone, her resolve hardening. "But I'm worried for your boatman, Thomas. He's no match for Bruce."

The man's expression softened slightly, though his wariness remained evident. "Has something happened? Thomas's a good man, but he's young. Naïve. He'll need to learn to steer clear if he knows what's good for him."

She shook her head, pressing her lips into a firm line. "And if he doesn't? What happens then?"

The man didn't answer, his silence heavy with implication.

"Thank you for your honesty. If there's any trouble, I hope you'll report it."

The man nodded once, a grim acknowledgment, before turning back to his work.

Madison stepped away, her thoughts spinning in a thousand directions as she walked back toward the concrete-slab path leading to the house.

Business that doesn't belong here.

The phrase stuck in her mind like a thorn. Illegal or worse? If Bruce was threatening Thomas, there was no telling what else he might be capable of. She couldn't let this go—not when others could be at risk.

Just as she stepped onto the main walkway leading to the house, a familiar figure appeared ahead of her.

Emmett leaned casually against a low stone wall, his arms crossed, his face lit with a grin that could rival the morning sun. "Top o' the morning to you, my lovely lass. Did you know these concrete slabs are to keep women's hems clean?"

"Good morning." Her lips tugged into a smile despite her heavy thoughts. "I did not."

He straightened, brushing a hand through his hair as if to tidy himself. "A useless tidbit, but I believe they'll pour proper concrete sidewalks on Heart Island before it's all done. Anyway, Mrs. Hazel mentioned you might have the afternoon free. Care to join me for a tour of the Boldt farms later? They've got new calves, and I thought you'd enjoy seeing them."

Her smile widened. "That sounds grand. After lunch, perhaps? I'd like to talk to you."

His grin softened into a more thoughtful smile. "I always enjoy our talks, Madison. Shall we say one o'clock?"

She curtsied playfully. "Until then, sir. Have a wonderful morning."

He replied with a quick bow before waving an arm to let her pass. As she walked away, she didn't dare look back as she felt his eyes lingering on her a moment longer than necessary.

Her thoughts churned as she made her way back to the Wellesley House, the world around her a blur of river sights and sounds. Distracted by thoughts of Emmett and the boatmen's warnings, she didn't appreciate the morning's beauty.

Bruce was dangerous.

Like a drumbeat in her head, steady and relentless, the warning held a keen certainty that time was running out to expose whatever dark secrets he hid. But how could she confront a man like Bruce without risking herself—or those she cared about?

Wellesley House came into view, its walls bathed in the warm glow of the rising sun. She headed straight for her favorite pondering place, the footbridge to Tennis Island, where she could view the river and take her cares to God. The scent of the abundant flowers on both islands swept over her like a blanket, but did little to settle her.

She tightened her shawl around her shoulders as a cool breeze swept her hair, its bite a sharp contrast to the morning's golden light. The chill pricked at her skin, but it didn't dim the fire blazing within her fueled by determination, by concern over the fear Bruce had instilled in others, and by a growing sense of responsibility.

Yet, should she be involved? A lady's maid to the fine Mrs. Boldt? Was that even proper? Would it endanger her job?

Her thoughts shifted briefly to Emmett. His easy smile and his steady presence had become unexpected comforts recently. He had a way of grounding her, of making her feel less alone in the face of uncertainty. What to make of the connection growing between them? His sincerity, his quiet strength, and the way he sensed her burdens without prying—all of it spoke to a character she wanted to believe in. Perhaps she'd found an ally she could trust.

She headed to the house but paused at the bottom of the steps leading to the veranda, turning back to glance at the footbridge and then the water. The sunlight spilled onto the river like liquid gold, yet shadows remained. Secrets always cast shadows. And Bruce's secrets were no exception.

With a deep breath, Madison straightened her spine and climbed the steps. The surrounding air was still, but her heart was anything but. Whatever lay ahead—whatever dangers, truths, or sacrifices awaited—she was ready to face them.

Because some secrets should be uncovered.

No matter the cost.

~ ~ ~

Emmett took her hand as she descended the steps. "Ready to explore the farm, my fair lass?"

They stopped as he gestured toward the canal construction in front of them. The silence of the steam dredge reminded him it was Sunday.

He led her to the middle of the footbridge and paused. "See that there, Madison?" His Irish brogue softened the edges of his words. "As you know, Mr. Boldt has such grand ideas, and this canal he's carvin' through the land is just one of those plans. 'Twas last August they started diggin' and look how far it has come. Daly and Hannan out of Ogdensburg brought their steam shovel. Quite a sight, isn't it?"

Madison tilted her head, surveying the dredge as it sat near the creek. "It's amazing. and this is one of my favorites spots. I saw all this in the works last summer but thought little of it. Somehow, your eyes give a new perspective of Mr. Boldt's dreams, and I can't tell you how much I appreciate it. It's like seeing the world in a new way. You cause me to think of things I've never considered before and see the result of his hard work, and I thank you."

"Thank you for the compliment." He folded his arms as he stood beside her. "This canal runs from Mud Creek all the way to Lake Waterloo. About two miles in length when it's done. I hear they'll have to blast through solid rock for a good stretch of it. That rock rises thirty, forty feet above the river in some spots." He clicked his tongue. "No small feat, I tell ya."

Madison's gaze drifted over the scene. "I always have to wonder, why would Mr. Boldt go to such lengths?"

He chuckled. "I reckon a man of such grand dreams can't help himself. This canal, when it's finished, will connect this summer home here on Heart Island with Lake Waterloo. It'll make the boating route shorter by far—quicker for his fishing trips and whatnot. And I'm sure you know that the fishin' is some of the finest you'll find in all the Thousand Islands, and he loves the sport."

Madison nodded. "I've been working for the Boldts for a decade now, and I never really considered all that he creates. Now, I'll forever look deeper at what he does, thanks to you."

His cheeks warmed as he glanced at Madison, noting her thoughtful expression. "The canal cost, they reckon, will be over a hundred thousand dollars, but Boldt seems to think it's worth every penny."

Madison shrugged, as if unflustered by the magnitude of the fortune required to fulfill her mistress's husband's dreams. "Mr. Boldt's ambition knows no bounds, but what about the land and the people nearby?"

He nodded. "Some folks welcome the progress—jobs and all that. Others feel it takes the wild beauty of the place. Me? I reckon it's a marvel to see what men can do when they set their minds to it, but I hope the land doesn't lose its soul in the process."

Madison's expression was thoughtful. "Mr. Boldt cares about others more than most. It's a fine balance, isn't it? Between progress and preservation."

"Aye. It is, indeed." He gestured toward the canal again. "Come on, lass. I'll show you around the farm."

As they walked together, Madison turned, her voice warm with admiration. "Did you know, Emmett, that the Wellesley House was originally meant to be a simple farmhouse?"

He raised an eyebrow, a playful grin tugging at his lips. "Aye, that's a hard thing to picture now, considerin' the grand place it is today."

She nodded, her hands clasped in front of her. "Back in 1899, the Boldts bought the land from the Cornwall Brothers, intending to build a modern farmhouse with stables for raising livestock. But instead of stopping there, Mr. Boldt built this magnificent summer home—over fifty-two rooms. It became one of the grandest residences in the Thousand Islands. Yet it pales next to the Castle, doesn't it?"

He let out a low whistle, glancing toward the house as if picturing the vast estate inside. "I betcha it's lovely inside."

Madison smiled softly. "It is indeed, but it's not just the size. It's the way the Boldts combined grandeur with charm. Mrs. Boldt calls it 'the farm cottage,' if you can believe that. I think it says something about their view of the place—it's not just as a symbol of wealth, but for them, it's a home, a retreat."

He chuckled, shaking his head. "Aye, leave it to the Boldts to call fifty-two rooms a 'cottage.' Still, I'll admit there's somethin' special about how they've made such a grand place feel rooted in the land."

Madison glanced at him, her expression thoughtful. "It really reflects their lives, doesn't it? Mr. Boldt's bold ambition, his ability to dream so big is like a glimpse into another world."

He met her gaze, his tone softening. "You've quite the way of paintin' a picture, Madison. Maybe you'll help me see the world through your eyes more often."

She laughed lightly. "Only if you promise to tell me more of your stories. I have a feeling you know this place even better than I do."

He led Madison along a path lined with stately trees that rustled in the summer breeze. Ahead, the sprawling fields of Wellesley Island Farms stretched as far as the eye could see, bustling with life and activity.

He tipped his cap toward her with a playful smile. "I'm surprised you haven't seen this before, since you've been here for the past three summers. Nevertheless, you're lookin' at one of the finest farms in the east. Mr. Boldt envisioned this place, and I reckon it's as grand as any of his fancy hotels in New York and Philadelphia."

Madison gazed at the landscape, wide-eyed. "It's enormous! I knew it was here—could smell it sometimes, too—but it's not the kind of place a lady's maid frequents. So, I've never really considered it. What do they grow here?"

"Ah, a little bit of everything. See that massive barn up ahead? That's the front farm. It's where the dairy cattle live, providin' milk, cream, and butter in abundance. Enough to feed the Waldorf-Astoria and then some."

He paused, pointing in the distance. "Now, the back farm, less than a mile yonder, is where you'll find the poultry buildin's and smaller livestock. Pheasants, ducks, chickens, even lobster are raised here, all to keep the tables of Mr. Boldt's hotels and homes well-stocked."

Madison raised an eyebrow, clearly impressed. "Lobster? On a farm?"

"Aye, 'tis true. The man doesn't do things by halves, does he?" He laughed heartily. "And here's somethin' that'll really knock your hat off—on an average day at the Waldorf-Astoria, I hear they need a thousand pounds of beef, another thousand of poultry, and six hundred gallons of milk. And that's without countin' the extra banquets they throw."

Madison gasped. "And this farm supplies it all?"

"Every last bit of it. And eggs? Over nine hundred dozen shipped out regularly. Fresh vegetables, fruit, flowers, maple syrup—you name it, Boldt's farms have it covered."

Madison furrowed her brows. "How can you possibly remember all these details? You're like a walking encyclopedia, and your aptitude for numbers is astounding."

He bowed teasingly to hide his burning cheeks. "Why thank you, my lovely lass. Mama said I was born with a steel trap for a brain, and it comes in handy sometimes. Other times it's a curse."

Thankfully, Madison didn't ask why it would be a curse, for he wouldn't know how to answer.

Soon they reached a rise in the path, revealing an expanse of manicured green stretching into the horizon. "And there is the grandest sight of them all—an 18-hole golf course in the works coverin' seventy acres of land, with a fine club house soon to be built. I reckon Mr. Boldt isn't only after productivity but entertainment as well."

Madison nodded. "Yet, with all he has done, I've paid so little attention to it, I feel ashamed."

"You mustn't scold yourself for not paying attention. You've enough on your plate carin' for the missus, and I suspect this development is not quite your cup of tea. It's overwhelmingly a man's world we're talkin' about."

"I'll pay attention now." Madison smiled warmly. "It must be exciting to be part of such a grand plan."

He returned her smile, his gaze steady. "It is, Madison, and it's grand to share it with someone who appreciates it. But you're part of this, too. If Mrs. Boldt didn't have you servin' her so faithfully, where would Mr. Boldt be?"

Madison blinked twice, pursing her lips, as if deep in thought. Did she think so little of herself as to only be a bystander and not a participant?

They continued walking, the farm's activity humming all around them. The distant cluck of chickens mingled with the rhythmic thud of horse hooves and the occasional cheerful shouts of workers. He told tales of Wellesley Island's grand farms, painting pictures of the determined men and women who had carved lives out of the rugged beauty of the Thousand Islands. Madison listened intently, her smile revealing a mix of admiration and curiosity.

By the time they reached the Wellesley House, the afternoon sun had sunk near the horizon, a warm glow hanging over the sprawling estate. A young boy sat outside on the steps, and as they reached him, he thrust a missive into her hands and ran away before she could question him.

She glanced at him and unfolded the note. Her eyes widened as she read its simple yet chilling words aloud: Mind your own business—or else.

A hasty hand scrawled the words, slightly smudging the ink as though written in a hurry—or with agitation. The color drained from her cheeks as she turned the note over, searching for any indication of who had sent it. There was none.

"Madison. What is it, lass?"

His voice was low, his brow furrowed as he looked between her and the note.

"Who would send this?"

She handed the paper to him silently, her hands trembling ever so slightly.

He scanned the message, his jaw tightening. "Bruce?"

"I don't know." She wrapped her arms around herself. "Bruce has been...difficult. It could be him. Or..."

Her voice trailed off as she glanced around, her eyes darting to and fro.

"Or someone else." He finished for her, his eyes scanning the grounds as if trying to locate the source of the unease. "Blathers! You've rattled someone's nerves, that's certain. Whoever wrote that note didn't reckon you'd have someone lookin' out for ya. But you do. If they're tryin' to scare you off, it's likely you're gettin' too close to somethin' they don't want found."

Madison nodded. "I won't let them intimidate me, Emmett. If something is being hidden on these islands, I'll uncover it. Truth matters."

He smiled faintly, his eyes filled with quiet admiration. "Whatever this mystery is, we'll solve it together."

CHAPTER 8

The Boldt's steamer, the beautiful *Kestrel*, chugged to a stop at the docks of Alexandria Bay, the nearby mainland village they frequented. Madison adjusted her mobcap, smoothing her apron as she balanced against the railing, readying herself to disembark. The yeasty scent of fresh bread mingled with the tang of the river, igniting her senses. The sing-song calls merchants selling their wares and the grunts, thuds, and occasionally even a cuss word of fishermen unloading their catches created a cacophony.

Madison stepped onto the dock first, turning to offer her hand to Mrs. Boldt. As the lady descended gracefully but enfeebled, the missus's gaze swept the lively market. Mr. Boldt joined his wife, taking her arm.

"Isn't it charming here, darling?" Mrs. Boldt remarked, her voice full of admiration. "I do love Alexandria Bay—it's a close-knit community. Far different than the city."

"Indeed," Mr. Boldt replied with a chuckle. "A perfect example of the wonder the river provides."

Today's plan was special—lunch with Mr. and Mrs. George Pullman, owners of the nearby Castle Rest on Pullman Island, at the Crossman House Hotel's dining room by the river.

The missus rallied to walk the mere two blocks, while Madison tossed up a silent prayer that this rare excursion wouldn't take the stuffing out of her ailing mistress. As her maid, she would remain close enough to anticipate Mrs. Boldt's every need but far enough away to respect her employer's privacy.

As they strolled toward the restaurant, Madison's eyes roamed the marketplace. She noted the cheerful chaos of children darting between carts, of vendors shouting their prices, and of the townsfolk chattering in clusters. The busy life of the town seemed worlds away from the peaceful Wellesley House.

Near a stack of barrels, two men caught her eye. Their quick, hushed tones stood in stark contrast to the open neighborliness of the market. Madison slowed, ears straining to catch their conversation.

"Bruce is playing a dangerous game," one man muttered, glancing around nervously. "If he keeps moving the goods like this, the authorities are bound to catch wind."

The other man huffed, folding his arms. "He's got too much at stake to slip up. But if he blows his cover, we'll all pay for it."

Bruce? The name hit her like a bullet. Could they mean Bruce from the island? She wouldn't put anything past the rogue.

Her heart quickened as questions swirled in her mind. What game were they talking about? What goods? And what risks? The possibility of Bruce being involved in an illegal business unsettled her deeply.

Madison looked away before the men noticed her eavesdropping. She hurried to catch up with the Boldts, her thoughts racing as she opened the door for the couple.

The Crossmon House Hotel restaurant overlooking the St. Lawrence River buzzed softly with the chatter of the elite Thousand Islands summer residents. George and Louise Boldt joined Mr. and Mrs. George Pullman, already seated at one of the finest tables, sipping tea as the gentle river breeze drifted through the open windows.

Soon, the couples' conversation became lively but cordial, circling around the projects and ambitions of the region's wealthiest families.

Madison lingered near the table, her hands folded neatly in front of her, her eyes and ears darting between her missus and the street outside, preoccupied with what she'd overheard.

Mrs. Pullman, her refined elegance notable, leaned forward slightly. "And how is the construction coming along at the castle?"

"Oh, it's progressing beautifully." Mr. Boldt's grin spread wide with pride as he addressed Mr. Pullman. "Every detail matters.

The billiard room alone will be a centerpiece—a place where men like us can talk business, smoke cigars, and enjoy a fine brandy."

Mrs. Boldt smiled indulgently at her husband's enthusiasm. "George is tireless with his vision. I sometimes think he dreams in blueprints."

Her quip elicited a soft laugh.

Mr. Pullman chuckled. "Ah, George, I can't help but see some of myself in you. As you well know, when I built Castle Rest back in 1899, I, too, poured every ounce of myself into the details."

Madison, standing discreetly nearby, listened. She had heard tales of Castle Rest, the first substantial summer home on the Thousand Islands, and its extravagant beginnings.

Mr. Pullman continued. "When I first set eyes on Pullman Island, I knew our summer home had to be special. The goal wasn't simply luxury." He waved a hand as if addressing a pesky fly at a picnic. "That we could have anywhere." His eyes sparkled, and his grin expanded with every statement. "It was about creating a retreat, a haven where the stress of the city simply melted away. I told my architects, 'Give me a castle that looks like it hatched from the rock itself.' And they delivered."

"Castle Rest is certainly a marvel," Mrs. Boldt said graciously. "We've passed it many times on our way through the channels."

Mr. Pullman nodded appreciatively. "It's our haven, and you must visit soon. But what you're building is on an entirely different scale. A European style castle with towers and turrets."

Mr. Boldt smiled humbly. "Romance is at the heart of it." He glanced at Louise. "This castle is for her and everything she means to me."

Mrs. Boldt's cheeks flushed softly, and she reached for her teacup, hiding behind its paper-thin china construction. "You spoil me, George."

Madison sighed. *Oh, how wonderful to be loved so deeply!*

Mr. Pullman chuckled. "As well you should, my friend. A man's success is measured by the joy he brings to those he loves. But let me offer a piece of advice—don't lose yourself in the grandeur. At the end of the day, it's the memories you make there that will matter most."

Mr. Boldt nodded thoughtfully, his gaze drifting out the window to the shimmering river beyond. "Wise words, George. I'll remember that."

As the conversation shifted back to mutual acquaintances and light pleasantries, Madison absorbed every word. She marveled at the interplay of ambition and affection that shaped these two grand projects. Yet, her own unease lingered. The grand castles and elegant luncheon loomed far from the secrets and tensions she battled.

As the group chatted, Madison grew anxious about the conversation she'd overheard. She glanced out the window, searching the market for the two men, but they were nowhere in sight.

Her chest tightened. Should she tell someone? But who? Was it even her place?

When the meal concluded, the couples strolled toward the dock before saying goodbye. She lagged, her gaze wandering over the charming town. At first, the intricate storefronts drew her eye. Then she spotted the same two men leaning against a barrel near the docks.

She slowed as her stomach tightened. A chill raced down her spine. Her mind reeled with the prospect of Bruce in cahoots with the shadowy men she'd overheard.

Her steps quickened as she caught up with the Boldts, her thoughts spinning. Could Bruce be involved in illegal activity? And if so, what did that mean for everyone on the island?

The ride home was quiet, the sun beginning its descent over the river.

Mrs. Boldt leaned back with a contented sigh. "Such a lovely afternoon. Don't you agree, Madison?"

She forced a smile. "Yes, ma'am. Lovely indeed."

But as she gazed out at the river, her thoughts churned. If Bruce truly was involved in danger, how far might it go?

The vibrant scenes of Alexandria Bay faded behind them, but her unease stayed. A shadow trailed her all the way home, spoiling the beauty of the day. As she prepared the missus for bed, she focused on her tasks, but every noise and shadow pressed on her nerves.

The missus quickly fell asleep, so Madison took a stroll in the garden, hoping to settle her mind. A twig cracked behind her, and the swish of a boot against the grass set her heart racing once more.

She turned quickly.

Bruce.

His dark eyes bore into hers, and his expression was anything but friendly. "Enjoy your little trip to Alexandria Bay?" His voice was low and menacing. "See something you shouldn't have?"

Her heart pounded. "What do you want, Bruce?"

He took a step closer, and she instinctively backed away. "Mind your own business, missy. Poking around where you don't belong could be...dangerous."

Her breath hitched. "Are you threatening me?"

Bruce smirked, and he leaned in, his breath hot against her cheek. "Did you enjoy the note I left you?"

She froze. *So, it had been him.*

Perhaps she could throw him off his game. "What note?"

A silent smirk confirmed her suspicions. His eyes flicked to the dark water beyond the shore, then back to her. "Keep your nose out of things, and you won't have any problems."

With that, he turned and disappeared into the shadows, leaving her quaking. The warning in his words—and the implied threat—settled heavily on her.

She had to tell someone, but who? *Emmett.*

A far darker web than she'd imagined ensnared her.

She needed help.

~ ~ ~

The morning light filtered through the tall, narrow windows of the Boldt Castle foreman's office, illuminating the meticulous blueprint sketches and scattered tools on Emmett's desk. As the project lead, he prided himself on order and efficiency, but this morning was different.

A courier had delivered a letter—thick parchment, stamped with the elegant insignia of his employer, G. W. & W. D. Hewitt, the prestigious Philadelphia architectural firm that oversaw his work on the castle's construction. His employers. The men to whom he was directly accountable.

He sighed, his Irish brogue expressing more than words could. "What do they want now?"

He opened the envelope and unfolded the neatly penned letter. His eyes scanned the words, his usual confidence giving way to a mixture of anxiety and fear.

Dear Mr. O'Connor,

I trust this letter finds you well and in fine spirits as you oversee the progress of Boldt Castle's construction. Your efforts, as always, are appreciated, and your skill is evident in the extraordinary craftsmanship displayed thus far. However, I write today with grave concerns that must be addressed without delay.

Firstly, it has come to my attention that Bruce—my wife's nephew—has been the subject of what can only be described as undue persecution by certain members of the construction crew. While I understand the importance of maintaining discipline and standards among the men, it is imperative that Bruce be treated with the respect befitting his position. He is family, Mr. O'Connor, and I trust you will ensure he is shielded from any further hostility.

Secondly, I have received troubling whispers regarding your personal conduct. Specifically, it has been suggested—though I hesitate to believe it—that you have been engaging in behavior unbecoming of your station with none other than Mrs. Boldt's lady's maid. Such impropriety, if true, could severely tarnish not only your reputation, but also the standing of this entire project.

Emmett folded the letter slowly, his jaw tightening as he stared out the window at the bustling construction site. All was in order until his gaze landed on Bruce—sullen and perpetually scowling, as usual—leaning against a stack of freshly quarried stone, chatting idly with another laborer.

He shook his head. "Family or not, that lad's got a knack for trouble."

As for the second accusation…his mind wandered to Madison. Such a kind-hearted soul, always quick with a smile or a word of encouragement. Friends, yes. But impropriety? Nonsense.

The letter dealt a blow to his integrity, but he still had to tread carefully. His position at Boldt Castle was hard-won, and he wouldn't allow vicious rumors—however unfounded—to jeopardize it.

He leaned back in his chair, the letter from George Hewitt clutched in his calloused hand. His eyes narrowed as his thoughts settled on a single name.

Bruce.

Bruce Clawson, the architect's entitled nephew, had been a thorn in his side from the moment he stepped onto the construction site. The man was lazy and only cared about boasting his relationship with the Hewitts, not the castle's progress. And now, this.

His jaw tightened as he replayed recent interactions in his mind. Bruce insulted the crew, favored connections over talent, and clearly ignored his authority. If anyone had a reason to spread whispers, it was Bruce.

"Morning, Emmett." Garrison's greeting jolted him from his thoughts. "You're lookin' like a man with a storm cloud followin' him."

He sighed, crossing his arms. "That obvious, eh?"

"Only to someone who knows you." Garrison clicked his tongue. "Something tells me this has to do with that letter you got. Word's got around. Seems the courier has a wagging tongue."

Emmett winced. The last thing he wanted was for the crew to think he'd lost control of the site. "Aye, it's about the letter. Hewitt's not happy with the way things are runnin'—or at least, he's been told he shouldn't be."

"And let me guess." Garrison raised an eyebrow. "That whelp, Bruce, is at the heart of it."

He nodded. "He's been stirrin' the pot, but it's more than just him. There's somethin' in the air, Gar. Tension among the men. Distrust. I can't have that—not if we're to finish this castle properly."

Garrison scratched his chin thoughtfully. "You're a good foreman, Emmett. The men respect you—most of 'em, anyway. But they're not mind readers. If there's trouble, you've got to lay it out plain. Let them know where you stand."

"You think I should talk to the crew?"

"Aye," Garrison said firmly. "They need to hear from you, not just see you stompin' around like a thundercloud. Address the rumors head-on, set the record straight, and remind them why they're here. If you don't, the whispers will only grow."

He wasn't one for speeches, preferring to lead through action. But Garrison had a point. The crew needed clarity—and reassurance.

"All right," he said finally. "I'll call a meeting at midday."

Just after noon, when bellies were full, he gathered the crew in the shadow of the castle's rising towers.

His voice rang out with authority as he addressed them. "Listen here, lads. I've heard whispers of discord among us, and I won't have it. Bruce Clawson is part of this team, same as the rest of you. Whatever grievances you've got, sort 'em out civilly and off the island. We've got a castle to build, not a schoolyard to bicker in."

As the men dispersed, he caught Bruce's eye and strode over to him, his boots crunching against the gravel. He stopped close enough to command attention without causing a scene.

"Bruce," he said carefully, his brogue laced with determination. "A word."

Bruce turned, his expression a mixture of irritation and apprehension. "What is it now, O'Connor? Another lecture about punctuality?"

He ignored the jab and gestured toward a nearby spot, away from prying ears. "Walk with me."

Reluctantly, Bruce followed, his hands shoved into his pockets. They stopped near a stone wall overlooking the St. Lawrence River.

"Bruce, I'll be straight with ya. I've received a letter from your uncle. A troublin' letter. Seems there's talk of… improprieties on my part." He fixed Bruce with a hard stare. "Care to tell me what you know about that?"

Bruce's brows shot up, and for a moment, he looked genuinely surprised. But the flicker of guilt that crossed his face didn't escape his notice. "Me? Why would I know anything about that?" Bruce said, his tone defiant. "I've got better things to do than gossip."

"Do you now?" Emmett countered, folding his arms. "Because it seems to me that someone's been flappin' their gums, and I can't help but notice you've had plenty to say about me and this project. Don't think I've missed your comments to the lads, Bruce. You've made it clear you don't respect my authority. But spreadin' lies? That's a new low, even for you."

Bruce's face reddened, and he shifted uncomfortably. "Maybe I mentioned a few things in passing. No big deal."

"Aye, and now it is," he snapped, his voice low but seething. "Let me tell you somethin', lad. Your uncle might've sent you here to learn a thing or two, but I don't think he meant for you to learn schemin' and backstabbin'. You've a choice to make, Bruce. Either you set this right, or I'll be writin' to Mr. Hewitt myself to let him know exactly what kind of troublemaker he's got for a nephew."

Bruce snickered, his bravado evident. "Go ahead. See if I care."

"From now on, you must show respect for the men on this crew—and for me. Because if ya don't, I'll make sure this castle stands long after you're sent packin'."

With that, he walked away, leaving Bruce to stew in his own shame. The confrontation hadn't solved everything, but perhaps it was a start.

Emmett would have to be careful in the days to come, but one thing was certain—he wouldn't let anyone—nephew or not—

endanger what he'd worked so hard to build. His reputation. This project.

Satisfied—for now—he returned to his desk. He had another matter to take care of. Taking up a clean sheet of paper, he began drafting his reply to George Hewitt. Aye, he'd address the accusations head-on, defend his character, and ensure that his leadership remained unquestioned.

As he wrote, a knock came at the door. He looked up to see Madison standing there, her face pale and worried.

"Emmett," she said softly, "What's wrong? I…I heard about the letter."

He set down his pen, meeting her concerned gaze. "Madison, there's always something wrong when it comes to bosses and letters. But don't you worry yourself—I'll set it straight."

Her lips curved into a small, grateful smile, and for a moment, the chaos of the day melted away. He'd tread a careful line between duty and honor, but he wouldn't back down.

Not for anyone.

CHAPTER 9

Golden light splattered on the stone floors as the sun poured through the arched windows of Alster Tower. Madison balanced the tea tray with practiced ease, even though the delicate porcelain rattled faintly. She approached the table where Mr. and Mrs. Boldt sat.

As usual, the couple gave an air of effortless elegance. George Boldt gestured as he spoke, while Louise, with her serene presence, listened intently.

Madison admired them, but today, her own turmoil clouded her esteem.

Mrs. Boldt smiled warmly as she set the tray down. "Thank you, Madison. It's such a lovely day, isn't it? Perfect for tea in the tower."

"Yes, ma'am." Madison curtsied, forcing a polite smile. She poured the hot beverage and arranged the cups, but inside, her thoughts churned.

Bruce's words and actions weighed heavily on her. She couldn't forget the way he had cornered her with veiled threats. She should tell someone—perhaps the Boldts—but the moment never felt right. And how could she accuse Bruce, the architect's kin, without proof? What if no one believed her? What if it only made things worse?

"I think we should expand the farm." Mr. Boldt's voice brimmed with enthusiasm. "It'll provide more for the castle and hotels and give us a sense of self-sufficiency. The locals would benefit too."

Louise nodded thoughtfully. "Maybe we should finish the castle first? The main hall still needs finishing touches and so do the other floors. I want it to feel warm, welcoming—a true home."

"It will, my darling," George assured her. "I won't settle for anything less than perfection."

Madison's chest tightened. The Boldts' vision for their grand estate was so beautiful, so full of hope. How could she shatter their peace with talk of threats and troubles? Her hand faltered as she passed Louise her teacup, and a single drop of tea spilled onto the saucer.

Mrs. Boldt laid a cool hand on her forearm. "Are you all right, Madison?"

"Yes, ma'am," Madison's cheeks flushed. "I'm fine. Just a bit distracted."

"If there's something on your mind, you can tell us."

Madison opened her mouth, the words floating on the tip of her tongue. Bruce. The rumors. The danger.

But Mr. Boldt's voice cut in before she could speak. "Distracted? Probably from all the work we've been piling on you." He glanced at her before smiling at his wife. "We're lucky to have someone so diligent, so caring, my dear wife."

Madison forced a laugh, her opportunity slipping away. "Thank you, sir."

She curtsied, retreating to the side of the room. Perhaps if she put distance between them, her problems would slip through the cracks.

The conversation returned to plans for the castle and the farm, but she barely heard a word. She scolded herself for her cowardice. They had given her an opening, and she'd let it pass. How many more chances would she have? And what would happen if Bruce's actions went unchecked?

As the Boldts finished their tea, Madison cleared the table with quiet efficiency. Her mind was made up—she couldn't stay silent forever. She'd find the courage to speak, even if it meant risking their trust or Bruce's wrath.

But not today.

She carried the tray back, her secret weighing heavily on her. The sunny tower stood tall and proud in contrast to her inner turmoil.

When Mrs. Boldt retired for her daily afternoon nap in the Venetian Room, Madison stole a few moments of quiet. Her mind was still a tangle of unease and indecision, so she hurried up to the castle. Emmett had invited her to see the progress, and she welcomed the distraction.

He greeted her just outside, his Irish brogue warm and inviting. "You must see the Billiard Room. It's comin' along nicely."

She followed him up the grand stone steps into the sprawling castle. Inside, her footsteps echoed in the unfinished halls. The scent of fresh timber and sawdust lingered in the air, mingling with the faint tang from the river through the open windows.

The soft creak of the oak floors echoed as he gestured her to step inside the Billiard Room. Her eyes widened as she took in its grandeur, even more impressive now than when she had encountered the altercation between him and Bruce.

"Welcome to Mr. Boldt's Billiard Room." His words carried a mix of pride and excitement. "I reckon it will be one of the finest in the house when it's finished."

She stepped forward, her boots clicking gently against the polished hardwood floor. The intricate inlaid patterns caught the light streaming through the tall windows, casting faint shadows that danced at her feet.

"It's beautiful already."

"Ah, but wait until you see it complete." His gray eyes sparkled as he walked to the center of the room. He gestured to the space in front of him. "Here's where the most lavish felt billiard table will sit, imported from across the sea, I 'spect."

She tilted her head, imagining the table in place. "And those inlaid patterns on the floor—they almost look like they're pointing to where the table should be."

"Exactly the point." He winked. "Craftsmanship like this is rare. Every detail was designed to draw the eye to the centerpiece."

She turned slowly, taking in the walls, their wood paneling rich and ornate, glowing warmly under the soft afternoon light. "And the ceiling." She marveled at the coffered design. "I have not seen one like it."

He leaned against the mantle of the carved fireplace on the left side of the room. "A palace might have more gold, but this room has somethin' better—character. Imagine it, Madison—a fire roarin' here on a cool autumn evenin', the game in full swing. Voices and laughter fillin' the air."

Her gaze drifted to the large windows. Beyond them, the greenery of the estate framed the room in natural splendor. "And these windows. It's as if the room and the outside world blend."

He nodded. "Aye, that's part of the charm. Sunlight by day, moonlight by night. And over here…" He motioned to the area across from the fireplace "…is where the viewin' chairs will be. A perfect place for spectators to watch the pool game, chat, and sip a drink or two."

"This is certainly a man's abode, so I'll not see it in person." She smiled, the image forming in her mind—the warmth of the fireplace, the thrill of competition, and the quiet elegance of the room itself, tying it all together. "But that's okay. It'll be Mr. Boldt's special place where friendships are made, deals are done, and visions are born."

"Aye. You see it well, lass—gentlemen gathered here with their brandy and cigars, talkin' business and politics."

She glanced at the ornate fireplace, its carved mantle standing like a sentinel. "And that's where a prize-winning musky will hang, isn't it? Mr. Boldt loves fishing."

"Aye, a proper St. Lawrence River Muskellunge. Big as your arms outstretched, I reckon."

She chuckled, trying to imagine the imposing fish mounted above the fireplace. But the lightness of the moment faded as her thoughts returned to the growing tension around the construction site. The workers had grown quieter, their usual banter replaced with wary glances and murmured conversations. Even Emmett, normally so cheerful, seemed more guarded.

"It's beautiful." Her voice trailed off. She hesitated before speaking again. "But have you noticed...things feel tense lately? Among the workers, I mean."

His brow furrowed, and he crossed his arms. "You've noticed it too, then. Aye, there's been a shift. Can't quite put my finger on it, but the lads aren't as easy as they used to be. Like they're waitin' for somethin' to happen."

She shivered. She wanted to tell him about Bruce—about the threats, the men she'd overheard in Alexandria Bay—but fear and concern knotted her tongue. Instead, she looked down at her hands, the prison of her silence growing heavier by the minute.

Before he could press her further, the sound of voices carried from the hallway. Workers were calling for him, their tones edged with urgency.

"Duty calls." His expression darkened as he turned toward the door. "Stay here if you like, Madison. I'll be back shortly."

She shook her head. "I'd better get back to the missus. Her sleep has been fitful of late, and she may need me. But thank you for the tour of the room. You certainly make it come alive."

He tipped his cap. "Best we both be on our way, then. Have a nice afternoon."

She curtsied. "And you, sir."

After he left, the castle, for all its grandeur, suddenly felt stifling. She turned back to the room, her eyes settling on the fireplace. The musky might one day hang there as a trophy of Mr. Boldt's achievements, but she couldn't help but think of the other things that could come to rest in these walls—the hidden deals, the whispered threats, and the secrets of those who walked its halls.

But what to do with her secret?

~ ~ ~

Bruce pretended to do a little extra work as he lingered in the shadows of the castle waiting impatiently for the last of the workers to head home. The site grew quiet as men packed up their tools and headed toward the dock for the last boat to the mainland.

He'd execute his plan tonight. Soon, Emmett O'Connor would no longer be his superior. That Irish Mick, with his easy grin and sharp attention to detail, drew praise like a bucket in a well. The workers admired him, the Boldts relied on him, and even Madison, with her doe eyes and quiet beauty, favored him.

Intolerable.

He gritted his teeth as he hauled a sack of mortar across the site, his shoulders aching under the strain. He didn't belong here. He was George Hewitt's nephew, kin to one of the most respected architects in Philadelphia. Wasn't that supposed to mean he had prestige? Yet here he was, toiling in the shadows, unnoticed and unappreciated, while that Irish Mick basked in the glow of every success.

The man's reprimand still stung. Pulled aside like a common laborer, Emmett speaking to him in that calm, measured tone. As if he were a child in need of a scolding.

Yes, he had nodded, mumbling a half-hearted agreement, but inside, his blood seethed. Who did Emmett think he was? Sure, he was foreman, but that didn't give him the right to talk down to him. *He* was the boss's kin, for Hades' sake.

That should count. But it never did. Not here. Not anywhere.

Bruce stewed that Emmett's sharp mind and steady leadership were impossible to compete with. The Mick had a knack for problem-solving, whether it was fixing a structural issue or mediating disputes among the crew. The men trusted him. Looked up to him. Even he could see it.

And then there was Madison.

The thought of her made his chest tighten. What a fine filly! But she clearly favored Emmett. Bruce hadn't missed the way she smiled when the foreman spoke to her. The way her eyes lingered a second longer on his face.

Their mutual admiration society drove Bruce near mad.

How could Emmett, an Irishman with calloused hands and dirt under his nails, command such loyalty and admiration? And why did Madison favor him? It wasn't fair. He deserved someone like her hanging on his arm. He deserved recognition, respect, a chance to step out of his shadow.

As the hours wore on, Bruce's resentment festered. He had to do something. All afternoon, he lingered near the other workers, dropping comments here and there.

"Funny how the foreman spends so much time near the Boldts' quarters." One of the laborers, Edgar, nodded. "You'd think he'd be more concerned with the work."

Edgar shrugged, clearly uninterested, but Bruce pressed on. "And that lady's maid of Mrs. Boldt's—what's her name? Madison? Seems like they are awful friendly."

The seed planted, Bruce walked away, satisfaction curling in his chest. If Emmett wanted to be everyone's golden boy, maybe it was time for a little tarnish.

As the sun dipped low and the workers packed up, Bruce stood at the edge of the site, staring at the towering silhouette of Boldt Castle against the fading light. For all his grievances, he couldn't deny the beauty of what they were building—or the skill it took to lead such a project.

Yet that wasn't enough to quell his jealousy. Unnoticed and unappreciated. His place in the grand scheme of things. And until that changed, it always would be.

Well, that stopped tonight.

He stood at the edge of the worksite, his figure cloaked in the shadows of the fading twilight, seething his whispered threat.

"That Irish Mick won't be telling me what to do. No siree! I'll teach him a lesson he'll not soon forget! I'll teach them all."

Bruce's sharp eyes tracked Emmett's every move as the Irishman meticulously inspected the newly constructed pine scaffolding. Ever the blasted perfectionist, that one.

Bruce ground the toe of his boot into the ground as the Mick ran his hands over the mortise and tenon joints, testing their fit and strength. He checked that the nails and bolts had been driven deep to add extra stability, and he tested the diagonal braces that crisscrossed the structure, ensuring all could withstand tomorrow's heavy labor.

Bruce mumbled past his grinding teeth. "Be on your way already, O'Connor."

Emmett gave the scaffold a good shake. It didn't so much as shudder. "Solid as the Rock of Cashel."

Footsteps approached, and Garrison joined Emmett, clapping him on the shoulder as he passed. "You've got an eye for the details, mate. Have a good evening."

"You too, my friend." Emmett waved as he climbed the scaffolding, his steps deliberate on the wooden planks.

The sight of the stable working platforms above made Bruce's heart race—not with fear, but with anticipation. The day was approaching when all of this—this hard work, this island—might become his biggest challenge.

Then the project manager descended, dropping the last step to the ground. One last glance around, then he headed toward the boats.

Still, Bruce waited a few extra moments. For the perfect time.

Bruce's breath was steady, but his pulse raced as he stood before the scaffolding. He ran his hand along the beams, feeling the smooth pine beneath his fingers. It was sturdy—too sturdy. Emmett had made sure of that. Of course, he had. The man could do no wrong.

Bruce's grip tightened on his tools. Tomorrow, they'd all see things differently. The men would finally realize Emmett wasn't infallible, and when the time came to choose someone to finally— and rightfully—take the leadership, Bruce's name would be on their lips. He'd finally have Emmett's job—as he so rightly deserved.

Glancing over his shoulder to ensure he was alone, he set to work, his actions calculated, his movements deliberate. A bolt here, a nail there—just enough to create instability without making it obvious. He paused only to wipe the sweat from his brow, the silence of the night amplifying the pounding of his heart.

As he worked, his mind swirled with fragmented thoughts. Would the scaffold collapse entirely? No, he reasoned. Just enough to make Emmett look careless, enough to tarnish his reputation.

Enough to tip the scales and get his job.

Bruce crouched near the base of the scaffolding where the sturdy vertical posts met the earth. He pulled out a small saw, its blade gleaming ominously in the dim light. His hands trembled, but revenge steeled his resolve. He sawed through a lower post, careful to make it appear to be a simple accident. Easy to overlook.

As he worked, he imagined the chaos that would ensue. Garrison's crew would arrive in the morning, ready to climb to heights they believed were safe. But the moment they stepped onto the planks, the entire structure would give way, sending them tumbling down. He pictured Emmett's face. The shock and disbelief as he realized his meticulous checks had failed.

Suddenly, the crackle of dry leaves interrupted his thoughts. He froze, the saw hovering inches from the wood. It was Garrison, finishing up some last-minute tasks.

Bruce quickly hid the saw behind his back, heart pounding in his ears. He forced a smile, trying to appear nonchalant.

"What are you doing out here, Bruce?" Garrison narrowed his eyes. "Shouldn't you be heading home?"

"Just checking things over." Bruce kept his voice steady despite the turmoil inside. "Thought I'd double check the inspection to make sure everything's ready for tomorrow."

Garrison nodded, seemingly satisfied, and turned away. Bruce let out a breath he didn't realize he'd been holding, but the moment of relief was short-lived.

What if he was caught? What if it all went wrong?

As Garrison headed to the skiff that would take him off the island, Bruce returned to his task, his resolve growing. He finished the cut, leaving the post weakened but not entirely severed. It would hold—at least for now. He stepped back, surveying his work with a mixture of pride and anticipation.

Emmett would be held responsible. And he would have the Mick's job.

As Bruce walked away from the scaffolding, the reality of his actions settled in his gut.

He had crossed a line.

A growing fear quickly replaced the thrill of sabotage.

What if he got caught?

CHAPTER 10

adison tossed and turned, her breath uneven when she forced herself awake, a strangled cry escaping her lips. Her body was slick with sweat, and her hands gripped the sheets so tightly her hands ached.

Moonlight filtered through the thin lace curtains of her small room, long shadows slithering across the wooden floor. The air in the room felt thick, pressing against her chest. It was dark but safe—no damp basement, no rusted door, no rats. Just the quiet hum of the Wellesley House at rest.

Another nightmare? A different one than usual, but equally as terrifying.

She willed herself to recall it, to make sense of it.

She stood alone in the grand halls of Boldt Castle, but something was terribly wrong. Torches along the walls flickered weakly, casting eerie, wavering shadows. Cracks marred the once-gleaming marble floors. Moths had eaten and torn the rich tapestries. The air smelled damp, thick with decay.

A cold whisper brushed against her nape. She spun around, heart hammering, but saw nothing—nothing but the endless corridors stretching into darkness.

Then came the footsteps. Slow. Deliberate.

She turned, and there he was—Bruce Clawson, his face half-hidden in shadow, a sickening grin curling at his lips.

"Madison." His voice growled, echoing unnaturally in the still night. "Did you really think you could ignore me forever?"

Fear clamped down on her throat, turning her breath into ragged gasps. She tried to move, but her feet wouldn't obey.

Bruce stepped closer, his eyes glinting with something sinister. "I want what's owed to me." He grabbed her wrist in a bruising grip. "And you, Madison, have been far too nosey and aloof. You'll be my insurance policy to get it."

"Let me go!"

She struggled, but the hallway shifted, and the walls closed in. A sharp gust of wind extinguished the torches, plunging them into darkness.

Then the ground disappeared beneath her.

She plummeted, falling into a black void, her screams swallowed by the abyss. She landed on cold stone, the impact knocking the air from her lungs. Dazed, she pushed herself up, her hands scraping against the damp, uneven floor.

A single candle flickered to life in the distance, revealing her surroundings.

She was in the castle's basement.

The walls were rough-hewn stone. The low ceiling dripped moisture into puddles on the ground. A rusted iron door slammed behind her. She spun, rushing to it, pounding her fists against it.

"Help! Someone, please!"

Her voice echoed, hollow and hopeless.

Bruce's laughter drifted from the other side. "No one can hear you, Madison. You're mine now."

Then, the scuttling began.

A scratching sound, faint at first, then growing louder. From the corners of the room, from the cracks in the walls, from the darkness itself—they came.

Rats.

Dozens of them. Their tiny claws scraped against the granite, their beady eyes glinting in the candlelight. They sniffed the air, their whiskers twitching, and then—they advanced.

She backed away, her breaths coming in short, panicked gasps. The first rat reached her ankle, its sharp teeth sinking into her skin. She shrieked, kicking wildly, but more swarmed, their hungry mouths tearing at her dress, her legs, her arms.

Pain flared through her body as the nightmare creatures gnawed at her flesh. She screamed, raw and desperate, as Bruce's laughter echoed around her, filling every inch of the wretched prison.

She pressed a trembling hand to her chest, willing her heart to steady. It was just a dream. A horrible, vivid dream.

But as she stood to dress for the morning, a terrible thought curled in the back of her mind.

What if it wasn't a nightmare?

What if it was a warning?

She tugged on her clothes and pulled her hair into a chignon, her heart racing wildly, her mouth dry. She had to tell someone today, and the missus was her most trusted confidant.

She'd expose Bruce as the villain he was, right after breakfast, after Mr. and Mrs. Boldt were fully awake and could take care of it. She'd summon her bravest courage, no matter what.

She pushed open the heavy door to Mrs. Boldt's chambers. The room was dimly lit, the curtains drawn to shield the fragile woman from the harsh morning light. A silence filled the space, broken only by the soft, labored breaths of the lady of the house.

As Madison stepped closer, her heart clenched. Mrs. Boldt lay against the fine embroidered pillows, her once-vibrant complexion more ashen than ever, her delicate features swollen. Her breathing was shallow, each breath a struggle.

Madison kneeled beside the bed. "Mrs. Boldt?"

The older woman's eyes fluttered open, clouded and weary. "Madison, dear," she rasped, her voice barely above a whisper. "Is it morning yet?"

Madison forced a smile, though tears burned the back of her throat. "Yes, ma'am. But it's early. Do you need anything?"

The missus gave a weak shake of her head. "Just to rest a little longer."

Despite her mistress's words, Madison knew rest wasn't enough. She had watched the slow decline for weeks—no, months now. The persistent breathlessness, the way Mrs. Boldt struggled to rise from bed, how she gripped furniture to move across the room. The fatigue that kept her confined, the swelling in her legs that worsened each day, the coughing that woke her in the night.

The progressive symptoms painted a grim picture. Madison had heard the doctors whisper it: heart failure.

And she was powerless to stop it. Her wonderful employer—no, her dearest friend—would be gone.

Fear gnawed at her. Not just for Mrs. Boldt's sake, but for her own. If the worst happened—if Mrs. Boldt passed—what would become of her?

The household would change, new staff would be brought in, positions reassigned or dismissed altogether. Would they send her away? Cast out from the only place she had called home?

Her fingers clenched the fabric of her apron. She couldn't bear to think about it.

A soft knock at the door startled her. She turned as Anna, a chambermaid, peeked inside, worry etched across her face.

The young woman glanced at Mrs. Boldt. "How is she?"

Madison sucked in a steadying breath. "Not well."

Anna stepped inside, her lips pressed into a thin line. "The doctor's been sent for again. Mr. Boldt is worried, so he wrote the children, too."

Madison nodded, her stomach twisting. She wished she could do more—wished there was some way to bring warmth back into Mrs. Boldt's cheeks, strength back into her voice.

But all she could do was wait. And pray.

She reached for Mrs. Boldt's frail hand, giving it a gentle squeeze. "I'll stay with you, ma'am. I won't leave."

Mrs. Boldt's lips curled into the faintest smile before her eyes slipped shut once more, lost in restless slumber.

Madison exhaled shakily. Whatever came next, she had to be strong. For Mrs. Boldt. For herself. For the uncertain future ahead.

Once the missus fell into a deep sleep, Madison moved around the dimly lit room, her mind heavy with worry. The ominous rumors, the growing menace that Bruce represented, and the ever-present fear for Mrs. Boldt's declining health consumed her thoughts.

Clearly, today wasn't the right time to expose Bruce—not yet. She had to tread carefully, but waiting worried her, making her feel restless and anxious.

Her hands trembled as she reached for the tray of linens, adjusting them absentmindedly.

Crash!

The sound echoed through the room like a gunshot. Mrs. Boldt stirred momentarily, but quickly returned to sleep.

Madison gasped, spinning around. The shattered remains of Mrs. Boldt's prized porcelain vase lay scattered across the floor. The delicate blue-and-white China, an expensive import from France, lay in jagged pieces.

Her heart pounded wildly in her chest. How could she be so careless? She fell to her knees, scrambling to collect the fragments, but her hands shook so badly she could barely touch them.

"What have you done?" Anna's voice came in a sharp whisper from the doorway. "You broke it."

Madison cringed. Dizziness came over her. "I—I wasn't paying attention."

"What was that?" Mrs. Boldt mumbled barely above a whisper. "Did something fall?"

Anna answered, her voice squeaky. "It's nothing, ma'am. Rest easy."

Moments later, the door to the adjoining study creaked open. Heavy footsteps followed.

Madison froze.

Mr. Boldt entered, his towering presence filling the room. His usual warmth was absent today, his face lined with exhaustion and grief. His gaze swept over the broken vase, then landed on Madison, his expression hardening.

"What is the meaning of this?"

His voice was clipped, restrained—too restrained—but still a whisper. He glanced at his wife, now resting quietly.

Her stomach twisted. "I—I'm so sorry, sir. It was an accident."

Mr. Boldt exhaled sharply, rubbing his temple as though he hadn't the patience for another mishap today. "That vase was an anniversary gift to my wife." His tone remailed low, controlled, but his jaw muscles clenched. "One of her most cherished possessions."

Her chest tightened. She inhaled, and her stomach clenched. This was all bad enough, but would she shame herself with vomiting as well? "I never meant to—"

He held up a hand, silencing her.

The room grew unbearably tense. Anna shifted uneasily beside her but said nothing.

Madison lowered her head, waiting for the inevitable. Surely, he thought to dismiss her on the spot. Could she truly lose everything over this?

The fear coiled in her gut like a viper.

Mr. Boldt let out a long breath, then shook his head. "Madison, I have more pressing matters to attend to than a broken vase. See that this mess is cleaned up."

She blinked, barely believing what she was hearing. "Yes, sir. I'm so sorry, sir."

As she scrambled to pick up the rest of the shattered porcelain, Mr. Boldt turned to leave, pausing in the doorway. Without looking back, he added, "Be more careful next time."

The door shut behind him, leaving Madison kneeling among the broken shards, her hands trembling with relief.

Anna crouched beside her, offering a sympathetic glance. "That could've been worse."

Madison let out a shaky breath, nodding. It could have been—but how many more mistakes could she afford? With so much uncertainty swirling around her, she wasn't sure how long her luck would hold.

And she still had Bruce to worry about.

~ ~ ~

Bruce's mind raced with anticipation as the sun rose. The workers arrived, and Emmett gathered the crew.

Emmett's voice boomed with authority as he gestured to the pile of granite blocks. "All right, everyone! Let's get those stones in place!"

Bruce folded his arms as the crew moved into position as Garrison climbed onto the scaffolding ahead of his team. That nosy mason deserved a broken leg or arm just as much as his Irish friend.

With each passing moment, Bruce's anticipation grew as the structure swayed precariously. Garrison paused, surveying the structure, but hauled a heavy hewn stone up for placement.

The structure creaked ominously, and Bruce's heart lurched. The moment of truth was upon him. Would it hold, or had he unleashed untold trouble in his pursuit of the Mick's envied position?

He held his breath. Just a few broken bones would teach them all a lesson. A loud crack echoed through the air, and the scaffolding buckled, sending a ripple of panic through the crew, who retreated from the debacle before them.

Bruce's breath caught in his throat as the scene unfolded, a curious combination of horror and satisfaction dawning on him. The structure collapsed, sending workers scrambling for safety, cries of alarm ringing out.

Emmett rushed to the scene, yelling for help, his expression a mixture of fear and fury.

Bruce grinned with the thrill of sabotage.

Dust choked the air, and the acrid scent of disturbed mortar filled his lungs. The splintering crash of wood and the tumbling cascade of stone had sent up a cloud of dust. Several men covered their mouths and noses as they ran—or walked—away. Blood dripped down one man's face, and another limped as he cradled his left arm against his chest.

Bruce's pulse pounded, not with fear, but exhilaration. Surely, this time, someone would hold Emmett accountable. As the foreman, the buck stopped there.

All around them, men assessed the damage amid the debris, their voices urgent and sharp. Some shouted orders, others cursed under their breath at the unexpected collapse.

But Bruce focused on one man. Emmett O'Connor.

The foreman stood rigid amidst the wreckage, his stance braced like a man ready for battle. His sharp gray eyes locked onto Bruce's with an intensity that sent a shiver down his spine. The storm of emotions in his gaze was unmistakable—anger, disbelief, suspicion.

Did he know?

No, not possible.

Had Garrison said something to the site foreman? Perhaps he should have taken care of the man last night.

Bruce's confidence wavered, but only for a moment. If Garrison had blabbed, Emmett would have accosted him first thing.

So, what had happened? Perhaps he'd been too bold? Had the sabotage been too obvious? He swallowed, his throat dry as sawdust.

Then, Emmett jabbed a finger straight at him, his voice ringing over the chaos. "Get over here and help us, man! Garrett's under the rubble!"

Bruce jolted as though struck. No accusations, no immediate blame—just an order. An expectation.

As if nothing had changed.

Suddenly, the gravity of what he had done settled in his chest like an iron anvil. He had wanted to undermine Emmett, to see the man struggle under scrutiny, but now, standing at the edge of the destruction he had caused, the reality was far less satisfying than he had imagined.

Men rushed past him, sweat-soaked and breathless. Even though some bled, still they lifted beams, pulled away rubble, checked for injuries. Their focus was on fixing, repairing, moving forward—not on blame.

Not on him.

For the first time, the thrill of sabotage curdled in his gut. He clenched his jaw, steeling himself. He had meant this to happen. He had wanted to make a statement. Hadn't he?

What he hadn't planned was that Garrison—or anyone—would die.

He had imagined the aftermath in perfect clarity—Emmett scrambling to control the damage, the workers casting blame, the responsibility falling squarely on the foreman's shoulders.

But as he drew near the site of his chaos, the world around him slowed. His stomach twisted as he pushed through the workers, the acrid scent of dust and mortar clinging to the back of his throat.

Then, he saw what had horrified Emmett.

Garrison Whitman lay motionless beneath a large, splintered beam, his broad chest barely rising and falling. Blood pooled beneath his head, staining the dirt a sickening shade of crimson. His usually strong, steady hands—hands that had carved stone with precision, that had built the very foundation of the castle—lay slack, lifeless.

No. No, no, no! This wasn't supposed to happen. No one was supposed to get killed.

"Get that beam off him!" The foreman's voice cut through the chaos, urgent and raw. He was already at Garrison's side, gripping his arm, shaking him gently. "Garrison, can you hear me? Hold on, man!"

Bruce stood frozen, unable to move. His mind reeled.

He had wanted Emmett to falter, to take the blame. He had wanted him to suffer, just for a moment, to know what it felt like to be the one struggling under scrutiny.

But this? This was not the plan.

Someone shoved past him—one of the workers—grabbing hold of the fallen beam. More men joined, muscles straining as they heaved it off Garrison's limp form. The groan of wood and dust of stone filled the air as they freed him, but he remained eerily still.

Emmett pressed his fingers to Garrison's throat, searching. The tension in his shoulders stiffened. A raw moan followed.

A moment later, his eyes snapped up, meeting Bruce's across the wreckage. The anger was gone. The suspicion remained. But beneath it all, he saw something far worse.

Recognition.

Emmett knew. He didn't say it aloud, didn't accuse Bruce in front of the men. But in that single, piercing look, he understood everything.

The ramification of his actions slammed into him, crushing any lingering sense of justification. He had wanted control. Power. Revenge.

Instead, he had blood on his hands.

And no matter what happened next, there was no undoing that.

Bruce's stomach twisted into knots as the reality of what he had done pressed down on him. Garrison lay still, his body slack in the arms of the men trying to rouse him. The blood pooling beneath his head was too red, too real.

His breath came in quick, shallow bursts. This wasn't how it was supposed to go. He had wanted that Irish Mick to stumble, to be taken down a peg, not…this.

But then, the thought slithered into his mind, dark and insidious.

No one saw me. Except Garrison.

No one had seen him loosen the supports. No one had watched him make the adjustments that weakened the structure. He could still come out of this unscathed.

If I say nothing…if I keep my mouth shut…

He swallowed hard, his heartbeat hammering against his ribs. His mind warred with itself—guilt and self-preservation battling like wild dogs.

Then, Emmett turned. Those sharp, knowing gray eyes locked onto Bruce, pinning him in place. There was no shouting, no accusation, not yet—but the foreman's stare was suffocating.

He noticed.

Bruce's hands balled into fists, but he forced his face blank. He needed to act fast. If Emmett suspected him, others would, too. And the only way to keep suspicion off himself was to redirect it.

His gaze flickered to a group of workers standing near the wreckage—new hires, men who barely spoke English, laborers Emmett had taken a chance on despite others doubting their skill.

Perfect scapegoats.

Bruce took a deep breath, steadied himself, and let his voice carry enough to be heard over the murmurs of concern. "Someone must've been careless." He shook his head as he crouched near the rubble. "Maybe one of the newer lads didn't brace the beams right."

The suggestion slipped from his lips with ease. He didn't dare meet Emmett's gaze again. Instead, he focused on the surrounding men, gauging their reactions.

A few nodded grimly, others exchanged uneasy glances. Doubt was easy to plant—especially in moments like this, when fear clouded judgment.

An older worker with deep lines in his face furrowed his brow. "The new lads worked under your supervision."

Bruce's stomach flipped, but he forced out a tight laugh. "If one of them made a mistake…"

He trailed off, letting the possibility linger. Giving the suggestion room to grow in the silence.

A younger worker—a Polish man who barely spoke English—looked up in alarm, his arm bleeding. "We do what we told."

Bruce didn't reply. He didn't have to.

Behind him, Emmett shifted. Bruce felt his disapproval, the slow burn of it, but he didn't look back. He couldn't.

This was survival. Even if it made him a coward.

CHAPTER 11

The morning sun streamed through the lace curtains of the missus's chambers with warm golden hues spreading across the room, infusing the very air—and Madison's spirits—with hope. Her hands trembled as she set down the tray of tea and biscuits, her heart swelling with relief.

Just the night before, she had feared the worst—that Mrs. Boldt's frail heart would not hold through the night. But here she was, sitting upright, her complexion rosier, her sharp eyes filled with purpose.

"You're feeling better this morning, ma'am?" Madison asked, unable to keep the relief from her voice. "You're surely looking as bright as a new penny."

Mrs. Boldt gave her a small, knowing smile. "Better enough." Still, her mistress's voice carried a note of weariness. She picked up her teacup but stopped short of raising it to her lips, instead looking her in the eye. "I need you to help me dress, dear."

She hesitated. "Are you sure, ma'am? Dr. Howard said you needed to rest—"

"Nonsense," Mrs. Boldt cut in, her tone firm. "George is going to Heart Island today, and I will not sit here like a wilting flower while men have suffered injury on my island."

Her stomach tightened. "But Mr. Boldt—"

"—will protest, as he always does," Mrs. Boldt finished for her, sipping then setting the tea aside. "I know my husband. He thinks he is sparing me, but he forgets that my heart is not so weak as my body might be. I *will* go."

She bit her lip. Mrs. Boldt's health had been precarious for months. The brief journey to Heart Island, across the choppy waters of the St. Lawrence, was no small endeavor for her, and the shock of seeing the accident site—Garrison's blood still staining the earth—could be too much for her.

"Ma'am." She couldn't help trying one last time. "I know you wish to support the workers, but your health—"

Mrs. Boldt placed a cool hand over hers, stopping her words. "My dear girl, when you have lived as long as I have, you learn there are things more important than one's own comfort. These men have given their strength and sweat to build this beautiful place. For me. Now, in the wake of tragedy, they need reassurance that their sacrifice is not overlooked."

Concern grabbed her, choked her, gagged her. "Yes, ma'am."

Mrs. Boldt squeezed her hand, then withdrew it. "Now, help me dress."

She moved to the wardrobe, selecting one of Mrs. Boldt's more modest gowns—deep blue with black trim, suitable for the morning chill. She helped Mrs. Boldt step into it carefully, securing the buttons along the back with steady hands. She worked quickly and efficiently, her mind still uneasy, but she could not deny the determination radiating from the woman before her.

As she secured the final button at Mrs. Boldt's collar, the bedroom door swung open.

"Louise." Mr. Boldt's voice was weary and laced with frustration. "I told you to rest."

Mrs. Boldt turned to face him, her expression gentle but unwavering. "And I told you, my love, that I will not sit idly by."

He sighed, rubbing his temple. "Heart Island is no place for you today. There is too much disorder. You don't need the strain."

"I need to be with you," she countered softly. "And with the men. I need to see what has happened with my own eyes."

Mr. Boldt's jaw tightened, but his resistance wavered. The love he had for his wife, the admiration for her resolve, was evident in the way his gaze softened. "And if you tire? If it is too much?"

Madison stepped forward, emboldened by Mrs. Boldt's resolve. "I will be with her every moment, sir. I won't let her overexert herself."

Mrs. Boldt beamed approvingly at her before looking back at her husband. "There. You see? You needn't worry so much, George."

Mr. Boldt let out a long breath, then finally nodded. "Very well. But you rest when I say, Louise."

"I always listen to you, darling."

Her teasing smile mocked his order.

Mr. Boldt scoffed but kissed her forehead, his affection clear. "Let's go to the dock."

Madison exhaled, knowing the morning would be difficult, but she could not deny the admiration swelling in her chest. Mrs. Boldt was frail in body, yes—but in spirit, she was unshakable.

That strength would be needed more than ever today.

The boat's slow approach toward Heart Island was thick with silence. The ordinarily breathtaking sight of the castle felt different today—its towering spires overshadowed by grief and concern.

Madison sat beside Mrs. Boldt, her hand near the older woman's arm, waiting to steady her if needed. Mr. Boldt sat across from them. He barely spoke, his expression grim. He always carried himself with an air of authority, but today, the tragedy of the situation pressed heavy on his shoulders.

When they docked, Emmett awaited them, his face drawn, his usual confidence dimmed. The wind tousled his dark hair, but he didn't move to fix it. Instead, he offered a brief nod to Mr. Boldt.

"Sir." His voice cracked. "You needn't have troubled yourself."

"Take me to the site." Mr. Boldt's order revealed his intention. He held out a hand for his wife. "Take *us*."

Emmett hesitated, his gaze flickering to Mrs. Boldt. "Are you sure—?"

Mrs. Boldt lifted her chin. "I—we need to see."

With a curt nod, Emmett turned and led them up the path toward the accident site.

As they neared the damaged scaffolding, Madison's breath caught in her throat. Her mind hadn't fathomed this much devastation. Piles of broken beams and splintered wood lay strewn across the ground. Several workers stood off to the side and whispered amongst themselves, their expressions somber.

Despite her intentions, her gaze shifted to the ground near the wreckage. The bloodstains had not yet faded.

Mrs. Boldt inhaled sharply, one hand clutching her shawl.

"Oh, Garrison…" Madison's voice—and her heart—broke for Emmett standing resolutely nearby, but as far away as if he resided in another county. "I never imagined…"

A worker removed his cap in silent respect, and Emmett cleared his throat. "He never had a chance. It happened too fast."

Mr. Boldt exhaled through his nose, his gaze sweeping over the site. "What do we know?"

"The detective will arrive shortly." Emmett's jaw clenched. "There are… concerns."

Mrs. Boldt tensed beside her, and Madison understood why. If the detective found fault with the structure—if they deemed it negligence—everything could change.

Mr. Boldt nodded stiffly, his voice laced with frustration. "I'll speak to the men. In the meantime…" He turned to his wife, his gaze softening. "Louise, this is no place for you."

Mrs. Boldt straightened. "George, I need to—"

"No." His tone was gentle but firm. "I won't have you standing in the middle of a worksite, breathing in death and grief."

He turned to Madison. "Take her to Alster Tower. Make sure she rests."

Mrs. Boldt opened her mouth to protest, but Madison knew better than to let this turn into a battle. She stepped forward, touching Mrs. Boldt's arm lightly.

"Come, ma'am." She held her arm out to her mistress. "Let me take care of you while your husband sees to business."

For several moments, Mrs. Boldt hesitated. She stared at the wreckage as though she would change what had happened if she could. But then, with a weary sigh, she relented, allowing Madison to guide her away, leaving Mr. Boldt and Emmett behind.

As they ascended the steps toward Alster Tower, Madison embraced the quiet reprieve from the chaos outside. Inside, the stone walls held onto the damp chill of the river air, and she quickly helped Mrs. Boldt into a chair near a window.

The older woman settled with a quiet sigh, pressing a hand against her heart. "Garrison." She shook her head, eyes unfocused. "How could this happen?"

Madison knelt beside her, clasping the frail hand gently. "The men said it was an accident. But…"

She hesitated, the words catching in her throat.

Mrs. Boldt's eyes, sharp despite her exhaustion, lifted to meet hers. "But?"

She bit her lip, then sighed. "I'm afraid of what the detective might find."

Mrs. Boldt exhaled shakily. "As am I."

A silence stretched between them, heavy with grief. She had known Garrison only in passing—his kind nods, his reassuring presence among the crew—but even now she felt the loss of him in the air.

Mrs. Boldt turned her gaze toward the window, staring up at the towering castle rising over the island. "These men have poured their lives into this place. Their hands have built it, stone by stone. And now, one of them has given his life for it." She closed her eyes for a moment, then whispered, "I wonder if it's worth it."

Madison's heart ached at the despair in her voice. "Ma'am…"

Mrs. Boldt shook her head, sitting up straighter. "No, I shouldn't speak that way. George meant this to be a place of love. A dream he and I shared. But love should never come at such a cost."

Her throat squeezed into a dry tangled rope. "What will happen if the detective finds fault? If…if someone is blamed?"

Mrs. Boldt sighed. "Then decisions will have to be made. Difficult ones."

They both fell silent again, and her thoughts tangled in worry. Outside, the low hum of voices drifted down from the accident site.

She reached for Mrs. Boldt's hand again, squeezing it gently. "We'll face it together, ma'am."

Mrs. Boldt gave her a weak smile. "Yes, dear. We will."

But in her heart, an unspoken fear remained.

Would this be the beginning of the castle's undoing?

And hers along with it?

~ ~ ~

Emmett remained behind as the steamer carrying the Boldts and Madison drifted away from Heart Island, disappearing into the mist rolling over the St. Lawrence River. He hadn't even had time to process his own grief over Garrison's death, and now he had to answer to the detective. At least he didn't have to be interrogated in front of Mr. Boldt who decided to accompany his wife back home. For that he was grateful.

A small skiff approached bearing a uniformed figure. The man wasn't tall, nor particularly imposing, but the sharp glint of his eyes told Emmett he missed nothing. His uniform buttons strained slightly against his midsection—years of good meals, no doubt—but Emmett would not underestimate him.

The detective stood near the bow, shading his eyes with one hand.

"Foreman O'Connor?"

Emmett nodded, tugging the boat closer to moor it. The man lumbered out of it while Emmett held the vessel steady, then he wiped his hands on his trousers before extending one in greeting.

The detective gave a firm shake before retrieving a small notebook from his pocket. "Detective Herold Fletcher." He flipped open the pages. "I understand there's been a fatal accident."

Emmett exhaled sharply, nodding. "Aye. Garrison Delaney. Stonemason. One of the best."

The detective hummed, stepping past Emmett to survey the collapsed scaffolding. "Walk me through it."

Despite the knot in his gut, Emmett nodded and led him to the site. Each footstep sounded like the pounding of a hammer on coffin nails. Garrison's coffin.

When they arrived, he motioned to the pile of debris. "The crew moved into position as Garrison climbed onto the scaffoldin' ahead of his team, but it gave way."

Fletcher crouched low, examining the ground. He ran his fingers through a pile of sawdust and thin wood shavings. "Fresh."

Emmett stiffened. "Aye, we noticed that too."

The detective rose, dusting off his hands. "But where's the piece that gave out?"

He frowned. "That's the problem. We can't find it."

Fletcher arched an eyebrow. "Convenient."

His jaw tightened. "What are you suggestin'?"

The detective didn't answer right away. Instead, he took a slow walk around the scene, scanning the area with a practiced eye. "Wood shavings suggest tampering. But the compromised piece itself isn't here." He turned back to him. "Either someone took it before we got here…"

"…Or it splintered into so many pieces it's lost in the wreckage." The knot doubled in size. "Difficult to prove one way or the other."

Fletcher gave him a long, measured look. "You think this was an accident, Foreman?"

He hesitated. His instincts told him no. But saying as much without proof wouldn't help anyone.

"I think," he said carefully, "somethin' doesn't sit right about it."

Fletcher studied him for a moment, then snapped his notebook shut. "Then let's find out why."

Together, they turned back to the wreckage, the import of the investigation settling between them.

Detective Fletcher walked the perimeter of the accident site, his sharp eyes scanning every piece of debris, every splintered beam, every footprint in the dust.

Emmett followed closely, arms crossed over his chest, his gut tight with worry. He had suspected foul play from the unnatural way the scaffolding collapsed. But without the missing piece of wood, or the tools, or an eye witness, he had no proof.

Fletcher kept his focus on the debris. "Did you oversee the construction of this scaffolding? Did you inspect it thoroughly?"

He stiffened. "Aye. I check every piece of equipment before the men use it."

Fletcher finally straightened, his gaze calculating. "Then you're either incompetent, or someone tampered with this after your inspection."

Emmett ground his teeth but held his tongue. The detective was simply doing his job, firing insinuations for effect, asking accusatory questions, seeing how people reacted. "The last time I checked, the beams were sound. But somethin' changed before the accident."

Fletcher huffed. "Then we need to find out who had access to it. Who was working around here before the collapse?"

He hesitated, his instincts screaming that Bruce was involved—but without evidence, he couldn't start throwing accusations, especially against the architect's nephew.

"I will make you a list."

"Good." Fletcher turned toward the workers still lingering around the site. His gaze settled on two of the Polish laborers who had only recently joined the crew. "Have them step forward."

Emmett frowned. "Why them?"

Fletcher pointed to the ground where the wood shavings had gathered. "Their boot prints are all over the fresh sawdust."

The shock of the accident pressed on Emmett like a millstone. Garrison was dead. The scaffolding had failed. And now, Detective Fletcher was here, sifting through the wreckage like a bloodhound on a scent.

He stood beside the lawman, arms crossed, gut twisted into knots. He had checked that scaffolding himself—every joint, every beam. It shouldn't have failed. But it had.

And now, he needed answers.

Fletcher flipped through his notepad. "I ask again. Who had access to this scaffolding before the collapse?"

He sighed, rubbing the back of his neck. "Everyone on the crew, but the men working closest to it were the stone team and the support crew."

Fletcher arched an eyebrow. "And who was in charge of overseeing those men?"

Emmett hesitated before answering. "Bruce Clawson."

That got Fletcher's attention.

The detective glanced toward Bruce, who stood just out of earshot, arms crossed, watching them with an innocent expression. "Bring him over."

Emmett turned, nodding at Bruce. "Clawson, over here."

Bruce approached at a measured pace, his face the picture of calm—but he didn't fool Emmett. He recognized that look. The same one Bruce always wore when covering his own hide.

Fletcher got straight to it. "Where were you before the scaffolding collapsed?"

Bruce blinked, then scoffed. "You think I had something to do with this?"

"No one's accused you." Fletcher tilted his head. "Just asking questions."

Bruce let out a short laugh, feigning insult. "I was working with the crew, same as always."

"Near the scaffolding?"

Bruce shrugged. "In and out."

Fletcher narrowed his eyes. "You weren't up there when it fell, but you were close, yes?"

Bruce hesitated just a beat too long before nodding. "I suppose."

Fletcher tapped his notepad. "And before that? The night before and the morning of the accident—where were you?"

Bruce exhaled sharply. "Helping oversee the work, just like I was told to do." He shot a glance at Emmett, his eyes darkening. That look made his skin prickle. "I only do what the foreman bids."

Fletcher squatted near the base of the wreckage, running his fingers through the pile of sawdust and fresh wood shavings. "Interesting thing here. Signs of recent tampering. Wood that's been deliberately weakened. But the piece itself—the one that gave out? Nowhere to be found."

Bruce folded his arms. "Sounds like poor management."

Emmett stiffened.

Fletcher glanced up. "You're saying this was negligence?"

Bruce let the words hang in the air before offering a slow, calculated nod. "I'm saying that if the scaffolding wasn't secure, then maybe someone didn't do their job properly."

The implication hit like a hammer.

Emmett's fists clenched at his sides. "You're sayin' this is my fault?"

Bruce didn't answer right away. He exhaled, shaking his head as if it pained him. "Look, I don't want to point fingers, Emmett, but…you are the foreman."

Emmett's pulse pounded in his ears. The sheer audacity of it.

Bruce had been there. He had worked on the scaffolding. And now, he was shifting the blame?

Fletcher watched them both, his eyes sharp. "That true, O'Connor? You were the last one to inspect the scaffolding?"

He forced himself to take a breath. "Aye. As I said, it was solid."

Fletcher gestured to the debris. "Then how do you explain this?"

He turned to Bruce, his gaze burning. "Maybe Clawson here can answer that."

Bruce held up his hands. "I don't know what you're implying. I only ever follow your orders, sir."

It was a masterful move—twisting the situation to redirect the suspicion. Bruce had laid the perfect trap, and he saw the way Fletcher's mind worked through the possibility.

Emmett was the foreman. The responsibility was his. Unless he could prove otherwise.

Fletcher scribbled in his notebook. "Until we find that missing piece of wood, I can't rule out foul play—or negligence."

He snapped the book shut. "And that means everyone stays on-site until I sort this out."

Bruce exhaled in mock relief. "Glad to hear it, Detective. We all just want the truth, after all."

Emmett wanted to knock that smug look right off Bruce's face. Instead, he took a slow, measured breath.

Bruce had played his hand, but this wasn't over. Emmett would find the missing piece.

And when he did, Bruce Clawson would regret ever trying to frame him.

CHAPTER 12

Madison sat across from Mr. and Mrs. Boldt, her hands folded tightly in her lap as the carriage rocked gently down Alexandria Bay's Church Street on the way to the small cemetery. Beside her, George Junior gazed solemnly out the window, while Clover, usually filled with a lively spirit, sat quietly beside her mother, her gloved hands resting in her lap.

While Madison was grateful Mr. and Mrs. Boldt's children visited, the certainty of loss hung over them. The overcast sky, thick with low hanging gray clouds, made it feel as if the heavens themselves mourned Garrison's passing.

It had been three days since the accident. Three days since Emmett had been placed under scrutiny. Three days since whispers of blame had spread.

On the walk to the graveside after the service, Madison fretted over the Boldts' sadness, but she ached for Emmett. She had heard the whispers and seen the way doubt crept into the workers, even though he held his ground against Detective Fletcher. And now, as they prepared to lay Garrison to rest, she shuddered at the feeling that even worse things might be on the horizon.

The funeral was a solemn affair. Mrs. Garrison and her young son proved almost inconsolable. Simple white linen draped Garrison's casket, surrounded by the men who had worked beside him building Boldt Castle. Some wept openly. Others kept their grief locked behind hardened faces.

Mr. Boldt stood beside his wife, his hand resting gently on her arm. When the minister spoke, his voice was filled with reverence for the man they had lost.

Madison remained a few steps behind the Boldts, hands clasped tightly, listening but unable to keep her eyes from drifting toward Emmett standing apart from the crowd, his face unreadable, his posture rigid.

But when she let her gaze wander, she noticed another figure—Bruce. Near the back, his expression carefully neutral. Too neutral.

Her stomach twisted.

When the funeral ended and the last shovels of earth covered Garrison's grave, the depth of sorrow still hung in the damp air. The workers and mourners lingered, exchanging quiet words of comfort.

Madison stepped away from the grieving crowd, needing a moment of air while the Boldts conversed with friends. As she rounded the side of the small chapel near the cemetery, hushed voices caught her attention. She stilled.

Bruce cleared his throat. "…won't be long now."

Her heart pounded as she moved closer, pressing herself against the stone wall, just out of sight.

Another voice—one of the crewmen, perhaps—responded, hesitant. "You really think Boldt will replace him?"

Bruce let out a short, amused chuckle. "He doesn't have a choice, does he? Detective Fletcher has his doubts, and Emmett's the one in charge of safety. If it wasn't sabotage, then it was negligence."

The other man shifted uneasily. "Still. He's a good foreman."

Bruce scoffed. "A good foreman doesn't let men die under his watch."

Her breath caught in her throat. So, this was Bruce's plan. He wasn't content just letting suspicion fall on Emmett—he was pushing the notion, molding it into certainty.

The worker hesitated. "And you? You think you're the best man for the job?"

"Who else?" Bruce chuckled. "I know this project inside and out. I know how Boldt thinks. I'm the architect's nephew. And, more importantly, I know how to make sure something like this never happens again."

The worker grunted. "And if Emmett doesn't step aside?"

A pause. Then, Bruce's voice, lower now. "He will."

A chill ran down her spine.

The conversation ended, but Madison remained frozen in place, her mind racing. Bruce was playing a dangerous game. And if Emmett didn't act soon, the man she'd grown to admire might lose everything.

She hurried to the graveyard's edge where Emmett still stood, her hands clasped together to keep them from trembling. She had to talk to him. To warn him.

He clenched his hat in his hands, his knuckles white, his shoulders rigid. Her heart twisted painfully. She understood that kind of grief.

That same grief had wrapped itself around her heart and soul when she lost her family. The kind of loss that left a person hollow, convinced no one could understand the weight they carried. She hesitated for only a moment before stepping toward him.

When she reached him, she stopped, suddenly uncertain. What could she say?

For a moment, she simply stood beside him, watching as his grip tightened around his hat. Then, quietly, she whispered, "I know what it feels like."

He didn't move.

She swallowed, her voice barely above a breath. "To feel like the world has gone on without you. To stand in a room full of people and feel apart."

Still, he didn't look at her.

She clenched her fingers together, pressing on. "I lost my family." The words ached as they left her lips, but she forced herself to continue. "My parents. My brother. And then my aunt, who took me in. One by one, they were taken from me. First, it was murder. Then the sea. Then sickness." Her throat tightened.

A muscle in his jaw twitched, his hands gripping his hat tighter.

Her heart pounded as she took a small step closer. "For a long time, I thought it was my fault. That if I had been stronger, if I had done something different, maybe they'd still be here." She let out a shaky breath. "I don't know if you feel that way now, Emmett. But if you do…I want you to know you're not alone. And I don't blame you."

The silence stretched between them. Madison searched his face, willing him to say something. Wondering if she should tell him about Bruce.

Instead, he turned.

He walked away, moving toward a stand of trees. She wrapped her arms around herself, biting her lip against the lump in her throat, helpless to stop him. She had reached out to him, but some walls were too thick to break in a single moment. All she could do now was wait.

And hope that, when he was ready, he would let her in.

The next day, the morning air was crisp, carrying the scent of the river as she stepped outside. A soft mist clung to the shoreline, the waters lapping gently against the rocks. The island was still quiet, the workers not yet stirring, the world wrapped in the hush of dawn.

That's when she saw him.

Emmett.

He walked along the shoreline, hands shoved deep into his pockets, head bowed. His steps, slow and, heavy, as if weighed down by the unknown.

She hesitated for only a moment before following. Taking careful steps across the damp earth, the crunch of pebbles beneath her boots loud and obtrusive. When she drew close, she spoke gently. "You're up early."

He didn't look at her, but he let out a low chuckle, one that held no humor. "Didn't sleep much. Can't stop thinkin' about him."

She remained quiet, letting him speak.

"I was the one responsible for safety. He trusted me. The men trusted me. And now he's gone." His voice cracked, and he shook his head. "How does that happen? How does a man wake up one mornin', go to work, and never come home?"

Her heart ached at the rawness in his voice. "At the funeral, I overheard Bruce say that he was going to have your job, that he was the man to replace you. He's scheming."

He ran a hand down his face, shrugging off her revelation. "Doesn't matter. Emmett does. I keep askin' myself—why? Why? And I keep comin' back to the same thing."

Her heartbeat thundered in her ears. "Which is?"

He finally turned to her, his gaze burning with unspoken turmoil. "Where was God in all this?"

The words hit her like a wave.

He let out a hollow laugh, shaking his head. "I know what people say—God has a plan, He works all things for good, His ways are higher than ours—but tell me, Madison, what good is there in a man bein' crushed under scaffoldin'? In a wife losin' her husband? In a son growin' up without a father?"

She lowered her eyes, wrapping her arms around herself. She understood his questions—she had asked them more times than she could count.

"Do you ever wonder," he said quietly, "if maybe God doesn't care?"

The pain in his voice almost broke her. She was silent for a moment, then took a deep breath. "Yes, I have wondered."

He turned his gaze back to the water, waiting.

She hesitated, then spoke. "When I lost my family, I asked the same questions. Where was God when that evil man killed my papa and brother? When my mother took her last breath? When I stood over my aunt's grave with nowhere left to go?"

He looked at her now, truly looked at her.

She exhaled. "I didn't find answers then. And I still don't have all of them now." She turned toward the river, watching the way the sunlight broke through the mist. "But I know this—evil exists, and God doesn't promise we won't suffer. He never said we wouldn't grieve."

He scoffed. "Then what does He promise?"

She met his gaze. "That He won't leave us in it."

His jaw tightened, his eyes searching hers as if grasping for something—anything—solid to hold on to.

She took a step closer. "I don't know why Garrison died, Emmett. But I do know that pushing God away won't bring you peace. And it won't bring Garrison back."

He groaned, long and low, looking away. For a long moment, they stood in silence, the gentle lapping of the waves and the calling of seabirds mere feet from them.

Then, finally, he let out a breath. "Maybe you're right. I just...don't know how to reckon it all."

She offered him a small, understanding smile. "Then let's reckon it together."

He didn't answer right away, but after a moment, he nodded.

And for the first time since the accident, a glimmer of hope shone in his eyes.

~ ~ ~

Emmett had always believed that a man's work spoke louder than words. But now, it seemed words had the power to drown out everything he had built.

The rumors started subtly—a quiet murmur among the workers, an odd glance from men he had known for years.

At first, he ignored them, too caught up in his own grief and guilt to take notice.

But then the whispers grew louder.

"He should've checked the scaffolding better."

"They say he's been cutting corners."

"A foreman's responsible for his men, and now Garrison's dead."

And then, the worst of them all—"What if it wasn't an accident?"

He clenched his fists as he strode through the worksite, feeling the omen of a dozen stares. He had spent years earning the respect of these men, proving himself a leader, someone they could trust.

But trust was fragile. And once doubt took root, it spread like wildfire.

It wasn't just the workers. The unease seeped into the village, around the storefronts, ripping into the very fabric of the community.

At the butcher's, the man behind the counter hesitated before serving him, his usual friendly chatter replaced with awkward silence.

At the blacksmith's, the apprentice barely met his gaze, mumbling about how folks were talkin'.

Even at church, where he had once found peace, the congregation's hushed voices followed him like ghosts. It didn't take long for him to figure out who was behind it.

Bruce.

That cladhaire had been busily planting seeds of doubt since the day of the accident, feeding men just enough speculation to make them question what they thought.

And now, he was the one staring down the consequences.

One evening, after a long day of work in which no man would meet his eye, Emmett found Bruce exactly where he expected him—leaning against the wall, doing nothing like always, a smug smile curling at the corner of his lips.

Emmett didn't stop to think. He grabbed Bruce by the front of his shirt, slamming him against the wall. "What have you done?"

Bruce didn't flinch. If anything, his smirk widened. "Careful, O'Connor. You wouldn't want anyone to think you've got a temper, now would you? Might make folks wonder what else you're capable of."

His grip tightened. "You're lyin' to the men. Turnin' them against me."

Bruce chuckled. "Am I? Or am I just voicing the concerns they already had?" He leaned in. "Face it, Emmett. People need someone to blame. I simply made sure they found the right scapegoat."

His stomach roiled with fury. His hands ached to retaliate— to shut Bruce up, to wipe that smug grin right off his face. But just as he tensed, a voice cut through the tension.

"Emmett?"

Madison. Her tone wasn't gentle. It was firm—concerned, but unyielding. She stood a few feet away, arms crossed, her brows drawn together in a mixture of worry and determination. "Don't!" She glanced between him and Bruce. "He's not worth it."

Bruce chuckled again, taking a step back and dusting off his shirt. "Listen to the little lady, O'Connor. You wouldn't want to lose what meager favor you have left."

His fists clenched, but he didn't take the bait.

Not this time.

Bruce gave her an almost mocking nod. "Good evening, Madison."

And with that, he sauntered off into the afternoon shadows.

Emmett stared after him, his pulse pounding in his ears. The anger inside him was like a roaring fire, consuming every thought. "You shouldn't have interrupted."

She huffed. "And what exactly were you planning to do? Beat him up in the middle of the workday?"

He whirled to face her, his frustration spilling over. "And why not? He's been lyin' to the men, turnin' them against me. He deserves worse than a few bruises."

She took a step closer, her voice intense. "And what happens when he shows those bruises to Mr. Boldt or the detective and plays the victim? You think that's going to clear your name?"

He opened his mouth to argue, but closed it just as quickly.

She shook her head. "You're letting your anger blind you. You know Bruce is behind this. He's the reason you're being blamed. He wants your job. But if you want to prove it, you need more than your fists."

He turned away, his blood still boiling, his Irish temper still burning through his veins. "Madison, you don't understand. This is my reputation. My life. I've worked years for it. And now, everywhere I go, I see doubt in their eyes."

She softened slightly, but she didn't back down. "Then fight back the right way, Emmett. Find proof Show that Bruce sabotaged the scaffolding. Stop this before it's too late."

He turned to her, shaking his head. "And how do you suggest I do that, then? Sneak around after him like a thief? Spy on him?"

"If that's what it takes. Yes."

His eyes flashed. "That's not how I work."

"Well, maybe it should be."

They stood there, locked in a silent battle, frustration thick between them.

She exhaled, her voice softer now. "I'm trying to help you, Emmett. But you must let me."

He looked at her then, really looked at her—the worry in her eyes, the way she had put herself between him and a mistake he'd regret.

Slowly, his rage settled. With a rough sigh, he pinched the bridge of his nose. "Fine. I'll do it your way."

She crossed her arms. "Promise?"

He met her gaze. "Aye."

When he returned to his office, he sat at his desk, a mess of papers spread before him. Half-finished reports, construction plans, supply lists—things he should have been focused on.

Things Garrison would be working on. But he couldn't focus. Not when Bruce had spent the past week poisoning everything Emmett had built.

The knock at his door came sharp and quick. "Telegram for you, Mr. O'Connor."

He pushed back from his desk, his jaw tight as he opened the door. One of the younger workers stood there, shifting awkwardly.

He took the telegram with a nod and shut the door behind him. He had a bad feeling about this. He hadn't received a missive from the Hewitts since the one confirming Garrison's passing.

He unfolded the paper, his pulse quickening as he read the message.

FROM: G. W. & W. D. HEWITT ARCHITECTURAL FIRM
TO: EMMETT O'CONNOR, FOREMAN
ARRIVING IN TWO DAYS. EXPECT FULL REPORT ON SITE CONDITIONS.
CONCERNS HAVE BEEN RAISED. EXPECT ACCOUNTABILITY. - HEWITTS

Emmett gripped the telegram until the paper crumpled in his fist.

Concerns have been raised.

He knew what that meant.

Bruce had gotten to them.

Bruce had been spinning his web all week—whispering in ears, sowing doubts, making him look like an incompetent foreman at best, a reckless one at worst.

Now, the Hewitts were coming. And they were expecting answers.

He paced the length of the room. If the Hewitts believed Bruce's lies, they could dismiss him. With no hope of a reference. No defense.

Replaced by Bruce.

The very thought made his stomach churn.

He had to act.

Now.

With renewed purpose, he yanked open the door, striding across the muddy worksite, his boots sinking into the damp earth up to his soles. He needed to think—needed proof.

As he neared the main path leading toward the docks, he almost ran straight into Madison.

She gasped, startled. "Emmett?"

He barely slowed. "The Hewitts are comin'."

She blinked. "What? When?"

"Two days." His voice was tight, his mind already racing ahead. "They want answers. Bruce's been feedin' them lies."

Her expression darkened. "Then we don't have much time." She fell into step beside him, her brows furrowed in thought. "You need proof, Emmett. More than just suspicions."

"Aye. And where do you suggest I start? The piece that failed is missin'. The detective has no proof of sabotage. And the men—" His jaw clenched. "They already doubt me."

She chewed her lip, thinking. Then, her eyes lit with an idea. "Bruce may have been careful, but he isn't—and wasn't—perfect."

"What're you gettin' at?"

She turned to him. "He had to dispose of the evidence somewhere. If he tampered with the scaffolding, he wouldn't leave it lying around for anyone to find."

His mind churned. She was right. If Bruce had removed the damaged piece, he'd have hidden it somewhere.

"We need to figure out where he might have put it."

He looked around the site. There were plenty of places Bruce could have stashed evidence that probably looked like scraps. It was like looking for a particular needle in a—in a needle factory.

His hands curled into fists. "Then we'd best start lookin'."

Madison nodded. "Before the Hewitts get here."

"Or Bruce gets rid of the proof we need."

CHAPTER 13

Madison had intended to spend the afternoon helping Emmett search for clues—anything that would prove Bruce's sabotage before the Hewitts arrived. But as soon as the Boldts awakened, she realized she wouldn't be leaving anytime soon.

The air was filled with laughter, warm and rich, the kind that had been absent for too long. Clover Boldt swept into the parlor in a flurry of satin, her face beaming as she giggled at Buster Brown's antics. The family dog yipped and bounced, his stubby tail wagging furiously as he chased after the ribbons on Clover's dress.

"Buster, behave!" Clover scooped him up. The dog wriggled in her arms, licking her chin, making her laugh. "Ooh, yuck. Stop that."

Madison's heart lightened at the young woman's girlish giggle. Clover had a special way of bringing joy to all of them.

George Junior leaned against the back of the settee, shaking his head with a knowing grin. "You'll never get that dog to sit still, Clover. He's got more energy than the rest of us combined."

Across the room, Mrs. Boldt sat comfortably on a velvet chair, a rare expression of peace easing her face. She watched her children, George Junior, twenty-four, and Clover, twenty, with a soft smile. The tension of the past weeks momentarily lifted from the missus's face.

Madison responded by smiling, too.

For the first time in days, the house didn't feel heavy with grief or unease. It felt alive. She had almost forgotten what that felt like.

"Madison, dear." Mrs. Boldt gestured to her. "Come sit by me."

She obeyed, honored to be included in the family moment.

Mrs. Boldt sighed, resting her hand over hers. "It's been too long since the house felt like this."

She nodded. "It's good to hear laughter again, ma'am."

Mrs. Boldt's gaze lingered on her children, her eyes glistening. "I worry about them, you know. For George, stepping into his father's world. For Clover, finding her place. And yet, when I see them like this…" She smiled wistfully. "I feel everything will be all right."

Madison squeezed her hand gently. "You've raised them well, ma'am. They love you."

Mrs. Boldt's fingers tightened around hers. "And I love them. More than anything." She sighed. "I only wish George was here to enjoy this."

Madison fidgeted in her seat. Mr. Boldt had been so preoccupied with the accident, with the detective, with the Hewitts' impending visit, he had scarcely been home. The notion Mrs. Boldt missed him after all their years together gave her hope for her own future. Someday.

As if reading her thoughts, Mrs. Boldt patted her hand. "I won't dwell on that today. Not when there's joy to be had."

Madison nodded, but her thoughts drifted to Emmett. He was out there searching—alone.
She had told him she would help, that she wouldn't let him fight this battle by himself.

Yet here she was, sitting in a warm parlor, while he combed the worksite by himself.

Guilt tugged at her, but then Clover sauntered up beside her, grinning. "Madison, you must help me convince Mama that Buster needs a new collar. A fashionable one."

She relaxed, allowing herself to be pulled into the conversation, into the warmth of family. Just for a little while.

Tomorrow, the fight would continue. But today was for rest. Joy. Something Emmett didn't have. Something she didn't have.

As the late afternoon sun dipped lower in the sky, Mr. Boldt returned. The family gathered for tea in the grand sitting room. Their laughter and quiet conversation drifted through the halls.

Madison spent most of the day with them, caught between the warmth of their company and the nagging guilt tugging at her chest.

But now she had an hour free. She slipped out of the house discreetly, her steps quick as she hurried toward a skiff to take her to the worksite.

Emmett needed her.

She stepped into his office, aghast at the sight before her. Papers, scattered across his desk. Rough sketches with notes scribbled hastily in the margins. A lantern burned low in the corner, casting long shadows over the cramped space. The air smelled of sawdust and ink, the scent clinging to every surface. And there he sat—leaning over a blueprint, his jaw tight, his brows furrowed in deep thought.

She hesitated at the doorway. "Emmett?"

He looked up, startled. He rubbed the back of his neck. "What are you doin' here?"

"Have you been working yourself to the bone?"

His expression softened slightly when he saw her, but the weariness in his eyes remained. "I asked you a question first."

"I have a little time. I want to help."

He huffed, sinking into his chair. "Help how? I've searched half the site, and I'm no closer to findin' that piece of wood than I was this mornin'."

She glanced at the mess of papers on his desk. "Then maybe we need to stop searching and start thinking."

He frowned. "Thinkin'?"

She pulled out a chair and sat across from him. "You've been looking where you think Bruce might have hidden it. But if he was smart enough to cover his tracks, we need to be smarter."

He exhaled sharply, leaning forward. "What do you suggest?"

She tapped her fingers against the desk, thinking. "Let's go over everything. Where was Bruce when the scaffolding fell?"

He sighed, rubbing his temple. "Nearby. But that doesn't mean—"

"No." She pursed her lips. "I mean, what did he do? Did he act guilty? Did he leave the site at any point afterward?"

His brow furrowed in thought. "Aye…he disappeared not long after the accident. Said he needed a moment."

Her heart quickened. "Where did he go?"

He sat back, realization dawning in his eyes. "Down by the docks."

She leaned forward. "And what's near the docks?"

He stood. "The supply shed."

She nodded. "That's where we start." She glanced at the clock on the wall. "I only have an hour."

He grabbed his coat. "Then let's make it count."

The docks were eerily quiet in the fading afternoon light. Most of the workers had already cleared out, leaving only the sound of the river lapping against the wooden pilings and the occasional cry of a distant gull.

They moved quickly, keeping their steps light as they approached the supply shed. The wooden structure sat at the far end of the dock, half-hidden behind stacks of lumber and barrels of mortar, stood solidly against wind and waves.

Did it now contain the evidence they sought? That they so desperately needed?

He tested the door handle—unlocked.

She laid a hand on his arm. "That's convenient."

He shot her a look. "Or suspicious."

Without another word, he pushed the door open, stepping inside first and lighting the lantern. She followed, wrinkling her nose at the musty scent of sawdust and damp wood.

Inside, crates and tool racks lined the walls, with stray planks stacked haphazardly in the corner. A workbench sat in the middle of the room, cluttered with old nails, a hammer, and a rusted saw.

He ran his hand along one of the wooden beams. "If Bruce hid the missin' piece of scaffoldin', this'd be the perfect place."

She nodded, her eyes scanning the room. "Let's split up—check everything."

They moved quickly, rifling through stacks of lumber, lifting tarps, and searching for anything out of place.

Then—"Here."

Madison turned as Emmett crouched near a pile of wood scraps, his hand resting on a short piece of beam that looked different from the others. The edges were rough, the grain uneven—like someone had hastily cut it.

Her breath caught. "Do you think—"

"Aye." He lifted the board carefully. "The break matches the kind that could cause a collapse." He turned the wood over in his hands, his jaw tightening. "This is it."

She exhaled in relief. "Then we have proof."

But before she could say more, a slow clap echoed from the doorway.

They both spun around.

Bruce stood there, silhouetted against the dying light, arms crossed over his chest. His smirk was lazy, but his eyes gleamed sharper. "Well, well." He stepped into the shed. "Looks like I've caught myself a couple of rats."

Her stomach twisted, and their predicament loomed before her like a chasm. Nobody knew they were here.

Emmett took a step forward, his fingers tightening around the piece of wood. "Funny. I was just thinkin' the same about you."

Bruce chuckled, shaking his head. "And what exactly do you think you've found, O'Connor?" He gestured lazily toward the piece of beam. "A bit of scrap? You can't prove anything."

She glanced at him. He was tense, coiled like a spring. If she didn't step in, this would turn into a brawl. She lifted her chin. "Maybe we can't—yet. But I'm sure the detective will want to see this."

Bruce's smirk didn't waver, but his eyes flickered. A flash of…amusement?

Then, in a single, swift motion, he reached for the lantern hanging beside the door and lifted it high.

Her stomach dropped.

"You really think you'll be able to show anyone?" Bruce growled. "Because it seems to me…you're on my turf."

He stepped closer, his fingers tightening around the lantern's handle. "And accidents happen all the time."

The threat hung in the air like smoke.

Her breath caught in her throat.

Emmett's grip on the wooden beam tightened. "If you so much as—"

Bruce tilted the lantern, the oil sloshing inside. His smirk widened.

He wasn't bluffing.

He fully intended them harm.

~ ~ ~

Emmett's pulse pounded like a war drum. His grip tightened around the broken wood as Bruce tilted the lantern just enough to let them know he wasn't afraid to use it.

The air inside the supply shed was thick, laced with sawdust and the sharp scent of oil. The flickering lantern cast wild shadows against the wooden walls, making Bruce's smirk look more sinister.

For a tense moment, no one moved. Then, just as suddenly as he had lifted the lantern, Bruce lowered it. He let out a slow chuckle, shaking his head as if amused by the whole thing. "Go on, then." He stepped aside. "Take your little piece of wood and scurry off."

Emmett didn't trust the cladhaire for a second. His body was still rigid with the need to fight—to do something—but Madison's hand brushed against his arm, grounding him.

Not here. Not now.

Bruce leaned against the doorway as they edged toward the exit.

Just as Emmett stepped past him, the man spoke again—his voice quieter this time, but far more dangerous. "Say a word of this,"

Bruce snarled, "and someone else will meet the same fate as Garrison."

Emmett froze. His blood turned to ice.

Slowly, he turned to face the man. Their eyes locked—blue against brown, fire against ice.

He had known men like him before—cowards who used power like a blade, cutting down anyone in their way.

But Bruce wasn't bluffing. He meant it.

Madison tensed beside him, but Emmett forced himself to breathe, to think. He understood what Bruce was doing—backing him into a corner, making him second-guess his every move.

But Bruce failed to appreciate one thing—Emmett O'Connor wasn't the sort of man to back down in the face of a threat.

He glanced at Madison before leaning in so only Bruce could hear. "You ever so much as touch her—or another man on my crew—and I'll make sure you regret it."

Bruce's smirk didn't waver. "Is that a threat, foreman? Threatening the Hewitts' kin? Not a good idea."

Emmett stepped back. "A promise."

With that, he took Madison's hand and led her up the path and away from the shed. She let out a shaky breath, glancing over her shoulder. "We need to tell someone."

His jaw clenched. "Aye. But not yet."

She frowned. "But—"

He shook his head. "We do this smart. Bruce isn't just runnin' his mouth—he's makin' actual threats. And I can't be puttin' anyone else in danger."

She exhaled, clearly frustrated, but didn't argue.

They had the proof. The game had changed. And he knew one thing for certain—Bruce would not let them win easily.

The cool air wrapped around them as they headed up the hill, the weight of Bruce's threat pressing down on him like a vise.

He didn't stop—not until they were well out of sight and into the shadows near the worksite. Only then did he let go of Madison's hand and exhale sharply, running a hand down his face.

She crossed her arms, her expression tight with frustration. "I still say we need to tell someone."

He shook his head. "Not yet."

"Not yet?" She stepped closer, her voice fierce but hushed. "Emmett, he just threatened us. Threatened others. You think he'll stop if we let this sit?"

He clenched his jaw. She was right. Bruce was the type who grabbed hold of every advantage and used it to his own. Every part of him screamed to march straight to the detective, to Mr. Boldt, to anyone who would put an end to Bruce's scheming.

But Bruce was careful. And careful men didn't leave loose ends.

"If we go to the detective now, what do we have?" He kept his voice level, holding up the broken beam. "A piece of wood that suggests sabotage—but no proof that Bruce touched it. No witnesses. No trail leadin' back to him."

She frowned but didn't argue.

He sighed, gripping the beam tighter. "And what happens if we go runnin' to Mr. Boldt with this and Bruce gets wind of it?" He turned to face her fully. "He'll cover his tracks even better. Or worse—he'll make good on his threat."

She looked away. He was right, even though she hated it. "So what do we do?"

He exhaled. "We get proof. Real proof. Evidence that ties Bruce to this mess so tight, not even his schemin' can get him out of it."

Her brow furrowed. "Like what?"

He thought for a moment, then looked down at the beam in his hands. "He had to have cut this somehow." He turned the wood over. "It's not from the scrap pile—it's from the original structure. If we can find the tools he used, if there's anything to connect him directly—bolts, nails, even marks on the saw—or a witness…"

Her eyes widened. "Then we can prove he tampered with it."

"Aye." His jaw tightened. "And that means goin' where Bruce thinks we're too afraid to go."

"The tool shed."

He nodded grimly. "The tool shed."

She shuddered, whether from the cold or the fear of what they were about to do, he couldn't tell. She met his gaze. "We'll have to be careful."

He huffed a dry laugh. "Careful isn't our way, is it?"

She smirked, though it didn't quite reach her eyes. "No, I suppose not."

He looked back toward the darkened path. "Tomorrow night. After the men have cleared out."

She hesitated. "You really think Bruce won't suspect us?"

"Aye, he suspects us." He exhaled. "But he thinks he scared us off." His expression hardened. "That's his mistake."

She nodded, determination flickering in her gaze. "Then let's prove him wrong."

They exchanged one last look before parting ways—she to the skiff to return to the Boldts, he to his office, the broken beam still clutched in his hands.

Tomorrow, they would find the truth.

One way or another.

Emmett returned to his desk, the castle eerily quiet. The short piece of beam in his hands felt heavier than it should have, as if it carried more than just wood and splinters—as if it carried Garrison's death itself.

He set it carefully on his desk and sank into his chair, elbows on his knees, fingers threading through his hair. His thoughts churned, tangled in the grief that hadn't left him since the day of the accident.

Garrison should be here. He should be laughin' with the men, sharing a *well done* after a long day's work. He should be plannin' the next phase of construction, grumblin' about the cold weather comin' in. He should be alive.

Emmett squeezed his eyes shut. The ache in his chest was a familiar one—loss, regret, and guilt. He had felt it before, in other ways, for other people. But this…this was different.

He had led these men. They had trusted him. Garrison had trusted him.

And now Garrison was gone.

And Bruce—that Skilamalink—was thrivin' off it, spinnin' his lies, poisonin' the workers and the town, creepin' his way into power while he—the foreman who had earned this position—stood accused.

Worse than that, Bruce was willin' to do more than ruin his name. He had threatened the people Emmett cared about.

Madison. The crew. The men who had worked beside him for years.

He saw her face in his mind—the way her brow had furrowed when she argued that they needed proof, the way her lips pressed together when she was thinkin'. She was stubborn, smart, and too fearless for her own good.

Bruce knew it too.

And that terrified Emmett more than anything.

Because now Bruce was aware that she was helping him. She wasn't just an innocent bystander…

He took a slow breath, pressing his hands together. "Lord, I don't know what to do."

His voice was hesitant. It had been a long time since he had prayed like this—not in the polite, practiced way he had been raised, but in the raw, desperate way of a man drowning in confusion.

He exhaled slowly. "I don't understand Your ways. I don't understand why You let good men fall and allow evil men to rise in their place. Why did Garrison have to die? I don't understand why people believe lies so quickly and truth so slowly."

His fingers tightened. "But You see what I don't. And right now, I need to know what to do. Because if I fail…someone else could pay for it."

He let the silence stretch, waiting—hoping—for some sign. Some whisper of guidance. The only sound was the wind against the window. Finally, he exhaled and sat back. Maybe God wasn't answering him tonight. Or maybe He already had.

Madison was right. They needed proof. Not fists, not accusations—proof. And if he had to walk into the lion's den to get it, so be it.

He glanced toward the broken wood on his desk, his jaw tightening. Tomorrow, he and Madison would find the truth.

But tonight, he would grieve. He would remember Garrison—not as a victim, but as a man who had worked hard, who had been more than just another laborer under his command.

Tomorrow was a fight.

But tonight… tonight, he mourned.

CHAPTER 14

The scent of fresh bread and warm tea filled the air as Madison sat across from Hazel in the cozy kitchen. The other staff had long since retired for the evening, leaving them alone in the flickering glow of the lantern. She wrapped her hands around her cup. The warmth grounded her, but her mind was anything but settled.

Hazel tilted her head, studying her with quiet concern. "You've been restless all evening, dear. Out with it."

She sighed, staring into her tea hoping for the answers she sought. "It's Emmett O'Connor, the castle foreman."

Hazel's brows lifted slightly. "What about him?"

She hesitated. She couldn't tell Hazel everything—not about Bruce, the threats, nor their plan they to uncover the truth.

But she could share what weighed on her heart.

"He's not himself. Since Garrison died, he's been…distant."

Hazel nodded slowly. "Grief can do that to a man."

"I know. But it's more than that. He's carrying it all alone—Garrison's death, the rumors, the scrutiny." She huffed, shaking her head. "It's infuriating."

Hazel leaned back in her chair, tapping a thoughtful finger against her chin. "Let me tell you about men like Emmett, dearie. They believe they're meant to bear burdens alone. They think if they let someone help, it means they're weak."

She frowned. "But that's ridiculous."

"Of course it is." Hazel shrugged. "But when has pride ever been reasonable?"

She bit her lip. "I don't want to push him too hard, but I can't simply stand back and do nothing, either."

Hazel reached across the table, squeezing her hand. "Then don't. But be careful, Madison. If Emmett is in the middle of danger—" She paused, her expression darkening. "I wouldn't want you caught in the middle of it."

Her stomach twisted. Hazel didn't know the full truth, but she recognized that things were amiss.

She exhaled. "I am being careful."

Hazel gave her a pointed look.

She managed a wry smile. "Mostly."

Hazel sighed, shaking her head. "You've got a good heart, Madison. Just promise me one thing."

She arched a brow. "What?"

Hazel's grip tightened slightly. "Don't let your determination blind you to trouble."

The words settled deep in her chest.

She thought of Bruce's threats. Of the risk he was taking. And of the way her heart clenched every time she saw the burdens Emmett carried.

Hazel leaned forward and looked deeply into her eyes. "Time for honesty, Madison. You're more than worried about him, aren't you?"

She sighed, rubbing her temple. "He's carrying too much, and it's affecting him."

Hazel tapped her fingers against the wooden table, her brow arching. "I don't doubt that. But this…this isn't just about concern for a fellow worker, is it?"

Her stomach flipped. She opened her mouth to protest, but Hazel gave her a knowing look.

"When did this start?"

She hesitated, staring down at her tea. "I don't know."

Hazel scoffed. "Oh, you do. You just don't want to admit it."

She exhaled. "It's not—" She paused, choosing her words carefully. "It's not what you think."

Hazel chuckled, shaking her head. "Oh, it's exactly what I think. You've been different since you met him, coming back distracted from your walks and your tours. And now you sit across from me, all worked up about Emmett O'Connor like he's your own burden to bear."

She chewed her lip. "He's my friend."

Hazel leaned in. "Yes, and I believe that. But is he more than that?"

Her heart pounded against her ribs like a hammer in the hands of a two-year-old She didn't have an answer.

Or rather, she had one, but saying it aloud made it real.

Hazel watched her carefully, then softened. "You don't have to tell me, dear. But you must be honest with yourself."

She exhaled, running a hand down her arm. "I don't even know what I feel," she admitted. "I just know I care."

Hazel nodded. "And does he know that?"

She frowned. "He knows I'm his friend, but anything more? I know the way of things. It's not proper for a maid, and anything more is not even a possibility. I know that. But even if it was, he's too caught up in everything else. Too focused on clearing his name, on protecting the men, on grieving. As he should."

Hazel tilted her head. "And yet, you care."

She sighed, rubbing at her temple. "I do."

Hazel reached for her hand, squeezing it gently. "Be careful, Madison."

The words weren't just about her concern for his turmoil.

She met Hazel's gaze, seeing the warning there, but also the understanding.

Hazel smiled softly. "Don't fight his battles for him, dear. But if you're going to stand beside him, make sure you know why. There's more at stake here than Emmett's reputation or the investigation or even Garrison's death. Your future matters, too. You know what being in service requires. And you know the consequences of breaking out of your station. Count the cost, dear Madison."

She nodded, her chest tight with emotions she wasn't ready to admit.

Hazel let out a breath, giving her hand one last squeeze before letting go. "Now, finish your tea before it gets cold. And maybe—just maybe—think about your future beyond this time of confusion."

She let out a small, shaky laugh. "Thank you, ma'am. I'll consider all you said."

But as she sipped her tea, she understood one thing for certain—she wasn't just fighting for the truth. She was fighting for him.

She hurried to her room, her shawl drawn tightly around her shoulders as the evening chill settled in. The conversation with Hazel still lingered in her mind, her words pressing against her like a weight she wasn't sure how to carry.

Don't fight his battles for him, dear. But if you're going to stand beside him, make sure you know why.

Why? Why had she risked caring so much? Why had she let his burdens become her own? Why did her heart ache when she saw him struggling?

She wasn't simply worried about him. She cared for him.

Deeply.

The realization almost stopped her in her tracks, but she forced herself forward. Now wasn't the time for emotions to cloud her mind. She had promised to help him, and she would see it through.

Madison sat on the edge of her bed, her hands clasped tightly in her lap, the room dimly lit by the flickering glow of her bedside lantern. The night outside was quiet, save for the occasional rustle of wind against the glass panes of her window.

She had watched his frustration grow, felt the load of his burdens press heavier upon him. And all the while, her own heart had twisted into ambiguity.

Her mission was to care for Mrs. Boldt. To serve. To be a lady's maid and do the best she could. But now, she found herself tangled in deeper feelings.

She exhaled and knelt beside her bed, resting her hands on the quilt. She hesitated, then bowed her head. "Lord…I don't know what to do."

Her voice was barely a whisper, but the intensity of her words filled the stillness.

"I'm here to work, to serve Mrs. Boldt, to fulfill a mission I believe You gave me. But now, I find myself drawn to Emmett in a way I never expected. I see his pain, his grief, his determination to stand alone. And I want to help him. I want to be strong for him."

Her fingers tightened around the fabric beneath her hands.

"But I don't know if this is my burden to bear. I don't know if I should risk losing my good standing with the Boldts or abandoning the missus in her time of need for a man I barely know, a man who could lose it all in a moment."

Her heart ached at the thought of stepping back, of letting Emmett fight this battle without her. A lump formed in her throat.

"And yet…I see glimpses of a man who is honorable, who cares deeply but doesn't know how to show it. A man who carries so much but never asks for help. A man who…"

She paused, her pulse quickening. "Am I falling in love with him?"

She squeezed her eyes shut. "I don't know if this is love. But if it is, I need You to guide me. I need You to show me if I should stand beside him, or if I need to let go before I lose myself completely."

A silence stretched through the room, thick and still.

Then, a soft breeze slipped through the window crack, rustling the flame. It wasn't an answer. But it was a start.

She exhaled, letting her forehead rest briefly against her hands. "One step at a time, Lord. One prayer at a time."

With renewed resolve, she rose, blew out the lantern, and slipped beneath the covers, her mind still tangled in emotions she didn't know how to face.

Tomorrow would come. And with it, a new chance to fight for the truth.

And for the man who didn't yet realize she was fighting for him.

~ ~ ~

The next morning, Emmett sat at his desk, hunched over a pile of notes, his brows knitted together in frustration. When Madison entered, he didn't look up right away, only grunted in acknowledgment. He had woken up on the wrong side of the bed and was in a foul mood, but he didn't know what to do about it. "You're late, lass," he muttered.

Madison arched a brow, before stepping inside. "I wasn't aware we were on a schedule. I got away as soon as I could. The missus is resting in Alster Tower, but I only have a few minutes to talk."

That made him glance up. He sighed and rubbed his temples. "Blathers! Sorry. It's just…I can't make sense of this." He gestured to the scattered papers. "I went back to the shed after we left last night—to see if Bruce had moved anything. But it was the same. Almost too untouched, if that makes sense."

She sat across from him, folding her hands in her lap. "It means he's being careful."

He huffed a bitter laugh. "Careful? No, Madison. It means he's winnin'."

She leaned forward. "Emmett, we found the wood. That's more than we had before, and he knows we're onto him."

He shook his head, rubbing a hand over his face. "And what if that makes him even more dangerous?"

Madison hesitated, searching his face. Sadness and confusion in her eyes reflected back at him.

And then, the truth slapped him in the face. This wasn't just about Bruce. It wasn't just about proving his own innocence. It was about the fear of failing—of letting another man—no, woman—down.

Of losing someone else. Again.

She reached across the desk, her fingers brushing against his. She planted her hand firmly over his, the warmth settling into him like liquid sunshine. "You're not alone in this."

He flinched slightly but didn't pull away, willing his hand to remain beneath hers and praying his trembling didn't expose his emotions. Emotions he must guard beyond anything.

A long silence stretched between them.

She breathed out her thoughts. "You don't have to carry it all."

He exhaled, glancing at their hands before lifting his gaze to hers, her expression compassionate and vulnerable.

Then, in a barely audible voice, he said, "What if I do? What if I can't bear the thought of you getting mixed up in this mess—or getting hurt?" He tugged his hand out from underneath hers. "The way Garrison did. I can't lose another person I care for."

He was afraid to accept her help. To care. Because if he did, it meant trusting someone with his pain. And maybe…trusting someone with his heart.

Madison inhaled deeply. "Then I'll remind you I'm here. For now, I need to head back to the missus, but I'll return this evening to help."

For the first time in days, the tension in his shoulders eased just a little.

She gifted him with a sweet smile. "See you later."

He sat at his desk, staring at the piece of wood, the flickering lantern casting jagged shadows across the room. He picked it up to examine it for at least the tenth time. The wood was rough beneath his fingertips, a reminder of everything that had unraveled in the past few weeks.

Garrison was dead. The men doubted him. The Hewitts were coming. And Madison….

He exhaled sharply, pushing back from his desk. His chair scraped against the wooden floor as he stood, rubbing a hand down his face. He couldn't think straight anymore—not about Bruce, not about the worksite, and certainly not about her.

She had come again, as always, standing beside him when no one else would. She had looked at him with that fierce determination, her voice steady when she told him he wasn't alone.

He clenched his jaw. She didn't understand. He had to carry it alone. Had to keep her safe.

That's how it had always been. A man did what he had to. He took responsibility. He bore the burdens. He didn't lean on anyone else—because people left. People failed.

But Madison…she was different. She didn't simply stand beside him—she pushed against the walls he had spent years building. She saw him in ways he didn't know how to handle.

And that was the problem. Because every time she touched his hand, every time she spoke his name in that quiet, determined voice, his heart lurched. He didn't have time for it. Didn't have time to protect her from danger.

He paced toward the window, staring out into the stormy day. "She can't be involved! I can't risk it!"

He had spent every moment since Garrison's death fighting to clear his name, to keep the men from turning against him, to make sure Bruce didn't win. And Madison—she had been at his side through all of it.

But she wasn't just helping. She was getting too close. And worse—he was letting her.

He closed his eyes, inhaling deeply. "Lord, I don't know what to do with her."

She was too kind for her own good. And she was walking straight into a fight that wasn't hers. He should push her away. He should make sure she stayed out of it.

But the thought of not having her there—of pulling away from her—made his chest ache.

His grip tightened against the windowsill. He had already lost too much. He couldn't afford to lose her, too. But if he let himself care—if he let himself fall—then what? Would she stay?

Or would she become another ghost in his past?

He drew a long breath, forcing the thought away. No, go back to the plan. Back to clearing his name. Back to the fight against Bruce.

Alone.

But now, as the rain rattled against the window, he acknowledged the one thing he had been too stubborn to admit.

He had fallen for Madison. And there was nothing he could do to stop it.

His jaw tightened, and his fists curled at his sides as he picked up the Hewitts' telegram.

He had to focus. They were arriving tomorrow.

Bruce had already poisoned them against him, already whispered enough doubts into their ears that Emmett would be walking into an interrogation, not a meeting. And Madison—blasted woman—was determined to stand beside him.

But she didn't belong in this.

He shoved the telegram into the drawer. She had done enough. The more she inserted herself, the more danger she was in. And he couldn't have that.

No. He *wouldn't* have that. He turned back to the desk, gripping the edges as he leaned over his notes. He needed a plan.

She wouldn't back down simply because he told her to. Tonight, he'd make sure she wasn't involved. He'd send her back to check in on Mrs. Boldt to keep her out of it. She wouldn't ignore that duty, not if she thought her mistress needed her.

And tomorrow, he'd meet with the Hewitts. By himself.

Tomorrow, he would control the conversation. Bruce would twist the narrative, spin more lies about his leadership. But he wouldn't rise to the bait. He'd keep his temper in check, stick to facts, make sure they saw him as a foreman who had everything under control.

Not a man desperate to clear his name. Not a man caught in a mess he couldn't untangle. And when the time was right, he'd press them. Ask them what, exactly, Bruce had told them. Make them say the accusations aloud. Because words spoken in the dark, behind a man's back, had a less power when forced into the light.

Once the Hewitts were satisfied—or at least off his back—he'd go back to what mattered—proving Bruce was a liar and a coward. And a murderer.

But Madison? She had no place in this fight. She'd done enough, risked enough. And the more she involved herself, the greater the chance Bruce would turn on her the way he had turned on Garrison.

No, he wouldn't allow that. If he had to lie to her—if he had to push her away to protect her—so be it.

He could live with that. He'd rather that than the alternative.

He pushed down the sick feeling that rose in his chest.

Tomorrow, he'd face the Hewitts and make sure Madison stayed out of it.

Tomorrow, he'd take back control.

Even if it meant losing the one person willing to fight for him.

CHAPTER 15

Madison's hands moved swiftly over the linens, folding them with more force than necessary. The crisp cotton edges were precise, almost rigid—an outlet for the tension she couldn't shake.

Her eyes flickered to the clock. The long afternoon made her anxious about her mission and Emmett's investigation.

She bit her lip, her fingers gripping the fabric in her hands. And then, the question she had been avoiding came crashing into her thoughts: How did she really feel about him?

Was this simply worry for a friend? A man she respected? Or was it more, something that might unravel her world completely?

Did she love him? Or did she just feel sorry for him?

Something twisted in her stomach. The idea of Emmett suffering alone, burdened by guilt, made her chest ache. But was it pity? Or couldn't she stand the thought of a world where he wasn't in hers?

She let out a shaky breath, shaking her head. Now wasn't the time to dwell on that.

Her gaze drifted toward the bed. Mrs. Boldt lay beneath the heavy quilt, her breathing shallow, pale hands clutching the fabric as if she was holding onto it for dear life. She'd had another hard day. Another decline.

Her throat tightened. How much more could her mistress take?

Madison had seen it before—the slow unraveling of someone fading, the helplessness of watching them slip further away no matter how she tried to keep them here. She had lost her mother that way. And her aunt.

And now, Mrs. Boldt slowly, painfully faded, too.

Her chest constricted.

If she lost her…

If she lost *him*…

Her breath hitched. What would happen to her if both were gone?

She cared for both of them. Loved them.

A chill ran through her. For so long, she had survived loss by clinging to duty, to her mission, by staying useful. First to her aunt, then to the Boldts, now to Emmett. But if all were taken from her, what would she have? Who would she be?

Her heart pounded, and she pressed a hand against her chest to steady the storm inside. She wasn't ready to face these thoughts.

Not now. Not yet.

She turned away from Mrs. Boldt's fragile form, folding the last linen with quick, precise movements. Then she smoothed her skirts, squared her shoulders, and took a slow breath.

She couldn't think about what-ifs. She wouldn't think about what would happen to the missus. Or Emmett. Instead, she'd focus on what she could do. Making sure Emmett didn't lose the fight he was in—whether he wanted her there or not.

When a firm knock at the front door sounded in the distance, she shoved her cares to the back of her mind. She set the fabric aside and hurried down the stairs, brushing a stray wisp of hair from her face before opening the door.

Thomas, the boatman, stood there, his usual timid expression more nervous than usual, a folded letter in his hand. "This is for you."

She frowned as she took the envelope, her name scrawled across the front in Emmett's familiar handwriting. Her pulse quickened.

He cleared his throat, shifting uncomfortably. "You ought to listen to what's inside."

Her concern deepened, but she nodded, stepping onto the porch, closing the door behind her, and breaking the seal with careful fingers.

Madison,

I need you to trust me on this. The investigation will have to wait. The Hewitts arrive in the morning, and I must prepare. Things are already uneasy enough without adding more to it. Stay away from the island while they're here.

I mean it, Madison. Stay away. There's nothin' more you can do right now, and I won't risk you gettin' dragged into this mess. Please, don't fight me on this. —Emmett

Madison's fingers tightened around the paper. Stay away? Postpone the investigation? Had he lost his mind?

She looked up at Thomas, her heart pounding. "Did he tell you to say anything else?"

He crossed his arms. "Only that he's handling it. That you're not to be involved."

She scoffed. "That's ridiculous. We're closer than we've ever been. He can't just—"

"He can." He sighed. "And he is."

She shook her head. "He's shutting me out."

Thomas's expression darkened slightly. "He's trying to protect you, Madison."

She let out a sharp breath, pacing away. "That's not his decision to make."

"No, but it's the right one."

She stopped, turning back to him. "You think I should stay out of this too?"

Another heavy exhale. "You're a nice girl with a good heart. Emmett is a man who's already carrying too much." He hesitated before dropping his gaze. "Bruce is dangerous."

Her stomach twisted. "You don't trust him either."

"No one with sense does." His voice was low. "But Emmett is right—this meeting with the Hewitts is going to decide what happens next. If you step into the middle of it, you might make things worse for him."

Her instinct was to fight. To demand he let her help.

But what if Thomas was right? What if her presence made things more difficult for Emmett?

Her fingers tightened around the letter.

He sighed. "Stay put, Madison. Just for tonight and tomorrow."

She didn't answer. Not because she agreed. But because she wasn't sure she could.

She crumpled the paper in her hand, the words sinking in like a stone in her chest.

Stay away.

His handwriting was unmistakable—bold, firm, and final. He'd left no room for argument, no space between the lines for her to slip through. No secret plea for help between the words.

Her pulse pounded as she looked up at Thomas, her brows drawn together in frustration. "This is absurd. He can't decide I'm not part of this anymore."

He shifted his weight. "He can, and he has." His voice was even, but his expression made her stomach twist. "He's doing what any decent man would do."

She folded her arms. "And what's that?"

"Keeping those he loves out of harm's way."

Her breath hitched. She shook her head quickly, dismissing the thought. "That's not what this is."

Thomas gave her a look suggesting he knew better. "Isn't it?"

She turned away, staring at the sky a dull gray in the late afternoon light.

"We've come too far to stop now. We're closer than ever to proving Bruce had a hand in Garrison's death. If we wait, we risk losing the only leverage we have."

He was silent for a long moment before he spoke again. "And what if Emmett's right?"

She turned back sharply. "Right about what?"

"About Bruce. About how far he'll go."

She hesitated.

He stepped closer, his voice quieter now. "You think I don't see what's happening? Bruce isn't just some troublemaker looking for a promotion. He's dangerous, Madison. He's got Mr. Boldt second-guessing his best man. He's got the Hewitts thinking Emmett's not fit to lead. And now, he's got you wrapped up in this, whether you realize it or not."

"I do realize it." She stomped a foot. "That's why I can't sit back and do nothing."

Thomas studied her for a long moment. "You care for Emmett. A lot."

The words landed like a punch to the chest. He knew? Her breath caught. "This isn't about me."

His gaze didn't waver. "Maybe. But it sure is about him."

Her heart raced like it did when a swarm of wasps had chased her last summer.

He crossed his arms. "Let me tell you what's happening here." His voice was calm but firm. "You're helping Emmett because you believe in him. And that's a fine thing. But you're also scared—scared of what happens if you walk away and he loses this fight."

Her throat tightened. He was right.

She was afraid. Afraid Bruce would win. Afraid Emmett would lose everything. Afraid if she stepped aside now, Emmett would push her away for good. Afraid he wouldn't need her anymore.

And she needed him.

Thomas sighed. "Listen to me, Madison. I'm not saying you give up. I'm saying you trust him. If he's asking you to stay away, it's because he thinks it'll make things easier for him to handle."

She clenched her jaw, looking down at the letter again. The page felt heavier, like it was pressing against her skin, leaving a mark she couldn't ignore.

He hesitated, then added, "But if you really think he's making a mistake…then that's something only you can decide."

Her hands quivered like her long-deceased granny. For the first time since, doubt crept in. She wanted to fight for him. But was forcing her way into this the right way?

Would she be helping him—or making it worse?

She took a slow breath, lifting her gaze to his. "If I stay put, it won't be because he told me to. It'll be because it's the right choice."

He gave a small nod. "Fair enough."

She looked back down at the letter one more time before folding it carefully and tucking it into her pocket. She wouldn't be giving up.

But maybe, just this once…she would wait.

For now.

~ ~ ~

Emmett stood at the accident site, waiting. The morning air was sharp and cool as the river lapped steadily against the docks in the distance. The steady rhythm did nothing to quiet the storm inside him. He flexed his fingers at his sides, keeping his face impassive, but his stomach churned.

This meeting would decide everything. He turned at the sound of approaching footsteps.

Mr. William Hewitt walked toward him, tall and deliberate in his movements, his coat neatly buttoned to fend off the chill in the air. He carried himself with authority—but not the blustering kind. Hewitt's authority was, in fact, calculated, precise, and unforgiving.

Beside him, Mr. Boldt strode along, his expression unreadable.

Emmett straightened, tipped his cap respectfully. "Mr. Hewitt. Mr. Boldt."

"Mr. O'Connor." Hewitt barely nodded before glancing around the site, his sharp gaze taking in every detail. "Let's not waste time. Show me where it happened."

He swallowed back his irritation at the clipped tone, then turned toward the skeletal remains of the scaffolding. Though cleaned, the accident's damage was still evident in the repaired beams and workers' nervous glances.

Mr. Boldt said nothing. Just took in the encounter with a passive frown.

Emmett stopped just beneath the area where the structure had collapsed. "This is where Garrison fell."

Hewitt surveyed the scene with a practiced eye, his brow furrowing. "And you were overseeing this part of the project? You examined it before the accident?"

His jaw tightened. "Aye."

Hewitt turned to him fully now. "Then how did this happen?"

A direct hit. No room for misinterpretation. He forced himself to stay level. "That's what the investigation will determine."

Hewitt raised a brow. "And what's your theory, foreman?"

Emmett met his gaze, steady and resolute. "The scaffolding was tampered with."

Boldt, who had been silent until now, turned sharply toward him. "Tampered with?"

He nodded, stepping toward the wooden beams. He put his hand on the repaired area. "When the collapse happened, this section broke too cleanly. The wood should've splintered unpredictably, but it came apart as if cut. I found a questionable piece of wood, but…"

Hewitt's expression didn't change, but his eyes flickered with…What was it?…Interest? Doubt? It was difficult to tell.

Boldt exhaled, running a hand down his face. "And yet, there's been no conclusive proof of sabotage."

"Not yet," Emmett admitted. "I believe the evidence was removed after the accident."

Hewitt narrowed his eyes. "And do you have this evidence?"

"Not yet."

Hewitt let out a humorless chuckle. "Convenient."

Emmett bristled, but bit back his frustration. "It's the truth."

Hewitt turned to Boldt. "I assume the detective has already reviewed this?"

"He has," Boldt said. "His report is included in the preliminary paperwork."

Hewitt nodded. "Then let's review it."

Emmett inhaled slowly, steadying himself. This was only the beginning. He led the men to his office, where he'd neatly arranged stacks of papers on the wooden table.

He stood across from Hewitt and Boldt as the architect sat in his chair and flipped through the detective's preliminary report. Hewitt read in silence, his fingers skimming over the neatly typed pages, his expression unreadable.

After what felt like an eternity, Hewitt set the papers down, took a seat, and laced his fingers together. "No official finding of sabotage. Yet you claim someone tampered with the scaffolding."

"Aye." Emmett's curt nod communicated his confidence. He hoped. "I do."

Hewitt tilted his head. "And who, exactly, do you believe is responsible?"

He hesitated for half a second. He knew the answer. Bruce. But saying his name here, now, without enough proof…it was too big a risk.

Boldt, watching him closely, cleared his throat. "Emmett?"

He forced himself to choose his words carefully. "Someone with access to the worksite intentionally weakened the structure."

Hewitt leaned back. "But you won't name names."

His jaw clenched. "Not without definitive proof."

Hewitt hummed, tapping a finger against the table. "A wise decision. And yet, this puts us in an unfortunate position, doesn't it? The firm has its reputation to consider, O'Connor. The Boldts are investing an extraordinary amount into this project, and we cannot afford delays—or controversy. If we entertain the notion of sabotage without proof, we open the door for liability, for scandal, for potential financial loss."

His stomach turned. "And if you don't entertain it?"

Hewitt's gaze sharpened. "Then I have to ask myself if you are the right man for this position."

Silence filled the room. He gritted his teeth. "You think I'd lie about this?"

"I think," Hewitt said smoothly, "that men in desperate situations see what they want."

Boldt let out a slow breath, glancing between them. "I trust you, Emmett. But I can't ignore the gravity of what Mr. Hewitt is saying."

His hands tightened into fists at his sides. This was exactly what Bruce wanted. Doubt. Uncertainty.

Hewitt sighed, pushing back from the table. "Until further evidence comes to light, the official position of the firm is that this was an unfortunate accident."

Emmett's stomach twisted. "That's a mistake, sir."

Hewitt stood. "It's my decision."

Boldt hesitated, then nodded reluctantly.

Emmett forced himself to stay still, to keep his expression neutral. But inside, his blood boiled.

This wasn't over. Not by a long shot.

As Hewitt and Boldt exited the office, he remained behind, staring at the scattered papers on the table. They wouldn't listen. Not yet. But he wasn't giving up. He had to get that proof.

And if Hewitt didn't stand by him now, then he would simply have to make it impossible for him to ignore the truth. One way or another, he would expose Bruce, even if he was the boss's nephew. Even if Hewitt felt an obligation to protect his kin.

He ran a rough hand down his face, then slammed his fist onto the desk.

Bruce—that cladhaire—had played this perfectly. He had spread his lies, cast doubt, and now he was sitting back and watching Emmett drown under suspicion.

He straightened, jaw tightening as he looked over the papers again. The report was useless—the detective had found no clear evidence of sabotage, which meant that, for now, it was Emmett's word against that scoundrel's. And Bruce had been whispering in the right ears for weeks.

He let out a slow breath, forcing himself to think. He couldn't charge forward, fists swinging, no matter how much he wanted to. He had already lost too much ground. This time, he must be smarter.

The broken beam was their best lead—until Bruce caught him and Madison snooping. He clenched his teeth at the memory. If he had hidden the evidence once, he might move it again. But what was that evidence? It had to be somewhere. He must find it. He needed more than a guess, more than a theory. He needed evidence so solid, so undeniable, that not even Hewitt could brush it aside for the sake of his kin.

But he couldn't go back to the dock alone, Bruce would be watching him now. If he wanted to find that evidence, he'd have to get creative. And for that, he'd need someone who would be discreet.

Thomas.

The quiet boatman had been wary of Bruce for weeks. He wasn't simply another worker who took orders. He saw things others didn't. If anyone could poke around without raising suspicion, it was him.

Bruce had poisoned the workers against him. At least, some of them.

But not all.

Thomas had been watching from the sidelines, quiet but not blind. If he could get the lads talking—maybe even questioning what really happened—he could turn the tide. A few workers speaking out wouldn't be enough to prove Bruce's guilt, but it would weaken his hold. Enough to plant doubt in the very men Bruce had manipulated.

Emmett inhaled deeply, pushing down the sick feeling twisting in his gut. Madison wouldn't like being sidelined from this. She would fight him on it. But he had to keep her safe.

Bruce had already threatened her once, and he wouldn't let that happen again. Madison had done more than enough for him already—more than he deserved. And if Bruce thought for even a second she was still involved, he wouldn't hesitate to turn his attention toward her.

He wouldn't risk that.

Couldn't.

Tomorrow, he'd talk to Thomas, set the plan in motion.

And if Madison involved herself? Then he'd make sure she stayed out of it. Even if it meant pushing her away.

Even if it meant hurting her in the process.

Because no matter how much he felt himself falling for her—

It wasn't worth her life.

CHAPTER 16

Madison had only meant to pass through the hallway, but when she heard Mr. Boldt's voice—low, serious—she hesitated outside the sitting room.

His tone stopped her in her tracks. "…I don't know what to think anymore."

She held her breath and stepped closer, careful to keep to the shadows.

George Junior sighed. "The detective's report was inconclusive. But I don't see how you would choose to doubt O'Connor. He's been running this project for years. He's never cut corners before."

Mr. Boldt exhaled sharply. "It's not about whether I doubt him. It's about the fact that the Hewitts doubt him. And if they doubt him, it puts everything we're building here at risk."

George Junior hesitated. "But…you don't actually believe O'Connor had anything to do with the accident, do you?"

"Of course not," Mr. Boldt snapped, then let out a weary sigh. "But that doesn't mean he handled this properly. He should have come to me first, not stirred up rumors about sabotage."

Madison's chest tightened.

Rumors?

Mr. Boldt continued, "We have no proof of foul play. If Emmett keeps pushing this theory without evidence, he'll make himself look desperate. And desperate men make mistakes."

George Junior hesitated. "Then what will you do?"

Mr. Boldt's voice turned grim. "We keep watching. If Emmett can't prove himself, we may have no choice but to replace him."

She pressed a hand over her mouth to stop the gasp threatening to escape. They were already considering replacing him? Her mind raced. This was exactly what Bruce wanted—to turn Boldt and the Hewitts against Emmett, to discredit him, to make him look reckless. And it was working.

She had to tell Emmett. But as she turned to leave, George Junior spoke again.

"There's another thing, Father. About the accident."

Mr. Boldt sighed. "Go on."

George Junior hesitated. "What if it wasn't just negligence? What if it really was sabotage?"

Silence hung heavy between them.

Then Mr. Boldt let out a breath. "If that's the case…then we need to know who."

Madison clenched her fists. She already knew the answer. And she couldn't wait for Bruce to tighten his grip. Even if Emmett didn't want her involved, she was.

She should burst into the room and tell them, but that wasn't wise. She was a lowly servant girl. Nothing more.

A few hours later, after George Junior and Clover left for New York City, the house felt like a tomb. Not silent—workers still moved about, still chatted in the kitchen. Daily chores still hummed along—but the liveliness was gone. The joy, the laughter, the little bursts of youthful energy that brightened the halls vanished with their departure.

Madison saw it in Mrs. Boldt immediately. The missus sat near the window of her sitting room, staring out at the water, her usually keen eyes dulled with sadness. Her hands, always so elegant, rested idly in her lap, as if she had no desire to needlepoint, to write, to do anything at all.

It worried Madison.

She saw worry in Mr. Boldt, too. Though not as expressive, he carried his unease for his wife in the tightness of his shoulders and in the way he lingered near his wife, watching her when he thought no one else was looking.

But just that morning, he'd announced his decision. They were staying.

"The Thousand Islands are our summer refuge. Louise and I planned to spend the summer here, and that hasn't changed. We love it here."

But love alone wasn't enough to lift Mrs. Boldt's spirits.

She found Mrs. Boldt in the parlor that afternoon, seated in her usual chair, gazing out toward the river. The tea tray beside her remained untouched, the delicate porcelain cup still full.

Madison hesitated for only a moment before stepping forward. "Would you like me to read to you, ma'am?"

Mrs. Boldt didn't turn, but her lips curved in a small, sad smile. "Not today, dear."

Madison clasped her hands in front of her, unsure how to proceed. She hated seeing the missus like this—withdrawn, lost in her thoughts. "It's difficult when they leave, isn't it?"

Mrs. Boldt let out a sigh, finally turning her gaze to Madison. "Every time. It never gets easier. Have a seat, dear."

She sat carefully on the small settee beside her. "But they'll be back."

Mrs. Boldt nodded. "Yes, of course. But life moves so fast. Clover is all grown up, and George has responsibilities in the city. One day, they will have families of their own. I know this is the way of things, and yet…" She trailed off, looking back toward the window. "I feel time slipping through my fingers."

She bit her lip, feeling the sadness of the moment seeping in. "I know that feeling."

Mrs. Boldt turned back to her, her expression softening. "Yes, I imagine you do."

They sat in silence for a moment before Madison reached out and gently touched her hand. "You've done so much for them, ma'am. The love you have for them—it's woven into every part of their lives. That doesn't fade just because they're away."

Mrs. Boldt gave her a wistful smile. "You sound as if you've lived far beyond your years."

She smiled sadly. "Grief teaches us things we never wanted to learn."

Mrs. Boldt squeezed her hand. "That it does."

A moment passed, filled with nothing but the distant lapping of the water and the occasional bird call from outside.

Then Madison spoke again, her voice quiet but steady. "Mr. Boldt said you both love it here. That this is home."

Mrs. Boldt's lips trembled. "It is."

"Then let yourself love it." Madison smiled and gestured to the grounds beyond the glass. "Enjoy these days, the beauty of the river, the peace of the islands. Trust that God has given you this time, not to grieve what is slipping away, but to cherish what you still have."

A tear escaped down Mrs. Boldt's cheek, but this time, there was something else in her eyes.

Hope.

She nodded, squeezing her hand once more. "You're right, dear. I must try."

Madison smiled, warmth filling her chest. "Not just try, ma'am. Trust."

And for the first time all day, Mrs. Boldt picked up her teacup and took a sip. "Would you please fetch a bouquet of fresh flowers to brighten the room? Perhaps that would help."

Madison stood and curtsied. "I'd be happy to, missus."

She headed to the garden with her basket, enjoying a moment of peace and quiet. Allowing the trill of songbirds to lift her spirits. The scent of the river to draw her eye to the horizon, wondering what life was like on the other side.

The air was thick with the scent of summer blooms—roses, lilies, and delicate Queen Anne's lace swaying gently in the breeze. She knelt near a patch of soft pink roses, handpicking the fullest blooms when a shadow fell over her.

A slow, measured voice broke the quiet. "Well, if it isn't Boldt's little lady's maid."

She stiffened, her fingers tightening around the shears.

Bruce.

She turned her head just enough to confirm what she already perceived. He stood a few feet away, arms crossed over his chest, watching her with that lazy, knowing smirk.

She forced herself to keep her expression neutral. "What do you want?"

He clicked his tongue, stepping closer. "Now, now. That's not a polite way to greet an old friend, is it?"

"You're not my friend."

He chuckled, shaking his head. His gaze flickered over her, calculating. "No, I suppose I'm not. But I am someone who'd hate to see you make a deadly mess of things."

A chill ran down her spine. She set her jaw. "I don't know what you're talking about."

He exhaled dramatically, as if disappointed. "Come now. You've been poking around where you don't belong. And, well…that sort of thing has consequences."

Her grip tightened on the flower shears. "Are you threatening me?"

His smirk didn't fade, but his eyes narrowed into slits just like her father's did before he took the strap to her. "I'm warning you. There's a difference."

Her heart pounded, but she refused to let him see her fear. "I've done nothing wrong."

Bruce tilted his head, taking another slow step forward. "Haven't you?" He let the question hang, his voice almost amused. "You see, people around here like their jobs. They like their place in things. They don't take kindly to someone upsetting the balance."

She squared her shoulders, feigning confidence. "If you're so certain I've done something wrong, go to Mr. Boldt and tell him."

He let out a low chuckle. "Oh, I don't think I need to do that." His voice turned silkier, more dangerous. "Because I don't think you want him knowing just how involved you've been. Do you think the Boldts would keep you around if they realized their little lady's maid has been sneaking about and carousing with a disgraced foreman?"

Madison's breath caught.

He stepped even closer, lowering his voice. "It'd be such a shame for someone like you to lose everything. Your reputation. Your position. Your security. Your precious Emmett."

Her stomach twisted. He wanted to rattle her. To make her doubt herself. She wouldn't let him.

Lifting her chin, she met his gaze with unwavering determination. "I don't scare easily."

He studied her for a long moment before letting out a slow, amused sigh. "Pity." Then, just as suddenly as he'd appeared, he took a step back, dusting off his sleeves. "Enjoy the flowers."

With that, he turned and strolled away, as if they had merely exchanged pleasantries.

She let out a breath she hadn't realized she was holding. Her hands trembled. She looked down at the roses in her basket, their delicate petals undisturbed by the tension.

But this was only the beginning. Bruce wasn't toying with her. He had made his intentions clear. If she kept pushing, if she kept helping Emmett…he would destroy her. She inhaled sharply, steadying herself.

She had never backed down before.

And she wouldn't start now.

~ ~ ~

Emmett stood near the dock, hands braced against the iron railing, staring out over the dark water. The river stretched endlessly before him, the gentle lapping of waves doing little to quiet the storm inside his head.

He clenched his jaw. "Blathers! You're a fool, O'Connor."

He had pushed Madison away. Again.

Not with sharp words or outright dismissal this time. No, something worse. He had been cold. Distant. He made sure she comprehended that he didn't want her in this fight. Not because she wasn't capable, but because he couldn't stand the thought of her being a target.

Because Bruce had already set his sights on him. And if she got any closer, she would be in the crossfire.

He let out a sharp breath, shaking his head, mumbling to the river, "And where did that get you? Did you think it would stop her? No. Would it really make her safer? No."

All he'd accomplished was hurt her. Thomas had relayed that fact clearly. "You're doing this for her, sir. To keep her safe."

Then why did it feel like he had made the biggest mistake of his life?

He rubbed a hand over his face, exhaling slowly. Aye, she was a stubborn lass. Had that faithful fire in her that made her care deeply. About Mrs. Boldt. About the workers.

About him.

And how had he repaid her? By treating her like a problem instead of a partner. By making her think she didn't matter to him. And that was the real problem, wasn't it?

Because she did. More than she should. More than he wanted her to.

He let out a bitter laugh. He had spent so much time protecting her, keeping her out of the mess Bruce had created.

But Madison wasn't a woman who could be kept in the background. She wasn't one who stood aside when another was hurting. And deep down, he had known that from the start.

He stared hard at the water. He needed to fix this. He couldn't take back the things he had written—or the way he had made her feel—but he could show her she wasn't alone. That she had never been alone. And that he wouldn't push her away anymore.

Not this time. Not when he was already losing the battle against his own heart.

He didn't waste time. As soon as he decided, he turned away from the dock, his long strides eating up the distance toward the Boldt estate. The air was thick with the scent of the river, the humidity clinging to his skin, but none of it mattered.

Only she mattered.

He had spent too many hours convincing himself he was doing the right thing—keeping her at arm's length, shielding her from Bruce, from his own burdens. But all he had accomplished was hurt her. And if there was one thing Emmett O'Connor couldn't stand, it was knowing he had caused her pain.

He had barely reached the Boldt's flower garden when he spotted her.

Madison shuffled along the path from the flower beds, her basket of roses clutched in her hands. But the way she carried herself was all wrong. Tension squared her shoulders. Like she was shaking off something that clung to her.

He slowed, his brows drawing together. "Madison? Are you all right?"

She startled slightly but quickly recovered, lifting her chin as she met his gaze. "Emmett."

He hesitated. He had planned what to say—or at least, he had thought he had—but now, standing in front of her, he was speechless.

She wasn't just upset. She trembled. And it had nothing to do with him.

His gaze flickered down to the way she gripped the basket, her knuckles white. His gut twisted. "What happened?"

His voice came out sharper than he intended, but she didn't flinch.

Instead, she took a steady breath, fixing her features expressionless. "Nothing I can't handle."

That only deepened his concern.

He stepped closer, lowering his voice. "Madison."

She sighed, looking away for a moment before finally saying, "Bruce."

His blood went cold. "What did he do?"

Madison hesitated, then shook her head. "He…reminded me how much I will lose if I keep sticking my nose where it doesn't belong."

He clenched his jaw. His pulse hammered in his temples, the familiar, searing anger curling in his chest.

Bruce had threatened her.

While he had been there, brooding over his own failings, that cladhaire had gone after her.

She sighed, setting the basket on a nearby stone bench. "I know what you're thinking." She folded her arms. "And I don't need you storming off to fight him."

He exhaled sharply through his nose. "You think I will let this go?"

"You need to be smart." She peered at him. "Bruce wants you to act reckless. To make a mistake he can twist against you."

He hated that she was right. And he hated that he had let this happen. He let out a slow breath, gathering himself. "This is exactly why I didn't want you involved."

She scoffed. "Oh, so I should sit back while he destroys you? While he turns Mr. Boldt against you? Is that what you want?"

"No!" He took a step forward, his voice lowering, rough with frustration. "I don't want you hurt because of me."

Madison's lips parted slightly, her breath catching. For a moment, neither spoke.

Then she shook her head, her voice quiet but firm. "You don't get to decide that, Emmett."

His chest ached. "Madison—"

"No," she interrupted. "You've been shutting me out, protecting me, and I understand that. But don't you see? You can't. I'm already in this."

His heart pounded. She was right.

And it terrified him. He exhaled slowly, rubbing the back of his neck before finally looking at her again. "I'm sorry."

She blinked, as if she hadn't expected the words.

He drew a deep breath. "I shouldn't have pushed you away. I thought I was doin' the right thing, but all I did was make you think you didn't matter. And you do, Madison." His throat felt tight, but he forced himself to continue. "More than I have any right to say."

She stared at him, her expression puzzling. Then, slowly, she let out a breath. "You're forgiven."

Relief flooded through him, but before he could speak, she added, "But I'm not stepping away from this."

He let out a low chuckle, shaking his head. "I didn't think you would."

She smirked slightly, but it faded as she glanced back toward the house. "Mrs. Boldt is waiting for these flowers. But later…we need to talk."

He nodded. "Aye. We do."

As she picked up the basket and walked toward the house, his chest constricted with emotions he wasn't used to. He had come here to apologize. But what he hadn't expected was to realize just how much she wasn't under his control.

She was his partner. And, whether he liked it or not…

He, most definitely, had fallen for her.

CHAPTER 17

Madison found Emmett in his office, the evening air thick with tension as he stood with his arms crossed, staring at the scattered plans on his desk as if he would will them into order. She had spent the past hour deciding how to approach him, but now that she was here, the frustration bubbling inside her left little room for caution.

"Emmett, we need to talk."

He barely looked up. "Not now, Madison."

He was shutting her out again. His words were clipped, taut with the mortar of rejection. The wall between them was solid, unmovable.

She stepped forward, undeterred. "Yes. Now."

He sighed heavily, rubbing the back of his neck before finally meeting her gaze. Exhaustion etched his face, darkening his eyes, and dulling his usual sharpness.

But his frustration still simmered beneath the surface. "There's nothing to say."

She set her jaw. She wasn't backing down. "I overheard Mr. Boldt talking with George Junior earlier this morning. They're questioning the investigation. They're questioning you, Emmett."

His expression darkened, but he didn't interrupt.

She pressed on. "Later, as you well know, Bruce cornered me in the garden. He threatened me again, but I can handle it."

"Nae, you shouldn't have to handle it!" His voice, rough with anger, echoed off the stone walls. "Blathers! You shouldn't even be in this mess, Madison. Stay out of it."

She flinched, but lifted her chin. "And I told you I won't."

Emmett exhaled sharply, shaking his head. "You don't understand what's at stake here."

"Oh, I understand perfectly! Bruce is winning. People are believing his lies. If you keep shutting me out, you're making it easier for him."

Emmett turned away, pacing a few steps before clicking his tongue. "This isn't your fight."

She crossed her arms. "Then whose is it? Yours? Alone? Because from where I'm standing, that's not working out too well for you."

His jaw tightened. "I don't need you distracting me. I don't need you putting yourself in danger for my sake."

"And what about your danger, Emmett?" She stepped closer, her voice lowering, her frustration giving way to deeper concern.

"Do you think I can stand by while you get dragged under? Do you think I can just watch Bruce destroy you?"

His silence was deafening.

Her heartbeat thundered in her ears. "I care about you, Emmett."

For a moment a flicker of raw, unguarded emotion crossed his expression. Then, just as quickly, it was gone.

His gaze hardened, his walls slamming back into place. "Caring about me is a mistake, Madison."

Her breath hitched. His words felt like a slap.

Had he seen the hurt his statement caused her? His face twisted with regret—but he didn't take it back.

She threw her hands in the air. "Fine. If that's what you really think, then I will stay out of it. Not because you told me to, but because I won't waste my time on someone who refuses to accept help."

She pivoted on her heel, storming away before he could say another word. The air outside was cold against her heated skin, but it didn't cool the fire burning inside. Wounded by his rejection, the sting settled deep into her bones. But as much as she wanted to walk away from the fight entirely, one thing was certain.

She wouldn't walk away from the truth, even if Emmett O'Connor was too proud to let her stand beside him.

Madison returned to the Wellesley House to find it quiet. She dressed for bed but stood at her bedroom window, her arms folded as she gazed into the darkness. This last encounter had tossed her heart about like a vessel in a storm, and she had decided—no, she had resolved—not to let it drift any longer.

Emmett was no longer her concern. She had spent too many days hoping, too many moments wondering if he thought of her as she thought of him. No more. From this day forward, she would turn her complete and focused attention to Mrs. Boldt and her duties, as she should have all along. There was plenty of work to do, and surely, if she poured herself into it, she could forget the ache Emmett's absence left in her chest.

A soft knock startled her from her thoughts. The door slowly creaked open.

Hazel stood in the doorway, concern in her eyes. The housekeeper, her friend, had a way of seeing past her silent fortress, and tonight was no exception.

"Madison, can we talk?" Hazel didn't wait for her to answer. "I'm worried about you. You've been too quiet. And not the peaceful kind of quiet. The sorrowful kind."

Madison forced a smile. "I've just been thinking. Nothing more."

Hazel tilted her head. "Sometimes, when we think too much, we carry burdens we aren't meant to." She paused, then added gently, "I'd like to tell you a story. One you may not have heard before."

She glanced back toward the window, but her curiosity won out. "Go on."

Hazel settled into a chair near the bed and gestured for Madison to take a seat, too.

When Hazel spoke, her voice carried the warmth of an old tale. "During the first winter that the Boldts owned Heart Island, the caretakers, George and Myrtie Edgerly Campbell, lived in the old summer cottage, the one they slid across the ice in 1900 to make room for the castle. The Dove Cote and the Alster Tower were already under construction. But during the winter, the island was quiet, blanketed in snow, and the river froze thick as glass. It must have been a lonely, isolated place to live in those months."

Madison listened, drawn in by the imagery Hazel painted.

"But in that stillness, a wonderful miracle happened. George and Myrtie welcomed their first child into the world—a baby girl, Gertrude. She was born right there, on Heart Island, in the midst of the cold and the silence. Can you imagine that? A new life, in a place that should have seemed barren and lifeless."

Madison's lips parted slightly, mulling the meaning of the story over in her heart.

Hazel smiled. "And do you know what the Campbells said about that winter? That this tiny new life made the island more than just a cold, empty land. It made it a home. It gave it a heartbeat. What could have been a lonely, difficult place instead became a place of love and joy."

Madison shifted from one foot to the other. "Why are you telling me this?"

"Because, Madison," Hazel reached for her hand, "sometimes, even in the hardest and loneliest of places, the new and beautiful can be born. Even when we think we've lost all hope, God is still at work, bringing new life where we least expect it."

A lump rose in her throat. She had been so determined to turn away from what hurt, so desperate to stop feeling the ache of longing, that she hadn't considered God might still be at work in *her* story.

Hazel squeezed her hand gently. "Maybe your heart isn't meant to be locked away. You need to hope again—even when it's difficult. I don't often welcome a different path for my servant girls, but I've come to see that you were meant for more. For him, and I can't deny it."

Madison let out a slow breath, her eyes returning to the window. In the darkness, the river stretched before her, restless yet steady, always moving, always changing.

Perhaps her heart was meant to do the same.

Madison shook her head, her voice quiet but firm. "It's impossible, Hazel." She exhaled sharply, looking down at her hands.

"Yes, my thoughts about Emmett shifted slowly. One day, it wasn't just admiration. No, it grew deeper. I cherished Emmett's presence, and it filled me with unexpected joy. Hope for something more."

Hazel remained silent, allowing her the space to speak what she had long kept buried.

"The more time I spend with him, the harder it has become to ignore these feelings. But here's the rub. He has now shut the door to further contact, and it's probably for the best. I am a mere maid. I can never be married. Besides, I am well below his station."

Her voice trembled slightly, betraying the sorrow she'd held back. "And I could never leave Mrs. Boldt. Never! She is my world, my family." Madison let out a bitter chuckle. "So perhaps Emmett was right to push me aside. Perhaps we should forget one another altogether."

Hazel studied her carefully, her expression concerned. Then, with a gentle shake of her head, she said, "Madison, change is hard. Sometimes what we think impossible is simply what we fear most."

Madison let Hazel's words settle, her breath catching in her throat. "But what if my fears are justified?"

Hazel's eyes softened. "Are they? I know you're worried about your position here, and I would miss you terribly, but are you protecting yourself from embracing a beautiful future?"

Her fingers tightened around the folds of her skirt. "I don't know. I have responsibilities here. I have a place here. A life here."

"And does that exclude love?" Hazel pressed gently. "Does it mean you must deny yourself the very thing your heart longs for?"

Tears stung Madison's eyes, but she refused to let them fall. "If I allow myself to love him, and it leads to nothing, I don't know if I could bear another loss."

Hazel reached for her hand again. "Loss is a part of life, Madison. You are braver than you think. And love is always a risk. One worth taking."

Madison let out a shaky breath, but she remained silent. Deep inside, her heart warred between reason and hope, fear and longing. She wasn't sure which would win—but she wasn't entirely certain she wanted to forget Emmett forever.

~ ~ ~

The letter to Emmett arrived in the early hours of the workday, carried by a courier who handed it over without a word. The envelope was crisp, the official seal stamped into the wax like a silent condemnation.

Emmett hesitated before breaking it open, his fingers rough against the fine parchment.

His heart pounded as he read the carefully penned words. The local authorities had launched a formal investigation. The outcry from the injured workers and their grieving families had reached the ears of those in power, and now, Emmett stood at the center of it all.

His jaw tightened. He had led the project with confidence, ensured the men were well-organized, that the structure would rise strong against the elements. But now, with the stress of the investigation pressing against his shoulders, doubt crept into the corners of his mind. What had he missed? Had he failed those who had trusted him?

The accusations weren't explicit, but they bled through the ink.

Negligence. Misjudgment. A failure of leadership.

Emmett rolled his shoulders, setting the letter on the worn wooden table. His gaze drifted to the window where the distant horizon met the river, calm and unwavering—unlike his thoughts.

He must face this. Stand before the authorities, before the men who had once followed his orders, and prove that he had done all he could. He still had no definitive evidence against Bruce, so he would take the fall.

But even as resolve settled in his chest, a whisper of uncertainty lingered. The truth had a way of surfacing. And whether it cleared his name or damned him forever—only time would tell.

Emmett paced his office, the wooden floor creaking beneath his boots, the sound echoing in the heavy silence. His hands trembled slightly as he reached for the letter again, rereading each line, as if the words might change. As if the ink might fade into nothing. But the truth remained.

A formal investigation. A summons. And the concern for the crew's suffering pressed upon his shoulders.

A sharp rap at the door startled him. He hesitated before beckoning the person in, revealing Liam Shepherd, one of his longest-standing crewmen, his face lined with concern.

Emmett stepped aside to let Liam in. "Ye've heard, then?"

"Aye." Liam pushed his cap back and sighed. "Word's spread like wildfire, just as everything does on this tiny island. Some of the men are on your side, Emmett. They know you wouldn't cut corners. But others…" He hesitated. "Well, they need someone to blame."

Emmett clenched his jaw. Nothing was private here. "And I'm the easy target."

Liam nodded solemnly. "The families of the injured—you can't blame them. They're scared. The papers are already calling it a disgrace. Some politician wants to make an example of whoever's responsible."

Emmett ran a hand through his hair. "Blathers! Responsible for what, Liam? I was there every day. I checked every beam, every bolt. If somethin' went wrong, it wasn't from negligence."

Liam exhaled sharply. "Then you'll have to prove it."

The thought sent a chill through Emmett. He wasn't just fighting to clear his name—he was fighting against a tide of fear and anger. And tides, once turned, were near impossible to stop.

Another knock came at the door, this one sharper, more official. Emmett and Liam exchanged a look before Emmett strode forward and pulled the door open once more.

Two uniformed officers stood before him, their expressions unreadable.

The taller one stepped forward. "Mr. Emmett O'Connor?"

"Aye."

"You are required to present yourself before the magistrate one week hence. The inquiry into the worksite collapse will begin then."

Emmett squared his shoulders. "I'll be there."

The officer nodded, handing him a document before stepping back. "Be prepared to answer for your leadership, Mr. O'Connor."

With that, they turned and left, their boots echoing in the Grand Hall.

Emmett stood there, letter in hand, the moment pressing down on him like the very stone and timber he had once commanded with confidence.

Now, the test of his integrity would begin.

Emmett closed up his office for the night, spent in mind, body, and spirit. The evening air was heavy with the scent of rain, the sky redolent with storm clouds as Emmett strode toward the dock.

Boatman Thomas Roberts barely looked up as Emmett stepped into the skiff. "Need a ride?"

Emmett nodded, a slow, long sigh escaping his lips as he plopped down on the wooden seat. "This is gettin' worse by the day. I have but a week to solve it."

Thomas pushed off the dock and rowed toward the Yacht House, stopping midway. He leaned in. "I've heard. Some say the collapse was bound to happen, that the beams weren't sound. Others swear they saw things—shadows in the night, tools missing before the accident. But no one's willing to speak up."

Emmett's gut twisted. He suspected Bruce, but suspicion wasn't enough. He needed proof. "I need your help, Thomas. If there's someone who knows somethin', we have to find them. The longer I wait, the worse this gets."

Thomas met his gaze, the starlight reflecting in his eyes. "I've been thinking the same thing. If this wasn't bad luck, someone wanted it to happen, and I suspect Bruce. He's the only varmint around here smelling of skunk. But why?"

Emmett exhaled slowly. "Could be lookin' to ruin me, or maybe he has a grudge against the project itself. Either way, I won't sit back and let him hang me for it."

Thomas nodded. "I'll keep my ears open. The men talk more freely in the skiff. They think I don't listen, but I'll do some digging. And there are a few who were near the site that day. If they saw anything, we'll find out."

Emmett clasped his shoulder. "Thank you, Thomas. I'll search again to see if anythin' was off about the supplies or the contracts."

Thomas gave a grim smile. "And if someone's hiding the truth, we'll dig it out."

The two men nodded, the importance of their task settling over them. The coming storm rumbled, mirroring the danger that lay ahead.

Emmett would uncover the truth. And when he did, he prayed it wouldn't be too late.

Thomas pulled up to the yacht-house dock but paused before mooring the skiff. "You know, there's more to this fight than clearing your name."

Emmett arched a brow, exhaustion weighing on him, ready to disembark. "Aye? And what else do ye think I should be worryin' about?"

Thomas tossed him a sly smile. "Madison."

The name sent a jolt through Emmett's chest, but he forced himself to remain silent, shifting in his seat instead of answering.

Thomas chuckled. "Act as indifferent as you like, but I see how you look at her. And more than that, I see how she looks at you. How she cares for you."

Emmett exhaled sharply, plunking into his seat with a dull thud. "It doesn't matter."

"Why?" Thomas folded his arms. "Because of class? Because she's a lady's maid, and you're what, a foreman?"

"Aye." Emmett shrugged the tension knot from between his shoulders. "And that's not all. She doesn't need to be in the center of this. To be in danger. She loves the Boldts and her position, Thomas. What could I offer her but a scandal and a reputation ruined?"

Thomas studied him for a moment before shaking his head. "You're a stubborn man, Emmett O'Connor."

He let out a humorless laugh. "So I've been told."

Thomas hopped out of the skiff and tied it up. "Madison's stronger than you give her credit for. If she wanted to turn her back on you, she would've done it already. But she hasn't, has she?"

Emmett sat silent.

"Don't decide her fate for her. You've got enough battles to fight as it is—don't make her another one."

The words settled in the air between them. Emmett wanted to argue, to say that loving Madison would only bring her hardship. But truth was, Thomas was right. Madison wasn't one to be told what to do, and if she had stood by him, who was he to deny her that choice?

He took a few steps toward the Yacht House but stopped. "I'll think on it."

Thomas grinned. "Yes, you do that. But don't take too long, Emmett. Not all things wait forever."

CHAPTER 18

Madison shifted in her seat in Mrs. Boldt's bedroom. Today they'd observe the Fourth of July Independence Day celebrations. In a few hours, they would be busy, attending the festivities, which were a particularly special time in the Thousand Islands.

But for now, she found comfort in the quiet moments of her day, particularly when the missus rested, which she did more and more of late. Her heart clenched at the memory of the once vibrant woman who now seemed unusually tired more often than not.

She touched her Claddagh locket, the one treasured possession she had left of her family. Nestled against her heart, her grandmother's locket was a symbol of the heritage that resonated deeply within her.

The design, with its heart representing love, the crown signifying loyalty, and the hands embodying friendship, spoke volumes of her grandmother's values. Each time Madison traced her fingers over the intricate etching, she harkened back to the rolling green hills of Ireland and the warmth of her grandmother's embrace.

Those memories brought a bittersweet comfort, a reminder of her roots and the strength of the bonds she had lost so long ago.

Inside the locket, a single pressed shamrock lay safely preserved—a fragment of her homeland. More than merely a botanical keepsake, the three-leaf clover was a bridge to her past. A reminder of the laughter shared and the tales told under the Irish sky.

In a world where she usually felt invisible, the locket was a tangible connection to her identity. It touched her deeply, evoking memories that brought both joy and sorrow. Ones of a Gran's love, but also of loss and sadness. And guilt and shame. Those recollections she shoved to the back of her brain, covered them with a black cloth, and refused to acknowledge them. Most of the time.

As she clasped the locket tightly, she remembered how it had become her anchor amidst the challenges of her new life in America. A small but powerful emblem of love, loyalty, and friendship, nurturing her spirit and guiding her through the trials of each day.

She'd found those virtues in the Boldt's household, a unique blend of caring that transcended class and careers.

Mrs. Boldt, only a decade older than she, had become more like an older sister—or strangely a mother—than a millionaire employer. Not once, no, not a single time, had she made Madison feel like a low-class servant. In public, they stayed in their stations, but in private, she was a friend, a mentor, a healer of her heart.

And Hazel, her direct superior who held power over her continued employment, was her closest friend, her confidant, a woman of wisdom. She touched her locket once again, grateful she'd found all three virtues in these women. How could she want—or need—anything more?

"Are you there, dear?" Mrs. Boldt rustled in her bed. "Is it time to get ready for the festivities?"

Madison frowned. The missus's voice held no joy, no energy, no life. That beautiful woman slipped away from her more each day.

"Madison?"

She jumped from her seat and hurried to Mrs. Boldt's bedside. "Sorry ma'am. I'm here. You have an hour before you need to get ready for the Fourth of July celebration. Rest awhile longer, if you'd like."

And she did, while Madison prayed for her, then laid out her clothing and prepared to assist her for the evening. Soon, the scent of lavender and rosewater lingered in the air as Mrs. Boldt stood shakily before a mirror, her reflection shimmering in the dim light.

Madison worked with swift but delicate precision, ensuring every detail of her mistress's attire was perfect for the evening's festivities. She adjusted the delicate lace-edged chemise beneath the layers of Mrs. Boldt's gown. The soft rustle of silk whispered through the room as she fastened the last row of tiny pearl buttons on the back of the bodice.

The gown itself was a masterpiece—midnight blue silk, the color of the river at dusk, embroidered with silver filigree that caught the light with every movement. A soft chiffon overlay gave the fabric an ethereal shimmer, while the scooped neckline, edged with lace, revealed just enough to be fashionable yet modest. Short, puffed sleeves, adorned with tiny seed pearls, framed her weak arms, which ivory gloves would soon conceal.

Madison stepped back, inspecting her work with a critical eye. "A moment more, ma'am." She reached for a sapphire brooch set in platinum and pinned it below her mistress's left shoulder, where it nestled against the rich fabric like a jewel against the night sky. "There. A touch of brilliance."

Mrs. Boldt offered a pleased smile before sitting at the vanity, where Madison set to work on her coiffure. Her hands swept her mistress's dark tresses into an elegant pompadour, securing the voluminous waves with pearl-studded combs. A few tendrils were left loose to soften the effect, lending an air of effortless grace.

"Now the final touch."

Madison reached for the long strand of pearls resting on a velvet cushion, looping them around Mrs. Boldt's neck with practiced ease. They gleamed against her pale skin.

Then Madison handed her a delicate fan of ivory and lace. "You are ready, ma'am."

Mrs. Boldt dipped her head in approval, the corners of her lips lifting ever so slightly. "Thank you, dear."

Within the hour, Madison stepped carefully off the Boldts' steamer onto the dock at Heart Island, the distant hum of conversations and laughter drifting from the Alster Tower. The night air carried the crisp scent of the St. Lawrence River, mingled with the faint sweetness of torches flickering along the walkways. She had looked forward to this evening, to the grand Fourth of July celebration on Heart Island, with fireworks set to light up the sky in a dazzling display of color.

Yet, even as she followed the Boldts along the path toward Alster Tower, her heart carried an unease she couldn't shake. She hadn't seen Emmett in a week. No letters, no word. Just silence. And it gnawed at her, the way a storm lingers on the horizon, just out of touch but impossible to ignore.

The lawns bustled with the dozen or so elegantly dressed guests, the ladies' gowns glowing in the lantern light, their skirts sweeping over the trimmed grass. Madison turned a corner, distracted by a sudden burst of laughter from a group near the gazebo where the Boldts would remain. In that instant, she collided with someone—firm, solid, familiar.

She gasped as strong hands steadied her, and she looked up into the shadowed face of Emmett.

"Madison."

Her name on his lips weighed heavily on the air, as though he could barely speak it. She stepped back, studying him. His usually lively gray eyes were dull, rimmed with exhaustion. The easy smile he normally carried was nowhere to be seen. Instead, his jaw was tight, his shoulders drawn as if the very air crushed him.

"Emmett." She stepped back, breaking contact. "Where have you been?"

He exhaled sharply, shaking his head. "Nowhere worth mentioning. Tomorrow's the day. The hearing."

His voice was thick, laced with more than worry. It was fear. And what else? Defeat.

Madison glanced at the Boldts, occupied in conversation with their guests.

She touched his sleeve gently. "I know. I've been praying."

Emmett let out a bitter laugh, stepping back. "Praying? Do you really think that'll change anything? The judge has already decided. I can see it clear as day. And what then? What happens after they strip away the little scrap of life I've built here for myself?"

She frowned. "Emmett, I—"

"Stay out of this. You deserve a life that isn't tangled in this mess."

A crack echoed across the sky, followed by a golden bloom of light bursting overhead, illuminating his face for a fleeting moment. The fireworks had begun, their brilliance reflecting in the dark river below.

She reached for his hand before he stepped away. "You're pushing me away because you think it'll protect me." She wouldn't let him leave without speaking her heart. "But Emmett, shutting out the people who care about you isn't protection. It's surrender."

He stiffened, his gaze flickering to hers.

She held onto him, refusing to let go, even with the Boldts just twenty feet away. "You've been fighting for so long you don't even see it anymore. But God does." She swallowed against the lump in her throat. "And I do. You are not alone, Emmett. Don't let fear make you forget that."

His shoulders shook slightly, and he looked away, staring at the dark water. Another firework lit up the sky in a dazzling spray of red and blue.

She squeezed his hand. "There's an old Irish proverb, 'God's help is nearer than the door. May the saddest day of your future be no worse than the happiest day of your past.'"

Emmett let out a shuddering breath, his grip tightening around hers.

His walls weren't gone.

But perhaps a door had opened.

~ ~ ~

Emmett clenched his fist, his jaw tight. Tomorrow, everything would change. The judge's gavel would fall, and with it, the course of his life.

He had spent years building a life of honesty and integrity. But it was never enough. No matter how hard he fought, the world had a way of dragging him back into the mire. And now, Madison—sweet, stubborn Madison—stood too close to the edge with him.

He wouldn't let her fall.

"You shouldn't be here with me." Perhaps if he kept his voice rough enough, she'd realize her precarious position. "Go back to the Boldts."

She stepped closer instead. "Not until you talk to me."

"There's nothing to say."

Madison crossed her arms, tilting her head slightly, studying him in that way that made him feel as if she could see straight through him. "You act as though I have no choice."

"You don't." She wasn't listening. He hardened his voice. Perhaps that would make her listen. "Because I won't let you or your reputation be ruined for my sake."

Silence stretched between them, filled only by the lapping of the water against the dock. And the pounding of his heart.

Finally, Madison spoke, her voice softer. "You think I'm afraid? Or that I don't care about the burdens you're carrying?"

He turned away from her, staring back at the water. "It doesn't matter. I won't let you get involved."

Madison sighed, her voice steady but firm. "Emmett, you are not the only one with choices. You think you're building a wall to protect me, but all you're doing is shutting out the very person who wants to stand by you."

A muscle in his jaw twitched. "Blathers, woman! It's not that simple."

"Yes, it is."

He turned to face her, frustration flashing in his eyes. "You don't understand, Madison. You do not know the load I carry. No matter what happens in court tomorrow, I'll never be free of it."

Her expression softened, and for a long moment, she stared at him.

Then she sighed and touched his arm. "I care about you, Emmett, and no matter what happens tomorrow, you are not beyond redemption. God can change it all in a moment."

Something inside him cracked. Just a little. The wall wasn't gone. But perhaps it wasn't as unbreakable as he'd thought.

The fireworks exploded overhead, their reflection dancing on the river. They stood near the water's edge, surrounded by the hum of the Boldts' Fourth of July celebration. He wanted to talk with her, to change the subject. To talk about anything but his predicament and her involvement in it. But his words were mechanical, as if he had rehearsed them for an audience.

But at the moment, it was the only thing he could think of saying. "I read in the paper that President Roosevelt ordered the removal of the White House conservatories. They're tearin' them down to build what will be called 'the West Wing.'"

She blinked, her brows furrowing. "What?"

He barely glanced at her. "The conservatories. The greenhouses. They'd been expandin' them for decades, startin' with the orangery in 1835. But now Roosevelt had them removed—just like that."

Madison folded her arms. "Why are you telling me this?"

Emmett shrugged. "Just news I read. It doesn't matter."

He had always been guarded by temperament, but tonight, he was worse. Distant. Removed. Perhaps downright cruel. He realized that. He was acting—and treating her—as if he was already gone. Acting as if he was stuck near her rather than wanting to be with her.

Madison's gaze pinned him in place, her quiet presence pressing in like the night itself.

"I see." Irritation he couldn't ignore tinged her voice. "You'd rather talk about tearing down greenhouses than what's really on your mind?"

His jaw tensed. He kept his gaze forward, watching the dark horizon, hoping she would let it go.

But of course, she didn't.

"You're not fooling me, Emmett. You think it doesn't matter if you act unaffected? But it matters. And you know it does."

He exhaled sharply, shaking his head. "Tomorrow is coming, Madison. Whether I want it to or not."

She stepped closer. The warmth of her presence provided a stark contrast to the cold fear pressing against his ribs. "And you think pushing me away will change that?"

"It's the only thing I can control."

She shook her head, her disappointment cutting deeper than he wanted to admit. "So, you're doing what Roosevelt did."

"What?"

She held his gaze, her expression steady. "You're tearing down something beautiful—something that took time to build—just because you think there's no place for it anymore."

Emmett's lips parted, but no words came. He stood there, frozen, as another firework burst above them, momentarily setting the world alight. The flickering colors caught in her eyes, softening the sharp edges, but not enough to hide the truth she saw in him.

Then, gently, she touched his arm. "God's help is nearer than the door, Emmett. No matter what happens tomorrow, He hasn't abandoned you."

Then he pulled back, shaking his head. "Blathers! It's not that simple."

"It is. She sighed. "You just can't see it."

He flinched at that, a crack in the walls he had built yawned wide before him. Concern for him showed in her narrowed eyes and down-turned lips. Determination tensed her jaw muscles.

She saw him. Not the man he pretended to be. Not the mask he wore. She saw everything—the exhaustion, the fear, the guilt.

And still, she stayed.

The Clock Tower rang out, its deep chimes rolling across the water, solemn and unyielding.

Madison flinched. He didn't.

Instead, he stared up at the tower, its presence settling over him like a shroud. "Three faces."

Madison crossed her arms, exasperation creeping into her voice. "What?"

"The clock." He gestured to the building. "Three faces. Added in 1900, the same year they finished the Power House."

The words came automatically, like reciting a history book rather than speaking to her as a living, breathing person. As the woman who'd stolen his heart, his thoughts, his dreams, and turned them into something beautiful. Before he'd acted the fool and dashed them to the ground.

She let out a sharp breath. "And what does that have to do with anything, Emmett?"

He turned to her then, his thoughts pressing against every syllable. "It means my time's up."

He saw the way her expression shifted. "Stop talking like that."

"It's true." He let out a slow breath, rubbing a hand over his face. "Tomorrow, I walk into that courtroom, and whatever happens—happens. I haven't found evidence that exonerates me or that proves Bruce's guilt. There's nothing left for me to do."

"So that's it? You're just giving up?"

"I'm accepting reality."

Hadn't she understood a word he'd said?

"No." Fire flared in her eyes. "You're running. From me. From yourself. From God."

His jaw tightened. "Madison, don't."

"Don't what? Call you out for treating me like I'm no one to you?" Her hands flew up in frustration. "You talk to me like I'm a guest at a dinner party instead of the person who—"

She stopped.

The silence stretched between them, heavy and charged.

Instead of the person who loves you. She didn't say it, but he felt it like a shot to his chest. Saw it in her eyes.

She shook her head, her voice thick with emotion. "You're acting like this is already over, but it's not. You still have a chance. But instead, you're building a wall so high I don't even recognize you anymore."

The clock struck again, the deep toll resonating through the night.

Emmett exhaled slowly, considering. Choosing.

"The Power House was built to bring light to the island. To make sure Mr. Boldt's dream would be possible." He looked at her then, his gaze steady. "But sometimes, even with all the power in the world, you can't stop it from going dark."

Her expression flickered, pain flashing in her eyes. "And what? You think this is how it has to be? That you must slip into the dark with it?"

He hesitated. Just for a second.

Then, as if shaking himself, he forced the moment away, burying it beneath cold resolve. "You should get back to the Boldts, Madison."

She inhaled sharply, hurt flickering across her face. Still, she didn't leave.

Instead, she step-stepped closer, her voice trembling but unshakable. "You can stand here and tell me history lessons all night, but that's not why you're doing this. You're scared. And instead of leaning on the people who care about you, you'd rather push us away."

The final chime rang out, the sound rolling over the island like a funeral bell.

Her next words came out sharp but barely above a whisper. "But you're wrong about one thing, Emmett. It's not your time that's up. It's your excuses."

Before he could say another word—before he could dismiss her again—she turned and walked away.

He stood there, beneath the darkness of the night, as the final chimes of the clock echoed across the river.

If time wasn't running out—and if she was correct—how did that change the outcome?

Because all the hopin' and prayin' in the world wouldn't change what the judge decided tomorrow.

Bruce had won.

CHAPTER 19

Madison wrapped her shawl around her shoulders, inhaling deeply, letting the cool breeze steady her thoughts. As the boat rocked gently across the dark waters, ferrying her and the Boldts back home, the memory of fireworks still shimmered in the rippling waves. But, like her hopes and dreams, their brilliance faded as swiftly as the evening's revelry.

She had spent too much time worrying about Emmett. His troubles loomed like a storm on the horizon, and though she longed to help, he had shut her out. It wasn't simply tomorrow's court appearance. The guilt he carried, the burden he refused to share—all shouted of a man intent on being in control.

She grunted. For a man determined to run—and perhaps ruin—his own life, his silence hurt more than she dared admit.

She clenched her hands in her lap. No, she could do nothing for him. Not when he didn't want her to.

Her duty, her purpose, was clear. Mrs. Boldt needed her now more than ever. The woman who had given her a home, a sense of belonging, grew frailer by the day. Madison would not waver—not in her devotion, not in her care. If she allowed her heart to stray, even for a moment, she feared she fail the one person who felt like kin.

Yet, the ache could not be silenced so easily. She thought she had steeled herself against hope when it came to Emmett. Hadn't she seen it in his eyes, that flicker of affection? Perhaps that's why his words and actions in recent days, and tonight especially, hurt so much? Because she understood, all too well, how it felt to love and lose.

She could not afford to succumb to that sense of despair again.

The boat docked at Wellesley Island, and she stepped onto the wooden planks, her heart heavy but her mind resolved. She had made her choice. The Lord would tend to Emmett as only He could. Madison had her own mission—to stand by Mrs. Boldt, to offer the love and loyalty the woman so richly deserved. And if the cost of that devotion also meant denying her heart, then so be it.

With one last glance toward Heart Island where Emmett secured the property before calling it a night, she turned toward the Wellesley House, each step firm, each breath a whispered prayer. *Let me be strong. Let me be steadfast. And let me not long for what I cannot have.*

Yet even as she walked away, a part of her knew the war within her heart was far from over.

When they returned to the house, Madison helped Mrs. Boldt prepare for bed.

As she tucked her in, Mrs. Boldt held her hand. "I'm too restless to sleep just now. Please tell me a story, perhaps, about your childhood?"

The request surprised Madison, though through the years, the missus often asked questions about her past. In those times, she fretted about how much to divulge, keeping the shameful parts hidden deep in the place she never spoke of.

Madison tugged the locket from under her shirtwaist and showed it to the missus. She had done so before, but it'd been years. "My gran gave me this locket. I spent many evenings with her by the hearth, where she told stories of our ancestors. Gran taught me the true meaning of the Claddagh symbol as she tatted lace. Love, loyalty, and friendship. And how these three virtues form the foundation of every meaningful relationship."

Mrs. Boldt sighed, settling deeper under the quilt. "She sounds like my grandmother."

Madison paused, her fingers brushing the locket before continuing. "As you know, when I was twelve, my mother decided we would emigrate to America to be with my Aunt May, her sister, your lady's maid. Gran stayed behind with my father's kin. For me, it felt like the end of the world. My mama was bitter and distant, while Gran was so warm and kind. How could I bear to leave her?"

Tears pricked at Madison's eyes as she recalled their parting. "I sobbed as I said goodbye, and Gran cried too. Mama, though, was sullen and silent. Gran pressed this locket into my hand, tears streaming down her cheeks. 'My darling granddaughter,' she whispered, 'I fear I will not see you in this life again, so take this with you to remember me. Remember your dear papa, my son. Remember your brother. Remember our beloved Ireland.'"

Madison took a shaky breath. "I held her so tightly. 'I will, Gran. I will remember. All of it! I love you.'"

She sighed. "At that moment, Mama huffed and yanked me away. 'Enough of this nonsense,' she snapped. 'Say goodbye and be done with it.'"

Madison fell silent, lost in the memories of the past.

Mrs. Boldt reached for her hand. "She gave you more than a locket, my dear. She gave you a piece of her heart."

Madison nodded, holding the locket close. "And I will never forget."

Mrs. Boldt squeezed her hand, her frail fingers trembling. "That is a treasure trove of memories." She paused, giving her hand a squeeze. "We share memories, too, and I hope you'll not forget. You know I'm not long for this world. I can feel it in my bones. My heart is failing—but you must stay strong."

Madison's eyes shimmered with unshed tears, but she forced a small smile, determined not to let sorrow overtake her. "Your kindness reminds me of my gran, ma'am. When I was a wee girl, I used to run my hands over the clumps of shamrocks in Gran's garden, feeling their delicate leaves between my fingers. She'd tell me stories as we tended to the plants, explaining how the shamrock was a symbol of blessings. How faith, hope, and love were in its very essence."

She covered her locket with her hand, her thumb running over its cool metal surface. "Before I left Ireland, I plucked a tiny shamrock and pressed it inside. It was a way to carry a piece of Gran and Ireland with me, no matter where life took me."

Mrs. Boldt gave her a gentle smile, urging her to go on.

"Gran's laughter lit up any room, and I hear it still. It echoes in my mind during the lonely moments, reminding me that joy can be found even in hardship." She smiled wistfully. "This locket became my comfort, holding not just her love but the resilience she instilled in me. Every time I faced adversity, I hold onto it and remember that I can endure."

Taking a deep breath, Madison unclasped the locket, carefully pulling out the tiny, fragile four-leaf clover. She reached for Mrs. Boldt's frail hand and pressed it into her palm. "I cannot give you rubies or gold," she said with a gentle smile, "but this is for you, missus. It'll bring you blessings and health."

Mrs. Boldt's eyes filled with emotion as she closed her fingers over the fragile clover. "Oh, my dear girl," she murmured, her voice thick with gratitude. "You've already brought me more blessings than I ever could have asked for."

The missus's hands trembled as she glanced at her. A soft smile touched her lips, and her eyes shone with a depth of emotion that made Madison's throat tighten.

"Madison," Mrs. Boldt said, her voice hushed, "you must understand. In all the years we've shared, through all the laughter and the burdens, you've become far more to me than a maid tending to my home. Titles and stations—maid and missus—those mean little to the heart. And my heart, Madison, sees you as a far greater gift."

Madison's breath hitched. "Missus, I—"

Mrs. Boldt brushed a curl from her cheek. "No, let me finish, child." Her voice was gentle, but insistent. "I see you as so much more than a maid, and if I could choose again, I would choose you. Time and again."

A lump formed in Madison's throat. She had spent her days in service, knowing her place in the grand order of things, never expecting such words. Never dreaming she could be loved like this.

Mrs. Boldt exhaled slowly, her frail shoulders lifting with effort. "One day, I will be gone, Madison. I do not say this to grieve you, but because I need you to remember something when that time comes. Remember you were cherished. Not by blood, but by choice.

By love." Her thumb brushed away the tear that slipped free. "And love, my dear, is what truly binds us."

Madison could no longer hold back the tears. She wrapped her arms around the woman who had become so much more to her than an employer. Mrs. Boldt returned the embrace, a haven of comfort reminding her of the love she had once known in Ireland.

"I will remember, missus," Madison whispered, her voice thick with emotion. "Always."

Madison bid her goodnight, and in the golden lamplight, the fragile clover became a symbol of hope, of love, of an unbreakable bond.

She had not only found a place of love in the Boldt household, but a place in a heart that could soon be gone.

~ ~ ~

Emmett stood outside the courthouse while he waited for the verdict. The hot July air pressed on him. The sun peeked through the clouds, casting a warm glow on the stone facade, but he felt none of its comfort. His heart raced as he replayed these last hours in his mind.

Inside the courtroom, the atmosphere had proven tense. The thorough investigation scrutinized every detail of the tragic incident. He sat in that stuffy room, surrounded by lawyers and officials, his hands clammy and his throat dry. Each question felt like a dagger, each comment a subtle accusation against him, probing the depths of his guilt.

Now, as the courthouse doors swung open, a wave of murmurs washed over the gathered crowd. Emmett's breath caught in his throat when the lead investigator stepped forward, a serious expression softening as he addressed the assembly.

The man stood on the top step, waiting until reporters held their pencils at the ready. He cleared his throat. "After careful consideration of the evidence and testimonies, we conclude that Emmett O'Connor acted in good faith. While the tragedy that occurred is heartbreaking, we do not find sufficient grounds for further prosecution."

A collective gasp echoed through the crowd, followed by a murmur of relief and disbelief. Emmett's knees almost buckled. He had braced himself for the worst, but this—this was a reprieve he hadn't dared hope for.

"Mr. O'Connor," the investigator continued, "we recommend you continue your efforts to uphold workplace safety, not only to honor Garrison's memory but to ensure no other family has to endure such a loss."

As the words sank in, Emmett's mind raced. Garrison. The haunting recollection of his colleague's face flashed before him, the memory echoing like a ghost. Tears threatened to spill, but he forced them back, knowing this moment was not about him. Instead, it was about the fallen and the injured. And he would keep his focus on proving Bruce's complicity in the disaster.

The crowd around him dispersed, some murmuring congratulations, others offering handshakes. Emmett turned at a hand on his arm.

Clara, Garrison's widow. Her eyes shone with unshed tears.

"Thank you for fighting for Garrison's memory," she said, her voice steady but laced with emotion. "I know it is hard, but we need to keep pushing for the truth. Someone tampered with that scaffolding. I know it. And so do you."

Emmett nodded, her words crashing over him like waves on a shore during a hurricane. "I will. I promise."

He glanced back at the courthouse, the building that felt like a cage just moments before. Now, it stood as a testament to a painful chapter—and the possibility of redemption.

As the sunlight broke through the clouds, Emmett's mood lifted with a renewed sense of purpose. He would honor Garrison not only through words, but through action. This was but the beginning. He would create a legacy of safety and compassion in the workplace, ensuring no one else would endure the same sorrow again.

And that started with finding the truth. It wasn't an accident. He knew that deep in his bones. But he had to find the proof. Proof that someone somehow tampered with the scaffolding. Proof that

Bruce was indeed the culprit. Not just for his own vindication or for Garrison's memory, but also for the protection of his workers. Without such a cladhaire locked up, no one was safe.

With a deep breath, Emmett stepped forward, ready to embrace the path ahead.

Bruce was still free. Still guilty. Still at large.

That evening, Emmett sat hunched at the small wooden table in the dimly lit Yacht House, stifled by unspoken words and the prick of old wounds.

Thomas stood over him with arms crossed, his eyes trained on him. "Emmett," Thomas said softly, breaking the silence. "You need to talk about this. You should be jubilant, but you're not."

Emmett's hands trembled as he clenched them into fists, his voice barely a whisper. His voice cracked, the memories flooding back like storm waves crashing against the shore of his mind. "Aye, I'm happy I'm acquitted, but it tears my guts up to think that you-know-who is still at large, is still able to cause mischief, or worse if he wants to. We must find the proof in order to prove Garrison's death wasn't in vain. If not, I'll go to my grave regrettin' it."

He paused, pondering if he should voice the deeper issues of his heart. Thomas had proven himself an honorable man, a man of faith. A man he could trust.

"And besides, how could God let this happen? I don't understand. If He is who He says He is, why did Garrison die? Why does the perpetrator go free? Why?"

Thomas stepped closer, his brows furrowed with concern. "God was there when all of that happened, Emmett. You couldn't see Him through your pain. You still can't. You believe the lie that He doesn't care, that He wasn't there. But He's with you every day. Waiting for you."

Emmett shook his head vehemently, a storm of emotions raging within him. "I haven't seen or heard God since the accident. He's been silent. Distant. And it's my fault. I don't blame Him for cutting me off. But God wasn't there to help when I needed him, and, truth is, I'm spittin' angry at Him."

Thomas clapped a hand on his shoulder before taking a seat beside him. "If you could only see how He cares. You're not to blame for the accident. If you let Him in, He'll show you that."

"How can I let God in when I'm responsible for not finding the evidence to convict the guilty party? Or to save my own family? It's too much. I'm no good, Thomas."

His head snapped up.

Wait! Had he revealed his darkest secret about not saving his family? It slipped out with Madison, but she was a pretty little thing, too sympathetic by far.

Now he told Thomas?

He slammed his fist on the table. "Forget I mentioned my family. That's none of your concern."

Thomas let out a slow, pensive breath before shaking his head. He handed him a glass of water and Emmett took a long draw of it. The cool liquid flowed down his throat, flooding his embarrassment and quenching the fire raging in his soul.

Thomas paused for several more moments as if deep in thought, then he looked straight into Emmett's eyes. "You're much more than the misplaced guilt you feel. God can settle this once and for all, Emmett, if you let Him. But sometimes His ways are not our ways."

"He could have prevented all of it, but He did not. And the buck stops with me."

Thomas held steady and resolute. "Misplaced guilt is a heavy and unfair burden to bear. It protects us from the hopelessness and helplessness we feel. But it also tears at the very fiber of our beings. It's numbing and confusing. It lies to us. Tortures us. Consumes us."

Thomas paused, allowing a brief moment while Emmett stood and paced the floor. "The longer you hide from dealing with the real problem, Emmett—the grief of losing your family, the sadness you've refused to feel, and the reality of being all alone in the world—the more you will suffer. You can't move forward until you let yourself feel again. Until you forgive God—and yourself."

Emmett stopped in his tracks, his eyes wide with uncertainty. "It can't be that simple."

Thomas stood and faced him. "Trust God that He can free your heart. That you can move forward, even if we never find the proof. Even if you never get the answers you seek. Even if we let you-know-who go free."

Emmett's jaw tightened, and he ground his teeth as he met Thomas's steady gaze. "That's difficult to even consider right now. Impossible perhaps."

"When God steps in, He makes everything new." Thomas's voice softened, filled with compassion. "Look to Him and find the strength and courage to forgive yourself. Trust Him to lead you on. Trust Him to be the vindicator."

Emmett's breath hitched, the flicker of hope battling against the darkness in his heart. "What if I can't?"

"I'm here for you, my friend. But I suggest you let Madison help you, too," Thomas said, his voice firm yet gentle. "She cares even more than I do, and you need her. Let her walk with you through this. I suspect she has a few ghosts of her own to deal with. Neither of you has to bear this alone. Neither of you is the sum of your past mistakes. You are both children of God, worthy of love and grace."

Emmett glanced into Thomas's eyes, searching for the truth behind the words. The flickering candlelight cast dancing shadows, but a glimmer of hope tugged at his heart. Perhaps, just perhaps, he could learn to forgive himself—and one day guide Madison to her own happy ending in the process.

But his friend's words still confused him. "Why Madison? Nae, I'd put her in danger if she is around me. I know it."

With a nod, Thomas smiled warmly. "Somehow, I think she holds the key to your heart and your future."

Could it be? Surely, life had to be more complicated than that. Is that why the lass was so insistent on walking alongside him?

Yet, had he burned one bridge too many to ask for her help again?

CHAPTER 20

A week passed, yet the shadows of sorrow still clung to the Wellesley House like a cold mist, refusing to lift. Madison felt powerless—unable to chase away the lingering shadows that haunted Emmett, nor to unseat Bruce from his wicked throne of deception.

Mrs. Boldt, once a beacon of health and grace, now dissolved a little more each day into the silken covers of her bed, her spirit waning like the last embers of a dying fire. Mr. Boldt, ever devoted, carried the burden of worry for his beloved wife, his eyes clouded with unspoken fears. And all around them, their island paradise, once filled with grandeur and dreams, lay shrouded in a suffocating veil of despair.

The missus had barely left her rooms these last few days. Madison worried more with each passing hour as the air around her mistress felt heavy with sorrow. The lively, gracious woman she had once known retreated into herself. Even the magical Thousand Islands, her beloved Wellesley House, and the rising Boldt Castle on

Heart Island—the grand monument to love—paled in comparison to her waning life.

The chambermaid, Anna, shooed her out of the room while the missus rested. No need for both to hover over her.

The sun was already high when Madison headed to the bright yellow and red rosebushes at the far end of the garden. The summer heat hovered over the manicured hedges and the trellis draped in climbing roses. A gentle breeze carried the scent of damp earth and blossoms, rustling the trees standing tall like silent sentinels over the grand home.

Late-summer blooms perfumed the air with their fragrance, and she took in a refreshing whiff, her spirit ticking up just a notch. Perhaps a bouquet would help.

With practiced hands, she clipped the fullest roses, careful to avoid their sharp thorns. Each bloom, velvety in texture and rich with color, dropped softly into her basket. The bouquet would be exquisite—one worthy of the grand halls of the Waldorf-Astoria where Mrs. Boldt once entertained the world's elite. But today, its only purpose was to bring comfort to a woman whose heart beat weakly, burdened beyond words.

Madison recalled how Mrs. Boldt once adored walking the gardens, delighting in the roses George Boldt planted especially for her. Now, she drifted through the days as though waiting for something—though what, Madison could only guess.

The late morning air was still, heavy with the scent of roses and damp earth, as she worked through the blooms. She had nearly finished gathering a bouquet, the rich reds and yellows vibrant in the soft light, when a rustle in the nearby hedges caught her attention.

A flicker of movement. A shadow stretching across the path.

Before she could react, a rough hand clamped over her mouth, cutting off her startled gasp. Strong arms wrenched her backward, dragging her swiftly through the winding paths of the estate. She twisted, fought, but her captor was too strong. The basket tumbled from her hands, roses scattering like drops of blood along the path.

Bruce.

She sensed it before he whispered into her ear, his hot breath against her neck. Intimately. As though he owned her. "Not a sound, girl, unless you want this to end badly."

Her heart pounded as he pulled her toward the Dairy House, the oldest structure on the Boldt properties. Madison knew the place well, though she'd never crossed its threshold. Here, dairy products and meat were processed for shipment to the Waldorf-Astoria in New York and the Bellevue-Stratford in Philadelphia.

But on Sunday, a day of rest in an otherwise busy week, it stood eerily empty.

The perfect place to hide in plain sight.

Bruce shoved open the door and dragged her inside, his grip tightening painfully around her arm. He forced her into a small office, the scents of milk and straw thick in the air. Only then did he release her, but not before slamming the door shut behind him.

Madison stumbled back, pressing a hand to her racing heart. Bruce loomed before her, his face twisted with anger, his dark eyes alight with a far more dangerous look—desperation.

"Think you'll get the best of me?" he sneered, his voice low and seething. "Not on your life."

Madison trembled as she forced herself to appear small, compliant. Not provoke him. Not when she was alone.

He ran a hand through his disheveled hair, pacing like a caged animal. "I've worked too hard for some little snippet like you to ruin everything. Do you have any idea what I've done to secure my rightful place? And you think you can just waltz in and upset my plans?"

He let out a sharp laugh, bitter and cold.

Madison remained silent, her mind working quickly. She hadn't realized just how unhinged he had become.

He stepped closer. "Get your nose out of my business, or I'll have you permanently taken care of."

He must've heard that she was snooping around, asking questions, gathering information. A shiver ran through her, but she refused to let him see her fear. Instead, she lowered her head, drawing in a slow, measured breath.

Then, feigning submissive defeat, she whispered, "I understand."

His eyes narrowed. "Do you?"

She nodded, adding a touch of hesitation to her voice. "I…I don't want any trouble. I never meant to cause trouble. I'll stay out of it."

He studied her for a long moment, then gave a satisfied grunt. "Good. See that you do."

She took a cautious step toward the door. "I should go. If I'm missing too long, people will come looking for me."

He smirked. "Fine. But remember—one word, and you won't live long enough to regret it."

With that, he reached for the door and yanked it open, giving her a rough shove forward. She staggered but quickly righted herself, keeping her eyes downcast as she stepped outside.

The moment she was free, she ran. Because one thing was certain. Bruce was desperate, and desperate men do dangerous things.

As she reached the garden, she paused, bending slightly to catch her breath. The basket and the roses she had gathered lay forgotten, their petals scattered on the path where she had been taken. But she didn't dare stop to collect them now. If Bruce saw her lingering, he might realize she wasn't as timid as she pretended to be.

Instead, she hurried up the veranda steps and slipped inside, pressing her back against the closed door. She needed to think—to decide what to do next. The house was unnervingly quiet, the only sound the distant ticking of the grandfather clock in the hall. A footman passed by, offering a polite nod but saying nothing.

Madison's heart pounded, her breath coming in brief gasps. She could still feel Bruce's rough grip on her arms, his words seared into her mind like a brand. *Permanently taken care of.*

She took a few steps, but suddenly, a figure slipped through the front door. "Miss Murray."

She gasped, her breath catching as Detective Fletcher stepped forward. His sharp brown eyes bore into hers, calm yet piercing. His presence should have startled her, but instead, relief flooded her veins.

He knew.

"You… you were there, in the garden."

He gave a brief nod, his voice steady. "I was."

She sucked in a breath, still confused. "You saw everything, then?"

"Enough," he confirmed, his tone cool, measured. "You and Thomas have been asking questions, seeking answers, so I've kept an eye on you. Truth is, Bruce Clawson is running out of places to hide."

A shiver ran down her spine. "Then why let him go?"

A flicker of worry passed across the detective's face. "Because men like him get careless when they think they've won." He stepped closer, lowering his voice. "And I want him careless. I want him thinking he has you frightened and out of his way."

Madison exhaled sharply. "You want him to make a mistake."

Fletcher nodded. "Exactly." He studied her, his gaze softening. "But that means you must stay out of it for now. Let me handle this. Can you do that?"

She hesitated. The very idea of sitting back, of not fighting to uncover the truth, felt unbearable.

But she had seen Bruce's rage, had felt his violence in the way he had dragged her to the Dairy House. If she pushed too far, she might not make it back next time.

At last, she nodded. "I'll do my best."

"Good." Fletcher's expression was firm, but there was an edge in his tone—concern, perhaps. "Stay close to the house today. No wandering off alone."

She wrapped her arms around herself and nodded again. As Fletcher turned and walked out the door, Madison pressed her fingers to her temple, willing the tremor in her hands to cease.

The bouquet would have to wait. The flowers meant to comfort Mrs. Boldt were still out in the garden, scattered and forgotten. There were bigger things at stake now.

Bruce was desperate. He was bound to make mistakes.

She only hoped Fletcher would catch him before it was too late.

~ ~ ~

Emmett sat beneath the sprawling branches of the grand oak just outside the castle, the leaves rustling softly as if whispering secrets of the past. He was grateful it was Sunday, and the island was empty—save Fred Shutieb, the chief electrician, who remained in the Power House like a hermit.

What he needed to do had tormented him all day. He'd fought it, but he couldn't go on with the bitterness inside, or it would destroy him. Whether he lost his job or kept it. He had to eliminate this bitter anger once and for all, regardless of whether he disgraced himself or was vindicated. It was eating him alive.

The late afternoon sun filtered through the foliage, casting dappled shadows on the ground, but all he saw were the blueprints scattered across his lap—plans for Boldt Castle that now felt like an anchor dragging him down into the earth.

His hands trembled as he clutched the drawings, the ink smudged with the sweat of his brow. The air was thick with remorse, and a heaviness wrapped around his chest, squeezing tighter with each thought of Garrison's last moments.

He still remembered his friend's face, lifeless under the collapsed scaffolding. Grief over losing his colleague and friend prevented him from feeling God's love and comfort. His bitterness had drowned out the heavenly whispers that now shouted in his mind. Garrison was gone, and with him, a piece of his soul had died.

"He's dead," Emmett choked out, a sob escaping his lips. "and before this is over, I still may lose my job."

The thought loomed insufferable, yet it paled in comparison to the truth that gnawed at him. Garrison had given everything—his time, his strength, his very life—for work that now felt hollow, meaningless in the wake of his sacrifice. The grief of the sense of loss and waste crushed Emmett's chest, a burden of grief too heavy to bear.

"Why?" The word tore from his throat, raw and bitter. He lifted his chin to the heavens. "Why didn't You save him, God? Why did You let this happen?"

His hands clenched around the blueprints resting on his lap—plans that once symbolized ambition, progress, his future. Now, they were nothing more than ink on paper, a cruel mockery of what should have been. With a sudden surge of anger, he shoved them aside. They fluttered to the ground like dying leaves, their intricate lines reduced to meaninglessness in the face of such loss.

King Solomon's words haunted him: Vanity. All is vanity.

His questions still reverberated in his mind, relentless, like a storm with no end. "Do You hear me, God?"

Then—a sweet whisper in the wind. A gentle breeze stirred his hair, soft as a mother's touch. Sunlight slipped through the branches of the great oak, dappling his face with warmth, a stark contrast to the cold despair that had taken root inside him.

And in that moment, he realized the truth. God hadn't taken Garrison. God hadn't abandoned him. No—God grieved with him. With all of them.

The realization settled deep, an ache both sharp and healing. How long had he nursed his anger, feeding it with his pain, directing it toward the only One who had never left? He had cursed heaven for its silence, blind to the truth that God had been weeping alongside him all along.

"Forgive me, God," he murmured, his voice cracking under the strain of his guilt. "My anger toward You has kept me from hearin' You, from findin' strength in You, from feelin' peace."

The words hung in the air, a fragile offering to the heavens. Inadequate against the enormity of his failure.

A sob rose in his throat, thick and unbidden. His fingers curled into his palms as he lifted his face to the sky.

"You didn't cause Garrison's death," he whispered, the words trembling on his lips. "You didn't take my friend. I—I'm so sorry, Lord. Sorry for blamin' You. For turnin' away in my anger. Forgive me."

The confession poured from him like a river breaking free of its dam, carrying with it the flotsam of bitterness, the jetsam of rage, the unbearable weight of guilt. His head dropped into his hands, his shoulders shaking as grief surged anew, but this time, it was different.

It wasn't simply sorrow—it was surrender. A desperate plea for mercy. "Please," he whispered, his voice barely more than breath. "Have mercy on me."

He glanced at the great oak standing firm above him, silent yet steadfast, its roots deep and unyielding. Under its branches, he understood—he had never been alone. And that truth, more than anything, would change him forever. If he allowed it to.

The sun dipped lower, casting long shadows across the ground. Emmett drew a deep breath, recognizing this new opportunity for what it was—his cue to rise from his despair. The world had not stopped turning, even if his own had come to a shuddering halt. Life pressed on, relentless and unforgiving, but now, resolve steeled his heart.

He would carry Garrison's memory with him, but without the chains of sorrow. His friend's life had meant more than his vocation or the sum of his earnings. Emmett would make sure his death hadn't been in vain. The fragility of life, the weight of responsibility—everything settled on his shoulders.

But for the first time, he did not shrink beneath it.

Yet, before he could move forward, he had to allow himself this moment—to bring an end to his mourning, to feel the full depths of his grief, and to let hope take root once more.

Beneath the sheltering arms of the oak, he whispered a last prayer, not of anger or despair, but of surrender. It was almost dark before he returned to his room in the Yacht House, spent, but at peace.

That night, as he lay in his bed, a calm he had not felt in weeks settled over him. And for the first time since the accident, Emmett slept without suffocating guilt pressing down on his chest.

And he dreamed.

A field stretched endlessly before him, golden and swaying in the gentle summer breeze. The scent of wildflowers carried on the air, warm and familiar. In the distance, laughter rang out—light and carefree, making his heart swell.

Garrison stood beneath a towering oak, his broad shoulders relaxed, his face radiant with joy. A small boy darted around him, giggling as he wove between the tall grasses, his curls bouncing with each step.

His son.

Garrison scooped the child into his arms, spinning him in circles, their laughter echoing through the open field. No burden, no sorrow—only love, pure and untainted.

Garrison turned to face Emmett, his smile steadfast. Silence conveyed the message clearly.

I am at peace. Do not grieve for me, my friend. Live!

Emmett reached out, as if he could touch the moment, hold on to it just a little longer. But the dream faded, and the golden light slipped away like sand through his fingers.

As he woke with the first rays of dawn filtering through the window, he did not feel the crushing loss. He felt hope.

The guilt that once consumed him—his relentless pursuit of justice, his need to expose Bruce, his desperate attempt to clear his name—no longer burned with the same obsession. The fire was still there, but it no longer threatened. Instead, he surrendered it, lifting his face to the heavens.

"Lord, it is Yours. The truth, the justice, the burden—I place it in Your hands."

The words were simple, but the act profound. The tight grip he had kept on his own plans, his own desperation, loosened. And in its place, peace flooded in—one that surpassed all understanding.

He would still seek the truth about the accident, about Bruce. He would still fight for justice. But he no longer carried it alone.

And above all, he prayed for protection—not only for himself, but for those who placed their trust in him. For his workers, honest men who deserved safety and fairness. For the men who followed him, believing in his integrity, even when the world cast doubts.

And for Madison.

An unfamiliar feeling settled in his chest at the thought of her—lighter, yet just as pressing. She had risked so much, faced so much, and still stood steadfast. A woman of quiet strength, of fierce determination. He wanted to protect her, to shield her from Bruce's wrath, from the dangers lurking beneath the surface.

And he would protect her still.

He loved her.

That realization humbled him. For the first time since the accident, he truly believed there was still life to be lived. And he would not waste it.

He rose to his feet, the morning light stretching across the floor, chasing away the darkness of the night. He dressed for the day, squared his shoulders, and took his first steps forward.

Not just toward justice, but to the life God called him to.

CHAPTER 21

It had been two days since Madison's altercation with Bruce and her promise to the detective to stay out of it, but now she and Thomas had everything in hand. Approaching the dock, she saw Emmett by the water instead of Thomas. He had been avoiding her for the past two weeks, but this morning, she wouldn't let him slip away.

She smiled in his direction, even though he couldn't see her yet. "Emmett."

He turned and let out a slow breath. "Madison."

She took a step closer. "Please stop avoiding me. This is no way to treat a friend."

The dim morning light cast shadows across his face, highlighting a confusing mix of worry—or was it peace—behind his eyes? "I don't know what to say."

Madison crossed her arms. "That's not true. You're still shutting me out, and I can't bear it. You're still pushing me away, but you've been acquitted."

Emmett shoved his hands deep into his pockets, growing frustration evident. "Madison, this isn't over yet, and I can't worry about your safety until it's settled."

She took another step forward. "Bruce didn't try to ruin your life—he's still putting our lives in danger, and he's out there, thinking he can get away with it. I must help."

Emmett clenched his jaw, his fists tightening as he tugged them from his pockets. "I'm just tryin' to protect you, lass. What do you want me to do? Walk into the sheriff's office with nothin' but my suspicions? That won't change a thing."

She exhaled slowly. "That's why Thomas and I are going to the authorities today. We'll give them everything we've gathered in the past few weeks. Hopefully, they'll take it seriously, Emmett, and we'll be free of this."

His expression held a stew of surprise, doubt, and perhaps a smidgen of hope, but still he shook his head. "Blathers! You foolish lass! What have you've been doin'? What if Bruce finds out you've been pokin' around? What if he—"

She reached for his hand, gripping it tightly. "Then we face it together."

Emmett stared at her, the loosening of his shoulders, release of his fists, indicating that the fight in him softened. For a long moment, he remained silent, the sound of the waves filling the space between them. Then, at last, he offered her a small nod, as if he had no more fight left in him.

"Aye," he murmured, his voice barely above a whisper. "Together."

Madison squeezed his hand, relief washing over her. It wasn't over yet. But for the first time in weeks, she felt like they weren't standing on opposite sides of the battle.

And that gave her hope.

Emmett motioned toward the Yacht House. "There's Thomas coming now. Please be careful, lass."

He slipped into his own skiff, his eyes brighter than she'd seen since the acquittal, and waved farewell.

She'd given him hope.

An hour later, Madison and Thomas climbed the steps to the courthouse, her heart pounding, the humid August air pressing thick against her. The past two weeks had been relentless—every free moment chasing whispers, collecting testimonies, and building a case strong enough to expose Bruce.

But even with Thomas by her side, the truth felt just out of reach. Today, that would change.

Madison tightened her grip on the stack of notes they had gathered. "Are you sure about this?"

Thomas met her gaze with resolve. "We have to be."

They had spent hours listening to the workers. Hearing murmurs of how Bruce ignored safety measures. How the men noted items disappearing from the construction site. How he dismissed Garrison's warnings. How his jealousy of Emmett twisted into evil, dark and dangerous.

She recorded every detail in a notebook, making sure everything was in order while Mrs. Boldt slept. The pieces of the puzzle were coming together, but they needed irrefutable evidence and still lacked it.

As they waited for the office to open, she prayed the authorities would take them seriously and finally discover the truth, and the detective wouldn't be vexed at her work.

Finally, the sheriff's office door opened, and Detective Fletcher faced them. "Come in."

The wooden floor of the sheriff's office creaked beneath her feet as she stepped forward, her hands gripping the notebook and bundle of notes she and Thomas had painstakingly gathered. The air inside was warm and heavy, filled with the scent of ink and leather-bound ledgers.

Detective Fletcher stood next to the sheriff, a broad-shouldered man with graying hair. He leaned forward, his gaze sharp and assessing as they explained everything thoroughly.

"You're saying Bruce Clawson had something to do with the accident?" The sheriff's voice was even, but Madison caught the flicker of surprise in his eyes.

"Yes." She forced herself to keep her voice steady. "We've spoken to several workers. The men say Bruce ignored safety precautions, dismissed warnings, and taunted Garrison just before the accident. It was intentional."

Thomas stepped in, placing their gathered testimonies on the desk. "He threatened Madison and me and some workers, too. He's reckless, Sheriff. More than reckless. People are afraid to speak up, but they know the truth. We're simply giving them a voice."

The sheriff's expression darkened as he flipped through the pages. Their words settled over the room like an approaching storm.

Madison watched his face, searching for any sign that he would take them seriously. Every second felt like an eternity.

Finally, the sheriff sighed, rubbing his chin. "These are serious accusations." He looked between them. "But accusations alone won't hold up. Do you have any real evidence? Proof that Bruce deliberately tampered with the scaffolding?"

Her heart sank. Testimonies were powerful, but they weren't enough. They needed more. She exchanged a glance with Thomas, her mind racing.

"We don't have it yet," she admitted, "but we will."

The sheriff tapped his fingers against the desk. Then he shook his head. "It's time for you to step away from this. We will officially reopen the case. Detective Fletcher and I will investigate this, but you need to be careful. If Bruce is as dangerous as you say, confronting him without proof could make things worse."

Detective Fletcher glared at her. "Yes. Stay out of it! Both of you."

Madison shivered, as if a cold wind accosted her. She had experienced the danger firsthand, the way Bruce carried himself with the confidence of a man who believed he was untouchable. But he wasn't.

She and Thomas had done all they could—now it was in the hands of the authorities. The weight of worry sat heavy on her chest, but she had to trust that justice would prevail.

She fell asleep that night praying just that.

The next morning, an urgent tapping on her bedroom window startled her. She rushed to open it, finding Thomas standing there, his expression jubilant.

"They found it," he said, breathless. "Everything. The saw that apparently cut the wooden beam Emmett found, the records of stolen supplies, even a notebook where Bruce foolishly kept track of it all. In a Dairy House office closet that the workers said Bruce frequented and kept locked."

Madison's heart pounded. She should've guessed. "Of course. Then they'll arrest him?"

Thomas hesitated. "They will, but there's a problem. We need to warn Emmett first."

Her stomach twisted. "Why?"

Thomas glanced over his shoulder before stepping closer. "Because Bruce is missing." His words slid out like an eel.

She gasped, throwing her hands up to her face. "Missing?"

Thomas nodded. "They checked his apartment this morning, and he was already gone. No one's seen him since last night."

A shiver ran down Madison's spine. If Bruce realized the authorities were onto him, he wouldn't merely disappear. He would strike first. And Emmett was his most likely target.

"We must find him. I'll be right out."

She threw on her clothes and shawl, combed her hair with her fingers and twisting it up as she hurried out the door. Her appearance didn't matter. And Anna would see to the missus at such a time as this.

She and Thomas rushed toward the docks, the morning mist clinging to the air. Emmett wasn't at the Yacht House—Thomas had checked—so they guessed he'd already be working at his castle office.

And if Bruce sought revenge, he would know that, too.

Madison's breath came in shallow gasps as they neared Boldt Castle. She spotted a worker and grabbed his arm. "Have you seen Emmett?"

The man shrugged. "Yes, he was headed toward his office about ten minutes ago."

Madison exchanged a glance with Thomas. "Let's go."

They took off running.

As they entered the castle, Madison's pulse thundered in her ears as she pushed forward, slipping into the dim interior.

She grabbed Thomas's arm. "We can't let Emmett face Bruce alone."

She wouldn't allow Emmett to think she didn't care about him.

It was time to end this.

~ ~ ~

Emmett sat at his wooden desk, his hands buried in his hair. The early morning light streamed through the castle window, casting long shadows as he scolded himself again and again. Why hadn't he noticed the discrepancies sooner?

The numbers had been right there in front of him—materials recorded as delivered, yet dwindling faster than they should. Little by little, the supplies disappeared into thin air.

It had to be Bruce. Who else had access? Who else had the opportunity? But proof. That was the problem.

No one reported him. No one had dared.

Emmett let out a frustrated breath and leaned back in his chair. He had spent the last two weeks searching for anything that tied Bruce to the missing supplies and Garrison's accident. He had come up empty-handed at every turn.

And now, Detective Fletcher expected a full assessment of the books and anything he uncovered. The two-and-a-half-hour inquiry the day before raised more questions, more concerns. The authorities were questioning Bruce, but they questioned him too, and that scared him. What if they didn't believe him?

What if Bruce found a way to twist everything back onto him?

Yes, just the week before, he had spoken with many of the men. Most played dumb, but their eyes sparked with fear. Why wouldn't they talk to him? Why wouldn't they be honest and tell him what they had seen or heard? Why was everyone silent?

Fear. It was fear. Bruce had them all under his thumb, and they feared what might happen to men who crossed him. He had seen it firsthand.

Emmett stood and paced, rubbing his chin as he recalled his conversations. The workers had been jittery, avoiding his gaze, shifting uncomfortably when he asked about Bruce.

First, he had spoken to Henry, an older man who had been working there for years. "Henry." Emmett pulled him aside while they stacked wood. "You've been here longer than most. You must've noticed something off with the supplies."

Henry's grip on the rope in his hands tightened. "Don't know what you're talkin' about."

Emmett narrowed his eyes. "Come now, Henry. Ye're smarter than that. We both know someone has been takin' things that don't belong to them."

Henry's face paled. He glanced around before shaking his head. "You don't want to be askin' these questions, Emmett."

"Aye, I do."

Henry let out a slow breath, his shoulders sagging. "Sir, you're a good foreman, and you mean well. But men who start pokin' around danger…" He trailed off, his voice barely above a whisper.

A chill crept up Emmett's spine. "What happened to Garrison wasn't an accident, was it?"

Henry shook his head vehemently. "I can't say."

"You mean you won't say."

Henry met his gaze, and Emmett knew. Knew Henry had seen something. Knew Bruce had made sure no one would talk.

"I got a family, Emmett," Henry whispered. "I can't afford to make enemies."

Emmett clenched his jaw, his hands tightening into fists.

Later that day, he approached young Will, one of the newer workers. Surely, Will, not yet fully under Bruce's influence, would be willing to talk.

"Will, can we speak?"

Will froze mid-step, his eyes darting nervously before nodding.

Emmett led him behind the storage shed, away from prying ears. "I need to know if ye've seen Bruce doin' anythin' suspicious. If he's been movin' materials that don't belong to him."

Will opened his mouth, then closed it again. He took a deep breath. "I…I don't know, sir."

Emmett sighed. "You know, lad. I can see it on your face."

Will bit his lip, then glanced over his shoulder as if expecting Bruce to appear from the shadows. "He…he told me to keep my head down. Said if I wanted to keep my job, I shouldn't ask questions."

Emmett's stomach dropped. "And if you didn't listen?"

Will hesitated, his throat bobbing as he swallowed hard. "He said accidents happen."

The threat turned thick, suffocating him, nauseating him, engulfing him. He had seen this kind of fear before, back home in Ireland, when men of power kept others in check through intimidation. The way Will's voice shook, the way Henry refused to meet his eyes—it was all too familiar.

Bruce had them all exactly where he wanted them.

Emmett exhaled sharply, rubbing a hand down his face. If no one talked, if no one dared stand against Bruce, then it was up to him. He had come up empty-handed at every turn. Until now.

The sheriff sent a note to the Yacht House early this morning disclosing they searched Bruce's apartment and a locked closet that Dairy House workers reported. And what they found was damning—receipts, records of stolen goods, even a saw that could have been used to tamper with the scaffolding.

He should have felt relieved. But instead, dread settled deep in his gut.

Bruce was gone, the note said. That meant one thing. He realized they were onto him. And if he was desperate, there was no telling what he would do.

Madison? Would he go after her? His blood ran cold at the very idea as he rose to go and find her.

A sudden noise snapped Emmett from his thoughts. A footstep. Slow, deliberate.

He stiffened, his hand moving toward the drawer where he kept a small hammer—nothing much, but enough if things went south.

Then, a voice. Low. Dangerous. "I was wondering if you'd figure it out."

Emmett turned, his blood running cold.

Bruce stood in the doorway, eyes dark, a cruel smirk twisting his face.

Emmett rose slowly, his muscles coiled. "You've got nowhere left to run, Bruce."

Bruce chuckled, shaking his head. "Maybe. But that doesn't mean I'll go down alone."

The door behind him creaked, and Emmett caught the faintest movement—Madison. Thomas. They had come. A mixture of fear and hope flared in his chest. He wasn't alone in this fight.

But now, they were in danger, too.

Emmett held his ground, his fists clenched as Bruce took a slow, deliberate step forward. The man's smirk was a mask, but Emmett noted the flicker of fear behind his eyes.

Bruce had lost control.

Before the man could say another word, the door creaked open, and Madison and Thomas stepped in. Madison's eyes locked onto Emmett's with silent determination, while Thomas and she moved to his side.

Bruce scoffed. "Ah, of course. The lot of you, always sticking together, always poking your noses where they don't belong." He chuckled darkly, shaking his head. "And for what? You think you've won?"

Madison lifted her chin. "We don't think. We know."

Bruce's smirk faltered.

Thomas stood straighter, his voice steady. "The authorities searched your apartment and the locked closet in the Dairy House. They found the receipts, the stolen goods records, the saw."

For the first time, Bruce hesitated. A muscle in his jaw twitched, and his fingers curled into fists. The fight drained from him, but pride was a stubborn thing. "You don't know what you're talking about," he growled. "None of you."

Emmett stepped closer, his voice low but firm. "Then say it yourself. Tell us why you did it."

Bruce's eyes darted between them, the gravity of his situation pressing in. His breath came quick.

He let out a bitter laugh. "What difference does it make?"

His shoulders slumped, the bravado cracking. "Fine. I took the supplies, sold 'em off. No one was paying attention, no one cared—except you."

Emmett stiffened. "That's why you tampered with the scaffolding? That's why Garrison is dead?"

Bruce exhaled through his nose, his smirk returning—though now it was hollow. "That was just supposed to be a warning. Thought if I rattled things a bit, made sure you knew who was in charge, you'd back off." His eyes darkened. "Didn't mean for Garrison to—not that it matters now."

Emmett's jaw tightened. "Aye, it matters." His voice was thick with restrained anger. "It matters to the man who lost his life. To his grieving family. To the workers you scared into silence. To every person you put in danger for your own greed."

Bruce opened his mouth to retort, but before he could, heavy footsteps echoed outside.
The door swung open.

Detective Fletcher and Sheriff Donnelly joined them, their expressions grim. The sheriff's sharp gaze locked onto Bruce. "That's enough."

Bruce froze.

The detective's voice was calm, but cold. "We heard everything."

Madison let out a breath, her hand brushing against Emmett's.

Sheriff Donnelly reached for his cuffs. "Bruce Clawson, you're under arrest."

Bruce didn't fight. He didn't argue. His shoulders sagged as the responsibility for his crimes finally settled on him.

As the sheriff secured the cuffs and led him toward the door, Detective Fletcher turned to the trio. "You did well. And you were right."

Emmett nodded, the tightness in his chest finally loosening. Justice was served.

As the sheriff escorted Bruce out, Madison turned to Emmett, relief and exhaustion in her eyes. "It's over."

Emmett exhaled deeply, his gaze softening as he looked at her. "Aye, lass. Thanks to you and Thomas."

Thomas clapped Emmett on the shoulder. "And now, maybe you can finally get back to work."

A small, tired smile touched Emmett's lips. For the first time in a long while, he felt hope.

And that was enough.

For now.

CHAPTER 22

The morning sun glowed over the veranda, splattering on the wooden floorboards with a warming light. A gentle breeze carried the scent of fresh flowers from the garden, mingling with the soft murmur of waves against the island's rocky shore.

Madison adjusted the cushions behind Mrs. Boldt's back, ensuring her comfort as the older woman sighed contentedly. It was the first time in many days that the missus had been outside, and Madison silently rejoiced.

Mr. Boldt, seated beside his wife, reached for her hand, giving it a tender squeeze. The quiet intimacy of the moment made Madison's heart ache with longing—for family, for love, for what felt out of her reach.

"You've been a great help to us, Madison." Mr. Boldt's deep voice carried both warmth and gratitude. "And not just with my wife." He turned to face her, his sharp eyes softening. "I must admit, I never expected you to uncover such a tangled web of deceit. Clawson's sabotage, the lies…I'm still reeling from it."

She lowered her gaze, hands folded neatly in front of her. "I only did what was right, sir. I couldn't stand by and let him tarnish what you've built—what you and Mrs. Boldt have poured your hearts into."

Mr. Boldt exhaled, rubbing his chin, his eyes half closed as if pondering the world's greatest dilemmas. But that was his way. Everything was a matter to consider and every problem his to solve. "Still, I worry about you. That was dangerous work. We did not know you used your free time for this." He gave her a knowing look. "Perhaps I've underestimated you."

She gave a small, shy smile. "I did what needed to be done."

Mrs. Boldt, her voice gentle but firm, chimed in. "She's more than a lady's maid, George. She's family."

Madison blinked rapidly, willing away the sudden rush of emotion threatening to surface.

Family.

The word wrapped around her like a warm embrace, filling a part of her that had felt hollow for so long.

Mr. Boldt nodded. "Indeed." He leaned forward, his expression kind but serious. "Madison, if ever you find yourself in trouble, if you ever need anything—you must come to us. You've proven your loyalty a hundred times over, and we will do the same for you."

The sincerity in his voice almost undid her. Swallowing the lump in her throat, she forced a smile and clasped her hands together. "Thank you, Mr. Boldt. That means more than I can say."

Mrs. Boldt reached out, patting Madison's arm gently. "Now, my dear, enough of this serious talk. Have a seat."

Madison smiled, grateful for the change in subject. As she settled into her chair beside them, a sense of belonging unlike anything she'd known in years filled her with peace and joy.

Perhaps, just perhaps, she wasn't as alone as she once thought.

But what about Emmett?

Mr. and Mrs. Boldt discussed their upcoming return to New York City. Though she had spent the last decade in their service as Mrs. Boldt's lady's maid, and the last seven traveling with them between the Thousand Islands and the city, there was always something bittersweet about leaving the Thousand Islands behind.

"I suppose it's time we return to the city." Mrs. Boldt ran her fingers along the armrest of her chair. "The city doctor will know how to help me recover better, and you have your affairs to tend to at the Waldorf-Astoria."

Mr. Boldt nodded. "Yes, dear, and we'll see the children again—George Junior, Clover, and of course, our sweet pup, Buster Brown. That should do you good."

A small, genuine smile touched Mrs. Boldt's lips. "Yes, I miss them." Then, she glanced at her. "And you, my dear? Are you ready to return?"

Madison hesitated, looking out over the rippling water that stretched to the horizon. "New York City is grand, but there's nothing quite like the Thousand Islands. The stillness, the way the light dances on the water at dawn—it's a beauty you can't find in the city."

Mrs. Boldt reached for her hand, giving it a gentle squeeze. "I know what you mean. There's a peace here that even the finest of city luxuries can't replace."

Mr. Boldt chuckled. "And yet, you never fail to remind me how much you enjoy the comforts of home once we arrive back in the city."

Mrs. Boldt gave a soft laugh. "That's true, isn't it?" She sighed, wistful. "Still, I'll miss the river and the castle. The quiet."

Madison smiled but kept her thoughts to herself. She would miss it, too—the scent of pine carried by the wind, the sound of water lapping against the shore, the feeling of belonging to a world untouched by time.

And Emmett.

"New York will be waiting for us." Mr. Boldt placed a reassuring hand over his wife's. "But we'll return to our Thousand

Islands paradise before you know it. And more of the castle will be complete."

Madison nodded. For now, she would simply enjoy these final days in the islands, soaking in every golden sunrise before the towering city skyline took its place.

With Mr. Boldt tending to his wife, Madison found herself with several hours of freedom. The realization they would leave in a few days weighed on her, and there was only one place she wished to go—Heart Island. And one person she wanted to see—Emmett.

She hurried down to the dock, where Thomas busily secured his boat, whistling a cheerful tune.

"Well now, look who's come for a ride." His sun-kissed face broke into a wide grin. "Thought you'd be too busy tending to the Boldts to visit a boatman like me."

She laughed. "How could I forget, Thomas? Especially after our adventures."

He chuckled as he helped her into the boat. "Ah yes, sneaking around, uncovering secrets, almost getting ourselves into trouble. Good times, eh?"

She shook her head with a smile. "You might call it that. I'm not sure I would."

As the boat cut across the shimmering water, the wind played with the loose strands of her hair, and she took a deep breath, etching the moment into her memory. The castle on Heart Island loomed in the distance, its grandeur growing day by day, yet things were different now. Soon, everything would change.

"So, what brings you out here?" Thomas guided the boat toward the dock. "Just takin' in the sights one last time before you're off to that big ol' city again?"

She hesitated before nodding. "Yes. We leave soon." The words felt heavy, as if saying them made their departure real.

He gave her a knowing glance. "And you're here to see *him*?"

She shot him a look, but his grin only widened.

"Ah, don't be giving me that." He nodded toward their destination. "A man would have to be blind not to notice the way you and Emmett look at each other."

She turned her gaze to the castle, warmth creeping into her cheeks. She didn't have a proper answer to that, so she simply said, "Thank you for the ride, Thomas."

He chuckled. "Anytime, friend."

She stepped onto the dock and took a steadying breath. She wished she knew what she would say to Emmett—perhaps nothing. But she needed to see him before she left.

With her heart pounding harder than she'd like, she made her way to his office. Would her arrival surprise him? Would he share his feelings?

Or would this simply be goodbye?

~ ~ ~

For the third time that morning, Emmett read the note from Detective Fletcher, letting the words sink in once more. *After thorough investigation, we have confirmed that Bruce was the perpetrator behind the scaffolding sabotage. He acted out of jealousy and ambition, endangering the lives of his fellow workers. I expect that the sentencing will be swift and harsh.*

He exhaled sharply, scratching his chin. Justice would be served at last. But despite the words' relief, he couldn't shake the lingering cost—what if Madison had been hurt? The thought tightened his chest.

A soft knock at the door pulled him from his thoughts. That feminine knock. Hers.

He stood and crossed the room in three quick strides, opening the door to find Madison standing there, the light breeze catching her hair.

"Madison." He beamed at her. "Come in."

She hesitated, glancing past him toward the open window. "Actually…would you walk with me? Just for a little while?"

He didn't even need to think about it. "Aye, of course."

Together, they made their way down the winding path toward Alster Tower, the sunlight casting golden patterns through the trees, as if lighting their way.

After a moment, Emmett spoke. "I have news." He pulled the folded letter from his pocket, offering it to her.

"It's over, Madison. Detective Fletcher confirmed it—Bruce is guilty. The sabotage, the danger…it was his doing. He let his jealousy and ambition turn into evil deeds, and now he'll face the consequences."

Madison's steps slowed as she read the note, her brows furrowing before her shoulders relaxed. "It's finally over, then." Her voice was quiet, as if she needed to say the words aloud to believe them.

"Aye." Emmett studied her face, searching for any sign of relief. "You need worry no more."

She let out a slow breath and turned to him. "It's strange, isn't it? Knowing the danger has passed. I should feel nothing but relief, and yet…"

She trailed off, folding the note carefully.

"And yet?"

She bit her lip before answering. "I suppose it's just the weight of it all. So much has happened, Emmett. It's not just Bruce—it's everything. The Boldts are leaving soon, and so am I. And I…" She shook her head, as if brushing away a thought she didn't dare voice.

Emmett's chest tightened. He knew this moment would come. She belonged to the Boldts' world, a world of fine city streets and elegant homes. And he—he belonged to the islands, to the land, to the quiet rhythm of life here.

Still, he couldn't ignore the ache in his heart. "Blathers, lass, you don't have to leave." His voice was lower, rougher than he intended.

Madison turned to him, eyes searching his. "Emmett…"

"No, hear me out." He stepped closer. "I know you have responsibilities, and I know your life is in the city. But if there's any part of you that wants to stay—" He broke off, shaking his head. "I don't want to say goodbye to you, Madison."

Her breath hitched, and for a long moment, neither spoke.

Then, just when he feared she would turn away, she reached for his hand. "I don't want to say goodbye either."

The wind rustled through the trees, the lapping of the waves a steady heartbeat against the shore. He held his breath, waiting, hoping. But after a long silence, she finally shook her head, her expression filled with sorrow.

"I can't leave Mrs. Boldt," she said softly. "She's in poor health, and it's getting worse by the day. I fear what might happen if I'm not there to care for her."

She exhaled, her fingers trembling slightly as she reached up, brushing aside a strand of his hair and tracing the scar over his left eye.

"And yet," she continued, her voice barely above a whisper, "I feel as you do, Emmett." Her eyes glistened as she looked up at him. "We've had a summer together, you and I, and oh, how I wish it could last forever. But I must go."

His angst danced a jig on her frayed emotions, searching for the right words, something to hold onto—anything that kept them from slipping into a final goodbye.

He reached for her hands, holding them between his own, rough and calloused from years of labor. "I understand, Madison. You have a duty, and I'd never ask you to abandon it. But this—" He gestured in the space between them, his grip tightening ever so slightly. "I can't just let you go."

As the wind rustled through the trees, carrying the crisp scent of the river, Madison hesitated. "Emmett, I—I don't know how this could ever truly work."

He frowned, his brow creasing. "What do you mean?"

She inhaled deeply. Was she gathering her courage? Did a possible future together frighten her as much as did him? Yet, the notion of not sharing their remaining years was inconceivable to him.

Tears welled in her eyes. "You're a foreman, a respected man here. And not just any foreman—you're trusted by Mr. Boldt himself. There will be more opportunities for you in the days ahead, maybe even a future far grander than you've imagined."

She lowered her gaze, her fingers twisting the fabric of her skirt. "And I am…I am just a maid. A lady's maid, yes, but nothing more. What can I offer you, Emmett? Nothing but a love that may not be enough in the eyes of the world. That may bring you regret."

Silence stretched between them, thick with unsaid things.

Then, he let out a low breath, stepping closer, his rough, calloused hands cupping her face. "Don't ever say that again, Madison Murray." His voice was rough with emotion. "Not to me, not to anyone."

She blinked up at him, startled.

"I don't care about stations or titles. You think I'm concerned about climbing some ladder, about rubbing elbows with men in fine suits? You think I think you less because you're in service? I've spent my whole life working with my hands, earning my place through sweat and skill, and so have you." His thumb brushed lightly over her cheek. "But none of it—none of it—means a thing if you're not beside me."

Madison let out a tiny sigh.

"You offer me nothing?" He let out a short, incredulous laugh. "Madison, you're the bravest woman I know. You've got more heart, more fire, than any lady in silk and lace. You see people—not for what they have, but for who they are. And if you think I'd trade that for what others think about status and stations, then you don't know me at all."

Tears ran down her cheeks. "Emmett…"

"I love you, Madison." He brushed the tears away with his thumb and spoke his heart from that strong, secret place. One that would never back down. Never walk away. Never stop protecting her. "And not in spite of who you are—but because of it."

She pressed a trembling hand over his. "I love you, too."

His heart pounded, causing his breath to shudder. He lowered his forehead to hers. "We'll find our way," he whispered. "Together."

He held her close, the warmth of her finally unfreezing that dark corner he'd hidden for so long. He never wanted to let go. The gentle rise and fall of her breath against him, the way she fit so perfectly against his chest—it all stirred life deep inside him, love he could no longer deny.

As he pulled back to look at her, his gaze drifted downward, catching the glint of the delicate chain around her neck. A simple, Irish pendant rested against the fabric of her shirtwaist. His breath hitched. He recognized that necklace.

His mother had one just like it—a cherished heirloom she carried from Ireland, passed down through generations. His fingers instinctively brushed over the pendant, a sense of familiarity wrapping around him like a memory brought to life.

Madison looked up at him, her cobalt eyes filled with questions. "What is it?"

His fingers lingered over the pendant before finally meeting her gaze. "My mother had one like this." He brushed aside moisture clouding his vision. "She used to tell me it signified faith, hope, and love, and it would bring protection to the one who wore it." His thumb traced the delicate design. "Seeing it on you…it only makes me realize how much I want you to be my family."

Madison's lips parted, her breath catching. "Emmett…"

He reached up, brushing a loose strand of hair from her face, his touch tender as if he handled a newly hatched chick. "I love you."

Please, God, let her hear the conviction in my heart.

He dropped his hands to his side, giving her space to make up her own mind. "And I'll wait an eternity for you if I must."

The moment stretched between them, heavy with emotion.

Then, slowly—tentatively—he leaned in, his lips barely grazing hers in the softest, most reverent kiss. Not hurried or desperate, but a promise. One whispered in the language of love that needed no words.

When he pulled back, his forehead rested against hers, their breaths mingling in the river breeze.

Madison's fingers curled into the fabric of his shirt. "I don't want you to wait forever."

Hope flickered in his chest. "Then tell me what to do, my love."

Fireflies twinkled in her eyes, lighting the way to his heart. "Just…wait for me a little while longer." Emotion dripped thick in her voice.

He nodded, pressing another kiss to her forehead. "For you? Always."

And, under the vast, endless sky, no matter where life took them, she would find her way back to him. Her lips parted as if she wanted to speak, but no words came.

"Will you write to me?" His gaze never left hers. "Let us carry on a courtship through letters until you return next summer?"

Madison let out a soft, breathy laugh, though her eyes were still misty. "A courtship through letters?"

He grinned, tilting his head. "Aye. I'd reckon I'm a fair hand at writin'."

She bit her lip, considering.

Then, a small nod, "Yes. Yes, I'd like that."

Relief flooded through him. He lifted her hands to his lips, pressing a kiss to her knuckles, lingering a moment longer than necessary. "Then we'll not say goodbye. Just farewell for now."

Madison blinked rapidly and nodded. "Farewell for now."

The wind stirred around them, carrying the scent of the river, the whisper of leaves, the echoes of a summer neither would forget. And as Madison turned to leave, Emmett let her go—knowing that, in time, the words they wrote to each other would bridge the distance between them.

Because some things—some loves—were worth waiting for.

CHAPTER 23

Autumn 1903

For Madison, autumn in New York City had always been a season of overwhelming beauty, a symphony of golds and reds, crisp air, and the scent of fallen leaves. But this year, was also a season of longing.

Every week, a letter arrived, written in Emmett's familiar penmanship. She recognized his handwriting before she even unfolded the paper, her heart fluttering as she traced her fingers over the seal, savoring the moment before she drank in his words.

My dearest Madison,

The river is quieter without you. The trees are turning, but none are so lovely as the memory of you standing beneath them. I miss you, lass. The islands feel emptier than they should. I look toward the dock each morning, expecting to see you, but you are not there. I remind myself that you will return, and until then, I will write.

Yours, always, Emmett.

The first letter made her weep, as she pressed it to her chest, curled up by her small window overlooking the city streets. How was it possible to feel both cherished and utterly sad all at once?

And then another arrived. And another. Each letter a lifeline. A whispered promise across the miles.

...I'm working hard on the castle, but without you here, it lacks warmth. Thomas keeps asking after you—says he never had so much fun ferrying anyone about. I told him to stop teasing, but you know Thomas. He doesn't listen. I laughed despite myself, but it isn't the same. Nothing is the same without you, Madison....

She clutched each letter, reading them over and over, memorizing his words, feeling his love in every stroke of ink. Emmett painted word pictures for her, describing the mists, whispering wind, and growing castle.

...The leaves are ablaze with color now, Madison. It's as if the entire Thousand Islands are aflame with gold and crimson, yet even in its splendor, they pales compared to the way your eyes light up when you smile. I wonder—are the leaves in the city as brilliant? Do they remind you of the river? Of me?

Yours, always, Emmett

She answered each letter with the same intensity, pouring her heart into every word, telling him how the city felt lonelier despite its crowds, how she missed the scent of the river, the sound of his voice.

Emmett, my dearest,

I see the changing leaves from my window, but I suspect they are not like the ones in the Thousand Islands. There, the air smelled of earth and water. The wind carried secrets through the pines. Here, carriages line the streets. Iron fences cage the trees. I long for the open sky. I long for the river. I long for you….

Despite missing Emmett and the Thousand Islands, she leaned into her mission. Mrs. Boldt needed her, and duty kept her bound to the city. But every letter, every word, made it more difficult to stay.

The days stretched on, golden leaves giving way to stormy days as autumn crept toward winter. Yet, her heart ached for something—someone—more. Dipping her pen into ink, she let out a quiet sigh and wrote another missive.

Dearest Emmett,

New York is even more alive with color. Central Park is filled with autumn leaves, and I watch them flutter from my window, but I'm sure it's not the same as standing by the river, watching the wind carry them across the water. The city is beautiful, but its fast pace makes people miss its natural wonders. Like the way light dances through the trees. Or how the water shimmers like glass.

I miss the quiet. I miss waves against the dock, the pines whispering when the wind moves through them. I miss the evenings when the sky turns to fire, and the world slows down, even if just for a moment. Yet, most of all, I miss you, Emmett.

Now, please tell me, what have you been working on?
Forever yours, Madison

She sealed the letter, pressing it to her lips for a moment before sending it off, knowing she would wait with bated breath for his reply. A week later, it arrived, thick with his familiar, steady handwriting.

My love,

The island is ablaze in gold. The river catches the light like a thousand diamonds. The mornings are colder now, and I wake to mist rolling over the water, settling around the castle like something out of a dream. It reminds me of the morning we walked to Alster

Tower together. Do you remember? You were shivering, and I offered you my coat, though you insisted you weren't cold. I knew better, of course...

Madison smiled, tracing the words with her fingertips as she continued reading.

At the castle, we installed the Great Hall window this week, artistically etched with the Boldt family crest. It is grand—heart-shaped, like the island itself, catching the light as the sun rises. It is a beautiful thing, Madison, but do you know what I thought of when I saw it lifted into place? You.

A heart, standing proud over this place, a symbol of love and devotion. And within it, a stag, strong and noble—a reminder of Mr. Boldt's heritage, but also a symbol of steadfastness. Seeing it there made me think of you, of the way you love so deeply, the way you have cared for Mrs. Boldt with such loyalty, and the way you have become part of this place, as much as the river itself.

You may be in New York City now, but your heart is here. Just as mine is with you. Write to me soon, my love. I count the days until you return.

Yours, always, Emmett

Madison clutched the letter in her hands, her breath shaky, her heart aching. How much longer could she bear to be apart from him? The city was beautiful. The Boldts needed her. But she had never felt the pull of love so strongly.

The light flickered beside her as Madison sat at her writing desk, her quill poised over the crisp parchment. She hesitated, staring at the blank page, her thoughts heavy with the weight of her responsibilities.

Louise Boldt had always been a force of nature—a woman of grace and strength—but now, as the weeks stretched on, Madison watched her seesaw between hope and despair.

Some days, the missus seemed brighter, her laughter returning, her energy restored. And then, without warning, she slipped into exhaustion, her body betraying her, the vitality dimming from her eyes. As if her reserves were depleted.

Madison had long learned to hope in quiet, measured ways. The doctors remained optimistic, as did Mr. Boldt and the children. George Junior and Clover spoke of their mother's recovery with assurance, as though sheer willpower and love alone could mend a failing heart.

And perhaps, for their sake, Madison believed it, too. But deep down, she feared the truth was different.

She dipped her quill into the ink, drawing a deep breath before she wrote.

Dearest Emmett,

Tonight, I find myself longing for the quiet of the Thousand Islands more than ever. The city is bustling as always, preparing for the holiday season, and yet my heart feels burdened beneath the noise. I cannot tell you how much your letters mean to me. Each word carries me back to the place I love, to you. Your grasp of the language is far beyond what you give yourself credit for—your words are as strong and steady as the hands that built so much of Boldt Castle. I cherish every single one.

Things here...they are difficult. Mrs. Boldt is holding on, though I fear she is slipping further from us. Some days, she is as bright as ever, speaking of springtime plans, of returning to the islands when the ice melts. And other days, she is weak, struggling even to sit up in bed. Mr. Boldt refuses to accept anything but her recovery. So do the children. And I pray they are right. But Emmett, I see it in her eyes. I see exhaustion that never quite leaves.

What will become of me, I wonder? My mission has always been to serve, to care for her. And if she—

She stopped, pressing her fingers to her lips, steadying the shake in her hands. She could not write those words. She would not.

After a moment, she continued.

I do not wish to think of such things just now. Instead, tell me more about the castle. What else have you added? Tell me of the island, of the river, of the way the world changes there in winter. I long to hear it from you. Until then, I will hold on to your words, as I hold on to hope.

Yours, always, Madison

As she folded the letter and sealed it, she let out a quiet sigh. She had never felt so pulled in two directions before—torn between the duty she had chosen and the love that chose her.

And as she stared out the window, the city glowing below her, she could not help but wonder—how long would she have to wait before her heart found its way home?

~ ~ ~

Emmett dipped his quill into the ink. The parchment before him sat empty, but his heart was full—too full. Eloquence had never been his greatest strength, but on paper, where he could take his time, he could say what pressed heavy on his soul.

He exhaled, leaning back in his chair for a moment, staring at the letter he'd received from Madison just days before. He had read it numerous times now. He smoothed the sheet where his calloused hands had worn the folds.

Each letter from her brought hope for a future. Each missive meant the time until they were together again drew shorter.

Setting his jaw, he dipped the quill again and let his heart spill onto the page.

My love,

The wind's whispering your name again. I hear it when I step outside before dawn, when the river is still but for the mist dancing on its surface. I hear it when the gulls call and even when Thomas goes on about some nonsense, laughing at his own jokes.

But it's empty here without you.

The castle is coming along just fine. The Boldt crest is a fine thing, but all I could think as we hoisted it up was how I wished you could've seen it first, standing beside me, your eyes filled with that wonder I love so much.

Every day, I dream of you. Of us. A future where we aren't living in letters and I'm not watching the dock like a fool, waiting for a ghost that won't come till spring.

I see a life where the first thing I hear each day is your voice.

Can you see it too, my love? Tell me you do. Tell me this waiting won't last forever.

Yours, always, Emmett

He set the quill down, rubbing at his bleary eyes. The words on the page felt like his soul spilled out before him. He had never been a man of grand gestures, never one to spout poetry. But for her, he'd found there was no end to what he wished he could say.

Weeks later, as he sat by the fire, he smirked to himself, shaking his head as he glanced at the well-worn Webster's Dictionary lying open beside him. He never thought he'd see the day when he'd pore over a book of words just to impress a woman.

Truth was, he owed most of his eloquence to Thomas, who, for all his teasing, had become a staunch friend. Their shared experiences over the summer—the danger, the secrecy, the risks—bonded them in a way neither expected. But more than that, Thomas had taken a great interest in Emmett's *courting abilities* as he called them.

With a chuckle, Emmett dipped his quill and wrote.

My dearest Madison,

You'll be glad to know that I've not been left to my own devices in this courtship of ours. No, I've got myself a proper advisor—and you'll never guess who. Thomas, of all people, has decided it's his duty to see that I don't make a fool of myself with you.

So, between Thomas and the Webster's Dictionary I bought just for this purpose, I reckon I've learned a thing or two. And if my words seem grander than before, you can thank the fine art of looking them up when I don't quite know if I'm saying things properly. But no amount of polished words can make the truth any truer—I love you. And I don't need a book of words to tell me you're the only woman I'll ever want.

Now, tell me, love—how are things there? Is the missus any better? And are you still thinking of the islands as much as I hope you are?

Yours, always, Emmett

With a satisfied nod, he folded the letter, sealing it with care. This waiting, this longing—it was an unfamiliar pain. But if each letter carried her closer to him, then he could endure it.

Two weeks later, before joining Thomas for a fine Thanksgiving meal at the Thousand Islands House hotel, Emmett dropped yet another letter into the post.

My dearest Madison,

Happy Thanksgiving, darling! I'm most thankful for you. Tell me, my love, do you still see the Thousand Islands when you close your eyes at night? Do you still dream of making this your home? I sure hope so.

And now, for news. The castle grows grander by the day, and though the work keeps my hands busy, it's the thoughts of you that keep my heart steady. We've been working on the Ballroom molding this week—Lord, you should see it, lass. It's a beauty, intricate and grand, the kind of work that makes a man stop and stare just to take it in. The ceiling's only half in place for now, but soon enough, it'll stretch across the entire room like a masterpiece overhead. And when I stand in the middle of it, I can't help but picture you there, Madison.

But I'll tell you a secret—I don't need to imagine you in finery, with chandeliers glowing overhead and a grand orchestra playing a waltz. I'd take you just as you are, standing by the river, your hair undone by the wind, laughing at something only you find funny. That's the woman I see, the one I dream of.

And there's something else that might interest you—the Otis hydraulic elevator in the Great Hall. Did you ever get to see it? You'd be surprised to see how we've been using it for carrying materials up and down, powered by water from a tank on the castle's roof—impressive, eh? I miss you, darling.

Yours, always, Emmett

Three weeks later, he'd gone to town for a Christmas concert, and he stopped by the post.

"From *her*," The postmaster tossed him an amused wink, and Emmett's cheeks burned.

That night, he responded to her.

My dearest Madison,

Ah, my love, how I wish I were with you this Christmas. To love and support you. To celebrate the Savior with you. Yet, I feel the weight in your words, the sorrow between the lines, and I wish more than anything I could be there with you, holding your hand through it all. I know how deeply you care for Mrs. Boldt, how you've spent your days tending to her, hoping and praying she'll regain her strength.

But Madison, you're stronger than you think. You've always been. And though I can't be there in the way I wish I could—I'm praying for you every day. For you, for Mrs. Boldt, for strength when yours feels like it's run dry. I ask the Lord to give you comfort, to fill your heart with peace even in the unknown. And I ask Him to bring you back to me when the time is right.

Still, I miss you something fierce. Every day, I wake up and wonder how many more mornings will pass before I see your face again, before I hear your laugh.

And yet, I struggle with myself, wondering if I'm doing enough, if there's any way I can help you when I'm so far away. I wish I could take the burden from you, ease your worry, and stand beside you when you need someone to lean on. But all I have are my words, my prayers, and the promise I'll be here when you return.

Take heart, my love. You are not alone, even when it feels like it. And when you find yourself weary, close your eyes and remember—there's a man here who loves you beyond reason, standing by the river, watching the horizon, waiting for the day he'll see you walking toward him once more. And there's a God Who already knows His good plans for you. Rest in our love.

Yours, always, Emmett

He folded the letter and exhaled slowly, his heart aching with the distance between them. He wished he could do more—be more. But for now, his words, his prayers, and his love would have to carry them through.

And until the day she returned, he would keep watching the river, waiting for her.

CHAPTER 24

January 7, 1904

Madison stood at the far end of Mrs. Boldt's grand yet solemn room, her hands clasped tightly at her waist, her breath shallow. The heavy velvet drapes muffled the bustling sounds of New York City beyond the tall windows, enclosing them in an eerie silence.

But the only noise that mattered now was the ragged breathing of Louise Boldt, the woman who had been Madison's world these past ten years.

Mrs. Boldt lay motionless in her grand bed, her frail frame barely visible beneath the ivory coverlet. Her once bright and commanding eyes had faded, her delicate hands now lifeless on the silk sheets.

Madison swallowed back the lump in her throat as Mr. Boldt devotedly knelt at his wife's side, his strong shoulders trembling with grief. George Junior and Clover clung to each other, their silent tears a testimony to their love for their mother.

Madison wanted to help the family, but she couldn't. Her station wouldn't allow it. Tears blurred her vision as the weight of grief settled on her chest, threatening to consume her.

This woman—so kind, so full of grace—took her last breath.

The room fell into a hushed ache broken only by Clover's weeping.

Mrs. Boldt had been Madison's life's work. She had found purpose in serving her, in offering comfort, in meeting her every need.

But now…

…Now, her mission was over.

She sniffed back tears, her fingers tightening around the embroidered handkerchief Mrs. Boldt had given her. Her employer, her friend, was gone. The family distraught. How could she help them? What could she do?

The future loomed ahead like a dense fog, uncertain and terrifying.

Her heart clenched at the realization—once her work here was concluded, she no longer had a place. Despite the Boldts' grand words about her being family, the truth overwhelmed her. Oh, yes, she'd be kept on while the family grieved. Through the funeral. And the work afterwards of sorting and disposing of Mrs. Boldt's personal items. All the work of a lady's maid must continue—in life and in death.

Yet, she was no fool. Without her position as Mrs. Boldt's maid, there was nothing tying her to this grand home, to this family. Serving her missus diligently, building this life as she sustained another's would come to an end.

But soon—far too soon—she'd find herself alone once more, adrift like she had been the day she stepped off the ship from Ireland, carrying only a satchel and the unbearable weight of loss. For the first time in years, Madison questioned everything. Her purpose. Her path. Her existence.

And where did Emmett fit into this? She closed her eyes, whispering a silent prayer for guidance. And in that still moment, with grief pressing in from all sides, a quiet resolve formed.

She would not let this be the end of her story. She would find her way. But to where—only God knew.

The room, once filled with the gentle presence of Mrs. Boldt, now felt hollow, as though her spirit had been the very heartbeat of this house. And now that heart had stopped. Just like her father, her brother, her mother, her aunt. One by one, they all left—her family, her aunt, and now Mrs. Boldt.

A shiver ran down her spine. Would Emmett be next?

She had dared to love again, dared to let her heart open to the warmth of his Irish lilt, the kindness in his steady gaze. But what if loving him meant losing him? Was she cursed? Destined to watch those she cared for disappear, taken by sickness, by the cruel hand of fate?

Her jaw clenched, her grief twisting into something darker—anger. If God was good, if He was truly loving, why did He take everyone she cared about? What kind of Father left His child alone?

She bit her lip hard, staring at the flickering candle beside Mrs. Boldt's bedside as the attending physician covered her head with the silk sheet. The flame danced, fragile yet steady, mocking the turmoil in her soul.

How could she trust a God who allowed this?

She had prayed for Mrs. Boldt to recover. She pleaded. Begged. And yet, the answer was silence. And now this.

Tears burned her eyes, and she turned away, pressing a hand to her stomach to keep herself from shaking. Maybe faith wasn't enough. Maybe love wasn't enough. Maybe it was safer not to love at all.

The thought sent a deep ache through her, but she pushed back the whisper.

No! This wasn't God's fault.

Madison slipped out of the room, grabbed her shawl, and stepped into the bitter January air, the wind biting through the thin fabric of her uniform. The world beyond the Boldt home in New York City bustled as if nothing had changed—as if the woman who had been her world hadn't just drawn her last breath. Carriages clattered over cobblestones, street vendors called out their wares, and pedestrians hurried past, wrapped in furs against the cold.

But all Madison heard was the silence of grief. The towering buildings, the relentless energy of the city, the sheer weight of knowing she no longer belonged here, it suffocated her.

She longed for the Thousand Islands, for the peace of the river, the solace of wide-open space and crisp, clean air.

And Emmett.

She stepped back inside the Boldt home and shook off the chill. She turned down the dimly lit corridor leading to her quarters when a voice stopped her.

"Madison." Mr. Boldt stood in the hallway. Grief carved deeply into his dignified face. Louise's death had visibly aged him, draining the vibrancy that made him a legend. "As promised." Exhaustion weighed down his voice. "I'd like you to stay on with us."

She dipped a curtsy in gratitude. "Thank you, sir."

The Boldts had always been fair to her. He could have dismissed her, but something in his expression told her it wasn't charity.

It was honor. A man keeping his word.

Still, when she sought Hazel later that evening to ask about her new position, reality struck a different chord.

"The only available position is as a housemaid." Hazel hesitated. "It won't be what you're used to, I'm afraid."

Madison forced a smile, though her heart sank. "I'll take it."

But nothing could have prepared her for the difference. For years, she had been Mrs. Boldt's lady's maid, her duties precise and refined. She dressed Mrs. Boldt in the finest silks and laces, fastened delicate buttons, styled her soft hair. She traveled with her, attended to her every need, enjoyed the quiet privilege of being close to a woman of grace and intelligence. Their relationship had been more than employer and servant—there had been trust, respect, even something like friendship.

But a housemaid? Scrubbing floors and polishing silver. Emptying chamber pots and dusting furniture. A housemaid was invisible.

Her first morning on duty, she tied on the plain apron over a rough wool dress and set to work making up the guest rooms. She smoothed sheets, fluffed pillows, and swept away the dust that would return by the next day. The elegance of her past role was gone, replaced by the mundane, repetitive tasks of maintaining a house too grand to ever truly be clean.

She was simply another servant.

And worst of all? This was not her calling.

As she scrubbed a stubborn stain from the parlor floor, the longing for the Thousand Islands surged through her like an ache.

Perhaps she had a new mission? One that entailed supporting the man she loved. Only time would tell.

Mrs. Boldt's funeral was a blur of black veils, somber voices, and the scent of winter roses clashing with the bitter cold air. Madison stood toward the back, hands clasped before her, as the minister's voice echoed through the cemetery. Snowflakes drifted down in quiet reverence, dusted the mourners' coats, settled on the polished wood of the casket holding the mortal remains of her precious missus.

Among the sea of sorrowful faces, the family dog drew her attention. Buster Brown, the family's faithful water spaniel, sat at the edge of the gathered mourners, his large brown eyes fixed on the casket. He did not whine, did not stir—only sat in silent, patient grief, his tail curled tight against his body. Madison had never seen an animal look so heartbroken.

Afterward, as the guests departed and the Boldt house fell into the heavy quiet of mourning, Buster Brown wandered from room to room, searching. He sniffed at the threshold of Mrs. Boldt's chambers, whimpering when the door remained shut. Curling up beneath the chaise where she used to sit, he refused to move for hours.

Everyone grieved in their own way. But the spaniel's sorrow was almost too much to bear.

Days later, Madison noticed the shift. She had just finished her morning duties when she spotted Buster Brown trailing at Mr. Boldt's heels as he walked through the house. The man who had been a pillar of strength through his wife's illness and death, who had remained composed even in the face of his own sorrow, now bent slightly to scratch the dog's ears. From that moment, Buster Brown never left Mr. Boldt's side.

And for the first time since Mrs. Boldt's passing, Madison felt a whisper of something beyond sorrow.

Perhaps even in loss, there could still be love.

And perhaps there was still hope for her, too.

~ ~ ~

The wind howled across the frozen St. Lawrence River, carrying a cruel, mournful sound across the wintery grounds of Heart Island. Snow swirled in thick drifts along the pathways, blanketing the walls of the castle in an eerie hush.

Emmett stood in the dim light of the foreman's office, the yellowed paper of the telegram trembling slightly in his calloused hands.

"STOP ALL WORK. LOUISE HAS DIED."

That was all. No explanation. No direction. Just six stark words bearing the weight of a dream lost.

Like an approaching storm, the words hit him, dark and ominous. Emmett gasped. He set the telegram down on the desk, staring at it as if more time might change the words.

It didn't.

In the Great Hall, the pounding of hammers and swishing of saws echoed faintly through the frigid air as the workers pressed on, unaware everything had changed in an instant.

Louise Boldt was gone. And with her, the castle she inspired—the very reason they worked tirelessly through the seasons—would now become nothing more than an unfinished monument to love and grief.

He ran a hand down his face, steeling himself before stepping into the hall. The men currently worked on the grand staircase. Bundled against the cold, the breath from their conversations formed *minuscule* clouds in the air. Another of his grand words learned from the dictionary.

They looked to him as he approached, their tools paused mid-air. Sam, one of the mason's, furrowed a brow. "What's wrong, sir?"

Emmett took a steadying breath. "Work's over." He exhaled, forcing out the next words that would forever change their lives. And his. "Mr. Boldt sent word. Mrs. Boldt has passed."

A heavy silence fell over the group. No one moved, no one spoke. Then, slowly, caps came off and heads bowed. Several wrung their hands. For a long moment, nothing but the sound of the wind swept through the castle.

And his future.

Emmett cleared his throat. "Go home to your families. I'm sorry, but there'll be no more work here. Not sure there ever will be. But I'll contact you if there is."

One by one, the men turned, making their way toward the shore, their shoulders hunched against the weight of the news. As they went, Emmett's own uncertainty gnawed at him.

What now? For years, he had poured his strength, his skill, his very heart into the stone walls rising on Heart Island. The castle took shape under his watch. He knew every curve of the turrets, every intricacy of the carvings. This building was a labor of love— not his own, but Mr. Boldt's. A love so grand it demanded something permanent, something lasting.

But now, it was over. There would be no grand unveiling, no welcoming of Mrs. Boldt to the castle built for her.

Instead, they would leave Heart Island unfinished, abandoned like a forgotten dream.

Emmett lingered a moment longer, taking in the towering, empty windows, the silent promise of what could have been. Then, with a last glance around the unfinished castle, he closed up his office and bid his life's work goodbye.

And Heart Island stood alone, abandoned in the cold. The wind cut sharp against his face, but he barely felt it. The weight in his chest was heavier than any winter storm. He was out of a job.

Just like that, everything he had built—every long hour, every careful stone laid, every dream for the future—was gone.

The telegram from George Boldt shattered any lingering hope, extinguishing the flicker of hope that had ignited for a future with Madison.

How could he ask her to marry him now? He had planned it in his mind, envisioned the way he'd ask her in the spring, when the river ice melted and gave way to new beginnings. He imagined taking her hand, telling her he wanted to build a life with her, a home where she would never feel lost again.

But now? What could he offer her except uncertainty?

He gritted his teeth, the thought nearly unbearable. He had nothing—not a job, not a future, not a place to lay his head at night. Not even the security to keep himself afloat, let alone provide for a wife.

Should he go to Philadelphia and find new work with the Hewitts? They were good to him before, and he was a skilled foreman. There would always be work for a man with steady hands and a mind for building. But the thought of leaving the Thousand Islands, of leaving Madison, tore at something deep inside him.

Would she wait for him? Did he even have the right to ask her to?

He crossed the frozen river and headed for the Yacht House he called home for the past few years. But which wasn't really his, was it?

By the time he reached his room, the reality had fully set in. He could not stay here—not without work, and no way to make a living. But neither could he bring himself to walk away without knowing where he stood with Madison.

He must talk to her. To know if she still saw a future for them.

With Mrs. Boldt's passing, they were both in the same row boat. Without a paddle.

The lass must be heartbroken. Adrift as much as he. Alone. Confusion coloring her world even more darkly than his own.

A letter arrived on a bitter morning as Emmett stood near the docks, debating his next move. He had all but convinced himself he would have to leave the Thousand Islands, to go where work would take him, to abandon whatever fragile hope he had clung to.

But when he broke the red wax seal and unfolded the crisp sheet of paper, his breath caught.

Mr. O'Connor,

I'd like to offer you a position. There is work to be done at Wellesley House and on the Boldt properties. For the winter, you'll stay in the Yacht House and begin repairs. Come spring, we'll discuss further responsibilities. I trust you will find this agreeable.

—G.C. Boldt

Emmett exhaled slowly, the letter trembling slightly in his grip. He had a job. Not the grand construction project of heart and soul at Heart Island, but it was steady work—a reason to stay.

Warm relief stirred in his chest. This meant he wouldn't have to go to Philadelphia. Wouldn't have to start over again in a place that felt nothing like home.

And more than that—if Madison returned to the islands in the summer, he would be here.
His fingers tightened around the letter as hope flickered to life once more.

Would she come back? He wasn't sure. But if she did, he would be waiting. And maybe this was God's way of keeping him where he was meant to be.

For now, that was enough.

A week later, the wind rattled against the Yacht House, whistling through the eaves as Emmett settled near the small desk in his quarters, Madison's letter trembling in his hands. He had read it twice already, but still, the sorrow woven between the lines gripped his heart.

She was lost. Her grief was raw, her words edged with doubt, as though she were lost in a sea of sadness, unsure whether God was still there, unsure whether she could still believe in love, in hope…in him.

He exhaled slowly, sipped his coffee, then reached for a fresh sheet of paper. Dipping his pen into the inkwell, he wrote.

Dear Madison,

I received your letter, and I sense the weight of sorrow sits heavy on your shoulders. I wish I could be there beside you now, to take your hand, to remind you that you are not alone.

Grief can be a cruel thing, making you question everything you once knew. It steals the light from the world and leaves you standing in shadows, uncertain if you'll ever find your way again.

But, Madison, even in the darkest night, the stars are still there—whether we can see them. Or not.

I won't pretend to have all the answers. I won't tell you that faith comes easy in times like these. It doesn't for me. Didn't, on the day Mr. Boldt canceled the construction at Heart Island. I, too, felt abandoned that day.

But God has proven Himself once again. And if you allow, He will step into your life and heart and soul as well. God has not abandoned you. You may not feel Him now, but He is in every moment, every breath, every tear you shed. And if you cannot find the strength to hold on to Him, trust that He is holding onto you.

As for me, I am still here, Madison. I have work at the Wellesley House and the Yacht House for the winter, and in the spring, I will still be here. Waiting. For you.

I don't know what the future holds, but I pray it holds you in it. Come back to the islands when the river thaws. Let the fresh air fill your lungs again. Let the river remind you that even after the coldest winter, life returns. And if you find your way back to me, Madison, I will be here.

Yours always, Emmett

He sat back, staring at the words before him, heart pounding. Would she come? Would she still believe in them? All he could do was send the letter, pray, and wait for spring.

And for her.

CHAPTER 25

May 1904

As the steamboat glided through the sparkling springtime waters of the St. Lawrence, Madison leaned against the rail, her fingers tightening around the smooth wood, relishing the breathtaking sight before her. The Thousand Islands stretched out in every direction, the familiar shores meeting the gentle lapping waves, the golden afternoon light casting a warm glow over the river.

Feels like home.

The truth whispered through her, unbidden yet undeniable. Despite the pain that followed her like a shadow, despite the grief that still clung to her heart, she could not deny the comfort of these waters. The way they welcomed her back like an old friend.

Yet, without Mrs. Boldt and her position as lady's maid, did any of it matter?

Then her gaze drifted near Wellesley Island, and another ache settled in her chest.

Emmett.

After dozens of readings of his letters over the past several months, each word proved a lifeline, pulling her from the depths of her despair. His warm and hopeful words became a quiet reassurance in her loneliest nights. He waited for her, as he'd promised. And now, after all this time, she would see him again.

Would he still look at her the same way? Would the hope in his eyes still burn as brightly?

Her nerves tangled into a knot of apprehensive anticipation. Their time apart had changed them both—she understood that. And yet, her heart beat faster at the thought of him standing on the docks, waiting, searching the horizon just as she sought him now.

But would she find the courage to face him?

Her station had changed. She was no longer Mrs. Boldt's lady's maid with the privilege of accompanying her mistress wherever she went. Now, she was a simple housemaid, expected to keep her head down, her mouth shut, and to work tirelessly behind the scenes. She had less freedom than before, fewer chances to slip away, to steal moments of laughter and conversation as they once had. Her station even lower than before.

Would he understand? Would he still want her?

"Madison?" Hazel's voice pulled her from her thoughts. The housekeeper stood near the gangway, ready to disembark, adjusting her hat against the wind. "Come along, dear. We've much to do before the family arrives."

With a last glance at the river, Madison inhaled deeply and nodded. The river had brought her back. Now, she must learn whether Emmett wanted her to stay.

She followed the others to Wellesley House, moving with the quiet efficiency expected of a housemaid, but her heart was anything but content. She got right to work, tugging off the sheets covering the furniture.

Late into the evening, the scent of lemon furniture polish and air-dried linens filled the air as she smoothed out the last wrinkle in Mrs. Boldt's old sitting room, frozen in time as though waiting for its mistress to return. Grief clung to the walls here.

And to her, too.

Mrs. Boldt's absence was a shadow stretching through every corridor, intertwined with memories of whispered conversations, shared smiles, and trust that had grown between them over the years.

Madison had served a woman of elegance and grace, and in return, she found her purpose. But now, that purpose loomed empty. Her world had changed, and no matter how tightly she tried to hold on to the past, it slipped through her fingers like river water. She had once been more than just a servant—to Mrs. Boldt and the family.

But what was she now? She still couldn't wrap her head around her present position as a housemaid. For the past four months, she floated like a shadow in the background. Another set of hands to scrub floors and make beds, not someone with the freedom to enjoy moments by the docks, to listen to conversations of important people like the Boldts, to share long walks along the shore, to laugh under the summer sky with Emmett at her side.

And what about her future? That was a mystery yet to be solved.

What would he think of her now? Would he see her differently? Would he—could he—still love her?

She could recite the words of his letters of devotion, his admission of love and caring by heart, the ink etched into her soul. He told her to come back. That he would be here, waiting. But had he truly understood that she would be returning as a lowly housemaid?

A fragile thread bound them together, but, for her, the weight of loss, of grief, of time apart, frayed the fabric of her identity.

She had lost her family. She had lost the missus. Would she lose Emmett, too?

Hazel mentioned that Emmett was off the island for the day, so she didn't see him. Surely tomorrow, they'd finally meet again. She ended her day with a quiet prayer for strength, for answers to her questions.

When the morning sun filtered through the trees and across the garden, Madison slipped away after breakfast to search him out. She hesitated near the garden path. The air was crisp, filled with the scent of damp earth and river breeze, but even the beauty of the

Thousand Islands could not ease the weight pressing against her chest. Making breathing difficult.

She had hoped to see him. And now, there he was.

Emmett stood alone near the weathered trellis, where empty vines curled around the wooden beams. He had his back to her, staring out toward Heart Island, where the unfinished castle stood in solemn silence. His hands, tucked deep in his coat pockets, suggested he waited in ease, but tension stiffened his broad shoulders.

She followed his gaze. She remembered, too.

Boldt Castle. Heart Island. The way Mrs. Boldt once walked the paths of the island, speaking of dreams that would never come to be. How she enjoyed the shade of the gazebo and napping in Alster Tower's Venetian Room. How her eyes lit up when she saw progress in the castle. Now, everything had changed.

Madison swallowed hard as she stepped forward, breathing a silent plea to heaven. A twig snapped beneath her shoe. At long last, this was the moment.

Emmett turned.

For a breath, they simply looked at each other, time stretching between them like the distance that had separated them for so many months. His eyes softened as they swept over her, taking her in as if confirming she was really there.

But his gaze held—what, exactly? Skepticism? Sadness? Disappointment? Regret?

"Madison."

Her name sounded like a whisper, a prayer. She clasped her hands tightly in front of her. "I hoped I might find you here."

His lips pressed into a faint smile. "I was beginnin' to think you were avoidin' me."

A nervous laugh escaped her, but it faded just as quickly. "I only now had a moment free, and I wasn't sure what to say."

He studied her, his expression warm. "Then let's not waste any more time, lass. Say what's on your heart."

Her heart raced. She had rehearsed this moment in her mind a hundred times. But now, standing before him, with the wind rustling the leaves and the river stretching endlessly beyond them, her carefully planned words crumbled.

She spoke from the rawest part of her soul. "I'm not sure I belong here, with you, Emmett. I don't know where I belong." Her voice wavered. "Not like I used to. Not without Mrs. Boldt. Not like this."

She fingered her simple housemaid dress.

A flicker of something—hurt?—crossed his face, but he said nothing.

"It was different last summer. I was Mrs. Boldt's lady's maid. Now, I make beds and sweep floors. I've lost everything I once was. I'm…I'm no one now."

He took a step closer, his gaze searching hers. "You think your worth is in a title? In what you do for a livin'?"

She shook her head, struggling to find the words. "I don't know. I'm not sure. I just know that I used to have a place. I belonged. And now, I don't."

Emmett's jaw tightened, and for a long moment, he was silent. When he finally spoke, his voice was soft but steady. "Do you think that changes how I see you, my darlin' lass?"

She held her breath, fear tightening around her ribs. "Doesn't it?"

A flicker of something fierce flashed in his eyes. He stepped even closer, close enough she could see the way the river breeze tousled his dark hair. Close enough she heard the steady cadence of his breath.

"Madison, if you think for one second I care about what station you hold in this world, then you don't know me at all." His gentle voice warmed her. "I never loved you for what you did. I love you for who you are."

Her breath caught. Loved. He had said it before. But it had been so long since she'd heard those words from his lips, in his wonderful Irish lilt.

Her eyes burned with unshed tears. "Emmett…"

His hand, rough and calloused from years of labor, yet warm and sure, wrapped around hers. "You don't have to prove your worth to me, lass. You were always enough. Always will be."

The worry she had carried for so long cracked, splintering under the warmth of his words. For the first time in months, she allowed herself to hope.

And as the wind whispered through the garden, Madison realized—perhaps she hadn't lost everything after all. Maybe she had found what truly mattered.

Perhaps loving Emmett was her new mission?

~ ~ ~

That evening, as the dark river stretched endlessly before him, restlessness niggled at Emmett beneath the moonlight. He leaned against the railing of the dock, his fingers curling around the wood as though it could anchor him against the tide of emotions threatening to pull him under.

He thought her presence would end his turmoil. That his letter writing would heal his heart. That time would ease the ache of what he'd lost. That if he worked hard enough, stayed busy enough, he wouldn't feel the melancholy pressing against his chest.

But grief is a stubborn thing. A dark shadow refusing to go.

The dreams he had once clung to so tightly—now he couldn't quite make them out. Like a fog surrounded them. Dreams of her. Of them. Of Garrison's friendship. Of completing the castle.

He had poured years of his life into the castle's very foundation, only to see it stand unfinished, a monument to a love that could never be fulfilled.

He had failed. Failed to protect. Failed to finish what he started. Failed to be the man he was supposed to be.

And now, Madison was finally here, offering him something he wasn't sure he deserved. He didn't share his deepest fears with her. This morning she needed his comfort more than he needed hers.

But now, he needed her understanding more than he realized.

She approached before he saw her, her steps light against the wooden dock. A part of him wanted to turn, to pull her into his arms, and pretend that none of these feelings of guilt, grief, and failure mattered. That he could be the man she believed him to be.

But what if she saw him for who he really was?

She softly sauntered up to stand beside him. The wind lifted a strand of her hair, brushing it across her cheek. She smiled but said nothing.

He tugged at his shirt collar but kept his gaze on the water. "You should be inside, lass. It's a chilly eve."

She ignored him, as he suspected she would. "I see the way you still carry the weight of it all. We both carry too much, and we have to let it go before we can move on."

A bitter chuckle escaped him. "Aye, and what would you have me do? Forget? I've tried, lass. It's not that easy."

She hesitated, then placed a gentle hand on his arm. "I'm not expecting you—or me—to forget, Emmett. I'm hoping that we can let God have it and move on. I'm trying to."

The words struck something deep within him, raw and aching. He clenched his jaw. "There are things I can't change, Madison. Things I can't fix." His voice was rough, edged with frustration—not at her, but at himself. "Garrison. His blood is on my hands. I should have gotten rid of Bruce long ago. The castle reminds me every day."

"I know how you feel. The regrets seek to drown me, too."

"Regrets? And what do you have tormentin' your soul and mind every minute of every day?" He exhaled sharply, pounding on the railing. "Nothin', that's what. Not like I do."

He turned back to the water, the only sure thing in his world right now. "You think I don't wish I could let it all go? That I don't wake up every day wonderin' if I could've done more? How can you love a failure like me, anyway?"

His voice broke slightly, surprising even himself. He had kept it all inside for so long, buried it deep where no one could see.

And now here it was, taunting him for the failure he knew himself to be.

But Madison saw. She understood. She always had. Her fingers tightened around his arm. "You didn't fail, Emmett."

He let out a humorless laugh. "Didn't I?"

She stepped in front of him now, forcing him to meet her gaze. "No. And you don't have to punish yourself for things beyond your control. Neither do I. You've helped me see that. Now I can hope for a future without regrets."

He searched her face, seeing nothing but honesty, nothing but love. And it undid him.

His throat closed as he whispered, "I don't know if I deserve happiness or if I can even hope for it, Madison."

Her expression softened, and she reached for his hand. "Then let me believe for you. Until you can."

The wind howled around them, but in that moment, standing in the moonlight with her fingers laced through his, he finally understood that what God said about her was true about him, as well. He wasn't as lost as he thought.

Emmett held Madison's gaze, unease pressing against his chest.

He had bared his soul to her, spoken of his fears, his failures, his doubts. Yet, here she stood—her presence as steady as the river itself.

He let out a slow breath. "I don't know what my future looks like. I've enough work for now, aye, but there's no tellin' if it'll last. I can't ask you to…"

She stepped closer, her hands reaching for his. Her fingers laced through his, quieting his words before they took hold.

"Emmett." She gazed into his eyes. "After you reassured me that my station doesn't matter, you still think because you're not the famous foreman of Boldt Castle that I think less of you? Never! After all you said, I see my future in your handsome eyes—you're a mirror into my very soul."

His breath caught, the depth of her words unraveling the pain deep inside him.

"You've always seen me, Emmett." Her fingers tightened around his hand. "Not as a maid, not as someone lesser, but as me. And now, I see you—not a man burdened by grief or fear, but the man who has always been strong, kind, and good."

Her presence wrapped around him like a warm blanket, seeping into the cracks of his doubt, soothing the ache of unworthiness he had carried for so long.

He shook his head. "You deserve more than what I can offer."

She smiled then, an expression holding both sorrow and hope. "Let me decide that, Emmett O'Connor."

He clenched his jaw, emotion thick in his chest. He had spent so long believing he had to be enough before he could love her the way she deserved. But here she was, telling him he already was enough.

The wind rustled through the trees, but Emmett only felt the warmth of her hands in his, the steady beat of his own heart answering hers.

He lifted one hand, brushing a loose strand of hair from her cheek, his touch lingering. "You truly see me, don't you?"

She nodded. "And I always will."

He sighed, contented. He did not know what the future held, but for the first time in a long while, he realized one thing…he wouldn't have to face it alone.

Madison tugged him back to her presence, unspoken words pressing between them, fragile yet full of a deeper surety neither could ignore any longer.

She inhaled slowly. "Emmett, I've spent so much of my life afraid. Of losing people. Of being alone. Of…" She hesitated, her voice faltering before she met his gaze, her heart hammering. "Of not being enough for you. Even as I wrote those letters. Dreamed those dreams."

His brow furrowed, his strong hands tightening around hers. "My precious Madison, how could you ever think that?"

Her lips pursed. "Because I've lost everyone I've ever loved. And I thought…if I let myself love you, I might lose you too." She patted his arm. "But when I saw you today, I realized that loving you is worth the risk."

The wind stirred around them, and Emmett stepped closer. Protecting her. Warming her. His brogue danced a jig on his frayed emotions. "Aye my love, I've spent months thinkin' I had to be better, to be more, before I could ask you to love me." He exhaled sharply, shaking his head. "But the truth is, I've loved you from the moment you walked into my life."

Her breath caught, tears shimmering in her eyes.

He took her face in his hands, touching her with tender steadiness. "I don't have riches to offer you, nor promises of an easy life. But I can promise you this—I will love you with all that I am, for all my days."

A single tear slipped down her cheek, and he brushed it away with his thumb.

She smiled up at him. "You're all I've ever wanted, Emmett. I don't care where we live or what work we do."

A slow smile touched his lips. He couldn't believe she was his to love. He pressed his forehead against hers. "Aye, my lovely lass, then let's build a future together."

She nodded, a laugh breaking through her tears. "A future built on faith…and love."

His arms wrapped around her then, holding her as if he never intended to let go. Surrounded by the quiet hum of the river, perhaps the ghosts of their past would cease to hold them captive.

They had chosen each other. And that was more than enough.

CHAPTER 26

July 1904

The Wellesley House kitchen buzzed with quiet purpose as the morning sunlight filtered through the lace-curtained windows. Madison folded napkins at the corner table, her thoughts far from the upcoming luncheon. The scents of vinegar, sweet onions, and chopped pickles filled the air.

Here in the Thousand Islands, she enjoyed the variety of work, away from the city. Here, she worked in the kitchen and in the garden. She wasn't constrained to making beds and cleaning. In the hustle and bustle in New York City with all the extra staff, her work was narrow and boring. Her life as a housemaid held no joy, not like serving Mrs. Boldt had. She glanced at her superior, Hazel, grateful for the comforting camaraderie she enjoyed.

Hazel stood at the wide wooden counter, whisking together a creamy dressing in a large bowl, her sleeves rolled up and her brow furrowed in concentration.

She paused her mixing, giving the contents of the bowl an approving glance before turning her eyes—sharp and knowing—on

Madison. "You're awful quiet today." She reached for the bottle of paprika. "That usually means something's brewing in that pretty head of yours."

She offered a small smile. "Just thinking, that's all."

Hazel added a dash of the spice, then stirred thoughtfully. "Is it about the luncheon? Or is it about a certain Irishman with kind eyes and calloused hands?"

Her cheeks burned instantly. She busied herself with a napkin corner that didn't really need folding. "It's..."

Hazel gave a soft, amused snort. "You know, this dressing may be rich and sweet, but it doesn't hold a candle to the look on your face when you think no one's watching. You saw Emmett yesterday, didn't you?"

Her heart fluttered. "I did."

Hazel paused, her whisk pausing mid-stir. "And?"

"It felt..." She struggled for words. "It felt like I'd been holding my breath for months, and finally I can breathe again. But it also felt precarious. We've both changed."

Hazel set the bowl down and crossed her arms, leaning back against the counter. "Love doesn't stay the same, Madison. It grows. Bends with the wind. But, if it's true, the roots hold fast."

She looked down at her hands. "I love him. I do. I see myself in his eyes, like a mirror to the part of me I thought I lost. But I'm only a housemaid now. And he's still searching for solid ground. What if that's not enough?"

Hazel moved to her side, wiping her hands on her apron. "Let me tell you something. This house, these rooms, the jobs we do—they don't define who we are. What matters is what we carry in our hearts. That man loves you. I've seen the way he watches for you, like he is waiting for his entire world to step into view. And the way he continually looks at you. It's as obvious as the smell of these onions."

Hazel's voice softened. "You've walked through sorrow, but don't let it make you blind to joy. God's not done writing your story yet, and it may be much different than you ever dreamed. Though I'd hate to see you go, I don't want to see you stay if you're miserable. And I've had a hunch you weren't going to stay here forever. Don't let fear keep you from the next chapter."

The kitchen stilled. Madison let out a slow breath, the warmth of Hazel's words settling over her like the scent of fresh bread—not onions.

She finished the napkin folding and leaned against the counter, picking up a towel to dry the crystal water glasses, her curiosity piqued by the scent wafting from Hazel's concoction.

Madison eyed the mixture. "That smells like something special."

Hazel grinned, not looking up. "It is. Thousand Island dressing. Figured it'd be a nice touch for the luncheon today."

Madison blinked. "The original Thousand Island dressing?"

Hazel chuckled. "That's the one. And do you know where it all started?"

Madison set the towel down, intrigued. "It's from this region, but I've heard two different stories."

Hazel nodded, her hands busy at work. "It goes back to Mr. Boldt, of course. He loves these islands like they are his own piece of heaven. Bought up land all over, including this very place. Entertained all his important friends here. But as proprietor of the Waldorf-Astoria Hotel in New York and the Bellevue-Stratford in Philadelphia, he is always thinking of new ways to make them an even bigger success."

Madison's smile warmed as the memory kindled. "True. Many of the Boldts' friends have visited here, including Oscar Tschirky from the Waldorf. He made the most innovative and improbable things. Waldorf Salad, Veal Oscar."

Hazel grinned. "You've got a good memory. He wasn't a chef, you know. People thought he was, but he was the maître d'. First one hired when the Waldorf opened. Loyal to Mr. Boldt like a shadow to the sun."

Madison leaned forward, enchanted now. "He came here a few times with Mr. Boldt."

"Often," Hazel confirmed. "Folks say that one summer, out on Mr. Boldt's yacht Louise—named after his wife, God rest her soul—Oscar realized the salad fixings had been left on the dock. So, he grabbed what he had on board, threw it together, and made this very dressing. George Boldt loved it so much he started serving it at the Waldorf. That's how it became famous."

Madison's gaze drifted toward the window where the river sparkled just beyond the lawn. "And to think…it all started right here. In these islands."

"As the result of an oversight." Hazel stopped whisking and looked over her shoulder at Madison, her eyes narrowing with quiet fondness. "Just goes to show, you don't need a palace or a fancy kitchen to make something special."

Madison's eyes met Hazel's, deeper understanding blooming in her chest. "You mean like how life doesn't have to be perfect to be good?"

Hazel smiled. "Exactly. Sometimes, the best things come out of a little improvising. A little faith. And maybe a whole lotta love."

Madison laughed, returning to her glassware. But her thoughts lingered on Oscar's unexpected creation, on George Boldt's love for his Louise, and on her own future. Love—improbable, imperfect, and unexpected—wasn't just for the grand.

It was for the brave.

Hazel poured the Thousand Island dressing into a delicate glass server and wiped down the counter with practiced ease. Madison, still drying the last of the glasses, drifted into thoughtful silence.

Hazel broke it first. "You know, Madison, you're a fine housemaid. One of the best I've ever trained. Quick, respectful, steady."

Madison looked up, blinking at the unexpected praise. "Thank you, Hazel. That means more than you know."

"But," Hazel continued, her voice gentler now. "This isn't who you are."

She paused, the linen in her hands forgotten. "What do you mean?"

Hazel turned to face her fully, her eyes kind but serious. "You've done your job with excellence. But I've watched you, day after day. You don't belong in the shadows, cleaning and doing the mundane. You've got more to give than folding sheets and polishing glassware. You've got purpose—a mission. You just haven't figured out what it is yet."

Madison gave a half shrug. "I've been trying. I thought it might be Emmett. But even that's dubious since his life's work is questionable."

Hazel nodded slowly. "Maybe it is. Or maybe it's something alongside him. Or something entirely different. What I do know,

Madison, is that you come alive here. In these islands. I see it in the way you breathe easier, the way your eyes search the river."

Madison glanced out the window, the sparkling water stretching far beyond the dock. "I've always felt at peace here. Like I belong to the river in a way I can't explain."

Hazel's voice softened. "That's why, when the family returns to the city after summer's end, you won't be going back with us."

Madison turned to her, wide-eyed. "What?"

Hazel gave a firm nod. "You need to stay. There's something here for you, Madison. Whether it's Emmett, or something else God's planned, I don't know. But I know you're at your best when you're surrounded by these trees and this water. And it's time you stopped trying to fit back into a life that's already moved on."

Her throat tightened. "But what will I do?"

Hazel smiled. "That's for you to find out. But you won't find it moping around the city or playing small as a housemaid. You'll find it here—where your heart beats steady."

Tears pricked at Madison's eyes, not from sadness, but from a sudden and overwhelming sense of clarity. Maybe she wasn't meant to go back. Perhaps her future really was unfolding here— among the islands, the river, and the people she'd grown to love.

And maybe…she was just beginning to discover the woman God intended her to be.

~ ~ ~

Emmett stood tall, his cap resting in his hands, fingers rubbing the brim as he waited just inside Mr. Boldt's office at Wellesley House. The morning sun filtered in through the wide windows, casting light across the polished floor and the expansive map of the Thousand Islands hanging on the wall.

Mr. Boldt sat behind his desk, a strong man with tired eyes. Grief still clung to him, but so did resolve—like a man who had decided that the only way through sorrow was to keep building something new.

"Emmett O'Connor." Boldt gestured to the chair across from him. "Thank you for coming."

Emmett nodded and took the seat, though his back stayed straight and his boots still hovered near the edge of the rug.

Boldt steepled his fingers and leaned forward. "I've watched your work for a long time now. Quiet, loyal, skilled. You've been faithful to me, even when the castle's construction halted. It's time we put your talents to better use."

He blinked, confused. "Sir?"

"I'd like you to serve as permanent foreman of all my properties here in the Thousand Islands," Boldt said plainly. "Almost three thousand acres under my name and more to come. It's too much for me to manage from afar and too valuable to neglect. I need someone I can trust—someone with vision."

For a long moment, he couldn't find the words. His fingers gripped the cap tighter. "That's…a mighty kind offer, sir."

Boldt gave a small smile. "It's more than just an offer, Emmett. It's the future—for both of us. This summer, finish the work on the Yacht House. Stay there through the season. After that, well…" He paused. "You'll likely need to find permanent lodging. We'll be leaving for the city after the summer, and I won't be maintaining the residence here year-round. But the work—that will remain."

He nodded slowly, still absorbing the weight of the offer. "And Florence Island, sir? I'd heard talk…"

Boldt's eyes glinted with the hint of a dream. "Yes. I'm acquiring Florence Island this season. Possibly a few more beyond that. The Boldt legacy isn't finished in these islands—not by a long shot."

Emmett's heart raced as the pieces aligned. A future here. On the river. With purpose again—not just labor, but leadership.

He cleared his throat. "It would be an honor, sir. I'll do right by you and your vision."

"I know you will." Boldt's gaze softened. "You're a builder, Emmett. Not just of structures—but of life. My plans need someone like you."

As Emmett stepped out of the study, the breeze from the river caught his jacket and lifted his spirits. The ache of lost dreams hadn't vanished, but they were no longer the whole of him.

There was work to be done, yes. But now there was something else, too. Hope. And if Madison stayed—as he now dared to believe she might—they could build a beautiful life together.

That evening, as the sun dipped low in the sky, the river sparkled, peaceful and alive, and the breeze carried the scent of pine and fresh earth. Emmett stood near the edge of the garden where it sloped down toward the water, hands tucked into his coat pockets and heart pounding with something he hadn't felt in months—anticipation.

After his meeting with Mr. Boldt, he'd sent Madison a message to meet him here when her work was done. He couldn't wait to tell her the news.

The soft crunch of her footsteps behind him alerted him to her presence, and he turned as she appeared at the top of the path. She looked radiant in the evening light, her hair caught in the wind, her eyes bright with the same searching wonder that always drew him in.

"Hope I didn't keep you too long, Emmett. Buster Brown spilled his water bowl. I had to clean it up."

He smiled. "Aye. Seems we always end up here when we've got somethin' important to say."

She tilted her head, her expression gentle. "What is it, Emmett?"

He took a step closer, heart steady now. "This mornin', I met with Mr. Boldt."

Her brow rose. "Oh?"

His heart pounded with delight. "He's offered me a permanent position—foreman of all the Boldt properties here in the Thousand Islands. Not just the Yacht House. All of it!" His voice held a quiet awe. "There's enough land and work here for a lifetime. He said he needs someone to carry out his vision. To build somethin' lastin'."

Her eyes widened, the news settling over her like the hush of a chapel. "Oh Emmett, that's…that's incredible!"

He nodded. "It is. And it means I'll have work. Here. For good."

A silence stretched between them, filled only by the rustle of trees and the rhythm of the river. He took her hand, the touch grounding him.

"I couldn't wait to tell you, love. I wanted you to know because…well, Madison Murray, more than this position, I see *you* as my future. Your heart is kind and strong, and you are my hope for a life full of love and blessin'."

She blinked back sudden tears, her breath catching.

He reached into his pocket and pulled out a simple ring—delicate, gold, and modest. "My mother's. It's not much. But it's precious. And it's yours, if you'll have it." He dropped to one knee in the soft grass. "My darlin' Madison, will you marry me?"

A breathless silence filled the space between them.

She took both of his hands in hers, her smile trembling with emotion. "Yes! I will. I want a life with you, Emmett O'Connor. I've hoped for it for a long time." She paused. "But I need to finish out the summer. The Boldts have been good to me, and I want to finish well."

He nodded, not disappointed, but proud. "Aye, I'd expect nothin' less from you, my love."

Then, slowly, gently, he leaned forward. Their foreheads met first, a soft pause in time. And then his lips touched hers—a sweet, reverent kiss, full of promise and quiet joy. Not rushed or grand, but rather tender and sure, like two hearts finally finding their rhythm.

When they parted, Madison smiled, her eyes bright with tears and wonder. They hugged, the ring now on her finger, their hands still joined. The river flowed behind them, steady and strong—just like the future they would build.

The next morning, Emmett stood outside Mr. Boldt's office at the Wellesley House, smoothing a hand over his neatly pressed jacket. All through the night, he'd had this conversation a hundred times in his head, but now that the moment had come, his palms felt slick, and his heart thudded like a hammer.

Mr. Boldt's voice called from within. "Come in, Emmett."

He stepped through the open door, as George Boldt stood, spectacles perched on his nose, a stack of property deeds piled on his desk. He smiled with the calm of a man who'd seen a great deal of life and carried more of it in his eyes than in words.

"Good morning, sir."

"Morning." Boldt sat as he gestured to the chair across from him. "Have a seat. You look like you've swallowed a bullfrog."

Emmett lowered himself into the seat, straight-backed and resolute. "Sir, I'd like to speak with you about something personal."

Boldt set the papers down, steepling his fingers. "Go on."

Emmett cleared his throat. "I've asked Madison Murray to marry me. And she's said yes."

Boldt blinked, then sat back, a grin spreading across his face. He guffawed, loud and free. "Well, thank the Lord above. I was wondering if you two would ever figure that out."

Emmett blinked, surprised. "You…knew?"

"Emmett," Boldt said with a chuckle, "a man doesn't build hotels and castles without learning how to read people. The way you looked at each other—it was never a matter of *if*, only *when*."

Emmett let out a sheepish smile. "Well then…I just wanted to ask for your blessing. She's served your household loyally. And I've worked under your name for years. It felt right, sir."

Boldt nodded, his gaze growing serious for a moment. "Madison is a remarkable woman. One of the finest to ever walk these halls. And you—" He pointed at Emmett, "—are a man I trust with everything I've built here. I can't think of a better match."

Emmett's chest swelled with quiet relief.

Then, Boldt smiled again. "When the season ends and before we go home, you two should marry here. And if Madison would have me, I'd be honored to walk her down the aisle myself."

For a moment, Emmett could say nothing. His throat tightened. "That would mean the world to her, sir. And to me."

Boldt extended his hand. Emmett rose and clasped it.

"Then it's settled," Boldt grinning. "A wedding in the islands before the leaves fall. The kind of ending Louise would've loved."

Emmett nodded. The healing of loss mingled with the sweetness of hope.

For his employer. And for himself.

And as he stepped back into the bright morning air, a thought dawned on him.

This was no ending.

This was just the beginning.

CHAPTER 27

The warm scents of fresh bread, simmering stew, and blackberry preserves filled the Wellesley House kitchen, where the heart of the home still beat strong on the eve of Madison's wedding. They set the old wooden table near the hearth simply but beautifully, using cloth napkins and delicate china, a nod to the celebration ahead.

Hazel stirred a pot on the stove while Anna, cheeks flushed with excitement, arranged a small bouquet of late-summer blooms in a jar at the center of the table. Anna loved service, every bit of it.

Madison, her hair loosely pulled into a chignon, sat with a contented smile, soaking in the comfort of this quiet moment before everything changed.

"Take off that apron and mobcap, girl. You'll not be working tonight." Hazel grinned as she ladled steaming stew into bowls. "You're no longer in service. Tomorrow you'll be a married woman, Madison Murray. Or should I say, Mrs. Madison O'Connor."

Anna clapped her hands lightly. "Have you decided what you'll do for your wedding trip?"

Madison's eyes sparkled as she reached into her apron pocket and unfolded a note. "Actually, yes. Mr. Boldt arranged a little surprise for us—a three-day stay at the Thousand Island House hotel in Alexandria Bay."

Hazel's eyes widened with delight. "Well, now. That's quite the extravagant gift. That hotel's seen many grand folk stay there. It'll be a mighty fine treat for you."

Anna leaned in, breathless. "Isn't that the one across the river, the one built right after President Grant came through with George Pullman?"

"That's right." Hazel nodded proudly as she sat with her bowl. "Finished in 1873 by Colonel Orin Staples. Built in less than a year, if you can believe it. The place holds up to six hundred people—fills up every summer with guests from all over—New York, Philadelphia, Boston. Fancy folk escaping the city heat for a little river magic."

Madison smiled, picturing the grand halls, the view of the river, the hush of water against the shore at night. "Mr. Boldt said our suite overlooks the river. He wanted us to have a view of Casa Blanca, Friendly Island, and even our dear Heart Island."

Hazel's eyes twinkled. "And if the skies are clear, you'll see the Sunken Rock Lighthouse lit up at night. And you've got to take one of the Searchlight Tours. I hear those nighttime boat rides are something else. Some say it's magical."

Anna turned to Hazel. "Didn't they add a whole recreation pavilion for hotel guests a few years ago?"

"They did." Hazel lifted her spoon. "Finished it just two years ago. That building you can see off the hotel on Staples Island? Built a bridge to connect it and everything. Billiards, bowling, dancing, card rooms. Even a nursery for the little ones. Men have their grill and tall tales. Women, their afternoon teas on the garden roof. You'd think you were in New York City with all the elegance they cram onto that little island, I hear."

"And tennis?" Madison asked. "I heard there were courts right by the water."

"Indeed." Hazel sighed. "Tennis, croquet, badminton—all of it. And music every night. But the best part?" She leaned forward slightly. "The views. No matter how grand the hotel is, it's the river that steals everyone's breath. That's what they come for. That's what they'll remember."

Madison grew quiet for a moment, her heart full. "Then I'll be in good company. Because the river's what draws me here. What keeps me here. And Emmett, of course." She giggled as she looked between the women, her voice softening. "And I'll remember this kitchen, this table, you two…just as much as anything else."

Hazel reached across the table, placing her hand gently over Madison's. "We'll remember you too, child. But it's time to step into the life waiting for you. And tomorrow, you'll do just that."

Anna beamed, already wiping her eyes. "And you'll be here when we return next summer with stories to tell—and maybe a little one to hold."

Madison face flamed, her smile trembling with joy. "Yes. But I'll write to you. I promise."

Hazel smiled, folding her arms across her apron. "First, we've got a beautiful garden wedding to get ready for. A fine place to start a life together. That old willow's seen enough seasons to bless a thousand vows."

Anna sighed dreamily. "It's going to be beautiful, Madison."

But Madison's smile faltered just a touch. "It is. And I'm so excited." She paused. "But I'm also a little sad to be leaving the two of you."

Hazel raised a brow.

Madison looked between them, her throat tightening. "You two have been more than coworkers. You've been family. You saw me through some of the hardest months of my life. You've been so patient, listened to me, laughed with me—even when I forgot how to laugh."

Anna reached over and squeezed her hand, her own eyes misty.

Hazel cleared her throat. "You may be leaving service, girl, but you're not leaving us. You'll always have a place at this table— and in our hearts."

Madison's voice wavered. "I'm not the same girl who walked into service a decade ago. I didn't know who I was then. But now…" She smiled. "Now I know. I'm a woman who loves deeply, who's been broken and mended, and who's ready to step into something new."

Hazel nodded, her face softening. "That's what we've hoped for you all along. That you'd find your way back to yourself."

Madison stood and wrapped her arms around both women in a tight embrace. "Thank you. For your friendship. For believing in me—even when I didn't."

They held one another like sisters, like kindred souls knit together by shared burdens and small joys. And as the breeze drifted in from the river, carrying with it the promise of tomorrow, Madison understood she wasn't leaving anything behind—she was taking it all with her.

A gentle knock at the door tugged Anna to answer it, and to her surprise, Emmett entered, walking down the hallway—his gait steady, his shoulders squared—as he waved and quickly stepped into Mr. Boldt's study.

Her heart fluttered. She didn't know what he needed to speak with Mr. Boldt about, but there was purpose in his stride. Something unspoken in the air.

A few moments later, Anna appeared at her side, breathless and smiling. "Mr. Boldt has asked for you. He's in his office with Emmett."

Madison blinked. "Now?"

Anna nodded. "Now."

Curious and slightly anxious, Madison smoothed her skirts and made her way down the corridor, her fingers brushing against the polished banister as she passed. The door to the study was already ajar, early evening light spilling across the richly colored rug.

Mr. Boldt stood behind his desk, and Emmett turned toward her the moment she entered, his expression surprised and touched with something warm.

"Come in, Madison." Mr. Boldt gestured her closer. "There's something I'd like to share with both of you."

She glanced at Emmett, who gave her a small, reassuring nod. She stepped to his side and laced her fingers in front of her.

Mr. Boldt paused, then smiled. "The two of you are building something more than a life together. You're building upon what Louise and I loved most in this world: this place, these islands, this community."

Madison's throat tightened at the mention of Louise.

"I've thought long and hard about how to honor not only Louise and your love, but also the work you've done—and will continue to do—here in the Thousand Islands."

He reached into a drawer and pulled out a folded document, laying it gently on the desk in front of them.

"This," he said, "is a deed to a piece of property just up the shore on Wellesley Island. Not far from the Yacht House and with a lovely view of the river. I'd like you to have it. And I'll provide the funds needed to build a home there—your home."

Madison gasped, a hand flying to her mouth. Emmett stared at Mr. Boldt, his brows drawn with disbelief.

He reached for the document. "You're…givin' us land?"

Mr. Boldt nodded. "You've earned it—with your loyalty, your integrity, and your commitment to this place. Both of you. It's a gift. But it's also a trust. Build something beautiful, something lasting. Make it a place where hope lives."

Tears filled Madison's eyes. She stepped around the desk and embraced Mr. Boldt without hesitation. "Thank you," she whispered, her voice thick with emotion. "We'll honor this gift. And all that you and Mrs. Boldt built here. I promise."

Emmett stepped beside her, his voice quiet and firm. "We'll care for the land like it was our own blood. And we'll carry on the vision you started here, sir."

Mr. Boldt gave them both a fond, fatherly smile. "That's all I could hope for."

As they stepped out onto the verandah, hand in hand, Emmett pecked the tip of her nose. "I can't help but sharing this Irish blessing that, my dearest, feels like it's coming true. 'To all the days here and after—may they be filled with fond memories, happiness, and laughter.'"

Madison nodded, accenting her agreement with a hearty laugh. The future stretched wide before them—rooted in legacy, nourished by love, and full of promise.

~ ~ ~

Emmett stood beneath the white trellis, its wooden arch woven with fragrant blooms and trailing ivy as the garden fell silent in anticipation. His heart raced, not with nerves, but with awe. He had waited for this moment, dreamed of it through countless prayers and quiet hopes.

Now, as Mr. Boldt gently guided Madison down the flower-lined aisle, sunlight danced through the leaves overhead like heaven's blessing, and Emmett could barely breathe for the wonder of it all.

Madison was radiant, her hair swept into an elaborate updo of soft curls that framed her face with grace. A few delicate pins glinted in the sunshine, catching the light like stars in a clear sky. Her gown—high-collared and Victorian in style—hugged her frame with soft pink cotton, matching lace details along the collar and bodice. She was every bit the picture of beauty and poise.

But it wasn't the dress or the hair that caught his soul—it was her smile. Wide and deep as the river, it spoke of joy, of long-awaited love, and of a heart anchored in faith.

Overwhelmed by the goodness of God, tears stung his eyes. The pain of the past—the losses, the longings—faded like mist in the morning light.

God had brought them here. And He was good.

As Madison reached the end of the aisle, her hand resting gently on Mr. Boldt's arm, Emmett stepped forward. His breath caught as their eyes met—hers shimmering with unshed tears, his full of reverent awe.

Mr. Boldt gave him a small nod, a silent benediction, then placed Madison's hand in Emmett's. Her fingers were warm, steady. She was his anchor now, just as he hoped to be hers.

The minister's voice rose over the gentle hum of the breeze and birdsong, but Emmett hardly heard the words. The world had narrowed to Madison's eyes, her hand in his, the faint scent of roses in the air. He glimpsed her trembling lashes and the subtle rise and fall of her breath, and his heart swelled. He squeezed her hand gently, grounding them both in the moment's sacredness.

Behind them, the river shimmered in the distance, flowing gently—always moving forward.

Much like them.

The minister began, "Dearly beloved, we are gathered here today in the sight of God, and before these witnesses, to join this man and this woman in holy matrimony..."

Emmett sucked in a steadying breath, humbled by the moment. After all he'd been through—leaving Ireland, so much grief—he was here. Whole. Loved. Restored.

Madison was his miracle. A living, breathing answer to prayer.

She smiled at him again. Deep down, deeper than words—whatever lay ahead, they would face it together. With faith. With grace. With love rooted not just in feeling, but in the goodness of the God who never once let them go.

After the ceremony, Hazel outdid herself with a bridal brunch fit for the Boldts' most famous guests. The long table on the veranda of the Wellesley House was set with crisp linens, delicate china, and sprigs of lavender tied with ribbon. Platters of warm scones, fresh berries, and savory tarts invited guests to linger and enjoy.

A feast fit for a king, not servants. But here, now, stations didn't matter.

From where they sat, the view was breathtaking—the blue waters of the St. Lawrence River shimmering under the late summer sun, with Boldt Castle silent, like a lost fairytale in the distance. Laughter drifted through the air as a small group of friends shared stories and toasts. Yet amid the joy, there was a quiet pause, a shared glance between him and his wife as they stepped away from the gathering for just a moment.

They stood together at the edge of the veranda, hand in hand, the breeze lifting a soft curl from her cheek.

"I wish Mrs. Boldt were here." Madison's voice held a tender ache of remembrance. "She would have loved this."

He nodded, his gaze fixed on the castle across the water. "Aye. She'd be sittin' right there beside Mr. Boldt, smilin' that big-hearted smile of hers."

"She would've loved this day." She leaned her head against his shoulder. "She'd believe in our love, even before we did."

He wrapped his arm around her, holding her close. "She'd be proud of you, darlin'. Of us."

They stood in silence for a moment, the river whispering below, the distant echo of laughter behind them. Silence filled with gratitude—for their love, for the people who helped shape it, and for the God who carried them this far.

Then Hazel called them back, her warm voice laced with delight. "You two can sneak off later—come now and cut the cake!"

He chuckled, kissed Madison's temple, and led her back to the table. The celebration wasn't over. In fact, it was only the beginning.

Later, as the sun shone brightly on the St. Lawrence River, he and Madison boarded a small boat waiting at the dock, Thomas in command, his grin wide. Hazel and Anna waved from the shore, Hazel's apron billowing in the breeze, tears of joy brimming in Anna's eyes. Madison blew them a kiss, and he offered a grateful nod before taking his bride's hand and guiding her to the boat's bench.

The river was calm, its surface sparkling, the same glitter that lingered in Madison's eyes. The breeze was gentle, and the hum of the motor a quiet companion to his thoughts as they crossed the water toward the Thousand Island House hotel—the place Mr. Boldt often took his beloved Louise, and now lovingly offered to them.

They sat close, Madison's head resting on his shoulder, her hand curled around his. "Can you believe we're really married?"

"Aye." He brushed his thumb across her fingers. "And I thank God for it. For you."

He waited until Thomas moored the boat and said goodbye as they stepped off the boat and onto the mossy path.

After bidding their dear friend a good night, he continued his thought. "Seems we're buildin' more than a life, my darlin'. We're buildin' a legacy. One made of love, yes, but also of faith, and of standin' firm through the storms of life."

She turned to him, her eyes shining. "A life rooted in trust. Fueled by purpose. And wrapped in grace."

He kissed her then, under the wide arms of an old maple tree, the river murmuring behind them like an old song. Their love was not born of ease but of perseverance, shaped by sorrow and refined by hope. As they walked hand in hand toward the hotel, he knew this was just the beginning.

A marriage that honored the past, embraced the present, and believed wholeheartedly in the future.

~ ~ ~ *The End* ~ ~ ~

HISTORICAL NOTES ABOUT BOLDT CASTLE

To my knowledge, there never was an accident in building Boldt Castle. But the true story of Boldt Castle on Heart Island began at the turn of the 20th century, when George C. Boldt envisioned building a magnificent summer home for his beloved wife, Louise.

Boldt had already fallen in love with the Thousand Islands, an enchanting archipelago straddling the U.S.-Canada border. He purchased Heart Island to serve as the canvas for his romantic dream and even reshaped the island into the form of a heart as a tribute to Louise.

Construction began in 1900. Boldt employed hundreds of workers to erect a Rhineland-style castle, complete with one-hundred-and-twenty rooms, several towers, multiple balconies, and a number of sweeping staircases. The project extended far beyond the main castle itself, including a powerhouse generating electricity for the island, a playhouse known as Alster Tower, a dove cote, Italian gardens, and a grand yacht house on nearby Wellesley Island.

Every element reflected both European elegance and the love Boldt held for his wife.

But in 1904, tragedy struck. Louise Boldt died suddenly at the age of 41. Grief-stricken, George Boldt immediately halted all construction and abandoned the project. The workmen dropped their tools and left the island, and Boldt never returned. For the next 73 years, the unfinished castle stood silent and decaying—an empty monument to a dream left unfulfilled.

Over the decades, Boldt Castle suffered from vandalism, harsh weather, and neglect. Yet despite its ruinous state, it continued to capture the imaginations of visitors who boated past its haunting silhouette. In 1977, the Thousand Islands Bridge Authority acquired the property for one dollar, with the commitment to restore and preserve the castle for public enjoyment.
What followed was one of the most ambitious preservation efforts in the region's history.

Restoration teams not only stabilized the structure, but finished the castle in the spirit of Boldt's original vision. The group installed lavish interiors, gardens, and restored auxiliary buildings like the powerhouse and Alster Tower. Millions of dollars transformed the neglected ruins into a world-class historical site.

Today, Boldt Castle welcomes thousands of visitors each year. Arriving by boat, tourists explore its rooms, stroll through the gardens, and immerse themselves in a story that blends Gilded Age opulence with timeless emotion. The castle is no longer a symbol of loss, but of beauty, preservation, and the enduring power of love.

Though George Boldt never saw his dream realized, his legacy lives on in the stone walls and spires of the castle that bear his name—a monument not only to his wealth and vision, but to the woman who inspired it.

And this story honors it all.

ABOUT THE AUTHOR

Susan G Mathis is an international award-winning, multi-published author of stories set in the beautiful Thousand Islands, her childhood stomping ground in upstate NY. Susan has been published more than thirty times in full-length novels, novellas, and non-fiction books. She has fifteen in her fiction line including, *The Fabric of Hope: An Irish Family Legacy, Christmas Charity, Katelyn's Choice, Devyn's Dilemma, Sara's Surprise, Reagan's Reward, Colleen's Confession, Peyton's Promise, Rachel's Reunion, Mary's Moment, A Summer at Thousand Island House, Libby's Lighthouse, Julia's Joy, Emma's Engagement* and *Madison's Mission*. Her book awards include four Illumination Book Awards, four American Fiction Awards, three Indie Excellence Book Awards, five Literary Titan Book Awards, two Golden Scroll Awards, a Living Now Book Award, and a Selah Award.

Before Susan jumped into the fiction world, she served as the Founding Editor of *Thriving Family* magazine and the former Editor/Editorial Director of twelve Focus on the Family publications. Her first two published books were nonfiction. *Countdown for Couples: Preparing for the Adventure of Marriage* with an Indonesian and Spanish version, and *The ReMarriage Adventure: Preparing for a Life of Love and Happiness*, have helped thousands of couples prepare for marriage. Susan is also the author of two picture books, *Lexie's Adventure in Kenya* and *Princess Madison's Rainbow Adventure*. Moreover, she is published in various book compilations including five *Chicken Soup for the Soul* books, *Ready to Wed, Supporting Families Through Meaningful Ministry, The Christian Leadership Experience,* and *Spiritual*

Mentoring of Teens. Susan has also written several hundred published magazine and newsletter articles.

Susan is past president of American Christian Fiction Writers-CS (ACFW), former vice president of Christian Authors Network (CAN), a member of Christian Independent Publishing Association (CIPA), and a regular writer's contest judge. For over twenty years, Susan has been a speaker at writers' conferences, teachers' conventions, writing groups, and other organizational gatherings. Susan makes her home in Northern Virginia and enjoys traveling around the world but returns each summer to the Thousand Islands she loves. Visit www.SusanGMathis.com for more.

OTHER BOOKS
BY SUSAN G MATHIS

Love at a Lighthouse *series*
Join the Row-family women, Libby, Julia, and Emma, as they navigate the isolation, danger, and hope for lasting love at three Thousand Islands lighthouses—Tibbetts, Sister, and Rock Island—in the St. Lawrence River.

Libby's Lighthouse
When the Tibbett's Point Lighthouse keeper's daughter finds a mysterious sailor with amnesia, the secrets she uncovers may change her life forever.

Julia's Joy
She came to Sister Island to claim her inheritance, but the mysterious lighthouse keeper, William Dodge, makes her question all her plans.

Emma's Engagement
A new wife for Rock Island's lightkeeper Michael Diepolder. A jealous daughter. Can love shine through the darkness?

A Summer at Thousand Island House
Addison Bell serves children of the Thousand Island House guests on Staple's Island. She meets Liam Donovan and Lt. Worthington, single father of mischievous Jimmy. When former President Chester Arthur finds Jimmy as a stowaway on his fishing boat, her job and

reputation are endangered. How can she calm the churning waters of Liam, Lt. Worthington, and the President, clear her name, and avoid becoming the scorn of the community?

Mary's Moment
As the first telephone switchboard operator for the Thousand Islands Park, Mary Flynn risks her life to call for help when fire blazes through the Thousand Islands Park Commons. Widowed fireman George Flannigan takes every opportunity to connect with Mary. But they both have secrets, and when he can't stop the Columbian Hotel—and almost a hundred cottages—from being burned to the ground, Mary is left homeless. Will she be consumed by her painful past or embrace the future? Will he?

Peyton's Promise
Peyton Quinn prepares the Calumet Castle ballroom for a summer gala. As upholsterer and suffragette, when her pyrotechnics-engineer father is seriously hurt, she takes over the fireworks display despite being socially ostracized. Patrick Taylor, Calumet's carpenter, hopes to win her heart, yet can Peyton ignore the prejudices and persevere or lose her job, forfeit Patrick's love and respect, and become the talk of local gossips?

Devyn's Dilemma
Devyn McKenna is forced to work in the Towers on Dark Island. But when Devyn finds herself in service to the wealthy Frederick Bourne family, her life takes an unexpected turn. Brice McBride, Mr. Bourne's valet, tries to help the mysterious Devyn find peace and love in her new world, but she can't seem to stay out of trouble—especially when she's accused of stealing Bourne's money for Vanderbilt's NYC subway expansion.

Katelyn's Choice
Katelyn Kavanagh finds herself in the service of none other than the famous George Pullman, and the transition proves anything but easy. Thomas O'Neill also works on Pullman Island and tries to help her

adjust to her new world, but she just can't seem to tame her gossiping tongue—even when it could endanger her job, the 1872 re-election of Pullman guest President Ulysses S. Grant, and the love of the man of her dreams.

Rachel's Reunion

Rachel Kelly serves the most elite patrons at the famed New Frontenac Hotel on Round Island. When her old beau, Mitch, shows up, he opens the wound she thought was healed. As captain of a touring yacht, his attempts to win Rachel back are thwarted, especially when a wealthy patron seeks her attention. Who will Rachel choose?

Colleen's Confession

Colleen Sullivan conceals secrets when she works on Comfort Island. She loves to draw and dreams of growing in the craft, but when tragedy strikes, her orphan dreams are dashed. Jack Weiss is smitten by the lovely Irish lass. Introducing her to the famous impressionist, Alson Skinner Clark, brightens her opinion of him. But rumors of war in Europe mean Jack must choose between war and a life with Colleen. If she will have him.

Reagan's Reward

Reagan Kennedy is governess to the Bernheim's twin nephews, but her life at Cherry Island's Casa Blanca is complicated. When Daniel, the island's caretaker-boatman, tries to help the alluring Reagan, her insecurities mount as her confidence is shaken—especially when she crosses the faith divide and when Etta Damsky makes her life miserable. As trouble brews, Daniel sees another side of the woman he's come to love.

Sara's Surprise

Sara O'Neill works as an assistant pastry chef at the Thousand Islands Crossmon Hotel where she meets seven-year-old Madison and her charming father and hotel manager, Sean Graham. But Jacque LaFleur, the pastry chef, makes her dream job a nightmare.

When Sean misreads Sara's desire to learn from the pastry chef as love, can Sean trust her and can Sara trust him—and can she trust herself to be an instant mother?

Christmas Charity
Susan Hawkins and Patrick O'Neill find that an arranged marriage is much harder than they think, especially when they emigrate from Wolfe Island, Canada, to Cape Vincent, New York, in 1864, just a week after they marry—with Patrick's nine-year-old daughter, Lizzy, in tow. Can twenty-three-year-old Susan Hawkins learn to love her forty-nine-year-old husband and find charity for her angry stepdaughter? With Christmas coming, she hopes so.

The Fabric of Hope: An Irish Family Legacy
After struggling to accept the changes forced upon her, Margaret Hawkins and her family take a perilous journey on an 1851 immigrant ship to the New World, bringing with her an Irish family quilt she is making. A hundred and sixty years later, her great granddaughter, Maggie, searches for the family quilt after her ex pawns it. But on their way to creating a family legacy, will these women find peace with the past and embrace hope for the future, or will they be imprisoned by fear and faithlessness?

Visit her at <u>www.SusanGMathis.com</u>
sign up for her newsletter and please consider writing an Amazon review. Thanks!

www.ingramcontent.com/pod-product-compliance
Lightning Source LLC
Chambersburg PA
CBHW020326010826
48973CB00005B/1147